'The literary love child of *One Day* by David Nicholls and *Life After Life* by Kate Atkinson. As moving as it is smart, Barnett's story is about one relationship in three versions, showing how the smallest coincidences and chances can lead to wildly different outcomes' Fiona Wilson, *The Times*

'Excellent . . . Barnett's clever and sophisticated plotting weaves the three outcomes seamlessly over a 60-year period . . . An affecting and thought-provoking read, *The Versions of Us* will keep you gripped until the tear-jerking conclusion'
Mernie Gilmore, *Daily Express*

'Barnett renders an irresistible concept in sweet, cool prose – a bit like a choose-your-own-adventure book in which you don't have to choose' Hephzibah Anderson, *Observer*

'Clever, but not showy, romantic but not schmaltzy, it's clear that the buzz around this book is justified'
Deirdre O'Brien, *Sunday Mirror*

'Truly enthralling – I simply adored this wonderful novel'
Jessie Burton, author of *The Miniaturist*

'It is an unusual and lovely thing to watch an entire romance develop across a novel, not just the fun early bits, or unpleasant mid-life startings-over, or male midlife crises disguised as literary novels. Its very scope is a joy, the technical achievement seamlessly done, and the ending – all the endings – suitably affecting'
Jenny Colgan, *Guardian*

'A classic summer read. *One Day* meets *Mad Men*' *Metro*

'I absolutely loved [*The Versions of Us*]. It's so elegantly and beautifully written . . . a really wonderful book'
Esther Freud, author of *Mr Mac and Me*

Laura Barnett is a writer, journalist and theatre critic. She has been on staff at the *Guardian* and the *Daily Telegraph*, and writes for a number of national newspapers and magazines.

Laura was born in 1982 in south London, where she now lives with her husband. She studied Spanish and Italian at Cambridge University, and newspaper journalism at City University, London.

Her first non-fiction book, *Advice from the Players* – a compendium of advice for actors – is published by Nick Hern Books. Laura has previously published short stories, for which she has won several awards. *The Versions of Us* is her first novel and has sold in 23 countries, with television rights optioned by Trademark Films. Laura is currently working on her second novel *Greatest Hits*.

@laura_jbarnett
www.laura-barnett.co.uk
www.versionsofus.com

THE
VERSIONS
OF US

Laura Barnett

WEIDENFELD & NICOLSON

A W&N PAPERBACK

First published in Great Britain in 2015
by Weidenfeld & Nicolson

This paperback edition published in 2015
by Weidenfeld & Nicolson
an imprint of the Orion Publishing Group Ltd
Carmelite House, 50 Victoria Embankment
London EC4Y 0DZ
An Hachette UK Company

1 3 5 7 9 10 8 6 4 2

Grateful acknowledgement is made for permission to reprint an excerpt from *Four Quartets* by
T.S. Eliot. Used herewith by permission of Faber and Faber Ltd.

Excerpt from *The Amateur Marriage* reprinted by the permission of HSG Agency as agents for
the author. Copyright © 2004 by Anne Tyler Modaressi.

Excerpt from 'This is Us' reprinted with the kind permission of Mark Knopfler.

'Tangled Up In Blue' Words and Music by Bob Dylan © 1975. Reproduced by permission of
Ram's Horn Music/Sony/ATV Music Publishing Ltd, London W1F 9LD

'Hearts and Bones'. Words and Music by Paul Simon.
Copyright © 1983 Paul Simon (BMI). All Rights Reserved.

A CIP catalogue record for this book is
available from the British Library.

978 1 4746 0089 7 (mass market paperback)

Typeset by Input Data Services Ltd, Bridgwater, Somerset

Printed and bound in Great Britain by Clays Ltd, St Ives plc

The Orion Publishing Group's policy is to use papers that are natural, renewable and
recyclable products and made from wood grown in sustainable forests. The logging
and manufacturing processes are expected to conform to the environmental
regulations of the country of origin.

www.orionbooks.co.uk

For my mother, Jan Bild, who has lived many lives;
and for my godfather, Bob Williamson, who is much missed

'Sometimes he fantasised that at the end of his life, he would be shown a home movie of all the roads he had not taken, and where they would have led.'

Anne Tyler, *The Amateur Marriage*

'You and me making history.
This is us.'

Mark Knopfler & Emmylou Harris

1938

This is how it begins.

A woman stands on a station platform, a suitcase in her right hand, in her left a yellow handkerchief, with which she is dabbing at her face. The bluish skin around her eyes is wet, and the coal-smoke catches in her throat.

There is nobody to wave her off – she forbade them from coming, though her mother wept, as she herself is doing now – and yet still she stands on tiptoe to peer over the milling hats and fox furs. Perhaps Anton, tired of their mother's tears, relented, lifted her down the long flights of stairs in her bath chair, dressed her hands in mittens. But there is no Anton, no Mama. The concourse is crowded with strangers.

Miriam steps onto the train, stands blinking in the dim light of the corridor. A man with a black moustache and a violin case looks from her face to the great swelling dome of her stomach.

'Where is your husband?' he asks.

'In England.' The man regards her, his head cocked, like a bird's. Then he leans forward, takes up her suitcase in his free hand. She opens her mouth to protest, but he is already walking ahead.

'There is a spare seat in my compartment.'

All through the long journey west, they talk. He offers her herring and pickles from a damp paper bag, and Miriam takes them, though she loathes herring, because it is almost a day since she last ate. She never says aloud that there is no husband in England, but he knows. When the train shudders to a halt on the border and the guards order all passengers to disembark, Jakob keeps her close to him as they stand shivering, snowmelt softening the loose soles of her shoes.

'Your wife?' the guard says to Jakob as he reaches for her papers.

Jakob nods. Six months later, on a clear, bright day in Margate, the baby sleeping in the plump, upholstered arms of the rabbi's wife, that is what Miriam becomes.

✳

It also begins here.

Another woman stands in a garden, among roses, rubbing the small of her back. She wears a long blue painter's smock, her husband's. He is painting now, indoors, while she moves her other hand to the great swelling dome of her stomach.

There was a movement, a quickening, but it has passed. A trug, half filled with cut flowers, lies on the ground by her feet. She takes a deep breath, drawing in the crisp apple smell of clipped grass – she hacked at the lawn earlier, in the cool of the morning, with the pruning shears. She must keep busy: she has a horror of staying still, of allowing the blankness to roll over her like a sheet. It is so soft, so comforting. She is afraid she will fall asleep beneath it, and the baby will fall with her.

Vivian bends to retrieve the trug. As she does so, she feels something rip and tear. She stumbles, lets out a cry. Lewis does not hear her: he plays music while he's working. Chopin mostly, Wagner sometimes, when his colours are taking a darker turn. She is on the ground, the trug upended next to her, roses strewn across the paving, red and pink, their petals crushed and browning, exuding their sickly perfume. The pain comes again and Vivian gasps; then she remembers her neighbour, Mrs Dawes, and calls out her name.

In a moment, Mrs Dawes is grasping Vivian's shoulders with her capable hands, lifting her to the bench by the door, in the shade. She sends the grocer's boy, standing fish-mouthed at the front gate, scuttling off to fetch the doctor, while she runs upstairs to find Mr Taylor – such an odd little man, with his pot-belly and snub gnome's nose: not at all how she'd thought an artist would look. But sweet with it. Charming.

Vivian knows nothing but the waves of pain, the sudden coolness of bed sheets on her skin, the elasticity of minutes and hours, stretching out beyond limit until the doctor says, 'Your son. Here is your son.' Then she looks down and sees him, recognises him, winking up at her with an old man's knowing eyes.

PART ONE

Puncture
Cambridge, October 1958

Later, Eva will think, *If it hadn't been for that rusty nail, Jim and I would never have met.*

The thought will slip into her mind, fully formed, with a force that will snatch her breath. She'll lie still, watching the light slide around the curtains, considering the precise angle of her tyre on the rutted grass; the nail itself, old and crooked; the small dog, snouting the verge, failing to heed the sound of gear and tyre. She had swerved to miss him, and her tyre had met the rusty nail. How easy – how much more *probable* – would it have been for none of these things to happen?

But that will be later, when her life before Jim will already seem soundless, drained of colour, as if it had hardly been a life at all. Now, at the moment of impact, there is only a faint tearing sound, and a soft exhalation of air.

'Damn,' Eva says. She presses down on the pedals, but her front tyre is jittering like a nervous horse. She brakes, dismounts, kneels to make her diagnosis. The little dog hovers penitently at a distance, barks as if in apology, then scuttles off after its owner – who is, by now, a good deal ahead, a departing figure in a beige trench coat.

There is the nail, lodged above a jagged rip, at least two inches long. Eva presses the lips of the tear and air emerges in a hoarse wheeze. The tyre's already almost flat: she'll have to walk the bicycle back to college, and she's already late for supervision. Professor Farley will assume she hasn't done her essay on the *Four Quartets*, when actually it has kept her up for two full nights – it's in her satchel now, neatly copied, five pages long, excluding footnotes. She is rather proud of it, was looking forward to reading it aloud, watching old Farley from the corner of her eye as he leaned forward, twitching his eyebrows in the way he does when something really interests him.

'*Scheiße*,' Eva says: in a situation of this gravity, only German seems to do.

'Are you all right there?'

She is still kneeling, the bicycle weighing heavily against her side. She examines the nail, wonders whether it would do more harm than good to take it out. She doesn't look up.

'Fine, thanks. It's just a puncture.'

The passer-by, whoever he is, is silent. She assumes he has walked on, but then his shadow – the silhouette of a man, hatless, reaching into his jacket pocket – begins to shift across the grass towards her. 'Do let me help. I have a kit here.'

She looks up now. The sun is dipping behind a row of trees – just a few weeks into Michaelmas term and already the days are shortening – and the light is behind him, darkening his face. His shadow, now attached to feet in scuffed brown brogues, appears grossly tall, though the man seems of average height. Pale brown hair, in need of a cut; a Penguin paperback in his free hand. Eva can just make out the title on the spine, *Brave New World*, and she remembers, quite suddenly, an afternoon – a wintry Sunday; her mother making *Vanillekipferl* in the kitchen, the sound of her father's violin drifting up from the music room – when she had lost herself completely in Huxley's strange, frightening vision of the future.

She lays the bicycle down carefully on its side, gets to her feet. 'That's very kind of you, but I'm afraid I've no idea how to use one. The porter's boy always fixes mine.'

'I'm sure.' His tone is light, but he's frowning, searching the other pocket. 'I may have spoken too soon, I'm afraid. I've no idea where it is. So sorry. I usually have it with me.'

'Even when you're not cycling?'

'Yes.' He's more a boy than a man: about her own age, and a student; he has a college scarf – a bee's black and yellow stripes – looped loosely round his neck. The town boys don't sound like him, and they surely don't carry copies of *Brave New World*. 'Be prepared and all that. And I usually do. Cycle, I mean.'

He smiles, and Eva notices that his eyes are a very deep blue, almost violet, and framed by lashes longer than her own. In a woman, the effect would be called beautiful. In a man, it is a little unsettling; she is finding it difficult to meet his gaze.

'Are you German, then?'

'No.' She speaks too sharply; he looks away, embarrassed.

'Oh. Sorry. Heard you swear. *Scheiße.*'

'You speak German?'

'Not really. But I can say "shit" in ten languages.'

Eva laughs: she shouldn't have snapped. 'My parents are Austrian.'

'*Ach so.*'

'You *do* speak German!'

'*Nein, mein Liebling.* Only a little.'

His eyes catch hers and Eva is gripped by the curious sensation that they have met before, though his name is a blank. 'Are you reading English? Who's got you on to Huxley? I didn't think they let any of us read anything more modern than *Tom Jones.*'

He looks down at the paperback, shakes his head. 'Oh no – Huxley's just for fun. I'm reading law. But we are still *allowed* to read novels, you know.'

She smiles. 'Of course.' She can't, then, have seen him around the English faculty; perhaps they were introduced at a party once. David knows so many people – what was the name of that friend of his Penelope danced with at the Caius May Ball, before she took up with Gerald? He had bright blue eyes, but surely not quite like these. 'You do look familiar. Have we met?'

The man regards her again, his head on one side. He's pale, very English-looking, a smattering of freckles littering his nose. She bets they gather and thicken at the first glance of sun, and that he hates it, curses his fragile northern skin.

'I don't know,' he says. 'I feel as if we have, but I'm sure I'd remember your name.'

'It's Eva. Edelstein.'

'Well.' He smiles again. 'I'd definitely remember that. I'm Jim Taylor. Second year, Clare. You at Newnham?'

She nods. 'Second year. And I'm about to get in serious trouble for missing a supervision, just because some idiot left a nail lying around.'

'I'm meant to be in a supervision too. But to be honest, I was thinking of not going.'

Eva eyes him appraisingly; she has little time for those students – men, mostly, and the most expensively educated men at that – who regard their degrees with lazy, self-satisfied contempt. She hadn't taken him for one of them. 'Is that something you make a habit of?'

He shrugs. 'Not really. I wasn't feeling well. But I'm suddenly feeling a good deal better.'

They are silent for a moment, each feeling they ought to make a move to leave, but not quite wanting to. On the path, a girl in a navy duffel coat hurries past, throws them a quick glance. Then, recognising Eva, she looks again. It's that Girton girl, the one who played Emilia to David's Iago at the ADC.

She'd had her sights set on David: any fool could see it. But Eva doesn't want to think about David now.

'Well,' Eva says. 'I suppose I'd better be getting back. See if the porter's boy can fix my bike.'

'Or you could let me fix it for you. We're much closer to Clare than Newnham. I'll find the kit, fix your puncture, and then you can let me take you for a drink.'

She watches his face, and it strikes Eva, with a certainty that she can't possibly explain – she wouldn't even want to try – that this is the moment: the moment after which nothing will ever be quite the same again. She could – *should* – say no, turn away, wheel her bicycle through the late-afternoon streets to the college gates, let the porter's boy come blushing to her aid, offer him a four-bob tip. But that is not what she does. Instead, she turns her bicycle in the opposite direction and walks beside this boy, this Jim, their twin shadows nipping at their heels, merging and overlapping on the long grass.

Pierrot
Cambridge, October 1958

In the dressing-room, she says to David, 'I almost ran over a dog with my bike.'

David squints at her in the mirror; he is applying a thick layer of white pan-stick to his face. 'When?'

'On my way to Farley's.' Odd that she should have remembered it now. It was alarming: the little white dog at the edge of the path hadn't moved away as she approached, but skittered towards her, wagging its stump of a tail. She'd prepared to swerve, but at the very last moment – barely inches from her front wheel – the dog had suddenly bounded away with a frightened yelp.

Eva had stopped, shaken; someone called out, 'I say – look where you're going, won't you?' She turned, saw a man in a beige trench coat a few feet away, glaring at her.

'I'm so sorry,' she said, though what she meant to say was, *You should really keep your damn dog on a lead*.

'Are you all right there?' Another man was approaching from the opposite direction: a boy, really, about her age, a college scarf looped loosely over his tweed jacket.

'Quite all right, thank you,' she said primly. Their eyes met briefly as she remounted – his an uncommonly dark blue, framed by long, girlish lashes – and for a second she was sure she knew him, so sure that she opened her mouth to frame a greeting. But then, just as quickly, she doubted herself, said nothing, and pedalled on. As soon as she arrived at Professor Farley's rooms and began to read out her essay on the *Four Quartets*, the whole thing slipped from her mind.

'Oh, Eva,' David says now. 'You do get yourself into the most absurd situations.'

'Do I?' She frowns, feeling the distance between his version of her – disorganised, endearingly scatty – and her own. 'It wasn't my fault. The stupid dog ran right at me.'

But he isn't listening: he's staring hard at his reflection, blending the make-up down onto his neck. The effect is both clownish and melancholy, like one of those French Pierrots.

'Here,' she says, 'you've missed a bit.' She leans forward, rubs at his chin with her hand.

'Don't,' he says sharply, and she moves her hand away.

'Katz.' Gerald Smith is at the door, dressed, like David, in a long white robe, his face unevenly smeared with white. 'Cast warm-up. Oh, hello, Eva. You wouldn't go and find Pen, would you? She's hanging around out front.'

She nods at him. To David, she says, 'I'll see you afterwards, then. Break a leg.'

He grips her arm as she turns to go, draws her closer. 'Sorry,' he whispers. 'Just nerves.'

'I know. Don't be nervous. You'll be great.'

He *is* great, as always, Eva thinks with relief half an hour later. She is sitting in the house seats, holding her friend Penelope's hand. For the first few scenes, they are tense, barely able to watch the stage: they look instead at the audience, gauging their reactions, running over the lines they've rehearsed so many times.

David, as Oedipus, has a long speech about fifteen minutes in that it took him an age to learn. Last night, after the dress, Eva sat with him until midnight in the empty dressing-room, drilling him over and over, though her essay was only half finished, and she'd have to stay up all night to get it done. Tonight, she can hardly bear to listen, but David's voice is clear, unfaltering. She watches two men in the row in front lean forward, rapt.

Afterwards, they gather in the bar, drinking warm white wine. Eva and Penelope – tall, scarlet-lipped, shapely; her first words to Eva, whispered across the polished table at matriculation dinner, were, 'I don't know about you, but I would *kill* for a smoke' – stand with Susan Fletcher, whom the director, Harry Janus, has recently thrown over for an older actress he met at a London show.

'She's *twenty-five*,' Susan says. She's brittle and a little teary, watching Harry through narrowed eyes. 'I looked up her picture in *Spotlight* – they have a copy in the library, you know. She's absolutely *gorgeous*. How am I meant to compete?'

Eva and Penelope exchange a discreet glance; their loyalties ought, of course, to lie with Susan, but they can't help feeling she's the sort of girl who thrives on such dramas.

'Just don't compete,' Eva says. 'Retire from the game. Find someone else.'

Susan blinks at her. 'Easy for you to say. David's besotted.'

Eva follows Susan's gaze across the room, to where David is talking to an older man in a waistcoat and hat – not a student, and he hasn't the dusty air of a don: a London agent, perhaps. He is looking at David like a man who expected to find a penny and has found a crisp pound note. And why not? David is back in civvies now, the collar of his sports jacket arranged just so, his face wiped clean: tall, shining, magnificent.

All through Eva's first year, the name 'David Katz' had travelled the corridors and common rooms of Newnham, usually uttered in an excitable whisper. *He's at King's, you know. He's the spitting image of Rock Hudson. He took Helen Johnson for cocktails.* When they finally met – Eva was Hermia to his Lysander, in an early brush with the stage that confirmed her suspicion that she would never make an actress – she had known he was watching her, waiting for the usual blushes, the coquettish laughter. But she had not laughed; she had found him foppish, self-regarding. And yet David hadn't seemed to notice; in the Eagle pub after the read-through, he'd asked about her family, her life, with a degree of interest that she began to think might be genuine. 'You want to be a writer?' he'd said. 'What a perfectly wonderful thing.' He'd quoted whole scenes from *Hancock's Half Hour* at her with uncanny accuracy, until she couldn't help but laugh. A few days later, after rehearsals, he'd suggested she let him take her out for a drink, and Eva, with a sudden rush of excitement, had agreed.

That was six months ago now, in Easter term. She hadn't been sure the relationship would survive the summer – David's month with his family in Los Angeles (his father was American, had some rather glamorous connection to Hollywood), her fortnight scrabbling around on an archaeological dig near Harrogate (deathly dull, but there'd been time to write in the long twilit hours between dinner and bed). But he wrote often from America, even telephoned; then, when he was back, he came to Highgate for tea, charmed her parents over *Lebkuchen*, took her swimming in the Ponds.

There was, Eva was finding, a good deal more to David Katz than she had at first supposed. She liked his intelligence, his knowledge of culture: he took her to *Chicken Soup With Barley* at the Royal Court, which she found quite extraordinary; David seemed to know at least half the bar. Their shared backgrounds lent everything a certain ease: his father's family had emigrated from Poland to the US, his mother's from Germany to London, and they now inhabited a substantial Edwardian villa in Hampstead, just a short tramp across the heath from her parents' house.

And then, if Eva were truly honest, there was the matter of his looks. She wasn't in the least bit vain herself: she had inherited her mother's interest in style – a well-cut jacket, a tastefully decorated room – but had been taught, from young, to prize intellectual achievement over physical beauty. And yet Eva found that she *did* enjoy the way most eyes would turn to David when he entered a room; the way his presence at a party would suddenly make the evening seem brighter, more exciting. By Michaelmas term, they were a couple – a celebrated one, even, among David's circle of fledgling actors and playwrights and directors – and Eva was swept up by his charm and confidence; by his friends' flirtations and their in-jokes and their absolute belief that success was theirs for the taking.

Perhaps that's how love always arrives, she wrote in her notebook: *in this imperceptible slippage from acquaintance to intimacy.* Eva is not, by any stretch of the imagination, experienced. She met her only previous boyfriend, Benjamin Schwartz, at a dance at Highgate Boys' School; he was shy, with an owlish stare, and the unshakeable conviction that he would one day discover a cure for cancer. He never tried anything other than to kiss her, hold her hand; often, in his company, she felt boredom rise in her like a stifled yawn. David is never boring. He is all action and energy, Technicolor-bright.

Now, across the ADC bar, he catches her eye, smiles, mouths silently, 'Sorry.'

Susan, noticing, says, 'See?'

Eva sips her wine, enjoying the illicit thrill of being chosen, of holding such a sweet, desired thing within her grasp.

The first time she visited David's rooms in King's (it was a sweltering June day; that evening, they would give their last performance of *A Midsummer Night's Dream*), he had positioned her in front of the mirror above his basin, like a mannequin. Then he'd stood behind her, arranged her hair so that it fell in coils across her shoulders, bare in her light cotton dress.

'Do you see how beautiful we are?' he said.

Eva, watching their two-headed reflection through his eyes, felt suddenly that she did, and so she said simply, 'Yes.'

VERSION THREE

//////

Fall
Cambridge, October 1958

He sees her fall from a distance: slowly, deliberately, as if in a series of freeze-frames. A small white dog – a terrier – snuffling the rutted verge, lifting its head to send a reproachful bark after its owner, a man in a beige trench coat, already a good deal ahead. The girl approaching on a bicycle – she is pedalling too quickly, her dark hair trailing out behind her like a flag. He hears her call out over the high chime of her bell: 'Move, won't you, boy?' Yet the dog, drawn by some new source of canine fascination, moves not away but into the narrowing trajectory of her front tyre.

The girl swerves; her bicycle, moving off into the long grass, buckles and judders. She falls sideways, landing heavily, her left leg twisted at an awkward angle. Jim, just a few feet away now, hears her swear. 'Scheiße.'

The terrier waits a moment, wagging its tail disconsolately, and then scuttles off after its owner.

'I say – are you all right there?'

The girl doesn't look up. Close by, now, he can see that she is small, slight, about his age. Her face is hidden by that curtain of hair.

'I'm not sure.'

Her voice is breathless, clipped: the shock, of course. Jim steps from the path, moves towards her. 'Is it your ankle?

Do you want to try putting some weight on it?'

Here is her face: thin, like the rest of her; narrow-chinned; brown eyes quick, appraising. Her skin is darker than his, lightly tanned: he'd have thought her Italian or Spanish; German, never. She nods, winces slightly as she climbs to her feet. Her head barely reaches his shoulders. Not beautiful, exactly – but known, somehow. Familiar. Though surely he doesn't know her. At least, not yet.

'Not broken, then.'

She nods. 'Not broken. It hurts a bit. But I suspect I'll live.'

Jim chances a smile that she doesn't quite return. 'That was some fall. Did you hit something?'

'I don't know.' There is a smear of dirt on her cheek; he finds himself struggling against the sudden desire to brush it off. 'Must have done. I'm usually rather careful, you know. That dog came right at me.'

He looks down at her bicycle, lying stricken on the ground; a few inches from its back tyre, there is a large grey stone, just visible through the grass. 'There's your culprit. Must have caught it with your tyre. Want me to take a look? I have a repair kit here.' He shifts the paperback he is carrying – *Mrs Dalloway*; he'd found it on his mother's bedside table as he was packing for Michaelmas term and asked to borrow it, thinking it might afford some insight into her state of mind – to his other hand, and reaches into his jacket pocket.

'That's very kind of you, but really, I'm sure I can . . .'

'Least I can do. Can't believe the owner didn't even look round. Not exactly chivalrous, was it?'

Jim swallows, embarrassed at the implication: that his response, of course, *was*. He's hardly the hero of the hour: the repair kit isn't even there. He checks the other pocket. Then he remembers: Veronica. Undressing in her room that morning – they'd not even waited in the hallway for him to remove his jacket – he'd laid the contents of his pockets on her dressing-table. Later, he'd picked up his wallet, keys, a few loose coins. The kit must still be there, among her perfumes, her paste necklaces, her rings.

'I may have spoken too soon, I'm afraid. I've no idea where it is. So sorry. I usually have it with me.'

'Even when you're not cycling?'

'Yes. Be prepared and all that. And I usually do. Cycle, I mean.'

They are silent for a moment. She lifts her left ankle, circles it slowly. The movement is fluid, elegant: a dancer practising at the barre.

'How does it feel?' He is surprised by how truly he wants to know.

'A bit sore.'

'Perhaps you should see a doctor.'

She shakes her head. 'I'm sure an ice-pack and a stiff gin will do the trick.'

He watches her, unsure of her tone. She smiles. 'Are you German, then?' he asks.

'No.'

He wasn't expecting sharpness. He looks away. 'Oh. Sorry. Heard you swear. *Scheiße.*'

'You speak German?'

'Not really. But I can say "shit" in ten languages.'

She laughs, revealing a set of bright white teeth. Too healthy, perhaps, to have been raised on beer and sauerkraut. 'My parents are Austrian.'

'*Ach so.*'

'You do speak German!'

'*Nein, mein Liebling.* Only a little.'

Watching her face, it strikes Jim how much he'd like to draw her. He can see them, with uncommon vividness: her curled on a window seat, reading a book, the light falling just so across her hair; him sketching, the room white and silent, but for the scratch of lead on paper.

'Are you reading English too?'

Her question draws him back. Dr Dawson in his Old Court rooms, his three supervision partners, with their blank, fleshy faces and neatly combed hair, mindlessly scrawling the 'aims and adequacy of the law of tort'. He's late already, but he doesn't care.

He looks down at the book in his hand, shakes his head. 'Law, I'm afraid.'

'Oh. I don't know many men who read Virginia Woolf for fun.'

He laughs. 'I just carry it around for show. I find it's a good ice-breaker with beautiful English students. "Don't you just love *Mrs Dalloway*?" seems to go down a treat.'

She is laughing with him, and he looks at her again, for longer this time. Her eyes aren't really brown: at the iris, they are almost black; at the rim, closer to grey. He remembers a shade just like it in one of his father's paintings: a woman – Sonia, he knows now; that was why his mother wouldn't have it on the walls – outlined against a wash of English sky.

'So do you?' he says.

'Do I what?'

'Love *Mrs Dalloway*?'

'Oh, absolutely.' A short silence. Then, 'You do look familiar. I thought perhaps I'd seen you in a lecture.'

'Not unless you're sneaking into Watson's fascinating series on Roman law. What's your name?'

'It's Eva. Edelstein.'

'Well.' The name of an opera singer, a ballerina, not this scrap of a girl, whose face, Jim knows, he will sketch later, blending its contours: the planed angles of her cheekbones; the smudged shadows beneath her eyes. 'I'm sure I'd have remembered that. I'm Jim Taylor. Second year, Clare. I'd say you were . . . Newnham. Am I right?'

'Spot on. Second year too. I'm about to get in serious trouble for missing a supervision on Eliot. And I've done the essay.'

'Double the pain, then. But I'm sure they'll let you off, in the circumstances.'

She regards him, her head to one side; he can't tell if she finds him interesting or odd. Perhaps she's simply wondering why he's still here. 'I'm meant to be in a supervision too,' he says. 'But to be honest, I was thinking of not going.'

'Is that something you make a habit of?' That trace of sternness has returned; he wants to explain that he's not one of *those* men, the ones who neglect their studies out of laziness, or lassitude, or some inherited sense of entitlement. He wants to tell her how it feels to be set on a course that is not of his own choosing. But he can't, of course; he says only, 'Not really. I wasn't feeling well. But I'm suddenly feeling a good deal better.'

For a moment, it seems that there is nothing else to say. Jim can see how it will go: she will lift her bicycle, turn to leave, make her slow journey back to college. He is stricken, unable to think of a single thing to keep her here. But she isn't leaving yet; she's looking beyond him, to the path. He follows her gaze, watches a girl in a navy coat stare back at them, then hurry on her way.

'Someone you know?' he says.

'A little.' Something has changed in her; he can sense it. Something is closing down. 'I'd better head back. I'm meeting someone later.'

A man: of course there had to be a man. A slow panic rises in him: he will not, must not, let her go. He reaches out, touches her arm. 'Don't go. Come with me. There's a pub I know. Plenty of ice and gin.'

He keeps his hand on the rough cotton of her sleeve. She doesn't throw it off, just looks back up at him with those watchful eyes. He is sure she'll say no, walk away. But then she says, 'All right. Why not?'

Jim nods, aping a nonchalance he doesn't feel. He is thinking of a pub on Barton Road; he'll wheel the damn bicycle there himself if he has to. He kneels down, looks it over; there's no visible damage, but for a narrow, tapered scrape to the front mudguard. 'Doesn't look too bad,' he says. 'I'll take it for you, if you like.'

Eva shakes her head. 'Thanks. But I can do it myself.'

And then they walk away together, out of the allotted grooves of their afternoons and into the thickening shadows of evening, into the dim, liminal place where one path is taken, and another missed.

VERSION ONE

\\\\\\

Rain
Cambridge, November 1958

The rain comes on quite suddenly, just after four. Over the skylight, the clouds have massed without him noticing, turned slate-grey, almost purple on their undersides. Raindrops gather thickly on the glass, and the room turns unnaturally dark.

Jim, at his easel, lays his palette down on the floor, moves quickly around the room, turning on lamps. But it's no good: in the artificial light, the colours seem flat, uninspired; the paint is too thick in places, the brushstrokes too clearly visible. His father never painted by night: he rose early, went up to his attic studio to make the best of the morning. 'Daylight never lies, son,' he'd say. Sometimes, his mother would mutter back, her voice low, but still loud enough for Jim to catch, 'Unlike *some* people around here.'

He puts the palette in the basin, wipes off his brushes on an old rag, places them in a jam jar filled with turps. Splashes of watery paint spatter the enamel: his bedder will complain again tomorrow. 'Didn't sign up to clean this sort of mess, now, did I?' she'll say, and roll her eyes. But she's more tolerant than Mrs Harold, the woman he had last year. In the third week of his first term, she had marched off to the head porter to complain, and before long, Jim had been hauled up before his director of studies.

'Have a bit of consideration, won't you, Taylor?' Dr Dawson

had told him wearily. 'This isn't actually an art school.' They both knew he'd got off lightly. Dawson's wife is a painter, and when the second-year ballot awarded Jim these enormous top-floor rooms, with their sloping ceilings and wide, uncurtained skylight, he couldn't help thinking that the old professor might well have made the necessary arrangements.

But when it comes to Jim's academic work, Dawson's tolerance is starting to wear thin: he's been late handing in all his essays this term, and not one of them has come back higher than a 2:2. 'We have to consider, Mr Taylor,' the professor had said last week, having called him back to his rooms, 'whether you really want to stay on here.' Then, staring at Jim meaningfully over his black-rimmed glasses, he had added, 'So do you?'

Of course I do, Jim thinks now. *Just not for the same reasons you'd like me to. You and my mother both.*

He runs a finger lightly over the canvas to see whether the fresh paint has dried: Eva will be here soon, and he must cover up the portrait before she comes. He says it's because it isn't ready, but in fact it very nearly is. Today, while he should have been reading about land trusts and co-ownership, he has been working on the blocks of shadow that define the contours of her face. He has painted her seated at his desk chair, reading (a trick to make the long periods of sitting mutually beneficial), her dark hair falling in loose coils across her shoulders. As soon as he had sketched the outline, he realised that he was bringing to life the vision he had of her when they first met on the Backs.

The paint is dry; Jim draws an old sheet down over the canvas. It is a quarter past four. She's three-quarters of an hour late now, and it's still pouring, the rain an insistent drumming on the skylight. Fear grips him: perhaps she has slipped on the wet-slicked road; or a driver, blinded by the downpour, has caught the wheel of her bicycle, left her drenched and twisted on the pavement. Irrational, he knows, but this is how it is now

– has been through the four weeks since each stepped into the other's life with the ease of old friends picking up the thread of a familiar conversation. Elation underpinned by fear: the fear of losing her; the fear of not being enough.

Eva had told Jim about her boyfriend, David Katz, on the night they'd met, after he'd fixed the puncture, fetched his own bike and then cycled out with her to a pub he knew on Grantchester Road. She'd met Katz six months earlier, when they were both performing in *A Midsummer Night's Dream*. (Katz was an actor, already carrying something of a reputation: Jim recognised the name.) Her heart wasn't really in it, she'd said; the next day, she'd tell Katz it was over. She'd have done it right away, but this was the first night of his new play, *Oedipus Rex*. She'd missed the performance, and it seemed unkind to compound the hurt by telling him why.

Jim and Eva had sat in a corner booth in the back room of the pub, while the landlord rang out for last orders. It had been precisely six hours since they'd met, and one hour and ten minutes since they'd first kissed. When she finished speaking, Jim had nodded and kissed her again. He didn't say that he had worked out why Katz's name was familiar: that he was a friend of an old classmate of Jim's, Harry Janus, now studying English at John's. Jim had met Katz once, at a party, and had taken an instant dislike to him for reasons he couldn't quite articulate. But from that moment on – even when Katz's professional success became such that his failure at anything would seem unimaginable – Jim would feel a certain compassion for his rival: a loose, winner's generosity. Whatever Katz ended up with, after all, Jim would still have the greater prize.

There, in the pub, Jim had admitted that there was also someone he'd need to let down gently. Eva hadn't asked her name, and he knew that were she to ask, he would struggle to recall it. Poor Veronica: could she really have meant so little? And

26

yet it was so: the following day, Jim had suggested they meet for coffee at a bar on Market Square, had told her it was over without even waiting for her to drain her mug. Veronica cried a little, silently – the tears loosened her make-up, sent a blackish trickle of kohl inching down her cheek. The depth of her emotion had surprised him – Jim was sure he hadn't misled her, nor she him – and inspired in him nothing but a distant, polite embarrassment; he had passed her a tissue, wished her well, and taken his leave. Walking back to college, it had occurred to Jim to wonder how he could behave so unfeelingly. But his discomfort was quickly displaced by other, happier thoughts – Eva's dark brown eyes, meeting his own; the pressure of her lips as they kissed. Jim would hardly ever think of Veronica again.

Eva had finished with Katz a few days later. The following Friday, she'd gone alone to London for her mother's birthday; she'd have liked Jim to come, but her parents had met Katz over the summer, and she didn't want to surprise them too quickly with news of this new relationship. Later that day, feeling at a loose end, Jim had found himself walking past the ADC Theatre, and buying a ticket for that evening's performance of *Oedipus Rex*.

Even under layers of white stage make-up, David Katz seemed a formidable opponent: tall, charismatic, with an easy swagger even Jim could see must be attractive. And, like Eva, Katz was Jewish. Though he would never have admitted as much, Jim – a nominal Protestant, baptised only at his grandmother's insistence, and with no sense of that common history, that loss – felt more than a little intimidated.

Afterwards, he'd slipped from the theatre, gone back to college and paced around his room, obsessing over what Eva saw in him, what he could possibly offer her that Katz couldn't trump. And then Sweeting had come, knocked on his door, and told him that a few of them were off to the JCR, so why didn't he stop moping and come and get drunk?

Now, the rain is pooling and sliding, and Jim's thoughts are circling, picking up speed: Katz has been to see Eva; he has won her back; they're lying together in her rooms, skin on skin. He reaches for his jacket, takes the stairs two at a time: he'll check the gap in the hedge – *their* gap – in case she's decided to avoid the porters' lodge. (The day porter is beginning to raise an eyebrow at how often Eva passes through; unfairly, Jim feels, as she is certainly not the only Newnham girl to spend a good portion of her time out of college.) On the ground floor, he almost collides with Sweeting, coming in as he's going out.

'Watch it, Taylor,' says Sweeting, but Jim doesn't stop, doesn't even notice the rain as it slicks his hair, slips beneath the loose collar of his shirt.

At the hedge, he stops, whispers her name. Says it again, louder. This time he hears her reply. 'I'm here.'

She climbs through the gap, wet branches tugging at her face, her coat. He tries to part them, to ease her way, but the tough boughs snap back, scratch his hands. When she stands in front of him – soaked, dirt-smeared, catching her breath, saying sorry, she got stuck talking to someone after lectures, she just couldn't get away – he could weep with relief. He swallows the urge, knowing it to be unmanly. But he can't help saying, as he takes her in his arms, 'Oh, darling, I thought you weren't coming.'

Eva slips from his grasp, wearing that same stern expression he is coming to love, rain dripping from her nose onto the ground. 'Silly boy. Don't be ridiculous. How could I ever want to be anywhere but here?'

VERSION TWO

||||||||

Mother
Cambridge, November 1958

'Must you go?' she says.

Jim, dressing in the half-light of her room, turns to look at Veronica. She has shifted onto her side; the twin mounds of her breasts are pressed together, solid, pale as china beneath her violet slip. 'I'm afraid I really must. I'm meeting the eleven-o'clock train.'

'Your mother,' she says flatly. She watches him as he pulls on his socks. 'What is she like?'

'You don't want to know,' he says, meaning *I don't want to tell you.* And really, any association between Veronica and his mother must be avoided: there's hardly ten years between them, a fact that, whenever he dwells on it, appals him, and must surely appal her even more.

Sensing this, perhaps, she doesn't press the matter, but follows him downstairs in her silk robe, offers to make him coffee. The morning is dull and overcast, threatening rain. In the blunt grey light, last night's detritus – the wine glasses, hers still carrying a bloom of pink lipstick; the dirty plates left festering in the sink – strikes him as impossibly sordid. He refuses the coffee, kisses her quickly on the lips, ignores her when she asks when he will see him again.

'Bill's back next week, remember,' she adds, her voice low, as he opens the door to leave. 'We haven't much time.'

29

The door firmly closed behind him, Jim retrieves his bicycle from the passageway at the side of the house. Next door's net curtains twitch as he wheels the bike out onto the road, but he doesn't bother to look round. There is an odd sense of unreality to all this – as if it isn't really him, stepping up onto the pedals, casting off onto the black tarmac of this unremarkable suburban street, leaving behind his lover (for want of a better word): a woman twelve years his senior, with a husband in the merchant navy. *Surely*, he tells himself as he turns onto Mill Road, skirts the steady flow of traffic filing from the city centre to the station, *it was all her doing?* Veronica had sought him out in one of the dustier corners of the University Library (she was doing an evening course in ancient cultures); Veronica had asked him if he would like to join her for a drink. She had done it before, of course, and she'll do it again. That doesn't make him an unwilling participant – far from it – but he is becoming keenly aware that he hardly knows her, and doesn't really care to know her better; that what once seemed exciting and illicit now carries the deadening ring of cliché. *It simply has to stop*, he thinks. *I'll tell her so tomorrow.*

Thus resolved, Jim feels a little better as he draws up in front of the station, leans his bicycle against a spare portion of wall. The eleven-o'clock from King's Cross is delayed. He sits in the cafeteria, drinking bad coffee and eating a Chelsea bun, until the train arrives with a great screeching of brakes. He is a little slow getting up, draining the last powdery dregs; from the ticket hall, he hears his mother calling. Her voice is brittle, over-loud. 'James! James, darling! Mummy's here! Where are you?'

Vivian is on one of her highs: he'd known it when she telephoned the porters' lodge two days before, saying she would be up to pay him a visit on Saturday, and wasn't that a lovely surprise? No use in telling her that it was almost the end of term, that he'd be home in two weeks, and had a mountain of work to finish before then if Dr Dawson was even going to entertain the possibility of allowing him to return next year. That is, if Jim decides he wants to return.

'Yes, that's a lovely surprise, Mum,' he'd told her dutifully. He tells her the same thing now, when he finds her out by the taxi rank, still calling his name. She is wearing a bright blue wool suit, a pink scarf, a hat entwined with red artificial roses. She feels tiny in his embrace: he fears she is tinier every time he sees her, as if, ever so slowly, she is evaporating before his eyes. That is how she had described the lows to him once – he was only little, nine or ten; this was before his father's death – as he sat beside her on her bed, the curtains drawn. 'It feels,' she had said, 'as if I'm disappearing, bit by bit, and I don't even care.'

He leaves his bike at the station, offers to pay for a taxi into town, but she won't hear of it. 'Let's walk,' she says. 'It's such a lovely day.' It's not lovely – they're only halfway down Mill Road when the first drops of rain brush their shoulders – but she's talking quickly. A stream of words. Her train ride up from Bristol yesterday – 'I met the *loveliest* woman, Jim. I gave her our number. I really think we could become great *friends*.' His aunt Frances, with whom she has spent the night in Crouch End – 'She'd roasted a *chicken*, James, a whole *chicken*. All the children were there – such sweet little things – and there was trifle for afters, just because she *knows* it's my favourite.'

Jim has booked a table for lunch at the University Arms. Vivian prefers to eat in college – 'so I can really feel what it's like to be you, Jim' – but the last time he took her to the buttery, she had approached the dons' table and engaged the startled master in conversation. It had taken him – a distinguished brigadier – almost half an hour to extricate himself. For Jim, it was just like being at school again – catching sight of Vivian waving at him from the gates in a red hat, a green coat: bright stabs of colour among the other mothers' muted plumage. The boys around him staring, nudging, whispering.

After lunch, they walk through town to Clare, cross the bridge with its great boulders of honey-coloured stone, and take a turn about the gardens. It has stopped raining, but the sky is still leaden. Her mood, too, is growing heavier. By the ornamental pond, she pauses, turns to him, and says, 'You will be home soon, won't you? It's so terribly lonely in that flat, all by myself.'

He swallows. Even the mention of the place feels like a weight around his neck. 'I'll be home in two weeks, Mother. It's almost the end of term. Don't you remember?'

'Ah, yes. Of course.' She nods, presses her lips together. She reapplied her lipstick – red, presumably to match the flowers on her hat, though it clashes terribly with her scarf – after lunch, but badly, in a smudged scrawl. 'My son the lawyer. The clever, clever lawyer. You're nothing like your father. You have *no* idea what a relief that is to me, my darling.'

The weight is growing heavier. Jim feels a sudden, over-whelming need to shout – to tell his mother he can't stand it here, that he's leaving. To ask her why she insisted he apply to Cambridge instead of going to art school: surely she knows that painting is the only thing that has ever truly made him happy. But he doesn't shout. He says quietly, 'Actually, Mother, I've been thinking about not coming back next year. I really don't think I . . .'

Vivian has covered her face with her hands, but he knows that she is crying. In a whisper she says, 'Don't, Jim. Please don't. I can't bear it.'

He says nothing more. He takes her to his room in Memorial Court so that she can splash her face, reapply her make-up. Her earlier ebullience has gone: she is falling back down to the trough of the wave, and he feels the old, familiar blend of frustration and helplessness, the desire to help tempered by the knowledge that there is no way for him to reach her.

This time, Jim insists on a taxi. He hands Vivian into a compartment on the five-o'clock train, lingers at the window, wondering whether he ought to get on board, go with her to his aunt's, make sure she gets there safely. Once, last year, in a state not dissimilar to this, she fell asleep in an empty compartment just past Potters Bar, and was only found by a guard long after the train had discharged its passengers and pulled into a siding at Finsbury Park.

But he does not go. He stays on the platform, waving uselessly at his mother's face – eyes closed, head tipped back against the antimacassar – until the train has receded into the distance, and there is nothing for him to do but retrieve his bicycle, and cycle back into town.

VERSION THREE

///////

Cathedral
Cambridge & Ely, December 1958

On the last Saturday of term, they wake early in Jim's college rooms, slip out unnoticed through the gap in the hedge, and take a bus to Ely.

The fens are lit by a thin, watery sun, so low in the sky that it seems to be almost touching the horizon. The wind is in from the east. It was there in town – they have felt it for weeks, drawn their scarves tighter around their necks, woken to see their breath form clouds of vapour in the freezing air – but out here, there are no buildings to break its passage, just acres of hard mud and low, twisted trees.

'When will you pack?' he says. They are leaving tomorrow: Jim on the midday train – he'll break the journey with a night at his aunt Frances's house in Crouch End; Eva after lunch, in her parents' Morris Minor, her brother Anton tired and testy beside her on the back seat.

'In the morning, I suppose. Shouldn't need more than an hour or two. You?'

'The same.' He takes her hand. His is cold, rough, his forefinger calloused by the hard wood of his paintbrushes, his fingernails framed by half-moons of dried paint. Last night, he had finally showed her the portrait; he removed the sheet with a magician's flourish, though she could see that he was nervous. Eva didn't admit that she had already taken a look a few days

34

before, while he was down the hall in the bathroom; had stared at her likeness. There she was, rendered in layers of paint, in his brushstrokes' swift, swallow shapes: both utterly herself and somehow elevated, other. It was a week since she had seen the doctor. She couldn't stand to look at the painting, to see such a tribute, and say nothing. And yet what was there to say?

She is silent again now, watching the great rolling blankness of the fens. At the front of the bus, a baby is crying, the sound low and guttural, as its mother tries to soothe it.

'Well over two months gone,' the doctor had said, fixing her with a pointed stare. 'Three, even. You'll need to start making arrangements, Miss Edelstein. You and your . . .'

He had let the ellipsis hang, and Eva had not filled it. She was thinking only of Jim, and the fact that she had known him for six short weeks.

If he notices her silence, Jim says nothing. He is quiet too, and pale, his eyes smudged with tiredness. Eva knows he isn't looking forward to leaving, to going back to the Bristol flat he doesn't think of as home — just the rented rooms that his mother, Vivian, occupies. Home, he has told her, is the Sussex house where he was born: rough grey flint and a front garden filled with roses. His father painting in the attic; his mother sitting for him, or mixing paints, swilling out jars with turps in the old pantry downstairs. That's where Vivian was, Jim said, when his father had stood clutching at his chest at the top of the stairs, and fell: she had come running from the pantry to find him broken and twisted on the bottom step. Jim was at school. His aunt Patsy had collected him, brought him back to a house that was no longer a home: a house filled with policemen, and neighbours making cups of tea, and his mother screaming, screaming, until the doctors came and everything was quiet.

In Ely, the bus lurches to a halt beside a post office. 'Everybody off,' the conductor calls, and they line up, still holding hands, behind the other passengers: the woman with the baby, sleeping now; an elderly couple, the man dour and flat-capped, the woman plump, her expression kind. She catches Eva's eye as they climb down the steps. 'Young love, eh?' she says. 'You both have a lovely day, now.'

Eva thanks her, draws closer to Jim. The cold bites their faces.

'We'll have a look at the cathedral, shall we?' he says. 'I saw a Law Society concert here last year, and took a tour. It's a beautiful place.'

She nods: anything Jim wants, anything to be close to him, to stave off the inevitable moment when she must tell him what she is, and what she has to do.

They start walking, huddled down into their scarves, towards the looming spires: two of them, square like castle keeps, their walls scarred, pockmarked, catching the winter light. Suddenly Jim stops, turns to her, his face reddening. 'You don't mind, do you? Going in? I didn't even think.'

She smiles. 'Of course I don't mind. As long as God doesn't.'

It's the space that strikes Eva first: the great pillars reaching up through the vastness to the distant, vaulted roof. Beneath their feet is a mosaic of polished tiles – 'A labyrinth,' Jim says, 'with God at the centre' – and ahead, under huge panes of coloured glass, is a golden screen, beneath which the altar sits, covered with a fine white cloth. They walk slowly along the nave, pausing to gaze up at another extraordinary ceiling, its ribbed panels painted red, green and gold. At its centre is a pointed star that reminds Eva of the one embroidered into her mother's Shabbat tablecloth – though that has six arms, and this (she counts them silently) has eight.

'The octagon.' Jim is almost whispering. Eva watches the quick, animated movements of his face, and loves him; is filled with a love for him so overwhelming she can hardly breathe.

How, she thinks, *am I to leave him?* And yet she must; sleepless in her college room, the building creaking and whispering in the night, she has allowed herself hope: imagined telling him, watching his expression change, and then resolve itself. *It doesn't matter*, he says – this imaginary Jim – and holds her close. *Nothing matters, Eva, as long as we're together.* It is a waking dream, but she knows it could become real, that this Jim standing here before her, staring up at the distant reaches of the roof (how she would love to reach out and cup his chin with her hand, tilt his face down to meet her lips) could really say it. And that is why – as morning creeps over the city, and the college begins to stir into life – she has resolved over and over again not to give him the opportunity, not to permit the man she loves, with his talent, his grand plans – the man already bearing the weight of his mother's illness – to be trapped by a situation that is not of his making. Father to another man's child: Jim would say he could do it, and he would do it well; but she will not allow him to make that sacrifice.

A few nights ago, Eva had sat on her bed in Newnham with Penelope, her head resting on her shoulder; and even her dearest friend hadn't tried to make her change her mind.

'And what if David refuses?' Pen had asked. 'What will we do then?'

How grateful Eva had been for that 'we'. 'He won't refuse, Pen. And if he does – well. I'll find a way.'

'*We'll* find a way,' Penelope had corrected her, and Eva had allowed the promise to stand, though she knew the burden was hers – hers and David's – and no one could carry it for her. Not Penelope, not her parents. She believed Miriam and Jakob would understand – how could they not, given their own history? – and yet she couldn't bear the idea of returning to her old room in Highgate, her studies abandoned, pregnant and alone.

In her notebook, she wrote, *I chose Jim, and I can't bear to leave him. But the choice is no longer only mine to make.*

Now, in the cathedral, Jim is still speaking. 'The monks built it after the original nave pillars collapsed one night. They thought there'd been an earthquake. It must have been their way of proving that the disaster hadn't defeated them.'

Eva nods. She doesn't know how to reply, how to convey the feeling welling inside her: love, yes, but with it sadness – not just for the pain of parting, but for the people they have lost. His father, splayed and broken on the bottom step. Her Oma and Opa, on both sides, and all her aunts and uncles and cousins, herded onto trains, thirsty and blinking, knowing nothing of where they were going – only suspecting, fearing, but still carrying hope. There must have been hope, surely, right until the very last moment, when they knew that there was nothing to be done.

As if sensing what she is thinking, Jim squeezes her hand. 'Let's light a candle.'

There is a stand beside the West Door: a dozen tapers glowing in the darkness. Others are stacked underneath, below a slot for coins. Eva takes a fistful of pennies from her purse and drops them in, picks a candle for each Oma, each Opa, and then lights them, fitting one after another firmly into a metal base. Jim chooses only one, for his father, Lewis, and then they stand and watch the wicks take light, his rough painter's hand in hers. She would like to cry, but tears are inadequate to express all that this means: to be here with him, remembering, hoping, when tomorrow she will be gone.

They eat thin vegetable soup in the refectory, then walk slowly back across town. The sun is fading, the wind whipping their hair; the warmth of the bus is a relief. Inside, Eva removes her shoes, thaws her freezing feet over the radiator underneath her seat. She isn't intending to fall asleep, but her head quickly lolls back against the headrest, and Jim lets the weight of it fall against his shoulder. In Cambridge, he wakes her gently. 'We're here, Eva. You slept all the way.'

It is only then, as they get off the bus, that Eva tells Jim she is sorry: she can't spend the evening with him; there is something she has to do. Jim protests: after tomorrow, he says, they won't see each other for four whole weeks. Eva says she knows. She really is sorry. Then she leans forward, kisses him, and turns and hurries away, though Jim is calling her, and it is all she can do to lift her heavy feet.

She doesn't stop until she reaches King's Parade. The tall towers of King's gatehouse are throwing their long, angular shadows across the cobblestones. Eva steadies herself against a lamppost, ignoring the curious stares of the men now stepping briskly past her in their black gowns. It is almost time for hall. She will be missing her own dinner at Newnham, but she doesn't care. She can't imagine being hungry for anything ever again.

Inside, the porter doesn't bother to hide his disapproval. 'It's dinner time, miss. Mr Katz will be going in.'

'Please,' she says again. 'It really is very important that I see him now.'

'Eva, what is it?' David says in an urgent whisper a few minutes later. 'Hall's just about to start.' Then, watching her face, his expression softens. She thinks of how he had looked when she'd told him it was over between them, how he had, in that moment, seemed utterly diminished. *But I chose you*, he'd said, and she'd had nothing to say but, *I'm sorry*. He shrugs off his gown, folds it over his arm. 'All right. Come on. We'll get something at the Eagle.'

Later, when the talking is over, when the plans have been made, Eva returns to her room in Newnham, and writes a letter. She takes her bicycle from the shed, cycles through the dark streets to Clare College, and asks another porter – this one older, kindlier, smiling at the television when she comes in, and then offering Eva the same smile – to place it in Jim Taylor's pigeonhole.

Then Eva hurries away, not wanting to look back in case she sees him. Not wanting to look back on everything that might have been.

VERSION ONE

\\\\\\

Home
London, August 1960

On the night of Eva and Jim's return from honeymoon, Jakob and Miriam Edelstein serve drinks in the garden.

It is the softest of English summer evenings: the last rays of sun still warming the terrace, the air placid, rich with the smell of honeysuckle and damp earth. Jim, sipping his whisky soda, is still sleepy, his head cottony and thick – but pleasantly so, his hand resting lightly on Eva's arm. She is smiling, tanned. Her skin is still, to his mind, carrying the heat of the island; the whitewashed veranda where they breakfasted on melon and yoghurt; the harbour-side where they sat with glasses of retsina as evening came.

'Well,' Miriam says, 'we must send you to Greece again. You both look so *well*.'

She is sitting to Eva's left, legs slender and bare beneath her summer dress. They are unmistakably mother and daughter: both so small and quick, birdlike – even their voices are similar, low and fluting, though Miriam's still bears the faint rough edges of her Austrian accent. Oddly, her singing voice – she was training at the conservatoire in Vienna when she fell pregnant with Eva – is a good octave higher: a bright soprano, clean and pure as pared bone.

Anton takes after his father: they are both tall, large-limbed, their movements slow, deliberate. He is nineteen, and has poured himself a whisky to toast his sister and brother-in-law – which he does now, lifting his glass to Jim's. 'Welcome home.'

Home, Jim thinks. *We live here too.* For they do, at least for now: the Edelsteins have cleared out the three-roomed flat – a bedroom, sitting-room with kitchenette and tiny bathroom – that spans the top floor of their wide, gracious house. It had been occupied, until his death last year, by Herr Fischler, a distant cousin of Jakob's from Vienna. Since then, it has become a repository for boxes of books, the overspill from the rest of the house, which, like its owners, is given over to music and reading above all other pleasures. Each room is lined with bookcases, and the front room with shelves of sheet music, presided over by a grand piano on which Anton grudgingly, and infrequently, practises his scales. (Eva, too, spent time at the piano as a girl, but proved so prodigiously untalented that the family has acknowledged her as a lost cause.) Over the mahogany bannisters hang sepia portraits of unspecified Edelstein relatives, high-collared, unsmiling. These photographs are precious less for their quality than for the difficult journey they made to London, after the war, sent by the kind Catholic friend to whom Jakob's father had, after Kristallnacht, entrusted those treasures that remained.

Eva – his *wife*; how new and wonderful that word is – takes Jim's hand. At first, when Jakob had suggested they move into the empty flat – they were having lunch at the University Arms, celebrating both Eva's twenty-first birthday and their engagement – Jim had been unsure. In his mind, he'd envisaged a place of their own, somewhere they could shut out the world. He had been offered a place at the Slade from September: with Eva's support, he had finally resolved to abandon the law. Eva went with him to Bristol to break the news to his mother, who cried, a little; but Eva poured the tea, and quickly, cleverly, distracted

Vivian with talk of other things, and Jim allowed himself to believe that the weight of his mother's disappointment might just be bearable after all. Several weeks of uncertainty followed, in which Jim was unsure whether the Ministry of Labour would allow him to defer his blasted national service again; the letter confirming that he was for ever off the hook finally arrived, to his great relief, in the same week as his last examination.

Eva, meanwhile, went down to London to interview for a job on the *Daily Courier*. 'It's really just dogsbodying on the women's page,' she reported on her return. 'Nothing remotely glamorous.' But Jim knew perfectly well how much the job meant to her. When the offer came through – it was just a few days after he'd had his own letter from the ministry – they climbed through the window of Jim's room in Old Court and stood together on the balustrade, looking out across the manicured sweep of lawn, at the punts idling downriver, drinking syrupy port (Jim's prize for winning a college art competition last term) straight from the bottle.

'To the future,' Jim said, and Eva laughed and kissed him. He seemed to see that future stretching out before them – their wedding, his art, her writing, the wonderful fact that he would go to sleep each night with Eva beside him – and he felt a rush of happiness so true, so overwhelming, that he had to clutch the stone balustrade with his hand to steady himself. And then one of the porters, crossing the lawn below in his bowler hat, looked up and saw them – 'You there, get down at once' – and they waved at him, hand in hand: young, untouchable, free.

Jim's vision of the future did not encompass living with the Edelsteins: he had pictured a flat near Hampstead Heath – they'd taken walks there over the summer holiday – with a wide bay window for his easel, a box room in which Eva could write. But Eva was more pragmatic. With only Jim's tiny stipend from the Slade, and the pittance she'd be getting at the *Daily Courier*

– at least at first – they'd be close to penniless. 'Better to be poor and warm with Mama and Papa,' she said, 'than poor and shivering in some damp basement flat, no?'

Jim smiled. 'That sounds rather tempting, actually. We'd have to huddle together for warmth.' Eva smiled back at him, and stroked his face; but he knew the decision was already made.

And anyway, Jim thinks now, looking around at his wife's family, *I have been lucky*. The Edelsteins have welcomed him with an easy, unforced generosity. Jakob, a first violinist with the London Symphony Orchestra, is a gentle, mild-mannered man, almost shy. On their first meeting, Jim had, on several occasions, caught Jakob watching him with a rather searching expression – he was, Jim supposed, sizing him up, and as he has never seen that expression again since, Jim can only assume that Jakob found in his favour. Anton was delighted to discover, at the wedding, that Jim's cousin Toby had been in Anton's own year at school – a fellow prefect, in fact, and much admired member of the first eleven. And Miriam has been kind to Jim from the first. If she or Jakob feel any residue of disappointment about the fact Eva has married outside the faith, they keep it well hidden. They seemed thoroughly happy with Jim and Eva's plans for a registry-office wedding (Eva in white silk, carrying a posy of blue anemones; a skiffle band playing in the hall downstairs); at no point did Jim feel they'd have preferred to have seen their daughter married in synagogue.

Not long after their engagement – still giddy on his proposal, and her acceptance – Jim had, during one of their whispered, early morning conversations, offered to convert; he had done so seriously, but Eva had laughed, gently, and told him not to even think about it. 'Mama and Papa are above all that,' she had said, her warm body tucked inside the crook of his arm. 'That tribalism, I mean. They saw where it could lead.'

By eight o'clock, it is still warm; the sky over Highgate is streaked with pink, the rising moon a faint disc on the horizon. They decide to eat outside – 'Seems a shame,' Miriam says, 'to be stuck in the stuffy old dining-room' – and Jim helps to carry out glasses, cutlery, candles. Miriam brings through plates of cold chicken, herring in dill sauce (Jakob's favourite), potato salad and fat tomatoes soused in the rough local olive oil Eva has brought home from Greece. Jakob pours the wine, and as they eat and drink, Jim is suffused with a heady blend of tiredness and warmth and the marvellous nearness of Eva, his wife, the woman who has chosen him above all others, with whom he has lain for most of two full weeks in a tangle of limbs, her warm, salty taste lingering on his tongue.

'Some letters came for you both,' Miriam says. 'I put them in the flat, on the mantelpiece. Did you see them?'

Eva shakes her head. 'Not yet, Mama. We went straight to sleep. We'll read them later.'

Miriam looks at Jim. 'One of them had a Bristol postmark. From your mother?'

Jim nods, and looks away. Vivian went back into hospital just a few weeks before their wedding, and even Eva, then, was unable to dissuade him that there could be no connection with his decision to abandon the law. The last time he saw his mother was just after finals. He'd gone straight from Cambridge to the Edelsteins', was occupying the flat upstairs while Eva slept in her girlhood room. One bright Saturday, he borrowed the Edelsteins' Morris Minor and drove west to Bristol, to the hospital. Vivian was sitting alone, before a window that looked out over a tall thicket of trees. He had said her name, over and over, but she did not turn round.

Jakob, sensing Jim's discomfiture, speaks for him. 'They'll have time to read them later, Miriam. Let them settle in first, eh?' Husband and wife exchange glances, and Miriam gives a quick nod, wipes her lips with her napkin.

'So which day is it that you start at the Slade, Jim? Are you looking forward to it?'

Later, lying together in the flat, Eva whispers into his ear, 'Let's go and see your mother, Jim, next weekend. We can take some wedding photographs. Make her feel as if she was there.'

He says, 'Yes, maybe we should,' and holds her closer. He falls into a deep, blackout sleep, dreaming that he is back on the night train, speeding through Italy, the fields dark beyond the half-open window, and his mother sleeping in the next compartment. Her head is lolling back against the seat, and he is watching her through the glass partition, unable to reach her, unwilling to try.

Gypsophila
London, August 1960

Eva Maria Edelstein and David Abraham Katz are married on a Sunday at the Central Synagogue on Hallam Street, with a reception afterwards at the Savoy.

The bride wears a full, stiff-skirted dress with a low sweetheart neckline, purchased from Selfridges at considerable expense by her mother-in-law, Judith Katz, and carries a bouquet of pink tea-roses and gypsophila. Later, all the guests will comment on how beautiful she looked – though truthfully, it will be the face of the groom they see. So handsome, his light grey suit so well cut, his hair perfectly coiffed. 'I hardly knew my own nephew,' one of the Katz aunts will say at the reception to anyone who will listen. 'I thought it was Rock Hudson himself.'

It is a sweltering day: the same aunt faints inside the synagogue during the ceremonial drinking of the wine, causing a short, anxious pause in proceedings, but is quickly revived with a lavender-scented handkerchief produced from her younger sister's handbag. Afterwards, the guests line up on the steps in the heat, carrying handfuls of pink and white rice paper. The couple emerge, blinking, into the light, laughing as the confetti lands on their hair, their eyelids, their shoulders, and the photographer clicks his shutter over and over again.

At the Savoy, there are drinks and dancing, and a great deal of rich food. Anton Edelstein and his schoolfriend Ian Liebnitz drink too much rum punch, and are discreetly sick in an ornamental urn. After the speeches, Miriam Edelstein sings a Schubert lied, accompanied by Jakob on piano. Privately, Judith Katz considers this a little *de trop*; but she smiles and claps politely, and is careful to hide any trace of disapproval as the wedding party takes to the dance floor for the hora, and Eva and David are lifted high on silver chairs, each clinging to the end of a white silk handkerchief.

And then, too soon, it is time for the bride and groom to retire. They are to spend their wedding night upstairs, in one of the hotel's grandest suites (another gift from Judith and Abraham Katz, along with the honeymoon: first thing tomorrow, Eva and David will board a BOAC flight for New York, spend a few days with his grandparents on the Upper East Side, and then take a train bound for Los Angeles). There are kisses, embraces; tears from the aunts and the two bridesmaids: the bride's best friend, Penelope (flushed and uncomfortable inside her tight satin bodice), and the groom's cousin Deborah (dark, rather haughtily beautiful, and noted, by keener observers, to have yawned twice while standing beside the chuppah). And then there is nothing but the upholstered silence of the lift, two hands intertwined, the bride's new ring a plain, shining band beneath her engagement diamonds.

The suite, too, is silent. The couple stands for a moment in the doorway, the bellboy hovering uncertainly behind them. 'Can I get you anything, sir, madam? There's champagne in your room, with our compliments.'

'How kind,' David says. 'Thank you, but you can go.' The boy obeys, after offering more congratulations, and a coy little half-smile that Eva chooses to ignore.

There is a gramophone in the suite, a stack of records. 'Shall we play some music, Mrs Katz?'

Eva nods, and David chooses an Everly Brothers album,

flushes away the silence. He takes her in his arms, moves her around the soft blue carpet. There is, as so often, something self-consciously performative in his manner – Eva has sometimes caught herself feeling more like his audience than his fiancée – but tonight she doesn't mind, because he is so handsome, and they are married, and David is the only man she has ever loved.

Or thinks she loves. There was a morning, soon after he asked her to marry him, when Eva woke filled with a kind of panic: a deep, nagging feeling that she did not love David, not as she should; or perhaps that she simply didn't know *how* to love. In the library, while she was meant to be finishing her essay on *Hamlet*, Eva took out her notebook and wrote – bending low over her desk, so that none of the girls nearby might see – *David is so clever, so brilliant, so charming. He makes me feel that with him, I could do anything, go anywhere. I do love him, I know I do. And yet this horrid, stubborn little part of me insists that what we have together isn't real, somehow – that it's some kind of shallow imitation of love. I've been thinking about Plato's cave, about that terrible idea that most of us spend our lives with our backs to the light, watching shadows on the wall. What if my life with David is just that? Suppose it's simply not the real thing?*

Eva had quickly dismissed the idea as absurd – she was surely complicating what should be utterly simple. But later, on her way to lectures, she asked Penelope, 'How do you know, Pen – I mean, *really* know – that you love Gerald?'

'Darling, I just know. It's instinctive.' She took Eva's arm in hers. 'But if you're worrying about David, don't. Doubts are natural too, you know. You must remember what I was like when I said yes to Gerald: a rabbit in headlights, desperate to know I was doing the right thing. "Anyone can see you're right for each other, Pen," you said: remember? Well, let me say that back to you. David Katz is a brilliant man, and he loves you, and I know you'll make each other happy.'

Eva had allowed herself to be reassured. She did believe that David loved her: he had taken, each Friday, to buying her a bouquet of red roses, which filled her room with their heady perfume. When he proposed (he'd booked a table at the University Arms: went down on one knee – it was a performance, of course, and the couple at the next table had started to clap) – he said he'd known, from the moment he first saw her, that he would one day make her his wife. 'You're not like other girls, Eva – you have your own ambitions, your own plans. I like that. I respect it. And my family loves you too, you know.'

The whole restaurant seemed to be watching as he slid the ring onto her finger. 'Even your mother?' she said.

David laughed. 'Oh, don't worry about her, darling. In a few months, *you'll* be the only Mrs Katz who matters.'

Mrs Eva Katz: she had written it down in her notebook, as if trying it on for size. With David, she was beautiful, weightless, free. Was this love? Eva had no reason, really, to believe it wasn't – and so she dismissed her doubts, putting them down to inexperience, to the lack of a yardstick with which to measure her feelings.

Now, in their hotel room, David pours two glasses of champagne. They move to the huge bed with its massed cushions and quilts, and make love a little clumsily – they've both had too much to drink. Then they lie together, sweat-sheened, silent; David falls asleep almost at once, but Eva is wide awake. She puts on her new nightgown and robe – one of the few things Miriam was permitted to buy her, amidst the trunkfuls of gifts issued by Judith Katz – finds her cigarettes in the front pocket of her suitcase, neatly packed for tomorrow's journey, and steps out onto the balcony.

Night is only just falling, and the air still carries the day's heat: there are couples walking along the Embankment, arm in arm, as the streetlights come on; lightermen drawing their boats across the darkening river. Bizarre to think that tomorrow they will be in the air, flying away from London, high above the unfathomable stretches of the Atlantic.

Eva lights a cigarette. She thinks of Jakob, of how, last night, before she went up to sleep in her old bedroom for the final time, he had taken her aside and said, in German, 'Are you absolutely sure, *Liebling*, about marrying this man?'

He had led her into the music room, sat her down beside the grand piano, the orchestra scores, the violins. It was not a room for inconsequential conversation; this, and the fact Jakob was speaking in German, had made Eva's stomach twist and leap.

'Why?' she shot back in English. 'Don't you like David? Don't you think you might have said something before?'

Jakob watched her steadily, his eyes dark brown, infinitely kind. Miriam always said those eyes were what first drew her to him on the train from Vienna: that, and the way Jakob had lifted up her suitcase without asking, carried it off into his compartment as if accepting without question the sudden intersection of their lives.

'It's not that I don't like him,' Jakob said. 'He is easy to like, and I can see that he cares for you. But I'm afraid for you, Eva. I'm afraid he will never love you quite as much as he loves himself.'

Eva had been too angry to speak: angry because Jakob had waited so long to tell her what he really felt, and angry because he was, in some way, giving voice to the fears she had already worked so hard to dismiss. Over the last few months, as their future plans came into focus, she'd had the unsettling feeling that they were all angled towards David's convenience rather than her own. In a month's time, he would be starting at RADA, and they'd be moving to his parents' house in Hampstead: Eva had suggested they take the empty flat in her parents' house, but David's mother had simply overruled her. 'He'll be working very hard, Eva,' Judith had said. 'Surely it's better if we're both there to look after him?'

Eva had waited a moment before answering, and then calmly pointed out that she, for one, had no intention of devoting herself to David's care. She'd applied for a job at the *Daily Courier* (just dogsbodying on the women's page, nothing glamorous), but the role had gone to someone else; her intention, now, was to read scripts for income – David had promised to pull some strings at the Royal Court – and start a novel. But in Hampstead, they would be confined to David's old room: a shrine to his schoolboy achievements, filled with his old cricket bats and drama-society trophies. Yes, there was a desk at which Eva would, in theory, be able to write, but she suspected that the time and space to do so would, if Judith had anything to do with it, be in short supply.

But there, in her parents' music room, Eva would not allow Jakob to revive her old anxieties; it was too late. She ran upstairs; in her bedroom, she lay awake for hours. It was almost dawn before she finally fell into a thin, fitful sleep.

Now, she smokes, watching the river, the lights, the bruise-purple sky. Then Eva goes back into the room, and slips into bed beside her sleeping husband.

VERSION THREE

//////

Tide
London, September 1960

Mid-morning, a Saturday: Eva is woken by the doorbell. At first, she doesn't recognise the sound. She is swimming up through layers of sleep, still semi-immersed in a disturbing dream: she and Rebecca, alone on a tiny island with the tide coming in; the blast of a foghorn echoing out from the empty harbour, and the child screaming and screaming, impossible to comfort.

Opening her eyes, she feels the waves recede: the island is the old chaise longue in their bedroom, the foghorn the trill of the doorbell, ringing at regular intervals.

'Anton!' Eva calls out, as Rebecca stirs and gargles in the crook of her arm. But there is no reply – too late, she remembers that her brother is at cricket practice. Her mother is giving her Saturday-morning singing lessons at the Guildhall; her father is away with the orchestra. And David – well, David is out, too. They are quite alone.

She lifts Rebecca to a standing position, balances her on her knees. Rebecca's eyes open sleepily, dark brown, all-knowing, and she stares frankly at her mother. She seems to consider whether to make a fuss – she has, after all, been roused unceremoniously from her morning nap – but decides against it, her tiny mouth cracking into a toothless smile. Eva smiles back, holds her daughter at arm's length as she stands, places her gently on the floor. 'Just let Mummy get dressed, and then we'll go downstairs and see who's making all that racket.'

It is Penelope. She's standing on the top step, her face flushed above her black houndstooth jacket, holding a posy of yellow roses wrapped in brown paper. She stares at Eva for the shortest of moments, then moves quickly towards her; as they kiss, once on each cheek, Eva catches her friend's familiar scents of lipstick and lily of the valley.

'Honestly, darling. Did you forget I was coming?'

Eva is about to reply, but Penelope is already bending towards Rebecca, heavy in Eva's arms. 'Oh goodness, Eva, I've only been away three weeks and it's like she's all grown up!' She places a hand on Rebecca's head, ruffles her baby hair; it is too long – Eva has been meaning to cut it for days – and sticking up at odd angles, giving the child the look of an oversized cockatoo. 'Aren't you a beauty, Becca? Will you give your aunty Penelope a smile?'

Rebecca obliges: Eva suspects her daughter of having inherited some of her father's willingness to rise to the expectations of an audience. She has his appetite for attention, too: she still wakes often in the night, wailing at some new, invisible affront. Eva and her mother have worn a threadbare track in the landing carpet from their pacing up and down, rubbing Rebecca's hot, twisting back, Miriam softly singing the old Yiddish lullabies.

In the kitchen, she hands Rebecca to Penelope. Then Eva sets about making tea, finding a vase for the flowers, a plate for the shortbread biscuits her friend has produced from the depths of her crocodile-skin handbag.

'Bad night, was it?'

'You could say that.' Filling the kettle, reaching into the depths of a cupboard for her mother's cut-crystal vase. 'David came home late – went to the pub with everyone after class. Of course, then he decided he wanted to see his daughter, so he woke her up. Rebecca got all excited, and then guess who had to spend the rest of the night getting her back to sleep?'

'Ah.' Eva senses that Penelope would like to say more, but she does not. She has stepped over to the sink, out of Eva's way; Rebecca, seizing her chance, now grasps a wooden spoon from the drainer, and taps it experimentally on the side of Penelope's head. 'Don't do that, Becca darling,' Penelope says mildly.

Eva winces. 'Sorry. Let me take her.'

'Why don't you both go and sit down? I'll make the tea.'

Eva is too tired to argue. She settles her daughter on the drawing-room floor, in front of the French windows, with her favourite doll, and a good view of next door's cat. She thinks of David as he had been last night, unsteady on his feet, reeking of beer and cigarettes. He had woken her coming in: woken the whole house, probably. Leaning over the bed, breathing out that stale pub smell, he'd said, 'Where's my favourite girl?'

Waking, Eva had been confused – had reached for him, thinking David meant her to take him in his arms; but he had pulled away. '*Rebecca*, I mean. Hasn't she got a cuddle for her daddy?'

At least, Eva thinks now, she can't accuse David of taking no interest in their daughter – if only when it suits him. And he is still sweet with Eva, too, sometimes. There was that day trip to Brighton last month, just the three of them, escaping the clammy, boxed heat of the city: fish and chips, and ice creams, Rebecca crying out with delight as David lowered her toes gently into the smallest breakers. Eva had watched them, her husband and her daughter, feeling the tension seep out of her. She had closed her eyes for a moment; later, she'd felt the soft press of David's lips on her cheek. '*How now, my love!*' he had whispered into her ear. '*Why is your cheek so pale? How chance the roses there do fade so fast?*' And she had smiled: they were Hermia and Lysander; there was the dust caught on shards of afternoon sunlight in the rehearsal room; there was David slipping his hand into hers in the courtyard garden of the Eagle. Back then – before Jim, before all the rest – they had been happy; and David had promised, that night almost two years ago when they had laid their plans, to try to make her so again. Surely it is too much to believe that he could have stopped trying so soon?

Penelope brings through the tea things, sits down next to Eva. 'I take it David's settling in all right at RADA?'

'Oh, he seems to be having a whale of a time.' Eva is trying hard to keep her voice bright. 'He's changed his name, you know. He's David Curtis now, professionally. The head tutor says he'll get more work that way.'

Penelope, halfway through a shortbread biscuit, widens her eyes. 'Why Curtis?'

'David *says* it's because his aunt in America married a man called Curtis, so the name is in the family. But I think it's because of Tony Curtis. You know, so that directors might think they're related.'

'I see. Well, good luck to him. We wouldn't want anything to stand between David and world domination, now would we?' Her tone is gently teasing; their eyes meet. Penelope laughs first, and then Eva does, and suddenly the morning seems sunny again.

'It's so good to see you,' Eva says, reaching for her friend's hand. 'Tell me all about the honeymoon. I want to hear everything.'

They went first to Paris, Penelope says: stayed in the loveliest little hotel in Montmartre, with a view of Sacré-Coeur. For a couple of days, they hardly left their room – this with a blush – except to wander down to the bistro on the corner, which was straight out of a Jean-Luc Godard film: gingham tablecloths, candles in old wine bottles, moules marinière and steak frites. ('Though not,' Penelope adds with a smile, 'any beautiful married couples loafing around looking thoroughly miserable, thank God.') Gerald bought her an antique bracelet in a flea market, they spent hours in the Louvre, and one night they stumbled across a basement jazz club, and danced under a cloud of Gauloises. 'They were all terribly serious,' Penelope says. 'While the band took a break, a man got up and read some dreadful poetry. I mean, really bad. I got the giggles. You should have seen the looks they gave us.'

From Paris, they drove out into the countryside, and found a cottage in the grounds of a crumbling old gîte. They stayed there for two weeks, swimming in the owners' pool and getting fat on salami and cheese – here, Penelope pats her belly. She has never been slender, and has indeed gained weight since her wedding, but Eva thinks it rather suits her. 'And now it's back to reality. Gerald started at the Foreign Office last week. I think he's rather in his element: using his Russian and all that. He doesn't seem to miss acting in the least.'

'I'm so glad, Pen.' Eva is watching Rebecca carefully: she has tired of her doll, struggled clumsily to her feet, and is now staring eagerly at next door's cat as it stretches out on the terrace, methodically washing its face. She thinks of Gerald, with his corduroy jackets and elbow patches and soft, boyish face; his utter, unashamed devotion to Penelope. She thinks of her own honeymoon: a week in Edinburgh, at the Scotsman Hotel, courtesy of Mr and Mrs Katz. *Tosca* at the Royal Lyceum, the streets wet and shadowed, and David's extravagant consideration of Eva's condition – still, thankfully, not too visible beneath a generous coat – fading to an impatience that wasn't quite so easy to conceal.

I will not *be jealous of my dearest friend*, Eva thinks. Aloud, she says, 'And you're starting at Penguin on Monday.'

Penelope nods. 'Rather exciting, really. Though they'll probably just have me doing all sorts of boring things to begin with.'

There is a charged silence, during which Rebecca decides to take a step towards the cat, without registering the obstacle of the French windows. She begins to wail, and Eva rushes over to soothe her. When Rebecca is quiet again, happy to sit back on the floor and play with her doll, Eva returns to the sofa.

Penelope says, 'What about you? What will you do?'

She knows exactly what Penelope means, and yet an odd obstinacy grips Eva: how easy a question it is to ask, and how difficult to answer truthfully. 'About what, Pen?'

'Well. About work. Have you been doing any writing?'

'What do you think? I'm hardly sitting around twiddling my thumbs.' Eva is snappier than she meant to be; Penelope looks away, her face reddening again – she has always worn her emotions close to the surface. But neither is she easily deterred. 'You had a baby, Eva. It's not a prison sentence. You have your mother here – Jakob, Anton, David, when he's around. David's parents. You could easily take on some work. Or find time to write. After all, I'll know exactly who to show your novel to soon, won't I?'

They are silent again. Eva, through her tiredness, knows that Penelope is right. She should be writing: she has half a novel upstairs, in notebooks, hidden away under their bed, not to mention her stuttering, lifeless attempts at short stories. But Eva's desire to write – the need to shape the world into a form she can understand, an impulse that had always seemed as natural as breathing – seems to have almost entirely deserted her since that terrible night when they had returned from Ely – she and Jim – and she had allowed him no explanation but that letter; had left it at his porters' lodge like the coward she was.

Jim hadn't tried to find her. Eva reminded herself that this was what she'd planned – that she'd presented him with a *fait accompli* because she hadn't wanted Jim to try to change her mind – but still, in the deepest part of her, she'd carried some small flicker of hope.

She had withdrawn from Newnham immediately. Eva was still unable to shift from her mind the expression her director of studies had worn as they talked – sympathy tempered by discomfort and the faint trace of distaste – as she delivered the college's official decision of rustication. Professor Jean McMaster was a brisk, plain woman, of the sort who would once have been called a bluestocking – and perhaps, in some quarters of the university, still was. 'I can't tell you how sorry I am for you, Eva,' she had said. 'I can only hope that the rules will one day come into line with life as it is actually lived, not as men wish women to live it – but I know that is of no comfort to you now.'

The wedding took place a few weeks later, in a back room at St Pancras Town Hall. It was a small, hushed affair, though Jakob and Miriam did their best to lighten the mood, making determined conversation with Abraham and Judith Katz: the former reciprocally jovial, the latter thin-lipped, clasping her new daughter-in-law in only the briefest of embraces.

Then, in January, Eva and David had moved back to Cambridge, into the married accommodation provided by King's: a damp, sour-smelling flat on Mill Road, which Eva did her best to make comfortable – sewing cushion covers, filling the rooms with books – but which remained resolutely dark, musty and cold.

Through much of that endless Fenland winter, Eva had stayed indoors, as her stomach swelled, and David came home later and later in the evenings – there was always a play, a reading, a party. She couldn't find a job. Soon after their return to the city, she walked into a bookshop, a café, asking for casual shifts, but each time the owner had looked her over, and then given her the same answer: 'Not in your condition.'

And so she tried to write. She lacked the energy to return to the novel she had started over the summer – her notebooks re-mained where she had put them, under the bed – but she began a short story, then another, only to find that she couldn't seem to get past the third or fourth paragraph. The characters Eva had grown so used to observing in her mind – shaping their thoughts, their physical appearance, their turns of phrase until she quite often struggled to remind herself that they weren't actually flesh and blood – no longer felt real to her; they had become fleeting, insubstantial. After a few weeks, Eva had given up trying to chase after them; and then there was nothing for her to do but read, listen to the wireless, work through the recipes in the Elizabeth David book her mother had given her (the mutton carbonade was a success; the dauphinoise potatoes, less so), and wait for the coming of her child.

No, she had not looked for Jim, and she worked as hard as she could not to think of him; and then one day, there he was. It was March, a few days before her twentieth birthday; she was six months pregnant. The sun was out for the first time in what seemed like years: Eva had wanted to get out, to feel its warmth on her face. She had walked into town, forcing her-self to pass along King's Parade, past the Senate House, from which she would never graduate, admiring the play of light on stone. At Heffers bookshop on Petty Cury, Eva paused – she was desperate for something new to read – and then she saw him, pushing open the door, carrying two books in a paper bag, wearing that same tweed jacket, that same college scarf. Eva hardly dared breathe. She stood still, hoping he wouldn't notice her; but hoping also that he wouldn't walk away without looking back.

He did look back. Eva's heart slipped into her mouth, and she had watched a curious expression cross his face: it was as if he were about to smile, but then remembered, and thought better of it. Jim had turned away, then, and she had watched his back as he walked the short distance to Sidney Street, and disappeared.

She saw him a few more times, after that – passing the flat on his bicycle one day; on Market Square in June the following year, on David's graduation day, as she stood beside her in-laws with Rebecca in her arms. And then David and Eva had packed their things into boxes and driven to London, to her parents' empty flat (she had drawn the line at moving in with the Katzes, insisting that she would need her mother's help with the baby) and that had been that: no chance of seeing Jim again, no chance at all.

The next day, unpacking, Eva had again placed her notebooks under their bed; and that is where they have stayed ever since.

'I did have a thought,' Penelope says. Eva recognises that voice: it is the one Penelope uses on Gerald when suggesting something she suspects he might not want to do.

Eva leans forward, pours the last of the tea. 'What was that?'

'Well. Publishers always need readers, don't they? People to tell them which manuscripts to take on, and which to reject.'

Eva hands her a cup.

'Thank you.' Penelope takes another biscuit from the plate. 'So perhaps I could put in a good word for you at Penguin. Tell them how brilliant you are, how nobody knows more about books than you.'

Eva is touched, despite herself: it seems a long time, suddenly, since she has thought of herself as brilliant at anything other than quieting her daughter, reading her moods, mashing last night's leftovers into something resembling a meal. 'Nobody other than *you*, you mean.'

Penelope smiles, relieved. 'Shall I, then? Mention you?'

At the window, Rebecca is whispering soft sounds into her doll's ear. Eva thinks of her mother, of their own whispered confidences, exchanged on this sofa a few weeks ago, when they had finally rocked Rebecca back to sleep.

'You really must find something to do with your time besides being her mother, darling,' Miriam had said. 'Motherhood is wonderful – important – but if you simply draw down the shutters on your creative life, you'll end up resenting her.'

Eva – delirious with lack of sleep – had looked down at her daughter, her eyes closed, her expression now absolutely serene. 'Is that how you felt when you fell pregnant? When you had to leave the conservatoire?'

Miriam had been silent for a moment. 'Perhaps at first, a little. But then, when he left me – when we understood what was really happening in Vienna – it was all about getting out, getting away. And once I had you – and Anton, of course – you were both the centre of my life. But still, when I could, I returned to singing.'

Eva had lain back, closed her eyes; she could see Judith Katz, presiding over the table at the last Friday-night meal (they had arrived late: Rebecca had been fussing as Eva put her to bed), and reminding her son and daughter-in-law that as it was *their* money – hers and Abraham's – that was facilitating their very comfortable life, the least Eva and David might do was show them the respect of arriving for Shabbat dinner on time.

Yes, Eva thinks now, *a little money of my own would make all the difference.*

She reaches across to Penelope, takes her hand. 'Thanks, Pen. It would be wonderful if you could.'

Bridge
Bristol, September 1961

On Fridays, the clerks have a strict arrangement to meet in the pub after work.

Today, Jim is a little later leaving than the others: he has stayed behind to tie up one of the many loose ends that sometimes, in his bleaker moments, he imagines as hundreds of thick, coarse threads, vine-like, wrapping themselves around him.

These excursions to the pub, he thinks as he walks the short journey from the office, are just another example of his colleagues' unwavering devotion to routine. Nine o'clock sharp – clerks arrive. Half past nine – clerks enter morning meeting. One o'clock – clerks exit to eat toasted cheese sandwiches at the corner café. Two o'clock – clerks return to desks. Five o'clock on Fridays – clerks repair to the White Lion to get tipsy on warm beer and try their luck with the barmaid, Louise.

Here they are now, bunched around an outside table. The week has been unseasonably warm, and the suspension bridge stands high and beautiful behind them, the lowering sun gilding the ironwork. *The lads*, their bosses call them, though there is nothing particularly laddish about these men, who are mostly university-educated, with soft hands and precision-parted hair: young men already beginning to resemble their fathers. At their desks, they trade jokes from *Beyond Our Ken*, or school-dormitory smut – but outside, confronted by other, more vigorous working men, their easy bonhomie seems to wither. There is only one – Peter Hartford: not a graduate, but the son of a stevedore, putting himself through his five-year articles by working Saturdays as a postman – whom Jim would tentatively call a friend.

He finds Peter inside, at the bar. Louise is leaning towards him, her large breasts splayed over the bar-top, her frosted-pink mouth curved into a smile. Seeing Jim, she snaps sharply back, readopts her customary *froideur*. Peter turns, smiles at him. 'What can I get you?'

They take their pints out onto the terrace, find a table at a discreet distance from the other clerks.

'Here's to another week at the coalface.' Peter lifts his glass to meet Jim's. He is short, stocky, with reddish hair and a broad, guileless face, the first in five generations not to follow his father onto the docks. *Cleverer than any of us*, Jim thinks, and he feels a rush of affection for him, decides anew not to confide too honestly, not to admit how deeply he despises the profession that Peter has worked so hard to enter, while he, Jim, has sleepwalked into it, pushed by . . . What? Fear, he supposes: fear and the centrifugal force of his mother's illness.

After graduation, he had hitchhiked to France with Sweeting, spent a happy fortnight pottering around villages and vineyards, painting watercolours – bare-legged girls drinking *citron pressé* at a pavement café; a cornfield, yellow-tipped, shimmering – with an energy he hadn't felt in years. He had returned resolved to inform his mother that he'd be applying to art school – to the Slade – but he had arrived in Bristol to discover that she was back in hospital. Her doctor would release her only on the condition that someone at home take charge of her day-to-day care. 'She mustn't be left alone, Mr Taylor,' the doctor had said. 'Not until we can be sure she's more stable, at any rate. Will you be living with her?'

'I suppose so,' Jim replied, watching his plans slip away into the distance, like a foreign landscape receding through the window of a train.

But then there was the matter of what he would *do*. In her more lucid moments, Vivian was insistent that he shouldn't abandon the law, and Jim himself could think of no other career that might keep him at home; but he still had his part-two exams to take, and there was no law school in Bristol. In the end, his aunt Patsy had come to the rescue: she'd move in with Vivian, leaving his uncle John to fend for himself in Budleigh Salterton, while Jim went off to Guildford to take his exams; then go home when Jim returned for the holidays. In a few weeks, it had all been arranged. Arndale & Thompson – the first firm of Bristol solicitors Jim found listed in the phone book – accepted him for his articles. After six months in Guildford – he was billeted with a widower named Sid Stanley, a rather sad, lonely figure, with whom Jim spent most of his evenings watching television sitcoms – he was back in Bristol, a fully fledged articled clerk, living with his mother.

It is not how Jim ever thought things would turn out – even when he allowed Vivian to persuade him to apply to Cambridge to study law. (He'd wanted to put down history of art, but there'd been a row, and he'd changed to law in a fit of pique, hardly thinking he'd get in; but it had turned out that, despite himself, he had an aptitude for the law's quiet logic, for the measured apportioning of right and wrong.) Perhaps, he thinks, his life would look quite different now if he'd met a woman at university – someone with whom he wished to start a life of his own. And there have been some, since Veronica – in his final term, he was briefly taken with an extremely pretty first-year history student named Angela Smith, but she'd broken it off, citing some old boyfriend from school – but no one about whom he has felt remotely serious.

'It's not such a bad place, really, is it?' Jim says aloud. 'Even old Croggan seems to be warming to me a bit.'

Peter nods. 'I find it's best to avoid him until early afternoon – he's usually just back from lunch then, and half-cut on port.'

They exchange weak smiles, sip their pints. Jim, facing the bridge, admires its great struts and curves, the way it seems to thrust out organically from the thick green foliage on either bank. Peter, like most of Bristol's natives, seems not even to notice it, but Jim is continually struck by the way Brunel's great construction hangs above the Avon like a huge, still bird, its grey wings outstretched.

The first time they came to the White Lion, Peter had told him a story: a factory girl, jilted by her lover, had thrown herself from the parapet and floated gently down to safety, her wide Victorian skirts billowing into a parachute. 'She lived to eighty-five,' Peter said. 'A legend in her own lifetime.'

Jim had shivered, thinking of the nights – how many had there been since he'd moved back to Bristol: three? four? – when he had run out onto the Clifton streets after his mother. Vivian was usually barefoot, her raincoat loosely belted over her nightdress. Once, she had already stepped out onto the parapet before he reached her. He had caught her by the collar like a cat, tried not to look down at the deep, silted darkness below.

Now, to dispel the memory, Jim asks Peter what plans he has for the weekend. 'Not much. Working tomorrow, of course. I might take Sheila out on Sunday. Clevedon, maybe, if it's still nice. Ice cream, stroll on the pier. All that jazz.'

Jim has met Sheila once, at Peter's birthday party: she is wide-hipped, tall (taller than Peter, in fact, though neither of them seems to mind), with a tumble of blonde curls and a low, infectious cackle. They are newly married, with a little house in Bedminster, a few streets away from where they both grew up. 'That's right,' Peter had said proudly when he introduced her to

Jim, 'I really did fall for the girl next door. How lucky was I that she fell for me too?'

'What about you?' Peter says now, eyeing Jim carefully over his pint glass. 'Up to anything? How are . . . well, things?'

Jim has sketched out the bare framework of his situation for Peter: his mother's illness; his decision – if Jim could call it that, for it had certainly not felt like one – to forget art school, forget London, and stay here with her.

'All right,' he says.

It's true, in relative terms: Vivian is back on an upswing. Last night, she woke him at three a.m., playing Sinatra at full volume in the living-room. '*Dance* with me, Lewis,' she said, her eyes unnaturally bright. And so Jim had danced with her, for a song or two, because he hadn't the heart to tell her for the millionth time that he was not his father, that his father was long gone.

'Find time to do some painting this weekend, will you?'

'Maybe.' Jim has set up his easel in a corner of his bedroom; the light isn't good, and he often wakes with a headache from the turps, but at least he can turn the key when he goes out. A month or so ago, when he forgot to lock the room, he came back to find great sweeps of paint smeared across the blank canvas he had left there, and the half-empty tubes bleeding stickily onto the carpet. 'Hope so.'

They are quiet then, enjoying the silence of men happy to leave the finer details of their feelings between parentheses. Soon their glasses are empty; another of the clerks, passing on his way to the bar, asks if they'd like another drink. Both say yes: Peter because he feels Jim could use the company, and Jim because it is a warm Friday evening, already carrying the sweet, resiny scents of autumn, and he wants to stay here, in the fading light, for as long as he can.

VERSION THREE

/////

Face
Bristol, July 1961

He sees her face on a Sunday afternoon.

He is out walking, carrying his sketchbook and pencils in his satchel: his aunt Patsy and uncle John have come up to see his mother, so he has the day entirely to himself. He is thinking of going down to the docks, sketching the lowered heads of the cranes, the still bulk of the William Sloan steamer, just in from Glasgow. Perhaps later he will see a film, or drive over to Richard and Hannah's for dinner: he has an open invitation to eat with them in Long Ashton whenever he likes. There will be roast chicken, salad from the garden, the cat curled on Hannah's lap. Richard will open a good bottle of wine, and they'll play records, and talk about art, and, for a while, he'll feel something akin to happiness: he'll forget about his mother and her vast, insufferable neediness; about the void that still lies at the very heart of him. All this Jim is thinking, idly, pleasurably – and then he sees her. Eva.

She is walking up the hill, on the other side of the road. Her face is cast in the shadow of a building, but it is hers: the same narrow, pointed chin; the same dark eyes, framed by full, arched brows. She is wearing a light summer jacket, unbelted, over a green dress. Her hair is pinned up, exposing her slender neck, the exquisite shade of her skin.

Jim stops still, collides with a woman coming the other

68

way. She scowls, tells him to look where he is going, but he doesn't reply. On the other pavement, Eva is walking on, her stride brisk, purposeful. She has her back to him now. He runs out into the road, narrowly missing a passing car, whose driver shouts, sounds his horn. Jim doesn't hear; he would like to call her name, but he can't seem to form the word. He falls into step behind her, marvelling at the physical fact of her presence. He can hear the blood pulsing in his ears.

The last time he saw her, she was standing on Market Square. The baby was a small, wriggling thing in her arms – pretty, as babies go, with her mother's dark hair and eyes. David Katz was beside her, in his fur-trimmed graduation hood. An older couple – the man glossy, foreign-looking; his wife hard-faced, unsmiling – stood at a slight distance, as if not quite sure whether to admit to being part of the group.

Katz's parents, he had thought: *they don't like her.* And over the deep muscle-memory of his own pain – the pain Jim has carried with him since that night, when he found her letter in his pigeonhole in the porters' lodge – he felt a rush of worry for her. It was the first time it had occurred to him to wonder what it was really like for *her*: until then, with the rampant egotism of the rejected, he had thought that the suffering must be entirely on his side. In fact, he had *wanted* her to suffer, had turned away when he saw her outside Heffers bookshop, her pregnant belly taut beneath her blouse. He had made sure she saw him looking, and then turned from her.

She is still walking, a few steps ahead. There is no child. Perhaps Katz has her, or perhaps – and Jim will feel a chill later, when he remembers how easily the thought came to him, how selfishly he had wished it were true – they have given her away.

He thinks wildly of what to say, of all the things he would like to tell her. *What are you doing in Bristol, Eva? How are you? Did you hear I quit my law course? I'm working as assistant to a sculptor now, Richard Salles. Perhaps you've heard of him? He's very good. I met him at an exhibition, and he's become a friend, a mentor, even. And I'm working, Eva, really working – better than I have for years. Do you miss me? Why did you end it like that, with that letter? Why didn't you give me a choice, for goodness' sake? Don't you know what my choice would have been?*

So loud are the words inside his head that Jim is unable to believe he hasn't spoken them aloud. He reaches out to tap her on the arm, and she swings round to face him, her eyes wide, furious. 'What on earth do you think you're doing, following me? Go away at once, or I'll *shout*.'

It is not her. Eva's face has melted into another's: broader, a little plumper, without her questioning, intelligent eyes. He has followed a stranger up the street, and terrified her half to death.

'I'm so sorry. I thought you were someone else.'

The woman shakes her head, turns away, half runs up the hill towards Clifton. Jim stands, watching her go. And then he walks on, in the opposite direction, down to the docks, the water, the deep quietness of ships at rest.

VERSION ONE

\\\\\\

Pink house
London, October 1962

It is a good house – not grand, but solid, foursquare: a pair
of windows on either side of the white-painted porch with its
twin colonnades; a large tree, heavy with russet leaves, almost
obscuring one half of the facade.

It was this, together with the colour of the stucco – an unusual salmon-pink – that had made the agent reluctant to show
it to them. The man – his name was Nicholls; he wore a rakish
checked waistcoat and a thin moustache – told them, doubtfully,
that the interiors hadn't been touched since the twenties. 'It's
going for a song,' he said. 'You'll see why. He was an *artist*, don't
you know? Didn't have a clue how to keep a place looking spick.'

That had been enough to make Jim put his foot down – they
would see the house, thank you, that very afternoon. It might
even have been enough to make them part with the money sight
unseen (and such a reasonable price, in comparison with most of
the other houses they'd been shown). They had the money in the
bank, after all: left to Eva, in a gesture not anticipated by any of
the Edelsteins, by her late godmother, Sarah Joyce – a soprano,
and the first real friend Jakob and Miriam had made in London.

But the garden was what had really sealed the deal. It was not
so much the plot itself, which tilted sharply, sliding down Gipsy
Hill – the dusty, forgotten corner of south London with which
Eva and Jim had, for reasons they couldn't quite explain, fallen

in love – but the building at the bottom: the deceased artist's studio. It was just a shed, really, but the artist had removed the original felt roof, and replaced it with glass panels that could be drawn back in fine weather, letting in the sky. It would no doubt be freezing in winter, and sweltering in summer – and, since the old man's death, it had fallen badly into disrepair. Weeds had sprung up between the floor-slats, and the glass roof was whitewashed with dried bird droppings. But Eva needed only to look at Jim to know that this was it: his place, her place; the place that they would make their own. They had told Nicholls they would have it there and then.

Now, as Eva stands at the kitchen window, peeling potatoes for fish pie, she can just make out her husband in his studio, over the grassy incline: the top of his head, the angle of his easel. Jim spent much of the summer working on the house, sanding down floors and cupboards, painting walls; Eva joined him most evenings, exchanging her office clothes for old shirts and paint-spattered slacks. She has hardly seen him since he finished preparing the studio. He is out there before she goes off to work, breaks to have dinner on her return, and then goes back out until the early hours, his old rule about only working in daylight forgotten. (His tutor at the Slade had quickly dismissed this as nonsense, and Jim had eventually come round to his way of thinking.)

The Slade has changed Jim's work, too: gone, for the most part, are his figurative paintings, the rich, textured renderings of land and sea and Eva herself. In their place is something much more urgent, untethered, almost feverish. 'Pure energy,' was how one enthusiastic critic had put it at the MA show – though he had not, in the end, found space to mention Jim in his article, and she had felt his disappointment for him, seen the way Jim offered his friend Ewan – the main subject of the piece – his sincere congratulations. She had wished there was something, anything, that she could do other than tell him she believed in him, that success would come to him in its own time.

The peeling finished, Eva slices the potatoes, places them in a pan, covers them with water. The fish is already poached, lying in its thick, creamy sauce; the trifle is setting in the larder. Only an hour until their guests arrive. She fills the kettle for tea, leans back against the worktop while she waits for it to boil, looks with pleasure around the kitchen they have furnished – barely – with a scrubbed pine table picked up at Greenwich Market, a brightly coloured rag-rug her mother had forgotten about, found rolled up in a corner of the cellar. 'No mod cons,' Nicholls had warned them. 'You'll be much happier in that new block I showed you.' They hadn't bothered to set him straight: how to explain the delight of bare floorboards, plaster cornicing, chipped Victorian tiles, to one who prefers gas fires, carpets, fitted kitchens? He thought they were barmy. Perhaps they were. They didn't care.

Eva carries a mug of tea down the garden to Jim. Before entering, she knocks twice and waits for his reply, as is their custom. He looks round, his eyes still glazed with concentration. She tries not to look at the canvas – he still prefers only to show her the finished work, though he no longer covers his easel with a sheet. She understands: she is the same about her writing; refuses to read him even a sentence before the story – or, these days, column – is complete. 'It's six o'clock, darling. They're coming at seven, remember? Do you want a bath?'

He shakes his head. 'No time. They'll have to take me as they find me, I'm afraid.'

'I'll go, then.' She moves towards him, hands him the tea, leans down to kiss him. She can taste the faint acrid tang of paint. 'You'll come in at seven, though, won't you?'

Back upstairs, Eva runs her bath, lays fresh clothes out on their bed. They'll be eight tonight – Penelope and Gerald;

Frank, Eva's editor at the *Daily Courier*, and his wife, Sophia; Ewan and his girlfriend, Caroline. *A motley group*, Eva thinks as she undresses, slips into the hot, scented water, *but they'll rub along all right, won't they?* She closes her eyes, leans her head back against the enamel. To think, their first proper dinner party in their new house: how absurdly grown-up it feels.

By half past seven, all but Ewan and Caroline are there. (Ewan is always late.) They sip dangerously strong gin martinis in the living-room: Jim has only recently taken to mixing cocktails, and hasn't quite got to grips with the concept of measures. By eight o'clock, when Ewan and Caroline finally arrive and they can sit down to eat, they are all more than a little merry. Penelope tells a story about the first time she and Eva tried to cook spaghetti at Newnham, on their one-ring electric hob: 'We went next door for cocktails – Linda Spencer had a bottle of gin – and forgot all about dinner. When we came back, all the water had boiled off, and the pasta was charred to a crisp. Then, of course, the fire alarm went off . . .'

Ewan, who has already finished his martini, makes Caroline blush by saying that she recently tried to serve him an uncooked egg, having forgotten to set the pan to boil. So then Sophia – a small-featured, rather dainty former debutante, with an unexpectedly rough-edged sense of humour – admits to the room that when Frank last offered to cook dinner 'to give her a night off', he presented her with a slab of raw mince, topped with an egg, and tried to persuade her it was steak tartare. 'I might have been convinced,' Sophia says, a forkful of fish pie hovering between her plate and her red-painted mouth, 'had I not recognised the mince as the stuff I'd put out that morning for the dog. It was off – I mean, really *grey* – and oh, the smell . . .'

Soon, the fish pie is finished, the trifle bowls scraped clean, and six bottles of wine stand empty on the dining-room table. After coffee, Jim suggests that they play some records. He and

Frank scrap good-naturedly about what to put on – before becoming the *Courier*'s women's editor (a title that surely only a man as vivid and masculine as Frank could pull off), he was its arts editor, and still reserves a particular affection for jazz. Frank carries the day, and they all dance clumsily around the room to the Dave Brubeck Quartet's slinking saxophone.

Later, Penelope and Eva, warm from the dancing, duck out to the garden for a cigarette. It is a cool, clear night, stars littering the sky above the city's sodium glow.

'Great party, Eva darling,' Penelope says, balancing unsteadily on her heels. 'I think I might be a bit drunk.'

'Maybe just a bit, Pen. Me too.'

They lean back against the brickwork, watching the burning orange tips of their cigarettes. 'Loved your column this week. Really *funny*, Eva. Funny and clever. Reckon they'll keep on with it?'

Eva smiles; she still can't quite believe her idea for a column has come good. She had pitched the idea to Frank just a few weeks before: 'An A to Z of modern marriage,' she said over a Friday-evening shandy in the Cheshire Cheese, 'covering everything from "arguments" to "zygote". We could call it "The Married Woman's Alphabet".'

Frank had spluttered into his beer. 'It's a great idea, Eva. I'll broach it with the Man Upstairs, but I think you'd do a great job. Just promise me not to use "zygote".'

Now, to Penelope, she says, 'I don't know. Hope so. Ask Frank.'

'Maybe I will.' Penelope beams, her teeth bright white in the darkness. 'No, all right, maybe not tonight.' She tilts her head, lays it on Eva's shoulder. 'Love this house. It's perfect. *You're* perfect.'

'Nothing's perfect,' Eva says, but she is thinking, *Perhaps this is as close to perfect as things will ever come. Right here, right now, there is absolutely nothing that I would want to change.*

75

VERSION TWO

||||||||

Hostess
London, December 1962

'Of course we all adore David. He really is so marvellously talented, isn't he?'

The actress – Eva is struggling to remember her name: Julia, perhaps, but she doesn't want to chance saying it aloud – stares boldly at Eva, as if challenging her to disagree. Her eyes are an arresting shade of pale blue, like Elizabeth Taylor's, ringed by a thick, upswept line of black kohl.

'Oh yes,' Eva says absently: her mind is on the kitchen, where she has forgotten a tray of sausage rolls; too much longer in the oven and they'll be good only for the bin. 'Marvellously talented. Will you excuse me?'

She makes her way across the crowded living-room, smiling at their guests – 'Thank you so much for coming' – as she goes. Her bump is impossible to disguise now, even beneath this great tent of a dress; it's not that she wishes to hide it, but she'd like to feel less ungainly, less like an oversized obstacle around which groups of guests are forced to part and re-form. That actress – not Julia, Eva recalls too late, but *Juliet*: she played Jessica to David's Lorenzo in *The Merchant of Venice* at the Old Vic – had actually wrinkled her nose at Eva, as if she were emitting an unpleasant smell.

'Oh, goodness, *look* at you, so enormous!' Juliet had said, without a trace of warmth. Eva had wanted to wrest the cocktail

76

glass from that dainty little hand and tip its contents over her head; the effort of not doing so had exhausted her reserves of self-control.

In the kitchen, Harry Janus is placing his hand on the thigh of a very young girl Eva doesn't recognise. He springs back as she enters, awards her one of his most charming smiles.

'Our gracious hostess,' he says. 'In full bloom.'

Eva ignores him. She moves over to the oven, bends to remove the tray. The woman hovers behind her, not offering to help.

'When are you due?' she asks shyly. 'Have you been very sick? My sister felt rotten the whole time with her first. It wasn't enough to put her off having another, though.'

She seems sweet enough, Eva thinks, as she transfers the hot rolls onto a serving-plate. *She's not to know what Harry's like. Not yet, anyway.*

'It was bad for the first three months,' she says aloud. 'Not so bad any more. I'm due next month.'

'How very exciting.' As Eva turns awkwardly, carrying the heavy plate, the woman seems to remember her manners. 'Won't you let me do that for you? My name's Rose, by the way.'

'Thank you, Rose, that's kind. I'm Eva.'

'I know.' Rose takes the plate as Harry lingers uncertainly by the door, unused to relinquishing the centre of attention. 'I love your flat, by the way. It's just gorgeous. So stylish.'

'Thanks.' Through the serving-hatch, Eva watches the guests milling and circling. A few of them are dancing, framed against the wide plate-glass windows, now black, but by day flooded with wintry light, offering up a landscape of leafless trees and frosted grass. The flat's proximity to Regent's Park was what had sold it to her. It had been David's choice, really – which meant his mother's. Eva would have preferred something more homely, less uncompromisingly modern; and she felt she had the right to make her own decision, not least because a portion of the money they were putting up for the flat was Eva's own, courtesy of her godmother's legacy. But Judith Katz was not easily disobeyed. She had simply walked into Eva and David's room without knocking – it was mid-morning; David and Abraham were out, and Eva was trying to concentrate on a tricky debut play by a young writer from Manchester – and said, 'Eva, you simply *will* tell me what on earth you have against that lovely flat. It's just perfect. I can't understand why you always have to pitch yourself against me.'

Eva – not quite three months pregnant, and still suffering from a nausea that, far from remaining confined to the mornings, seemed to last well into the afternoons – had opened her mouth to argue, and found that she simply didn't have the strength. All right: they would take the flat. And it would be wonderful, Eva had to admit (though she did not give Judith the pleasure of doing so aloud), to be just a few yards from the park once the baby was born, and the blossom was back on the trees.

The baby. Though Eva has not spoken, the baby seems to hear her: she feels a sharp responsive kick, as if something at her very core is struggling for release.

'Eva, why are you hiding out here? Come and mingle, won't you?' David is at the kitchen door; she turns to him, puts a finger to her lips, beckons him over. 'What is it?'

She lifts his hand, places it on her stomach. He feels it then, taut and quivering beneath his hand, and his face creases into a smile. 'God, Eva, sometimes I still can't believe he's really in there. Our son. Our little boy.'

He leans forward to kiss her. So unexpected is the gesture – David has barely kissed her for weeks, and certainly hasn't attempted anything more intimate – that Eva resists pointing out that they have no idea whether it *is* a boy. In fact, with an inexplicable certainty that she has shared only with her mother and Penelope, she knows the baby to be a girl.

They had waited a good while before trying for a baby – 'I'd like to get myself established first, Eva,' David had said, 'and you're busy enough with your script-editing, aren't you?' Eva was busy – too busy, some weeks – and there was the fast-flowing slipstream of David's work: the auditions, the read-throughs, the first-night parties. His was a world of people, of social-ising, of collective endeavour, while hers was shrinking to fit inside four walls. She collected a fresh stack of play scripts from the Royal Court once a fortnight or so, delivered them again a few weeks later, and was otherwise rarely required to leave the house. Once, unable to stand another moment alone in the house with Judith, she had decided to drop in on David at re-hearsals, unannounced; the director had barked at her to leave at once, and David had sulked for days afterwards. The world that had once seemed to her so glamorous, so mysterious – the magnificent conjuring trick of the theatre; the audience and actors co-operating in a glorious spotlit illusion – was already, through familiarity, losing its allure.

Meanwhile, her own writing was, as Eva had feared, coming to nothing: she had started a novel, but it had come undone halfway through. She showed what she had written to Penelope, who was kind – 'There's real potential here, Eva, but it's not quite coming to life yet, is it?' – and went over and over the pages, searching for the thread that might weave her words into a cohesive whole. But she couldn't find it; in the back of her mind, a voice said, *You'll never be a real writer, Eva. You're just not good enough.*

As the months went on, she began to reach less and less for her notebooks, and to think more and more about how much she would like a baby; this was one of the few subjects on which she and her mother-in-law concurred. 'I can't think why you're waiting so long to get pregnant, Eva,' Judith Katz had said one Shabbat dinner. 'You're rattling around the house with absolutely nothing to do.'

'Hardly, Judith,' Eva had replied tartly. 'I am working, you know.'

'Motherhood is a woman's only real work,' Judith had said – a familiar refrain, uttered with all the mustered hauteur of a Victorian dowager. Cousin Deborah had rolled her eyes at Eva, and Abraham had reached out and touched his wife's arm.

'Now, Judith – I'm sure David and Eva will work it all out in their own time. David does have his career to think of.'

When it did eventually happen – when a week of constant sickness was, to Eva's joy, confirmed as a symptom of pregnancy – David was every bit as delighted as Eva. Within a few days, Eva had already secretly chosen a name – Sarah, after her godmother Sarah Joyce, whom she had loved, and whose last gesture had been so unexpectedly generous. This would be one point on which Eva would brook no argument from Judith Katz, or anyone else.

'Come on, darling. You're missing the party.'

David takes her hand, leads her back out to the living-room. Someone has changed the record, put on the album Eva bought specially for tonight: Ella Fitzgerald singing the old Christmas songs. (Never mind the fact that at least half the guests celebrate Hanukkah.) The first piano chords skitter across the room, syncopated, feather-light; Ella sings of snow and fields and open sleighs, and more people join the dancers at the window. Someone – Penelope – takes Eva's other hand, and then she is half shuffling, half twisting around the floor, the baby kicking and spinning to a rhythm only she can feel.

At first, Eva doesn't notice Juliet, across the room, standing a little apart. But when she staggers to a halt – dizzy, flushed, catching her breath, Sarah's kicks coming faster now, like a second, juddering heartbeat – Eva becomes aware of Juliet's gaze: not smiling, not frowning, but watching her unblinkingly, as if challenging her to be the first to look away.

VERSION ONE

\\\\\\\

Dancer
New York, November 1963

The first thing Jim notices about her are her feet: her toes are long, sinuous, slightly simian; her ankles are starkly pale against her black leotard. He watches her body too, of course: the broad curve of her hips; her tapering waist; her breasts pressed tight against her chest. But it is her feet that hold his attention as she dances, tracing skittish patterns across the floor, her rhythm unsettled, unpredictable, obeying an inner metronome that only she can hear.

Other dancers cross the stage – a man with a pouched, lugubrious face; a thin woman with red hair, the cleft of each rib visible through her costume – but he sees only these two feet. In his slightly inebriated state – it was another wasted day: a morning in the apartment, failing to paint; an afternoon drinking bourbon in the bar on Charles and Washington – he thinks they might well be the most beautiful thing he has ever seen.

Afterwards, the audience seems reluctant to leave. A small crowd gathers on the steps of the church, as if after a service, though the wind is blowing cold, sending the last of the fallen leaves tumbling across Washington Square. A girl in a blue mackintosh, her eyes carrying an unnatural, burnished sheen – *Stoned out of her tree,* Jim thinks – turns to him. In a small, high voice, she says, 'Wasn't that just the *best* thing you've ever seen? Don't they just change your life?'

Jim hesitates. He enjoyed the performance, found something liberating, hypnotic, in the way the dancers moved and twisted around the floor. He was reminded of the Matisse paper cut-outs with which he had, at the Slade, become briefly obsessed: their kinetic lines, their giddy, infectious energy. But he doesn't quite know how to explain this to a stranger. 'It was great, yes.'

The stranger beams at him. 'You're British!' This said triumphantly, as if he might have forgotten.

He smiles back, without warmth, and thrusts his hands deeper into his pockets – he has left his gloves in the apartment, overlooked the face-aching chill of the New York City winter. 'I am indeed.'

The girl in the blue mackintosh – her name is Deana – is still talking when the dancers emerge: tall, shapeless figures, thickly wrapped in coats and mufflers. That dancer's long, pale feet are now encased in leather boots, but he recognises her face; he can't help smiling at her, though of course she doesn't know him. She doesn't smile back; why should she? The male dancer with the long face greets Deana with a kiss, throws an arm around her shoulders. Deana raises an eyebrow at Jim, as if in apology, but he barely notices. He is still looking at the woman in the leather boots.

They are all going on to a bar on Cornelia Street. Jim falls into step with them: it's only ten o'clock, and Eva won't be home from the theatre for a few hours yet – there's a party afterwards at the Algonquin. At the thought of her standing with David Katz, his old rival – talking, laughing, sharing memories of old times – a tightness draws across Jim's chest. Perhaps he should have gone to the play with her; he can see now that not going was a rather childish decision on his part. And yet when Eva said that Katz had been in touch, that Harry's play had trans-ferred to Broadway, Jim's refusal to go had been instinctive: self-preservation, he supposes, or just plain old jealousy. It is five years now since Katz had any claim on Eva – five years in which she has become Jim's *wife*, for goodness' sake, has bought a house with him, become the bedrock of his life. But still there is a nasty, snarling chorus in the back of his head that he can't quite ignore. *Katz is a star now – what have* you *done? Who are* you? *You're just a kept husband, wafting around New York while your wife goes out to work. You're not an artist. You haven't sold a painting since you left the Slade. You can't give* your *paintings away. You're nothing.* It is only in the bar on Charles and Washington that he has been able to silence that chorus: there, he sits with a bourbon as morning slips into afternoon.

The bar on Cornelia is a basement dive, black walls and sticky floors; a small platform with a chair, where a man with a guitar may or may not appear. The Judson dancers occupy a booth. Jim is late joining them, returning from the gents' – he can't quite believe his luck when the only remaining seat is next to her. She is looking at him now.

'Pamela,' she says, as he slides onto the bench.

He will not remember much about the night: just the sooty semi-darkness of the room; the red wine that arrives in fat, raffia-covered bottles; the deep, rough-edged voice of the musician who at some point takes to the stage singing Woody Guthrie. Pamela he will recall mostly in still frames: a lock of black curls, pushed behind her ear; a glass lifted to her lips; the bright whiteness of her naked body, slatted with shadow. And her feet, of course: the cool length of them, pressing against his legs when she comes.

He will not remember leaving her apartment, or getting home, though he must have done somehow: the next day he wakes late, in their bed – his and Eva's – the sound of the telephone cutting painfully across what may well be the worst hangover he has ever had. He stumbles across the bedroom to the landing, fumbles for the phone. It is Eva, ringing from work

– she has a cubicle in the *New York Times* offices; files her new column, 'An Englishwoman in New York', to the *Courier* from there, along with reports on news, fashion, culture – to tell him that the president has been shot dead. A motorcade shuffling through a Dallas square. Three shots. Blood seeping across Mrs Kennedy's neat pink suit.

Beneath the shock, there is a heady, shaming sense of relief: this is the story now. This is all anybody will be talking about for days, weeks, months. Eva will be busy filing to London: too busy to wonder where her husband was last night; why he came in sometime before dawn, showered, and then slid into bed beside her, his mind still jumbled with images of another woman. Later, there will be guilt, of course – but not yet. Not now.

VERSION TWO
||||||||

Algonquin
New York, November 1963

After the show, the producers throw a first-night party at the Algonquin.

It is, by British standards, a swanky affair: liveried waiters, a jazz trio, an apparently endless flow of champagne. The Oak Room's wood-panelled walls lend the occasion an intimate, faintly medieval air; a series of heavy iron chandeliers punctuates the thickly plastered ceiling, their dim, guttering bulbs offering the guests the flattery of semi-darkness.

Paul Newman and Joanne Woodward stand together in one corner; in another, Rex Harrison bends his head towards Burt Lancaster, his crisp, theatrical baritone faintly audible beneath the general hubbub. At the centre of it all are Harry, David and Juliet, the play's young director and stars. David's hand is light in the dip of Juliet's bare back as they make a slow, beaming circuit of the room.

Eva stands a little apart, holding a glass of champagne. Her shoes are rubbing – she bought them yesterday at Bloomingdale's, along with her floor-length gown. She had left Sarah with David's grandparents on the Upper East Side. It was the first time she'd been away from her daughter for more than half an hour, and she could barely concentrate for worrying, so she chose the first dress she tried on. Now, catching her reflection in the bar's mirrored siding, Eva wonders whether she made a bad decision: the green silk has gathered in unflattering ridges across her stomach, still soft from her pregnancy. She stands a little straighter.

'It went really well, didn't it?' Rose is at Eva's elbow, bride-like in a draped white dress; it occurs to Eva that she may be trying to drop Harry a hint. But that is unkind: she likes Rose, is glad that her relationship with Harry seems to have stuck. Over the last month, marooned with Sarah in the tiny walk-up the show's American producers rented for them – David refused to stay with his grandparents, insisted he needed his own space, though their disappointment was palpable – Rose has become a friend, perhaps Eva's only friend in this maddening, beautiful city, with its neon gaudiness and sidewalk awnings and shuf-fling, unheeded beggars. On the long walks Eva has begun to take, pushing Sarah in what the Americans so charmingly call a 'stroller', the beggars are the only people who seem to have the time to stop and talk. A few weeks ago, while watching the pigeons with Sarah in Washington Square, Eva had been ac-costed by a tiny, wizened old woman wearing blue plastic bags for shoes. 'Watch yourself, missy,' the woman had hissed as Eva pushed Sarah briskly away. 'I might *bite*.' Eva has been unable to quite shift the woman's face from her mind ever since.

'Yes, I don't think it could have gone any better,' she says now. 'Though I did worry John might miss his cue – you know when he asks David for a light, just before the curtain? He was a few seconds late.'

Rose stares at her, impressed. 'I didn't notice. You know the script better than they do.' She sips her champagne. 'But of course, that's your job. To read carefully, I mean. To notice things.'

'Yes, I suppose it is. Or it was.'

Since having Sarah just over ten months ago, Eva has given up her script reading: the Royal Court announced, soon after

Sarah was born, that they were taking someone on full-time, and she has not made enquiries at other theatres. She has been happy to lose herself completely in motherhood: in its daily routine, minutely attuned to her daughter's needs. And yet a part of her still wonders – especially in the sleepless hours of the night, when David buries his head beneath the pillow, and she must walk up and down the apartment's tiny living-room, quieting Sarah as best she can – whether it will be enough. It is certainly not how she had imagined her future with David: she had seen them rising in tandem, his success as an actor complementing hers as a writer. And yet now, her free moments are so few, and when she does sit down to write, her mind feels loose, ragged, full of holes, and she is filled with the conviction that nothing she has to say is worth committing to paper. When she tries to raise the subject – to seek anew the warmth of David's all-encompassing confidence – his answer is usually, 'Well, darling – you have Sarah to think about now, don't you? I'm sure you'll find time to go back to writing when she's older.'

Eva, has, in a weak, exhausted moment, confessed her frustration to Rose – who says now, as if reading her mind, 'You could leave Sarah with David's grandparents again, you know. Give you some time to get on with your writing.'

Eva looks over at David, now reaching out to shake Lancaster's hand. Juliet is still standing close to him. Eva watches Lancaster's eyes slide from the perfect oval of her face to the low V-shape of her neckline.

'Or couldn't David mind her sometimes? He'll be free in the daytime now, won't he? They all will. You could leave Sarah with David, go off to the library.'

Eva considers this: leaving her daughter in David's care; tripping off down Fifth Avenue to the public library, a whole day stretching out in front of her; coming home to a clean apartment, a happy, rested baby, dinner bubbling away on the stove (or at least a couple of boxes of Chinese takeaway). It is unimaginable; David loves his daughter, there's no doubting that, but he's about as capable of changing her nappy as flying to the moon.

They are interrupted by Harry, approaching with a man Eva doesn't recognise. His hair is neatly slicked, his suit charcoal-grey, loose-fitting, a little square. Not an actor, then – a money-man. But as they come closer, Eva reconsiders; there is something oddly familiar about the cast of his face.

'Darlings.' Harry is exuberant, high on his success. He slips an arm around Rose's waist. 'Here's someone I'd like you both to meet. Jim Taylor. Jim, this is my darling English Rose – and this is Eva, David's wife.'

Jim offers his hand to Rose, a little formally; stifling a giggle, she leans towards him and kisses him once on each cheek. 'Much better than a boring old handshake, isn't it?'

His cheeks colouring, he turns to Eva. As she also leans in to kiss him, she notices that his eyes are a very deep blue, almost violet, and framed by lashes longer than her own. In a woman, the effect would be called beautiful. In a man, it is a little unsettling.

Harry's attention is already wandering; his duty done, he steps back, seeking more useful company. 'You'll look after Jim for me, won't you, darlings?' He turns away without waiting for a reply.

There is a brief, rather awkward silence. Then Jim says to Eva, 'David was great tonight. It's a brilliant play.'

The man, Jim, has a very straight gaze, made even more intense by the uncommon colour of his eyes. 'Yes, he *is* good in it, isn't he?' Another short pause. 'And what about you – how do you know Harry? Are you an actor?'

'Oh no, nothing so glamorous, I'm afraid. I'm a solicitor.' He lifts his palms, as if in apology. 'Harry and I were at school together – and Cambridge, though I didn't see so much of him there.'

'Which college? I was at Newnham.'

'Clare.' Jim looks at Eva again, more closely, this time. 'Do you know, I have the strangest feeling that we've met.'

Rose gives an exaggerated sigh. '*Please* don't start one of those Cambridge conversations. I can't bear it. I get enough of it with Harry.'

Eva laughs. 'Sorry. You're right. It's tedious.'

For a few minutes, they talk of other things – Rose's modelling; Sarah; what Jim is doing in New York (a two-month exchange programme, he says, organised to 'further Anglo-American relations'). Then Rose, catching sight of Harry as he edges closer to a young woman in a tight black cocktail dress, slips away. 'Nice to have met you, Jim.'

A passing waiter stops to fill their glasses. When he has moved on, Jim says, 'I wish I could work out where I've seen you before.'

'I know. It's so odd, isn't it? I can't work it out either.' Now that they are alone, Eva suddenly feels a little shy.

They are silent for a moment, and then he says, 'Would you like to sit down?'

'God, yes. These shoes are killing me.'

'I thought so. You've been shifting from foot to foot ever since I came over.'

'Have I?' She watches him, alert to the possibility of ridicule, but he is smiling again. 'How embarrassing.'

'Not at all.'

They choose a corner booth. Discreetly, Eva kicks off her shoes. There is another silence – a little charged, now that they have chosen to separate themselves from the rest of the room. Jim breaks it. 'How long have you known David? Did you meet at Cambridge?'

'Yes. We were in a play at the ADC: *A Midsummer Night's Dream*. I was Hermia; he was Lysander.'

'So you were set on acting too?'

'No, not really. My friend Penelope was auditioning, so I went along for the ride. It was good fun.' The dry, chalky smell of the old store room in King's, where they had rehearsed; drinking warm shandy in the Eagle courtyard afterwards; David taller, brighter, somehow *more* than any man Eva had ever seen. 'I thought he was insufferably arrogant at first.'

'But he won you round.'

'He did.' Eva falters, cautious of disloyalty. Carefully, she says, 'What about you? Are you married?'

'No. I'm rather ... Things have been difficult. My mother, she's ...' Jim is looking at her again, with that disconcerting, unwavering stare, as if he's weighing up how much to tell. 'She's not well. The last time she was discharged from hospital, the doctors said she shouldn't be living alone. My father died, you see.' He pauses, and she senses how much it costs him to go on. 'My aunt went to stay while I finished my law training in Guildford, but then it was down to me. So I moved back to Bristol to live with her.'

'I see.' On the other side of the room, the jazz trio has started up again, the saxophone rising mournfully above the soft shimmer of hi-hat and bass. 'And how is she now?'

'Not good.' Jim's expression shifts, and Eva regrets having asked. 'Not good at all. She's back in hospital. I wouldn't have come all this way, but ... Actually, her doctor said I should come. He thought it would be a tonic. For me, anyway.'

'And has it been?'

'Yes. Yes, I think it has. To be honest, I'm feeling better than I have in a good while.'

They move on to New York: the city's unstoppable pace; the dizzying height of the buildings; the eeriness of the steam-plumes rising ghostlike from the pavements. ('The first time I saw it,' Eva says, 'I was sure the subway must be on fire.') Jim is impressed by the fact that Eva and David are staying in Greenwich Village – his own apartment is in Midtown, boxy and nondescript, a few blocks from the law firm. But he has, he says, spent most of his free time in the Village, drinking it all in. 'There are some amazing galleries – in basements, shopfronts, old garages. All kinds of work, too – sculpture, installations, performance art. Even dance, over at the Judson church on Washington Square. There's a real vibe.'

'Perhaps that's where I saw you, then. In the Village.'

He nods. 'Yes. Perhaps that's where it was.'

From there, they sidestep to Jim's father – Eva saw his last retrospective at the Royal Academy – and to Jim himself: his own love of painting, the fact that he had always wanted to go to art school rather than Cambridge, but his mother wouldn't hear of it. 'My father died when I was ten – well, perhaps you knew that, if you know his work. After that, she got a lot worse. She sold the house in Sussex, almost all of his paintings. She couldn't bear to think that I'd turn out like him.'

A waiter is hovering by their table; they are silent while he tops up their glasses. Then Jim says, 'There was a woman, you see. Sonia.' His finger traces the stem of his glass. 'In fact, there'd been a lot of women.'

As they talk, Eva has the sense that she is drifting further and further from the room, into a borderless place where time fractures, loosens, and there is only this man, this conversation, this inexplicable sense of profound connection. There is no other way she can describe it, though she is not yet trying to describe it to herself – she is simply here, intensely aware of the moment (the nearness of him, the soft rise and fall of his voice) as the rest of the world drops away.

She tells him about her writing, about her faltering attempt to finish a book: describes the plot, the characters, the setting. 'It's about working women, I suppose,' she says. 'Four women who meet at Cambridge, and then take a house together in London. Careers, friendship, big dreams.' She pauses, offers him a smile. 'And love, of course.'

He returns her smile. 'Sounds fascinating. Do you have a title yet?'

Eva shakes her head, and tells him that she is worried she will never finish it, that she is too busy with Sarah; but that, if she is truly honest, she thinks she is afraid to finish and then find it isn't good enough.

At this, Jim leans closer, his uncommon blue eyes fierce. His hand meets the tabletop with a dull thud. 'Good enough for whom, Eva? Surely it only ever needs to be good enough for you.'

It is, in its glorious simplicity, possibly the most interesting thing anyone has ever said to her. Eva sits back against the leather banquette, fighting the desire to reach out and touch him, to take his hand in hers.

'And you?' she says with a new urgency. 'Are you still painting?'

'No.' She can see how much it pains him to tell her the truth. 'Not really. I'm just . . .' He sighs. 'I really have no excuse.'

'Well, Jim Taylor, Lewis Taylor's son,' Eva says quietly, 'I'd say you'd better get back to it too.'

'What *are* you doing, darling, hiding out over here?' David, looming tall over their booth, extends his hand to Jim. 'I'm not sure we've met. David Curtis. I see you've been taking care of my wife.'

Jim gets to his feet, shakes David's hand. He is a little shorter, and his grey suit looks decidedly shabby next to David's slim-cut Savile Row, but he has no trouble meeting David's eye. 'Jim Taylor. I'd say that she was taking care of me. I don't know anyone here other than Harry.'

David does not remove his gaze from Jim's face. 'Harry, eh? How do you know my old mucker?'

'We were at school together. And Cambridge. In fact, you and I have met. Graham Stevenson's birthday party at the Maypole. You came with Harry.'

'Is that so? I really don't remember you at all.' David looks from Jim to Eva. Hatefully, she feels herself colouring, though she has done nothing wrong, has just been talking to an interesting man, while David paraded around the party with Juliet. Eva is gripped by righteous anger (and jealousy, though she won't name it as such; but the fact is not lost on Eva that, a few years ago, *she* would have accompanied him around the room). She says nothing, however; a waiter is again approaching their table. This time, though, he isn't carrying champagne.

'Mrs Curtis?' Eva nods: on theatrical occasions, she adopts David's stage name. 'There's an urgent phone call for you at reception. Would you please step this way?'

The hotel lobby is cool and quiet after the clamour of the party. The receptionist – a trim, efficient-looking woman, her hair teased into a neat blonde bob – hands Eva the telephone with an expression of remote, professional concern.

Rachel, David's grandmother, is on the line, her voice high and tight: Sarah has a fever, and won't stop crying. She hates to disturb Eva, but she thinks she ought to come home.

Eva leaves at once, her pulse quickening. She asks the receptionist to tell David where she has gone, to follow her – which he does, after an interval of several hours that she will later find difficult to forgive.

It is the middle of the night by then – two a.m., the blank windows of the emergency room admitting the sickly neon glow of the city. They sit together on hard metal seats, Eva and David still in their evening dress, Rachel and Simeon swaddled in coats: David's grandparents have insisted on coming, though they are grey with worry and tiredness. Eva can see nothing but a kind of whirling blankness. She doesn't speak, except to refuse a third plastic cup of watery coffee from the kind candy-striper passing with her trolley. She holds David's hand, and doesn't think that an hour before she had wanted to hold Jim's. All thoughts of their conversation, of anything at all, have fallen from her mind – she can see only Sarah, puce and bawling, kicking her tiny arms and legs, disappearing through the maw of the emergency-room doors in a stranger's arms.

Just after three a.m., the doors open again, and a nurse approaches. Sarah is fine, she says – it's just an ear infection, a nasty one, but nothing to worry about. The doctor has given her something to help her sleep. They can take her home.

By unspoken consent, they share a taxi back to Rachel and Simeon's apartment. In bed, Eva settles Sarah into the crook of her arm. Her daughter is breathing slowly and evenly, her damp hair slick against the fragile armature of her skull.

David falls asleep quickly, and Eva listens to the sound of his breathing, overlaid by that of their child. It is only then, in the darkest hour of the night, that she allows herself to think of Jim Taylor: of that dizzying sense of connection, so strange, so unexpected. It is his face Eva sees as she falls gratefully into a deep sleep, dark enough to blot out the stars.

Algonquin
New York, November 1963

Jim had not been intending to go to the play. He already had plans for the evening – a performance by the Judson dancers at the church on Washington Square. Richard and Hannah were going with a crowd from MoMA; afterwards, there'd be a party at some painter's apartment in the Village. Artists, writers, sloe-eyed girls swaying to the music, and someone in the kitchen doling out amphetamines from a paper bag.

But the posters have been tracking Jim's movements around the city ever since they arrived: on the subway, on news-sellers' booths, pasted to brick walls and lampposts. 'David Curtis' and 'Harry Janus' printed in thick black type. 'The new smash-hit London play.' He resolved to ignore the posters as best he could, to pretend that neither of those names was familiar. And then that day, after leaving the gallery – he is supervising the installation of Richard's exhibition – he finds himself passing the theatre, asking if there are any tickets left for tonight's performance of *The Bohemians*.

'Just one, sir,' the teller says. 'Would you like me to book it for you?'

Jim is seated in the back row of the mezzanine. He can't see the stalls below, and is disappointed – he is sure she must be here, had hoped to scan the rows for a glimpse of her. From here the stage, with its stark, realist set – a toilet, a pallet bed, a sink – is rendered miniature, a toy theatre.

He has read about the play, a loose adaptation of *La bohème*, set among the pushers and prostitutes of postwar Soho: the London notices were glowing, and its Royal Court run was extended twice. But Jim was not expecting its impact: he is captivated, even at this distance. Katz – or Curtis, as Jim supposes he must call him now – as the poet Rodolfo (here named Ralph), is transformed: shivering, bone-thin, clutching his Mimì (Mary, here, played by an actress of an uncommon, sensuous beauty: Juliet Franks) as she chokes out her last breath. Jim can't deny that Katz is good – so good he almost forgets to hate the man.

After the curtain, the crowds pour out onto Broadway. Jim hangs back, looking for Harry (and, of course, for her). It is some years since he last saw Harry – not since their graduation; they were never particularly close, even at school, and Jim has no New York number for him, no means of telling him he was coming. He waits until the lobby is empty and echoing, a cleaner in crisp striped livery manhandling an enormous vacuum cleaner from a cupboard.

'Looking for someone, sir?' An usher is approaching from the stalls door, the gold buttons on his uniform polished to a high shine.

'Yes, actually. I'm a friend of Harry Janus, the director. Do you know whether he's . . . ?'

The usher's expression softens. 'A friend from London? You've come a long way, sir. There's a party at the Algonquin. Want me to hail you a cab?'

'It's all right – I'll get one myself. But thank you.'

On Broadway, the air is cool and sharp – a wind has got up, whipping the awnings, sending a stray news-sheet skipping across the sidewalk. Jim draws his scarf tighter around his neck; with a certain self-consciousness – the act still feels oddly unreal, like something a character in a film would do – he steps out into the road to hail a cab. He is lucky: a passing yellow saloon slows, stops. He climbs in.

'The Algonquin, please,' he says.

At reception, he gives Harry's name. A bellboy takes his jacket, leads him down carpeted corridors, silent as churches, pushes open a door, waves him through. He hands the boy a quarter, steps inside. Suddenly, all is light and noise: dark panelled walls lit by ugly iron chandeliers, a jazz trio rattling through a Stan Getz number. People – glossy, fashionable, laughing – are standing in impenetrable groups, clutching glasses of champagne. He takes a glass of his own from a waiter's tray, scans the room for Harry. And for her.

He sees her first. She is standing alone in a floor-length green dress. Her hair is coiled and pinned, exposing the naked brown skin of her neck; her arms are also bare, lifting her glass to her lips. Confronted by the real, undeniable presence of her, Jim realises how wrong he was to have seen her face in that girl on the street in Bristol: Eva's face is hers, and hers alone. The tapered sharpness of her chin; the twin arches of her eyebrows; her quizzical brown eyes. He is willing her to look up, to notice him, but he is also seized by the desire to turn and run.

'Jim Taylor! What on earth are you doing here?' Harry is jovial in his penguin suit, beaming, all-powerful. He has thickened out since university: his face is soft, his cummerbund pulled taut. He beats Jim on the back, in lieu of an embrace, and Jim returns the gesture.

'I'm here for work. I saw your play was the talk of the town, so I bought myself a ticket.'

'You clever, clever chap.' Harry's quick blue eyes watch Jim carefully. 'What is it you're doing these days, then? Still painting?'

Jim nods. 'Yes, actually – when I can. And I work for a

sculptor: Richard Salles. Perhaps you've heard of him? He has an exhibition opening at MoMA next week.'

'Does he? That's great, Jim.' But Harry isn't really listening: he's already looking over Jim's shoulder, smiling a greeting at another face. 'You'll forgive me, won't you – so many people to talk to. But we must catch up while you're here. Call the theatre, ask for my New York number. And thank you for coming.'

Harry moves away, and then – though he is no longer facing Eva – Jim can feel her eyes on him. Panic rises in him: to meet her expression, whatever it may be – friendly, or the opposite – suddenly seems more than he can manage. He forces himself to turn. She is still there, and she is looking at him – he has not forgotten the intensity of her gaze – but she is not alone: a slender girl in a white dress is standing with her. Eva is not smiling, but she nods, as if in invitation. And then he is crossing the space between them until they are only inches apart, and he is leaning in to kiss her cheek.

Eva introduces the other girl as Rose Archer. Harry's girlfriend, she adds, and he kisses Rose's cheek, too, registering her beauty automatically, as if looking at her picture in a magazine. She is not truly present for him – not as Eva is.

Jim watches Eva for as long as he can without seeming rude. She is carrying a little more weight, but it suits her, has softened her sharper angles. She looks tired, as any mother might – how old must the child be now? Five? The skin beneath her eyes is smudged with shadow. He remembers that first morning, after they met on the Backs, waking before her in his rooms; neither had slept much, but she was sleeping then, her closed face greyish in the dawn. He had been seized again by the need to paint her, to capture her exactly as she was, and would never be again. But instead he had dropped back into sleep, and that moment had rolled off irretrievably with all the others, into the past.

They are talking – Jim, Eva and Rose. He is aware that their lips are moving, though he barely registers what they are saying: plain, inconsequential things – how much he enjoyed the play, how long they have been in New York. Rose looks from Jim to Eva. If she wonders how well they really know each other – Eva has called him only 'an old schoolfriend of Harry's', a description so inadequate that Jim struggled to resist the temptation to correct her – she does not say. After a time, Rose excuses herself: she must go and find Harry; it was wonderful to meet him. Jim fires back the same dusty pleasantries, hearing his own voice as if from a great distance. And then they are alone.

'It's good to see you,' Eva says.

Jim stares at her. *Surely*, he thinks, *she could have found a better word than 'good'*. He has inherited from his father a hatred of imprecision, in language and in art. He remembers quite clearly a Sunday afternoon – Jim couldn't have been older than seven – when he had been allowed into the attic, shown a painting of a wooded landscape, swaddled in whiteness. 'Look,' his father said, 'you think snow is white, but it's not – it's silver, purple, grey. Look closely. Every flake is different. You must always try to show things as they are, son. Anything else is just smoke and mirrors.' It was years before Jim really understood what his father meant, but he understands it perfectly now.

'I'm sorry,' Eva says. She must know what he is thinking: she was always able to read his face. 'I don't mean "good". It's as bad a word as "nice". There's just nothing that's quite right, is there?'

To write him that letter; to leave it in his pigeonhole. It occurs to Jim that perhaps he hated her, for a time, even while wishing he could find the words that might bring her back to him. But it would be useless now to pretend that there is any hatred left.

'No,' he says. 'It's true. Nothing's quite right.'

'Jim Taylor.' Katz (he can't get used to thinking of him as Curtis), slender as a toreador in his black suit, hair slicked just so. 'Well, this is a surprise. What are you doing in town?'

Jim extends his hand. 'I'm assistant to a sculptor. Richard Salles. He has a retrospective opening at MoMA.'

Katz lifts an eyebrow. 'Really? Oh, I know his work. Very interesting. Eva and I will have to see if we can make it.' Behind his carefully composed expression, Jim can sense the whirring and clicking of the man's brain. He has never liked Katz, for reasons he could not, before Eva, quite articulate. Afterwards, there was time enough to find those reasons: Jim had tried to do so in the only way he knew, with charcoal and paper and slashes of oil paint. He never painted Katz himself, but men who looked like him, men with cruel, handsome faces and unseeing eyes. Men who always won the game, without even bothering to learn the rules.

It strikes Jim, with some force, that of course Eva must believe that he never tried to change her mind. It isn't true: after he found her letter, Jim wrote her sheet after sheet in reply. He wanted her to know that she didn't have to do this; that it didn't matter; that he would love her – love the baby – just the same. But he posted none of the letters; he simply couldn't find the courage. Christmas came and went – his mother was barely functioning; Jim addressed himself to the daily minutiae of helping her to rise, dress, eat. By the time the new term began, he felt empty, purged, in the grip of an emotionless, numbing sense of calm. Eva had made her choice. Surely the most loving act was to set her free?

Now, with her standing before him, he feels the full weight of his mistake. He should have gone to her. He should have held her to him until she understood.

But there is nothing left to do now but excuse himself, say he really must be getting home. At the door, Jim turns again to the space where Eva was standing, but sees only empty air. He sets off alone down the corridor. And then, quite suddenly, a hand is clutching at his arm, tugging him back. Eva. She slips a scrap of paper into his pocket. Then, just as quickly, she is gone.

Jim walks on, waits until he is in the lobby, and the bellboy is fetching his jacket, before opening the note. The letters are fat, smudged, charcoal-black.

Tomorrow. The public library. Four o'clock.

PART TWO

VERSION ONE

\\\\\\

Exhibition
London, June 1966

'Gilbert's brought that bloody parrot in again,' Frank says.

Eva, lost in the middle of a paragraph – should that be 'maybe' or 'perhaps'? – doesn't look up from her typewriter. 'Has he?'

Frank gets up from his desk, goes over to the open door. 'Can't you hear it squawking?' He leans out into the corridor. 'Gilbert! Shut that bloody thing up, won't you?'

From the office opposite, Gilbert Jones, the obituaries editor – a thin, desiccated man who has recently taken to bringing his pet macaw to work – gives a muffled, 'All right, all right, no need to shout.' Then comes the dull thud of a door slamming shut.

'That's better.' Still standing, Frank reaches into his trouser pocket for a cigarette. 'Want one?'

She has settled for 'perhaps'. 'Oh, go on, then.'

They perch uncomfortably on the windowsill, as is their custom: Bob Masters, the literary editor, with whom they share an office, has an unaccountable hatred of cigarette smoke. It is late afternoon; the air is clammy, weighted, carrying the familiar scents of frying onions and unemptied bins. Their office, at the back of the *Courier* building, is not envied for its uninspiring view of fire escapes and fan-shafts; it is, however, usefully placed next to the main stairwell – usefully, at least, for Frank, who adores gossip, and usually prefers to leave the door open.

Whenever a pair of secretaries passes, chattering loudly, he will rush to the doorway, cock an ear towards the stream of their conversation. In this way, Frank has managed to confirm both that Sheila Dewhirst, the chief secretary, is sleeping with the editor, and that his wife is fully appraised of the matter, and has effectively given them carte blanche.

'No sign of Bob, then?' Eva says, looking over at his empty desk, his lonely typewriter marooned among great stacks of books, miscellaneous collections of paper, envelopes, string.

Frank stretches out his legs, emits a chain of perfect smoke-rings: one, two, three. He is in shirtsleeves, as he usually is after lunch; his thick, unruly hair – once a glossy black – is now rather dashingly shot through with grey. He's a handsome man – Eva has heard the secretaries giggling about him in the canteen – but still touchingly devoted to Sophia; Eva doesn't think he's the type to stray.

'Not likely,' he says. 'Lunching at the Arts Club, some writer or other. Usually turns into dinner, doesn't it? You know what *writers* are like.' He elbows her gently in the ribs, and she smiles. 'How're you getting on, anyway?'

'With the feature?' Eva is writing about a women's commune in East Sussex; she drove up there earlier in the week, spent the night. The de facto leader – there was, in theory, no hierarchy – was a stout, plum-voiced woman named Theodora Hart. She had inherited the large house from an aunt, and decided, with an idealism that was either touching or profoundly naive, to found a 'new matriarchal co-operative community'. Eva was sceptical: how, she had asked them, could a truly co-operative community exclude half the population? The women were patient with her, answered all her questions over a delicious stew made with vegetables from their own garden. Afterwards, they had sat in a relaxed circle, playing records, passing round joints. 'I don't know how you can stand to be married,' one of the women said. 'A man telling you what to do all the time.' And Eva – drowsy with dope – had laughed and replied, 'Oh, don't you worry. I give as good as I get.'

'No,' Frank says now. 'How are you getting on with the novel? The writing that matters.'

'Oh.' She takes a slow drag on her cigarette, enjoying the soft sensation of unfurling smoke. 'Not bad at all, thanks. Nearly there.'

'When can I read it?'

'Soon. After Jim, of course.'

'Of course.' Their cigarettes have wasted to stubs. Frank crushes his into the ashtray. 'Right. Another hour knocking Yvette's blasted copy into shape, then off to the Cheese for a swift half. Coming?'

'No. It's Jim's exhibition opening tonight.'

'Of course! I'd forgotten.' He throws her an apologetic glance. 'Should Sophia and I be coming?'

'No. He hasn't invited anyone. It's really just for the school. Though I think it's open to the public on Saturdays.' Eva hates the way she sounds: as if she is apologising for the show's modest scale; and, by implication, for the modest scale of Jim's ambition. She sits back down at her desk, keeping her eyes on the typewriter.

'Well.' Frank sits too, crossing his legs beneath his desk. 'Perhaps we'll see if they'll let us in one Saturday, then.'

An hour or so later, her feature finished, copy stacked neatly on Frank's desk for him to read first thing tomorrow, Eva steps out into the evening. Fleet Street is busy – women like herself, neat in print dresses, striding efficiently towards bus stop or Tube; men smartly suited, carrying rolled copies of the *Evening Standard*; others (hacks, copywriters, marketing executives: the standard-bearers of this new media age) younger, looser-limbed, their hair creeping over the collars of their sports jackets.

The train from Victoria is delayed: it is almost half past seven when she arrives at the school. The exhibition is in a corridor adjoining the main hall – Jim has told her about the difficulty he had in hanging his paintings while the boys scurried back and forth, dumbly curious. She felt for him, pictured a narrow passageway, dimly lit. But in fact it is a wide, bright space, his paintings arresting flashes of colour against the white walls; and she wonders again why he feels this need to play down every achievement, each small step that might carry him closer to success. Though she's not even sure what that word means to him any more: the man she met at Cambridge – the man she fell in love with – with his grand ambitions, his all-encompassing desire to paint, to fit the world to the frame of his own vision, is, she feels, fading before her, like a photograph left too long in the sun.

'Perhaps,' he had said to her a few months ago (they'd been to the theatre, were sitting up late, sharing a bottle of wine), 'this is all there is for me, Eva: teaching, dabbling with painting on the side. Perhaps I've reached the end of the line.'

'No.' She'd reached for him: attempted to convey, in the pressure of her hand on his, the extent of her belief in what he could achieve. 'Don't say that. It's a struggle – you know it is – to create anything of real value. You've just got to keep at it, Jim. You mustn't give up.'

He had looked at her then – really looked at her, and his expression had raised goosebumps on her skin: there, in those dark blue eyes, was the trace of something she'd never seen before. Distance; disbelief; his cool acknowledgement of the growing disparity between her achievements and his. Eva had wanted to shout at him then: *No, Jim! Don't do this. Don't use my success as a weapon against me. We're a team, aren't we?* But she had said nothing, and neither had he; after a silence, she had told him she was going to bed, and he had made no move to follow her.

Now, she finds Jim standing with a small group: other

teachers, a few she knows; parents; a couple of governors. 'Sorry, darling,' she says in a low voice. 'Trains a nightmare.'

He frowns, whispers back, 'Wish you'd been here.' But she squeezes his hand, and Jim's face, as they rejoin the group, re-arranges itself, finds its usual easy charm. The headmaster, Alan Dunn – a tall, spare man, with a neat moustache, and the de-flated air of an army colonel on furlough – tells Jim, rather unconvincingly, that the exhibition is a 'triumph'. Then he turns to Eva, informs her that her last column (on their return from New York, she was given both a new job title – features writer – and a larger slot on the women's page) had caused quite a stir at home. 'I'm not at all sure you should be telling the nation's housewives to hang up their aprons. Eleanor is threatening to go on strike.'

Eva opens her mouth to frame an appropriate response – she can't imagine Eleanor Dunn, a minor aristocrat whose preferred conversational topics are horse-racing and the mat-rimonial arrangements of the European royals, ever having to lift a finger around the house. But Alan continues: 'Of course, I'm only joking, my dear. We think you're quite marvellous. Not our usual newspaper, you understand, but still – marvellous.' He beams at her, and she smiles back, almost expecting him to issue her with a gold star.

When the sherry is finished (a reluctant pair of sixth-formers has been making a dutiful round, offering thimblefuls in plas-tic cups), the corridor echoing with the loud, expectant silence of an empty school, a few of the teachers go on to the pub. Eva has met most of them before – there is Gavin, from the English department; Gerry, Jim's fellow art teacher; Ada, the French mistress, who wears black and chain-smokes Gauloises as if unafraid of conforming to caricature. Jim – grateful for the fact they all stayed to the end – buys a round of beer, and a few packets of crisps.

Eva is dizzy from drinking too quickly on an empty stomach, and from the tension of knowing how much tonight matters to Jim, though he will not show it. When he'd told her, back in May, that the school was to mount an exhibition of his work, it had been with a shrug. 'It's just a consolation prize, isn't it?' he'd said. She had disagreed with him, insisted they go out for dinner to celebrate – and they had gone, eaten steak and chips in their favourite French restaurant in Soho. He'd rallied then – ordered a bottle of Chianti, seemed more like his old self. But over dessert, he'd grown maudlin; returned to the idea that this couldn't be all there was to look forward to.

'I've been thinking, Eva,' he'd said, suddenly animated, taking her hand, 'that I'd really like us to have a child. Wouldn't you? Isn't it time? Haven't we waited long enough?'

Eva had drained her glass; waited a few seconds before replying, 'You know I want a child, Jim – of course I do. But not now. Not yet. I'm so busy at work, and I'd still like to—'

His reaction was brisk, dismissive. 'Finish your magnum opus – yes, I know. How could I forget?'

He'd been so full of excitement about teaching, at first. He'd come out with the idea while they were still in New York. It was a week or so after Kennedy's assassination – Eva had been busy interviewing, summing up, but had still noticed his withdrawal. For weeks, he'd avoided his easel, his paints; in the evenings, when she came back from the *Times*, he was often out, and had left no note. Worry had begun to gnaw at her: worry not only for his loss of creativity – she felt that deeply; couldn't bear the idea that his desire to paint, always natural, instinctive, might have been suddenly extinguished – but that perhaps the unthinkable was already happening to their marriage: that perhaps he was having an affair. But Eva did not voice her anxieties, afraid that in doing so she would call them into life; and then one evening, she came back to find him home, boxes of Chinese takeaway spread across the dining-table, a bottle of wine just opened.

'I've made a decision, Eva,' Jim said. 'When we get back to London, I'm going to start teaching.'

She knew what it cost him – his dreams of earning a living only from his art, at least for now. Ewan was already making a name for himself: he had been taken on by a major Cork Street gallery; *he* certainly didn't have to teach. But Jim was heady with newfound enthusiasm: teaching would, he said, be a far better option than, say, returning to the law; he'd still be immersed in art, and he'd have the holidays to paint. And so Eva had allowed herself to be swept up in his plans. *Thank God it's this*, she thought. *Thank God it isn't another woman. Thank God we're all right.*

Now, in the pub garden, it is still warm, the night velvety, smelling of beer and cut grass. The teachers are a little drunk, bursts of laughter punctuating their horror stories about pupils they have known and loathed. Ada, the oldest of the group, recounts her memory of the time a notorious fifth-former sent a series of obscene notes to Alan's secretary, purporting to be from Alan himself. The poor woman, she says, was frequently seen crying at her desk until the deception was finally discovered. 'I've never seen Alan so furious,' Ada concludes with an approving nod. 'It was like a scene from – what is that film with the angry gorilla? *King Kong.*'

Jim is quiet, holding Eva's hand under the table. She thinks of his paintings, arranged neatly on the white walls: the cut and swipe of them, their vivid swirls and streaks, caught inside trim black frames. On their return from New York, he had seemed galvanised, excited once more by the possibilities of paint. Out in his studio at the bottom of the garden, he had begun working furiously – in the evenings, and at weekends, after starting at the school; the private boys' school in Dulwich, whose headmaster, Alan, seemed delighted to have Jim on the staff. Now, two years on, Jim is painting with less intensity – on Sundays, on the odd evening, when he isn't too tired – and the work he is producing is moving deeper and deeper into abstraction. But where, with other painters, that abstraction becomes its own language, in Jim's work the meaning remains knotted, indistinct. Really, Eva believes he should return to his earlier, figurative style: he is wonderful at portraits and landscapes; many of his early paintings, including two of her, line the walls of their house.

She tried saying this to him once, as tactfully as she could, but he turned on her, snarled. 'Nobody wants to see *technique* any more, Eva. For God's sake – can't you see that stuff's way out of date now? The world's moved on.' Eva knew perfectly well what he meant by 'that stuff' – his father's paintings. She had rarely seen Jim so riled, and she did not press him further.

At closing time, they walk home: their car is parked at the school, but they are both too drunk to drive, and it's not a long walk, though it is mainly uphill. Halfway, they pause to catch their breath. The suburban street is dark, silent, the lights of the city spread out below.

'It went well, I think,' Jim says. 'Maybe I'll get Adam Browning to come and have a look.'

Adam Browning is Ewan's gallerist: Ewan has kindly told him about Jim, and Browning has written him a note, offering to come and see Jim's next exhibition.

'Good idea,' Eva says. She leans forward to kiss him. Jim loops his arm around her shoulders, and they walk on, uphill, towards home.

VERSION TWO
||||||||

Warehouse
Bristol, September 1966

The exhibition is in an old warehouse, down by the docks. The building has no name, and Jim wonders how he will ever find it: the flyer – rough, hand-drawn, the letters curling around the image of a woman, hair thick and flowing as a pre-Raphaelite muse – says only 'Warehouse 59'.

But as he nears the river – still, glassy, mirroring the tall, lumbering bulks of ships and abandoned grain-stores – he sees he needn't have worried: there is a chain of people leading the way across the cobblestones. They are around his age, the women in long skirts, their hair loose, much like the picture on the flyer; the men in jeans, bearded, their shirts louchely unbuttoned. 'Hippies', they are calling them in San Francisco – and even in Bristol, now. They are shouting to one another, and laughing: loud, peacock-bright. Jim falls into step with them, wishing he'd had time to change out of his suit.

'Hey, man,' somebody says. 'Going to the show?'

The man is nodding at him, eyes half closed, his mouth carrying a slow, private smile. Stoned, of course – or something. Jim nods back, and the man says, 'Groovy. Should be a blast.'

As they skirt the dockside, passing piles of pallet boxes, container stacks, the rusting hulls of old passenger ferries, Jim can feel his mood lifting: he is sloughing off the working week, the dust and grime of it, the hours spent poring over statutes, reading title deeds, sitting in airless rooms with fat-necked businessmen. He likes the law no more than he ever did, and yet it seems to like him: he is good at his job, more than he cares to be; and the less he cares for it, the more he seems to succeed.

Perhaps he would like his work better were he not navigating his days at Arndale & Thompson from inside the dreamlike fog of the chronically sleep-deprived. For months, his nights have been broken by his mother's unpredictable wanderings. One day a few weeks ago, he woke at four. The flat was unnaturally silent: he rose, saw Vivian's room empty, dressed, rushed out onto the dark Clifton streets, and found her walking up and down Whiteladies Road in her nightdress, sobbing, shivering. He wrapped her in his jacket, walked her home, and put her to bed like a tired child.

In that moment, Jim felt something shift in him: he resolved to care a little less. Whether his mother has noticed the change, he can't say – and yet things have started to improve. Her doctor has prescribed a new medication: the high dosage leaves Vivian puffy-eyed and lethargic, but it seems to be evening out her extremes, and she has begun to sleep through the night. And anything is better, surely, than hospital, than ECT. (Jim can remember, quite vividly, going to visit her that first time, after his father's death. The cool white corridors. The kindly nurse who had poured his orange squash into a plastic cup. The terrible, uncomprehending blankness of his mother's face.)

His sleeplessness is not aided by the fact that he has begun painting again: late at night, usually; Bob Dylan or Duke Ellington on the record player, turned down low. His time in New York seems to have reinvigorated him. The other lawyers there were fast-talking, obsessed with money, cars, drink. Jim had nothing in common with them; he had spent most of his time at MoMA – the British sculptor Richard Salles, whose work Jim had seen before in Bristol, had a retrospective there; he went along, intrigued, and returned twice more, drinking in the swoop and thrust of bronze, granite, poured concrete. Or he wandered the streets of the Village, peering into gallery windows, walking through open doorways and finding himself part of some spontaneous 'happening'. Once, in a basement gallery on Christopher Street, he stood among a small, solemn crowd as a young woman removed her clothes and began, slowly and reverently, to cover herself in liquid clay.

At first, painting in his room in the Bristol flat (how he hates the place, longs to get away; but while her night-time escapades continue, Jim knows how dangerous it would be for Vivian to be left alone), he feared his mother's reaction; he remembered, too well, the times he'd come home from the office to find his canvases spoiled, his oil paints ruined. But she has not reacted with the vitriol he was expecting. Last weekend, she even came into his room, sat on his bed and watched him working, her legs curled under her like a girl's. He let her stay, though he hates an audience. After a while, she said, 'You're good, you know, darling. You'll never be as good as your father. But you're really not bad at all.'

Warehouse 59 is easy to spot: someone has painted flowers over the rough brick, sent them spilling from the window frames, over the chipped pediments. Inside is a large open space, divided by an iron staircase. The walls are lined with paintings, the stone floor crowded with sculptures and installations: to Jim's right is an old supermarket trolley, twisted and soldered into an animalistic skeleton; to his left, a mound of rubble on a plinth.

Jim sees right away that most of the art is second-rate – though as soon as the thought has formed, his confidence deserts him: who is he to judge, after all? A solicitor, a Sunday painter. The son of a great artist, but a man too fearful, too tied to the ebb and flow of his mother's illness, to lay any claim to the word 'artist' himself.

He takes a beer from a trestle table at one end of the room, in exchange for a few coins, and begins a slow circuit of the room, aware that he recognises no one: he had seen the flyer in the White Lion, left Peter and the others finishing their first round. He asked Peter to come, but Sheila was expecting him for dinner, and it wasn't quite his thing.

Jim can't deny that he is jealous, sometimes, of his friend's marriage: of their easy intimacy; of the instinctive protectiveness, the love, that he senses in Peter every time his wife's name is mentioned. There have been women, of course – in New York, a secretary named Chiara, Italian-American, with a wide, generous body; Diane, a student actress, pale-haired, thin; several others in Bristol, including, most recently, a primary-school teacher named Annie. They have spent several months circling each other, neither quite ready to show their hand, though Jim knows, with what is surely insufferable arrogance but also nothing less than the truth, that Annie is falling for him, and that he doesn't, won't ever, feel the same. Sometimes, when he looks at her, it is as if he is looking at someone else: a woman with a small, intelligent face, dark eyes, skin lightly tanned, as if spun under a glaze.

Eva. Eva Katz – or should that be Curtis now? Married to the man they're calling the next great British actor, heir to Olivier. Jim had spoken to her at the Algonquin for what, half an hour, before she rushed away? He had asked someone – that pretty girl in the white dress – where Eva was going; looking at him curiously, she had told him that Eva's daughter was unwell. At the mention of the child, Jim had felt shame wash over him – what kind of man was he to sit exchanging intimacies with another man's wife, some poor sick child's mother? And yet he had done so, and her face has stayed with him; and her words.

Are you still painting? ... No ... Well, Jim Taylor, Lewis Taylor's son, I'd say you'd better get back to it.

One painting holds his attention more than the rest. It is that most unfashionable of things, a seascape – the canvas layered in shades of blue and grey; the merging wash of sky and sea. Jim stands in front of it, trying to place the view: there is a crop of rock in the foreground, sprigged with coarse, bleached grass. *Cornwall*, he thinks, and a voice behind him says, as if in response, 'St Ives.'

He turns. The woman is tall – her eyes are almost level with his own – with clear, pale skin. Her long brown hair is parted neatly at the centre. She is wearing a loose white top that reminds him of his father's old painting smocks. Blue jeans and brown suede boots, fringed like a cowboy's.

'Helena,' she says, as if he'd asked her name. 'That one's mine.'

'Is it? It's very good.' He gives his own name, extends his hand. She doesn't take it, just smiles. 'What are you – a banker?'

He feels his cheeks colour. 'A solicitor. But don't worry. Dullness isn't contagious. At least, I don't think it is.'

'No. Maybe not.' She regards him for a moment. She has blue eyes, a wide, sensual mouth; a kind of freshness seems to come from her: the scent of clean linen, sea air. 'Are you hungry? There's food upstairs.'

They eat cross-legged on the floor, in an upstairs room hung with cheap Indian tapestries and dyed cotton sheets. One corner of the room is equipped with a small kitchenette; in another stands a record player, balanced on a stack of bricks. Someone has put on music, turned it up: Jim can hardly hear what Helena is saying, but he enjoys watching her lips move, and the way she eats, neat and efficient, not a mouthful going to waste.

Later, they move outside, where the music dulls, and the quayside is dark, the empty boats casting long shadows across the water. Helena has a joint in her bag, ready-rolled. She lights it, offers it to Jim, and they sit down on the cobblestones, backs against the warehouse brick, smoking. She lives in Cornwall, she says; not in St Ives itself, but just outside – they have a community there, an artists' colony. The old one in St Ives is dying, killed off by in-fighting and old age. Theirs is a new way, free of ego, just artists living together, sharing thoughts, ideas, techniques. No art-world cronies telling them what to paint, how to think, how to sell their work: just a crumbling old house, a vegetable garden to tend, the limitless freedom of sea and sky.

Jim says it sounds wonderful, idyllic – a world away from painting at an easel in the spare room of his mother's flat. And Helena looks at him and says that it is wonderful – that he should come, stay for a while: visitors are always welcome.

He says he might just do that, though he's not sure he means it. Not yet.

When he kisses her, she tastes of garlic, tobacco and the sweet, cloying undertow of marijuana – and, yes, he is sure of it, though later he will admit it was fanciful, there is also the soft, salty tang of the sea.

VERSION THREE

////////

Sandworms
Suffolk, October 1966

For Miriam's birthday, Eva treats her to a weekend in Suffolk.

Penelope and Gerald have recently spent their anniversary in Southwold, in a smart seafront hotel. They returned with the telephone number of a local woman who had an old fishermen's cottage to let right on the coast – 'The loveliest little place you ever saw, Eva, really – Rebecca would love it.' It is a long time, Eva realises, since she and Rebecca have had a holiday – even longer for her mother. With Jakob so often away on tour, her parents seldom travel; they prefer to spend their rare weekends together pottering, gardening, nodding silently in twin armchairs to their beloved stack of opera LPs.

This birthday, it will be just the three of them – Eva, Miriam and Rebecca. Jakob is in Hamburg with the orchestra. Anton is on a work trip to Glasgow. (He has, much to the bemusement of his family, settled on shipbroking for a career.) And David – well, David is also away, of course, filming: when, these days, is David not away?

They drive up on Friday, after school, in Eva's new Citroën (a present from David, bought with his pay-cheque from the last film; much as she is grateful for the car, she can't help thinking of it as the symptom of an uneasy conscience). Rebecca is breathless, excited – she insists that Oma sit with her on the back seat, look at the drawing she did that afternoon. The teacher, Rebecca explains at length, asked each child to imagine their perfect weekend. She has drawn herself, her mother and her grandmother as stick figures on a beach, against a strip of sky; each wave a pencilled curlicue, the sun an orange ball, rays fanning out like wheel-spokes.

'You see, Oma, this is what I'll *actually* be doing this weekend. Miss Ellis said I was a very lucky girl.'

Miriam, laughing, says she does see. She asks after a fourth figure: taller, placed some distance away from the others. 'That's Daddy, silly,' the child replies scornfully. 'In my imagination, he will be there too.'

'Don't call Oma "silly", Rebecca.' Eva speaks firmly from the driving-seat. 'That's not nice.' Rebecca bites her bottom lip, a gesture that always threatens tears. In the rear-view mirror, Eva catches her mother's eye.

'I know a song about going on an adventure,' says Miriam. 'Do you want to hear it?'

It is dark when they arrive at the cottage. Eva edges the Citroën down the narrow path between the terraces and into the cottage's tiny courtyard, which is barely wider than the car.

'I don't fancy doing that again,' Eva says when she has brought the car to a shuddering halt.

Miriam nods. 'We shan't need to drive much. Now, shall we wake Rebecca, or carry her in?'

Eva looks over at her daughter, curled on the seat, her face perfectly composed. She is small for a seven-year-old – she takes after Eva and Miriam in that respect, though her features are more like David's: she has his persuasive black eyes and wide, expressive lips. It seems a shame to wake her.

'I'll carry her. Can you manage the bags?'

The cottage is flat-fronted, boxy, with a scrubby front garden stretching down to the seawall. Inside, it is freezing, the cold undercut by the strong, vegetable smell of damp. For a moment, standing exhausted in the doorway with Rebecca in her arms – she had two manuscripts to finish for Penguin before lunchtime, and their bags to pack – the prospect of making it habitable seems too much for Eva to bear. Thank heaven, then, for Miriam, striding in with the bags, issuing instructions. 'Make up a bed for Rebecca, *Schatzi*. Open all the windows for ten minutes – just keep your coat on – and then I'll light a fire. We'll have the place *gemütlich* in no time.'

Quickly, deftly, Miriam sweeps out the grate and lines it with crushed newspaper and kindling, while the open windows flood the rooms with the fresh chill of the sea. Upstairs, in the small back bedroom – she has insisted Miriam take the larger room at the front – Eva smoothes sheets and blankets across the double mattress, and lays her sleeping daughter down.

Then she sits awhile with her mother before the fire, sharing a bottle of Riesling. The smell of damp has been overlaid by the deep, peaty scent of firewood, and the room is dark but for the fire's orange flare and the greenish light of the table lamp. They talk of family matters – Jakob's last concert; Anton's latest girlfriend, a brittle blonde secretary named Susan whom both Eva and Miriam are struggling to like; Miriam's health - she has suffered for years, uncomplainingly, with the drawn-out after-effects of a chest infection caught in her thirties, during a lengthy recital tour.

They do not talk of David, though he is there, lurking at the fringes of their conversation. Eva last saw him the night before he left for the shoot. It was late – Rebecca had been asleep for hours – and David was just back from some party to which Eva had not been invited. She had sat on the corner of their bed, smoking, watching him pack.

David had loved her once – he had told her so, that night in the Eagle pub. (How long ago it seemed now; how spent and deflated all that panic, that urgent making of plans.) He had never hesitated, never taken advantage of the balance of power now tipped decisively in his favour, in which he might – many men had done it before him – have refused to acknowledge her, or their child.

And Eva had believed, then, that she could love him too: this beautiful, clever, charming man, with his absolute belief in his own talent. She has come to love David, in her way, as he has her; and yet Eva feels now – she has considered the matter in her mind, examined it from every angle as if it were an object under glass – that he has never truly allowed her to know him, to slip beneath the various masks he presents to the world.

That night six weeks ago, as David moved silently around their room, she'd found herself wondering whether it was all simply a role he was playing: a part he'd once liked the look of – dutiful husband and father – and of which he'd grown tired. Or perhaps, more likely, the fault was hers; how could she be a proper wife to him, form a proper family, when he knew – he must know – that she had left her heart with another? And yet she had tried – oh, how she had tried; and she couldn't forgive David easily for simply stepping away, absenting himself with the easy excuse of work. And of course it wasn't only for work that he was absenting himself; of that she was fully aware.

The next morning, Miriam's birthday, Eva wakes to wintry sun, the smell of woodsmoke, voices carrying faintly from downstairs. There is a space in the bed where Rebecca should be. Eva brushes her hair, pulls on clothes. She finds her mother and daughter in the kitchen preparing breakfast, a fresh fire already burning in the grate.

'Happy birthday, Mama. What time is it? I should be making breakfast for you.'

Miriam, at the stove, waves a hand. 'Don't worry, darling, I don't need waiting on. It's ten o'clock. I thought you could use some sleep. Anyway, Rebecca and I have been having a fine old time.'

Rebecca tugs at her mother's sleeve. 'Come and sit here, Mummy. I set a place for you.'

They breakfast on fried eggs and milky instant coffee, thoughtfully left for them in the larder. From her suitcase, Eva produces her mother's gifts. A silk Liberty scarf from herself and David. A pair of woollen gloves from Rebecca, bought with the carefully hoarded contents of her piggy-bank. A bottle of Fleurs de Rocaille perfume from Jakob. The 1964 Joan Sutherland recording of Bellini's *Norma* from Anton, acting on his father's advice.

'What riches,' Miriam says, and she fastens the scarf around her neck, sprays the perfume and slips on the gloves, so that Rebecca cries out, outraged at such a breach of protocol, 'Oma, you *can't* wear your gloves indoors!'

Later, they walk down to the beach. The tide is out, the sea a distant glimmer; the coarse sand is wet, littered with the discarded cases of sandworms. Rebecca runs ahead, towards the waterline, her arms flung wide. Eva calls her back, afraid of quicksand or other unknown dangers, but Miriam places a restraining hand on her arm. 'Don't worry so much, *Schatzi*. Let her play.'

Eva takes her mother's hand, links her arm through hers. An image slips into her mind: her mother and Jakob, walking arm in arm along another eastern seafront, another beach. The tale of their arrival in England – and Eva's own arrival a few months later – is as worn and familiar to her as an old photograph carried in a wallet. Docking in Dover; boarding a train for Margate, the address of Jakob's cousin's boarding-house written on a slip of paper. The cousin had found jobs for them both – Miriam cleaning, Jakob washing dishes. Two young musicians with a new baby, tidying up after an assortment of oddballs in a dilapidated dosshouse at the very edge of the world.

And yet they had been happy, Miriam always said; even later, in the camp on the Isle of Man, where they had organised evening concerts, and Miriam had taught rudimentary English to those who spoke only German, Polish, Hungarian, Czech. Then, they had still believed, despite the gathering weight of reports from across the Channel, that their families would eventually be able to join them in England: Miriam's brother, Anton, and their elderly mother, Josefa, whose poor health had prevented them from leaving with Miriam; Jakob's parents, Anna and Franz; his sisters, Fanny and Marianne; and all their cousins, uncles, aunts.

There was pain later, of course, a pain that never left them, only softened its edges with time. But Eva has always envied her mother's ability to be happy: a facility for making do, for making better, that must surely spring from having had to leave everything behind.

'Does this remind you of Margate?' Eva says aloud. 'Of how England looked when you first saw it?'

'A little.' Miriam is quiet for a moment. 'The sky, perhaps – how huge it is, how pale, like a watercolour. A Turner. Your father would like it here.'

'He would,' Eva says, knowing she means Jakob, not that other father, his face shadowy, unknown. Just the idea of a father, really.

They walk on in silence, their shoes slapping faintly against the sand. Eva thinks of David, wherever he may be: in Spain, somewhere south of Madrid. He is due home in a fortnight. It is a long, complex shoot – a version of *Don Quixote*, directed by David Lean, with Oliver Reed in the title role. David has telephoned twice, spent most of each short conversation talking to Rebecca; told Eva only that Lean is working them hard, but he is enjoying himself – he and Reed stayed up till dawn the previous night, drinking rough local liquor. David did not mention Juliet Franks, though her name loomed large between them: she has a small part in the film, and was due to arrive halfway through the shoot. They both know who put her forward for the part, and why.

Seven years into her marriage, an uncomfortable awareness has settled over Eva: that it should never have happened. At this distance, she can hardly account for her own fervent belief, shared by David, Abraham and Judith (how clearly she recalled her mother-in-law's air of martyred resignation), that her pregnancy meant they should marry at once. Her own parents certainly never pressured her. ('Just be sure, *Schatzi*,' Miriam had said. 'Please just be absolutely sure.') How could they, when Jakob had married Miriam knowing that he would be the father to another man's child: believing that, as he loved her, it was the right, indeed the only, thing to do? Eva had known that Jim would make the same decision, if she had only given him the chance. She had believed that not allowing him that chance – not permitting his grand plans to buckle, lose their shape, under the weight of fatherhood – was an act of love. And yet, in New York, she had seen Jim's face, and known at once that their parting had hurt him much more deeply than she had ever imagined.

At the thought of Jim, Eva feels a vertiginous sickness, as if she is standing at the very edge of a cliff. That nausea is there at night, too, sometimes, when she wakes in the early hours. (Last night, in the cottage, she slept better than she has in months.) To run after him at the Algonquin, hand him that note, and then not to go – the cruelty of it appals her; she would never have thought herself capable of such a thing. And yet she was. That New York morning had dawned bright and uncompromising, and Eva's fear had been such that she could not go.

She could not conceive of a version of that day in which she would leave Rebecca with her great-grandparents and stroll off in the autumn sunshine to the public library, and into – who knew what? An affair: a new beginning. The taking apart of everything in favour of an uncertain future.

That fear still shames her – though she wonders, too, whether Jim even went to the library. She has not heard from him. He does not have their London address, but it would be easy enough to find: he need only ask Harry, or even his cousin Toby, still part of her brother's extended circle of friends. So perhaps – and Eva isn't sure whether the thought makes her feel less wretched or more so – Jim didn't go. Perhaps her very presumption disgusted him. Perhaps he tore her note into small pieces, and threw them away.

'You are unhappy, *Schatzi*,' Miriam says suddenly, as if Eva had spoken aloud. 'You are unhappy in your marriage.'

Eva opens her mouth to protest. She has never discussed her true feelings about David with her mother – but of course Miriam must have some knowledge of them; she is too intuitive to be deceived. She and Jakob have always said they liked David – that they find him dynamic, charming. But Eva is aware that they are becoming increasingly frustrated with the long absences that are, in effect, leaving Eva to bring Rebecca up on her own, with all the difficulties and frustrations that this entails – the constant parrying of Rebecca's questions about David's return; the soothing of Rebecca's tears, late in the night, when she comes running into her parents' bedroom, looking for her father, and finds her mother alone.

She works so hard to protect her daughter: tells Rebecca how much David works; how greatly he is in demand. Each postcard from him is pored over; each long-distance phone call a cause for celebration. And in the meantime, she, Eva, is just the workaday parent, the constant presence – loved, yes, but so familiar as to hold little interest; certainly not the glamorous, remote figure swanning back into Rebecca's life with gifts and kisses, whenever he so desires. And as for Eva's own career – her writing, so much more important to her than her hack-work for Penguin – there is simply no time. She might, of course, give up her job – David is making good money now – but she refuses, on principle, to be entirely dependent on handouts from her husband, just as her mother has never been on Jakob, however much she has relied on him in other ways.

Now, on this beach, against this wide, empty sky, Eva no longer sees any point in burying the truth.

'It's true, Mama. I am very unhappy. I think I have been for a while.'

Miriam squeezes her arm, pressing Eva's gloved hand tighter against the thick wool of her coat. 'You have made a cage for yourself, my love. You think it is impossible to get out. But it is not impossible. You need only to open the door.'

'Like you did, you mean?'

Miriam does not turn her head; she keeps looking out to sea, to where Rebecca is tracing a broad circle in the sand with the heel of her shoe. Her mother's profile is neat, handsome, bearing only the faintest tracery of wrinkles around her eyes, spanning down from the corners of her mouth.

'Yes, like I did,' she says. 'And like anyone can who is lucky enough to have a choice.'

VERSION ONE

\\\\\\

Miracle
London, May 1968

Jennifer Miriam Taylor is born at nine a.m. on a fresh spring morning, clouds sculling through a watercolour sky, blossom weighting the tops of the trees outside the maternity ward.

Years later, his daughter's timing will strike Jim as entirely in keeping with her character: she will be a neat, ordered child, and then a neat, ordered woman – a solicitor, in fact, and a better one than he would ever have made. But now, holding her in his arms, feeling the fractional rise and fall of her breathing, he is barely aware of time. The minutes, the hours, seem to have slipped their usual markers and turned loose.

He had wanted to stay with Eva – to somehow share her pain, make it bearable – but the midwife had clucked at him and sent him home. He'd spent the night at the kitchen table with the cat, drinking coffee, anxiously watching the clock, waiting for the call that would tell him it was time to return. It was just after nine when the telephone finally rang; morning was settling over the street as Jim went out to the car, drove back to the hospital. He found his wife asleep.

'Don't wake her,' the sister warned, wagging a finger at him. He feels powerless before the nurses, who all seem like minor variations on the same woman, each brisk and capable in her white starched cap.

The sister allowed him to see his daughter, though. Peering

through the window of the baby unit, it took him a moment or two to find her, and Jim panicked, fearing the significance of this, fearing that he might already be failing. And then he saw Jennifer, and realised he would have known her anywhere: that miniature skull with its translucent covering of skin; that sweep of dark hair, unexpectedly thick; those wise, lucid eyes – blue, like his, he saw, and the discovery delighted him, though the sister told him they would likely turn dark as she grew.

Now Eva is awake, her face unnaturally sallow, etched with tiredness. But she is smiling, and to Jim, she seems somehow transformed: he is a little in awe of her, in awe of the conjuring trick she has performed. This tiny miracle. He sits beside her bed, on the uncomfortable plastic chair, Jennifer staring up at him with her startling blue eyes, opening and closing her tiny fists. He has heard about the strangeness of newborns, how they seem like shrunken old men and women, carrying as they do the inchoate knowledge of what comes before; Ewan spoke of it when his son, George, was born last year. But Jim hasn't known it himself until now, hasn't experienced the unworldliness of looking into a newly minted face, and understanding that the child knows all there is to know of life's great mysteries, but will quickly forget it all and have to start over again.

During the long wakeful night at the kitchen table, Jim's excitement had been tempered by a hot sense of shame: he had found himself thinking of that woman in New York, the dancer. Pamela. He hadn't seen her again: the guilt had risen in him as quickly as the hangover had faded, and he realised how casually, how easily, he had betrayed his wife and everything she meant to him. *A mistake*, he had told himself by way of comfort. *It won't happen again*. And yet it had, a year or so later, when Eva was away on a story: and in their own bed, with Greta, the young German assistant at the school. She was nineteen, her body soft and pliant, her breasts full; she had clung to him

129

afterwards, cried a little, and he had realised the depth of his mistake. Luckily for him – for all of them – she had returned to Munich a week later, citing a family illness; wrote him two heartfelt letters, which he managed to intercept before anyone noticed the German postmark, and then fell mercifully quiet. For weeks, Jim had been disgusted with himself; could barely meet his own eyes in the mirror; couldn't understand how it was that Eva carried on as if everything was just as it had been. But eventually the guilt faded, became something like tinnitus: a low-level white noise, always present, but liveable with. Not life-threatening.

He began to wonder whether his father had always lived with that feeling, too. Lewis Taylor, bright star of the postwar English art scene, fallen from fashion now, though he had still loomed large in the minds of Jim's tutors at the Slade. Some had even studied with him; they remembered him as a skinny boy with a lopsided smile and a cigarette always dangling from his mouth. Jim had always had the impression that his tutors were especially hard on him for being Lewis Taylor's son. One, in particular, had seemed to take pleasure in accusing Jim of drawing too heavily on his father's work; the slight had made Jim stubborn as well as angry, reluctant to please. He had wanted to set himself apart – and yet he had known, at the same time, that the only approval he would ever crave was from his father, and that was the one thing he would never have.

Jim is old enough now to know that Lewis had never been faithful to Vivian: he had slept with the majority of his models, and fallen in love with several. Jim can remember, as a boy, watching his father pack a suitcase as Sonia, the girl from the paintings with the dandelion cloud of orange hair, sat outside in the car, and his mother raged, running up and down the stairs, her screams drawing out Mr and Mrs Dawes from next door. The timid voice of Mr Dawes from across the garden fence.

'Now, now, Mrs Taylor, I'm sure there's no need for all this.'

But his mother was inconsolable: she had cried for days after his father had placed his cases in the car, gently wrested her grip from his arm. Jim had had to make their meals, take them up to her on a tray. He was only nine years old; it did not occur to him to blame his father, who had returned a few weeks later, without explanation. Vivian had got up again then, painted her face. Jim could hear her singing tunelessly in the kitchen as she cooked, and other, deeper night-noises coming from their bedroom that he didn't understand. All was normal again, it seemed – and then a year later, his father was dead, and a few days after that, the hospital van came to take his mother away for the first time.

Jim had, for a while, consoled himself with the fact that he had never subjected Eva to such indignities. He had not loved Pamela, after all; and he had certainly not loved Greta. His desire for them had been purely physical – a reflex action; this, at least, was what he'd told himself at first. But more recently, he has found himself considering the fact that there was something else behind his infidelities: the need, perhaps, to meet a woman's body anew, free from the sedimented strata that underpin a marriage – the memories, the disagreements, the highs and lows; and yes, the love. Of course he loves Eva: after betraying her, he had felt washed through with love, overflowing. And yet he is aware of the growing distance between them, and he hates himself for it. Hates himself for the resentment that he can't swallow, however hard he tries. Resentment of the fact that her career is set on an upward trajectory, straight and true, while his lies trapped beneath the tedious demands of teaching.

Eva's refusal to have a child had lain between them for years: a grenade picked up and lobbed, at intervals, to cause maximum damage. He had thought it selfishness, even called it so to Eva's face, and then, seeing how much he had hurt her, regretted the words he was unable to retrieve. And then, one wonderful day last summer, she had told him that she was pregnant (they had been careful, but not, it appeared, quite careful enough) and had seemed as delighted by the news as he. And now Jennifer is tumbling into the world: their daughter; their love – the hope and promise of their marriage – made manifest.

Towards four, the cat had stretched out on the table in front of him, twitching through some deep animal dream, and Jim had fallen into a fitful doze, still sitting upright in the chair, his head resting on his hand. He had seen himself in his studio in the garden – 'the shed', he calls it now; 'studio' seems too grandiose a word for the inconsequential work he does out there on Sunday afternoons. In the dream, he was finishing a self-portrait. The canvas was blurred, impossible to make out, but he knew that the painting was good, perhaps the best he had ever done, the work that would finally get his stunted career off the ground. He had called for Eva, wanting to show it to her, and she had come running down from the house; but when he looked round, it was his mother standing there, not his wife. The painting had resolved itself: in the place of his eyes were two ragged, gaping holes. 'Not good enough,' he heard his mother whisper sharply behind him. 'Not good enough at all.'

At the hospital, he drinks watery coffee in the canteen, leaving Eva to sleep, telling anyone who will listen – a harassed-looking doctor in a suit and bow tie; an elderly woman with a sad, pinched face – that he is a father. Sometime in the afternoon, Jakob and Miriam arrive; they are beaming, rapt, taking turns to hold Jennifer. When visiting hours are over – all is well, the sister says, but they'll keep mother and baby for another few days 'to get them shipshape' – the three of them linger uncertainly at the hospital doors.

Jakob clears his throat. 'It seems a shame just to go home now, doesn't it, Jim? Perhaps we could have some dinner?'

They find a French restaurant a few streets away, where the

men order steak frites and red wine, Miriam a bouillabaisse. They raise their glasses, toast Jennifer's future, and Jim looks from Miriam, elegant in a pale yellow blouse, a silk scarf knotted at her throat, to Jakob, easy, large-featured, the shadow of a beard already creeping across his freshly shaved chin. He has been a good father to Eva, Jim thinks, and he is not even her flesh and blood. Perhaps fatherhood is not just biology; perhaps it is simply a decision.

'And your mother?' Miriam says. 'Will she be coming down?'

Fleetingly, Jim sees his mother as she was in the dream last night: young, about the age she had been when his father died, her skin smooth and unlined, her arms bare. There has been an improvement in her condition: a new medication, a levelling out of her extremes. He telephoned her just after Eva went into labour, and found her a little strange: her voice seemed dulled, as if heard in echo. But dulled, echoing, was better than the alternative. Perhaps he would invite her to stay.

'I'll telephone her tomorrow,' he says. 'I didn't want to make too many plans – you know, in case Eva doesn't feel up to it.'

Miriam nods. Jakob, next to her, smiles at him, sips his wine. 'You have a daughter now, Jim,' he says. 'Nothing will ever be quite the same.'

'I know,' Jim says, and he smiles back at Jakob, overwhelmed with the newness of his baby daughter, with the sense of a life stretching before her like a blank page, waiting to be filled.

VERSION TWO

||||||||

Leaving
London, July 1968

Eva gets home from the *Daily Courier* to find David in the bedroom, his suitcase splayed open on the bed.

'You're back early,' she says.

He looks up at her. He is wearing a short-sleeved shirt that she doesn't recognise. The white cotton is stark against his tanned skin – after a month in Italy, he could pass for Italian himself. Meeting his gaze, she feels oddly shy: it's been weeks since he was last home – he went straight to Italy from New York – and they have hardly spoken on the telephone; each time he calls, he talks mainly to Sarah. When they do speak, Eva finds herself struggling to think of anything to say: the world David inhabits – one of call-sheets, sides, days in trailers, late nights of drinking – is so distant from her own. It feels increasingly as if neither speaks the other's language, and each lacks the impetus to learn.

'The shoot wrapped two days early. I changed my flight.'

'Oh.' Irritation flares in her: Penelope is coming for dinner, and Eva has been looking forward to their evening on the terrace, catching up, each filling the other in on the office gossip. It is two years now since Eva started at the *Courier*: not under the editor – Frank Jarvis – for whom she'd interviewed in her final term at Cambridge, but as a junior editor on the books pages. (Penelope had called in a favour to secure Eva the interview.)

She has employed a girl to look after Sarah, now five, in the hours between school and work: a rather indolent French girl named Aurélie; sweet enough, though prone to settling Sarah in front of the television while she telephones her boyfriend in Reims, or paints her nails. But Aurélie has gone home to France for a holiday, and Eva would have liked some time to prepare for David's return – cleaning, tidying, explaining to Sarah that her beloved daddy is on his way. 'You might have let me know.'

He is silent for a moment, watching her. Something passes between them – something coded, unspoken – and the realisation hits Eva with a force that leaves her winded. David is not unpacking.

'Let's go and have a seat,' he says evenly. 'I think we could both use a drink.'

She goes out onto the terrace. The sun is still hot, and she lifts her face to it, closes her eyes, listens to the faint cries of children in Regent's Park, to the throb and hum of passing cars. She is oddly calm: it is as if, she thinks when David emerges carrying the gin and tonics (too strong, no doubt, when Eva is due to collect Sarah from Dora's house in an hour – but hang it, Dora's mother can think what she likes) this is happening to other people, and she is observing them. A young couple sitting in the sun – the man dark-haired, elegant, each movement as precise and measured as a dancer's; the woman small-featured and slight. The man hands the woman a glass, and they drink, looking anywhere but at each other.

'Where will you go?' she says. And to show she fully understands – to say the woman's name first, and in doing so to dispel its power – she adds, 'You and Juliet.'

He looks at her then, but she doesn't meet his eyes. Eva would like to think that even now, even here, she still has the capacity to surprise him. 'You know, you're not at all as I thought you were when we first met,' David had said to her, a few years into their marriage. Eva had taken it as a compliment, but recently she has wondered whether the version of her that emerged in its place has proved a disappointment: a dull, tarnished facsimile of the woman who had once so captured his attention.

But if he is surprised, now, David doesn't show it. 'She has a flat in Bayswater. But we're thinking about Los Angeles.'

'And Sarah?'

'She can come out to visit in the holidays.' There is the briefest hesitation, in which Eva allows herself to hear regret, anxiety – though she knows her husband well enough to be aware that he is a stranger to such feelings. *If they are there now*, she thinks unkindly, *it is because he has learned them ahead of time; because he has prepared the script.* 'If that's all right with you.'

Eva says nothing, and David goes on, more urgently, 'I have to do this, Eva – you do understand, don't you? I think you do. I think you know our marriage has been dead for a long time.'

An image slips into Eva's mind: the two of them laid out on concrete slabs, quietly sleeping, like the stone effigies on Christian tombs. What was it Jakob had said, in the music room the night before the wedding, as the grandfather clock ticked on in the hallway? *I'm afraid he will never love you quite as much as he loves himself.* She had known it then, has always known it, really, and yet surely this is too much. To move to Los Angeles, with *that woman*; to leave it to Eva to tell his daughter that David has gone, and will not be coming back. The anger will come, Eva knows – she is already dimly aware of it, but from a distance, as if viewed from the wrong end of a telescope. For now, there is only this deadening sense of calm.

'Eva.' She looks at him, and instantly recognises his expression: it is the one David Lean had lingered on in close-up in the last film. At the screening, her husband's face had been six feet high, his cheeks damp with summoned tears. She had never seen him cry. 'I did love you, you know. I'm sorry for how it's turned out. I'll make everything as . . . easy for you as I can.' He places a hand on her shoulder.

'Please don't. Please just go.'

He stands; swallowing, she adds with as much dignity as she can muster, 'We'll work everything out later.'

Eva waits on the terrace while he packs, finishing her drink, her eyes closed against the sun. He is done in what seems like no time at all. 'I'll call tomorrow,' he says from the living-room. 'Please try to explain things to Sarah.'

Surely that is your job, she thinks, and yet of course it will fall to her: who else is there?

David hovers uncertainly for a moment. She wonders whether he will step back out onto the terrace, perhaps kiss her goodbye, as he has done all the times he has left for rehearsals, shows, auditions, shoots; as if his leave-taking were only temporary. But he doesn't come.

'Goodbye, Eva,' he says. 'Do take care of yourself, now, won't you?'

She doesn't reply – just waits for the conclusive click of the front door. After a moment or two, he emerges again on the street below. She watches the top of her husband's departing head as he drags his case off down the pavement.

Halfway down the street, David stops beside a parked car, opens the boot, stows his case inside. There is a woman at the wheel: Eva can just make out a tangle of dark curls, a pair of tortoiseshell sunglasses, a slick of pink lipstick. Juliet: she must have been waiting out there all this time, watching them. At the thought of their marriage ending so quietly, with such a lack of ceremony, while that woman sat outside watching them in dumb-show, the tears threaten to spill, and Eva steps quickly back inside.

In the kitchen, she allows herself to cry, clutching the sink for support, until it is time to collect Sarah. Then she splashes her face with cold water, reapplies her make-up with care, and goes down to their car – *her* car, now, she supposes, assuming the settlement is fair. She can't imagine it won't be: David has always been, beneath his arrogance and bluster, reasonable; kind, even, in the distracted, blurred way of a man primarily devoted to his own happiness.

It occurs to Eva, with a blunt shock of pain, that she will miss him, despite everything – despite the distance between them; despite his infidelity; despite her knowledge that their romance should never really have been made to last more than a few months; that the deficiency she had perceived in her love for David was, in fact, more than the product of her inexperience. She will miss his laugh, the way he taps out a Morse code pattern on his leg when he is restless. She will miss his hands on her body (though it is many months since they last made love), the way he made her feel – beautiful, all-powerful – when he told her that he loved her. She will miss watching him make their daughter breakfast: a rare occurrence, and yet it strikes her with some force that she is unlikely ever to see him do it again. She will miss hearing the rise and fall of his deep, sonorous voice lulling Sarah to sleep. All this, and more, they have shared; and now it is simply to fade to black, and disappear.

Eva waits for a moment, sitting motionless at the wheel, taking in great gulps of air. Then she starts the engine and edges the car out onto the road, past the space that Juliet's car has just left.

VERSION THREE

/////////

Frost
Cornwall, October 1969

There was a frost last night. *The first of the year*, Jim thinks, standing at the kitchen window, a mug of coffee warming his hands.

It is seven fifteen. He is the first up – he has taken to rising early again, as he used to, as his father did, to make the most of the morning light: so pale here, unfiltered; brighter than any other place he knows. Today, he woke later than usual, burrowed deeper under the bedclothes, drew Helena's warm body to him, as if sensing that outside the frost was settling, the tall grass of the back lawn stiffening into peaks, the lettuces huddling in rows under their plastic sheeting. Somebody – Howard, he supposes – had the presence of mind to draw the tunnels over them: he must have seen the forecast, or more likely just read the wind, the precise shade of the darkening sky, in his uncanny, countryman's way.

Before moving to Trelawney House, Jim might also have considered himself a man of the country: as a boy, he was accustomed to the rhythms of the Sussex countryside, to its colours and smells, its sudden noises and deep silences. But he knows now that Sussex is not real countryside, not in the same way as Cornwall – not as it seems, at any rate, on this windblown patch of land, a few miles from St Ives: sea before them, fields behind them, and the cliffs their own lunar landscape of black rock, scrub-grass, flowers whose names Howard has tried to teach him, though only some of them will stick: milkwort, eyebright, lady's bedstraw.

This last is a four-petalled flower of a vivid, waxy yellow. On a walk that first summer, soon after he'd arrived, Helena lay down in a patch of it, and the flowers were beautifully bright against her red hair. (It was that colour – the same shade, he thought, as Lizzie Siddal's, at least as Rossetti had captured it – that had first drawn Jim to Helena; he would be disappointed to discover, later, that it was dyed.) There, on the clifftop, he gathered a bunch of the flowers, brought them back to the house, placed them in a jug beside his easel. Helena had cleared a corner of the studio for him – an old barn; freezing in winter, though they draw Indian bedspreads across the doors, bring out an ancient oil heater on the coldest days. That was the first painting Jim had produced in Cornwall: a clutch of lady's bedstraw, a blue and white jug, a table. It was not much, but he knew instantly that it was better than anything he'd painted in a long time.

He pours himself another cup of coffee, finds the bread – one of Cath's tough, seeded loaves – and cuts himself a slice, layers on butter, jam. He can hear someone moving about upstairs: Howard, probably. He is usually the second one up, and they have spent many early mornings out in the studio, just the two of them, Jim mixing up his paints, drying off brushes, Howard dragging in wood from the yard – driftwood, pared and bleached by the sea; great logs of burnished oak from the sawmill at Zennor; stacks of twigs that he has gathered and roped together, thick and spindled as a witch's broom. Howard is a sculptor of wood, and his section of the studio resembles a carpenter's workshop, with its workbenches and lathes, and its clean, medicinal scent of resin and wood shavings.

At first, Jim was distracted by the sound of Howard at work – the drag and whirr of the saws, the hammering of nails. He had said as much, discreetly, to Helena; asked whether he might colonise one of the empty attic rooms. But she shook her head: the whole idea was that they should all share a workspace, let ideas flow. She had told him this on the night they met – it was at Richard's fiftieth birthday party, at his house in Long Ashton; Jim had noticed Helena standing by the fireplace in a green dress, her flame-red hair loose across her shoulders. He had walked straight over and asked her name, with a directness that had surprised them both. They'd had to shout at each other to be heard – someone had put on a Led Zeppelin record – but as she described where she lived, the 'colony' in St Ives, it had sounded to Jim like a kind of paradise.

The following week, he'd got into his battered old Renault and driven down to Cornwall to see her; a few weeks after that – high on love, on lust, on the late-night conversations he'd had with them all at the colony, passing round joints, talking about art, sex, everything – he'd told both Richard Salles and his mother that he was leaving. 'Go, make work,' Richard had said, 'and may you find the happiness you deserve.' Even Vivian had sent him away with what he took to be a kind of blessing. 'You're Lewis Taylor's son, Jim, and you've got your father's stubbornness in you. Just mind that you keep a little part of yourself back for the woman who loves you, won't you?'

She had stepped forward, cupped Jim's chin with her hand, and for a moment he'd been transported back to the Sussex house; to the afternoons when he had often returned from school to find his mother sitting motionless in her armchair, smoking cigarette after cigarette, while his father worked away, oblivious, upstairs.

Once he was actually living at Trelawney House, Jim wasn't sure it was really practical, all of them working in the same room, but he let it go. It was Howard's house, after all; had belonged to his late mother, a society dame and patron of the original St Ives colony. Now, at the distance of more than a year,

Jim can see the logic of the rule: his own work has changed, become more muscular, somehow, as if drawing confidence from Howard's hard, inviolable forms.

There is the sound of footfall on the stairs. The kitchen door swings open: here is Howard, bear-like in his woollen dressing-gown, his eyes still gummed with sleep. He is an extraordinary-looking man: six foot two in his bare feet, bald, his features huge, fleshy, and ill suited, as if woven together from three different faces. And yet there is something about him – charisma, Jim supposes, though the word seems inadequate to describe the raw, silent power that Howard commands, especially over women. Jim suspects that Howard and Helena were once lovers, though he has never asked, aware that he mightn't like the answer. If they were, it would have been kept very quiet: Howard and Cath have been together for years. And anyway, it is not *that* kind of place – Howard had made that very clear when they first discussed his moving in.

'This is not,' he told Jim, his eyes burning holes in his face, 'the sort of set-up you read about in the papers. We do not pool our money, and we do *not* –' this said with the emphatic thump of a fist on the kitchen table '– pool our lovers. We are artists here. We work, we garden, we cook together. If that sounds like the way you'd like to live, then you are welcome to join us.'

'Pour me a mug, would you?' Howard says now, landing heavily on one of the kitchen chairs. Jim does as he asks. 'Good man.'

'There was a frost last night,' Jim says. 'The first.'

Howard sips his coffee, closes his eyes. 'Yes. I covered the lettuces. Firewood'll need drying out, though. You on wood today?'

'I think so.' There is a duties rota pinned to the cork-board by the door, written in Cath's small, neat hand. 'Helena's cooking tonight. She said something about cassoulet.'

142

Howard nods slowly, his eyes still shut. With his bald head and cowl-like robe, he has the look of a monk at prayer. 'And Stephen's coming at twelve, I believe.'

'So he said.' Jim has spent the last week in preparation: finishing the last of the canvases, sorting through the others, though Stephen said he would make the final selection himself – and Jim wasn't to worry about packing them; he would bring a man with him to do that. Privately, Jim fears that it can't really be happening, that Stephen Hargreaves can't possibly be arriving today to load a clutch of his paintings into a van, and drive off with them back to Bristol, back to his gallery. But he knows such fears for what they are: night-terrors, irrational. For the exhibition is all arranged, the posters printed, one of them pinned proudly by Helena onto the cork-board: *Jim Taylor – Paintings, 1966–69.* The private view is in three days' time – they will all be going up, all eight of them, Josie and Simon and Finn and Delia too, in Howard's shuddering old van. Jim's aunt Patsy and uncle John are coming, and even his mother, with Sinclair. Jim can't quite bring himself to call Sinclair her 'boyfriend'; he could not have been more surprised when Patsy gave him the news, by telephone, a few months after he left for Cornwall. 'Your mother has met someone. I haven't seen her this happy – this *calm*, Jim – since she met your father.'

'Did you and Helena work things out?' Howard sips his coffee. 'About the picture, I mean.'

Jim's mug is empty. He lifts the coffee jug, hoping to pour another, but it is empty, too. 'Yes. At least, I think so. She says she's all right about it now.'

It was their first proper argument, a painful, drawn-out one that began six months ago, when he started work on a new painting, the largest he had ever done. A portrait, painted from memory, though he asked Helena to sit for the hands and feet (perhaps there lay his error): a woman, curled on a window

143

seat, reading, the light falling in pale shafts across her face. The woman was small, her hair dark and shining, a half-smile playing on her lips as she read: Eva, of course it was Eva; he knew it would be her before he began.

It hadn't occurred to him that Helena would be jealous – she is an artist, too; surely she would understand that some ideas emerge fully formed, beyond conscious control. But she *was* jealous. For days Helena would barely speak to him, wouldn't allow herself to be comforted – though what comfort, really, could he give her? He had been honest with her from the first; she knew how much he had loved Eva, and how deeply she had wounded him.

He should never, he supposed during that uncomfortable time, have started the painting – though it was the best portrait he had done; he knew it and Helena knew it. When they mounted their exhibition in St Ives, it had dominated the room, drawn most of the visitors to it as if by some imperceptible magnetic force. One man had stood in front of it for almost a quarter of an hour; this was Stephen Hargreaves, an old friend of Howard's from the Royal College. His Clifton gallery was, as it turned out, just a few streets away from Vivian's flat; Jim had walked past it many times. 'There's some very good work here, Jim,' Stephen had said, shaking his hand. 'We really must think about giving you a show.'

Of course the Eva portrait (as he called it privately; its official title was *Woman, Reading*) would be the centrepiece of Jim's exhibition, but Helena hadn't allowed herself to think about that; yesterday, as she helped him sort through his canvases, she had seen it again, propped against the studio wall, and grew suddenly upset. Later, in bed, when she was calmer, she said, 'I'm sorry, Jim. I know I'm being ridiculous. But I can't help feeling that she haunts us, somehow. I know you still think about her. I can tell.'

He denied it, of course, held her close, whispered soothing words into her ear. And yet he knew that she was right, and he was angry with himself, and with Eva above all.

Two hours he had stood there, outside the New York Public Library: one hundred and twenty minutes ticking by with extravagant slowness while the city traffic clotted and flowed, and disappointment settled on him like a weight. Walking back to his apartment, he'd promised himself that he would finally leave Eva, and everything that might have been, behind. He would, again, stand by the decision she had made.

He has remained true to his word – and yet now here she is, in the painting, soon to be wrapped and coddled and driven the two hundred miles to Bristol. He places his empty mug in the sink and looks over at Howard, who is leaning back against the wall, his eyes half closed. 'Still coming to, Jim, my man. That dope was strong stuff.'

'It was.' Jim didn't smoke much: he had left them to it and gone upstairs to Helena, who had not joined the party. 'I'm going out.'

Howard nods. 'Won't be long myself. Turn the heater on, will you? It'll be freezing.'

It is: the cold hits Jim as he crosses the yard, and he draws in its freshness, the morning smells of sea and damp earth. He will never tire of the view down to the sea: the cove's gentle shelving of rock, the mosaic of pebbles, and the water, restless, changeable, this morning a dark, inky blue, the sky lightening at the horizon. He stands for a moment before opening the studio door, looking down at the beach, flooded with a disorientating happiness; and he savours it, drinks it in, because he is old enough now to know happiness for what it is: brief and fleeting, not a state to strive for, to seek to live in, but to catch when it comes, and to hold on to for as long as you can.

Thirty
London, July 1971

They are almost two hours late for Anton's party.

First the babysitter – Anna, the rather petulant teenage daughter of a neighbour – arrived half an hour after they had asked her to come, without explanation. Then Jim, already several sheets to the wind (he poured them each a gin and tonic as they dressed, and downed another two while they waited for Anna) suddenly announced that he didn't like what Eva was wearing.

'You look like an oversized baby in a romper-suit,' he said, while she, stung, looked down at the black jumpsuit that had seemed so elegant last week in the shop, paired with her new rope-soled wedge shoes. How could Jim not know how cruel he was being? He was smiling as he spoke; seemed surprised, affronted even, when she clattered back upstairs to change: 'I was only joking, Eva – where's your sense of humour?' And yet as she changed – found the long dress she'd worn to the school leavers' barbecue last weekend; he'd seen nothing to complain about in *that* – she found that she was crying a little.

'Let it go,' she told herself in the bathroom mirror as she swept a fresh layer of blusher over her cheeks, reapplied her kohl. And yet she couldn't deny that she was wounded by this new sharpness in Jim; where once he couldn't compliment her enough (how many times, in their early days, had he told her she was beautiful?), he was becoming barbed, critical; especially when he'd had a drink or two. And he couldn't seem to see it: she'd tried to confront him a few weeks ago, asked why she seemed to irritate him so. He'd stared at her, eyes innocently wide (she'd chosen her moment poorly: they were just back from a drinks reception at the *Courier*, and neither of them was sober), and told her that he had no idea what she was talking about. 'Surely I'm the one who irritates you,' he'd said. 'Your husband, the artist that never was. Not exactly something to boast about, is it?'

As she repaired her face in the bathroom, Jennifer had come waddling in on her sturdy little legs – 'Mummy go party' – with Anna following sulkily behind. So Eva bent to kiss her daughter, and then went back downstairs to tell Jim they had better get going, or there'd be no point in going at all.

'You've changed.' He sounded resentful. 'I didn't say you needed to change.'

She drew a deep breath. 'Just let's *go*.'

They took a taxi to Anton's house: a narrow Georgian terrace on a leafy square in Kennington. He and his wife, Thea – an angular, strikingly blonde Norwegian barrister – bought the house as soon as they returned from their wedding in Oslo. Thea immediately set about knocking through walls, ripping up the tattered linoleum, planing away imperfections, so that every corner of the house was soon modern, luxurious and understated – rather, Eva thinks, like Thea herself.

Eva finds her sister-in-law in the garden, where coloured lights are hanging from the trees, and a trestle table is laid with the remains of a feast: platters of cold meats and cheese; herring in dill sauce; potato salad and Coronation chicken; a huge Sachertorte, baked by Miriam.

'Have we missed the food?' Eva says, kissing Thea lightly on each cheek. 'I'm so sorry we're late.'

Thea dismisses her apology with a manicured hand. 'Please. Don't worry. We're only getting started.'

Anton is in the kitchen, dispensing rum punch from a metal tureen. '*Meine Schwester!* Have some punch. Your husband's had a head-start.' He nods in the direction of the hallway, where Jim is talking animatedly to Gerald – where, in that case, is Penelope?

Eva accepts a glass from Anton, leans in to kiss him. 'Happy birthday. *Thirty?* How does it feel?'

He shrugs, ladles out another dose of punch, hands it to a passing guest. She watches his face – his dark eyes, much like her own in colour and shape, framed by thick, heavy brows (Jakob's), his wiry, untameable crop of hair – and sees her brother as a boy, two years younger and always wanting what *she* had, to be just like her. Once, aged three, Anton had borrowed Eva's favourite doll and carried it around for the rest of the day, insisting she was *his*, until Miriam intervened. He laughs when reminded about this now.

'I'm not sure yet, sis. Much the same. How does it look from the other side?'

Eva is prevented from replying by a sudden influx of new guests: Anton's friends from work, men with loud voices and flushed, beery faces. The professional world Anton inhabits – a world of regattas, mooring rights, the gleaming hulls of newly launched yachts – is as unfamiliar to Eva as hers must be to him. Smiling politely at the men, mouthing, 'Hello,' she moves away, Anton's question still loud in her ears. *How does it look from the other side?*

She is thirty-two; married to the man she loves; mother to his child; writing for a living. She is halfway through a novel, and she hopes – believes – that it is good. She is asked, with increasing regularity, to appear on television talk shows, discussing anything from nuclear disarmament to the rights of working mothers. As her appearances on screen have become more regular, Eva has grown accustomed to being noticed, to having the eyes of strangers trail after her, visibly puzzled as to where they might have seen her before. The first time it happened – she was wheeling Jennifer to the park on her tricycle – she found it disconcerting, and still professes to find it so; but in a deep, private part of her, Eva is aware that she finds it rather gratifying.

But what, then, of the most vital thing, the foundation on which all else rests – her marriage? The facts are becoming starker: Jim is unhappy, she fears desperately so, and she is unable to reach him. She has tried – of course she has – but he bats away every attempt. Last Sunday, for instance, when she left him at work in the studio and took Jennifer to lunch at Penelope's, she had returned to find him slumped in his chair, an empty whisky bottle upended at his feet.

'Daddy *sleeping*,' Jennifer had said. Quickly, Eva picked her daughter up, took her inside, set her down to play with her toys in the living-room, where Eva could still keep an eye on her through the patio doors. Back in the studio, she shook Jim awake. Roused, he stared at her, his expression so nakedly bleak that Eva was suddenly afraid.

'What *is* it, darling?' she said. 'What can I do?'

He closed his eyes. 'Nothing. Nothing at all.'

She had moved closer to him, placed her hand on the back of his neck, stroked his down-soft hair. 'My love. Don't do this. Why are you punishing yourself? You have your work; you have time to paint; we have Jennifer; we have each other. Isn't that enough?'

'It's easy for you to say, Eva.' He spoke softly, without venom, and yet she felt the weight of every word. 'You have everything you've ever wanted. How can you possibly know how I feel?'

'Eva.' Here is Penelope, in a paisley-patterned dress; she has

149

gained more weight since having Adam and Charlotte, and it gives her a rather fetching, queenly air. 'Where on earth have you been?'

Eva smiles, grateful for the interruption to her thoughts. She has made her way out to the garden again; the night has come on, and Thea has lit candles, placed them all round the perimeter flower-beds in glass jars, a second string of lights beneath the coloured bulbs. 'Babysitter was late.'

'Not that sulky girl from down the road?'

Eva nods. 'She's not so bad, really.'

'So you think. Do you know, when Gerald was off sick last week – some kind of stomach bug; poor thing couldn't move for two days – Luisa actually went into our room in a bikini top and shorts, and asked if there was anything she could do for him?'

'Perhaps she was concerned . . .'

'Not likely.' The topic of Luisa, Penelope's Spanish au pair, is a familiar one: Penelope suspects her of nymphomania. Eva cannot imagine loyal Gerald – who is also starting to turn plump, while his hair grows thinner – succumbing to temptation or, indeed, of a lissom twenty-year-old with eyes like molten chocolate choosing to tempt him. But she supposes that you never know. Eva would never have thought it possible of Jim, either.

'That woman's a menace,' Penelope adds.

'Now, now, Pen. That's not very sisterly.'

'She doesn't make me *feel* very sisterly.' Penelope sips her drink; she has rejected the punch in favour of white wine. Eva, already starting to feel a little drunk, begins to wish she had done the same. 'But no, you're right. I shouldn't go on about her. She's a godsend, really. Have you thought any more about getting someone in?'

'An au pair?' Eva has thought about it often: with both she

and Jim out at work, arranging care for Jennifer is a haphazard, piecemeal affair, and she knows that she depends rather too heavily on Miriam. Jakob said as much, tactfully, last Sunday: he mentioned Juliane, the granddaughter of some old friends from Vienna, who was planning to come to London to study. 'She's worked with children before. It could work out well, *Liebling*.'

Eva had nodded, said it could, though she still feels the same reluctance to bring a young stranger into their home. It is a nasty, private thing that she can't bring herself to say aloud. She had found a letter once, with a German postmark, when she was cleaning his studio; it was from Greta, the recently departed language assistant at his school. Her English was stilted, Germanic: *I am wondering when my body you will touch again. My heart calls at you.* Eva had felt sick; she had actually run inside, to the bathroom, and bent low over the toilet bowl. But she had not been sick; instead, she had sat at the kitchen table, working her way steadily through a packet of cigarettes. By the time she'd smoked the last stub, she'd resolved to put the letter back where she'd found it, and say nothing: she could think of nothing to say that wouldn't bring a response she couldn't stand to hear. To imagine that Jim had loved that girl – that his decision to stay with Eva and Jennifer, rather than leave with Greta, had sprung from duty rather than desire – was impossible enough; but to have that fact in any way confirmed would, Eva felt, be too much to bear.

'Papa says there's a girl coming over in September from Vienna,' she says now. 'Juliane. The granddaughter of some friends of theirs – remember the Dührers? I might meet her. See what she's like.'

'Good idea. Now let's get another drink.'

They do so – Eva deciding, against her better judgement, to stick with the punch. As she drains her second glass, she is suffused with a giddy, infectious warmth. Anton ladles her out another, and then leads her back to the garden to dance. Everyone is there: Anton's old schoolfriends (there, dancing close together, are Ian Liebnitz and his new wife, Angela); his shipbroker colleagues; Thea and her barrister friends; Penelope and Gerald; Jim's cousin Toby and his friends from the BBC – and Jim, coming up behind her, taking her in his arms so that they are dancing together to the Rolling Stones – 'Wild Horses' – her back against his chest. She turns to face him. He is drunk, of course, but so is she, and they are smiling, moving in time with the music.

He draws her face close to his, so that his features are huge, magnified: his blue eyes, so startling when she first saw them, are snatches of sky, and she can feel the rough texture of his beard against her cheek.

'I'm sorry,' he says into her ear. 'I love you. Always have, always will.'

'I believe you,' Eva says, because she does, despite her doubts, despite her nagging fears. And because really, if she can't believe in that, then what is there left to believe in?

VERSION TWO
||||||||

Thirty
London, July 1971

He meets his cousin Toby, as arranged, in a pub off Regent Street.

Toby is with friends at a table in the small courtyard garden – relaxed in short sleeves, laughing over a pint of beer. He gets up as Jim approaches, and the men shake hands, their touch warm but a little uncertain: it is some years since they last saw each other, and the thought of contacting his cousin, of arranging to meet him, had only occurred to Jim quite late the previous day.

His aunt Frances had telephoned a few weeks before to congratulate him on his first London exhibition: she'd seen the article in the *Daily Courier*. 'We'll all come,' she said. 'Do call Toby, won't you, when you're up? I know he'd love to see you.' And so, last night, just before Helena drove him to St Ives to board the sleeper, that is what Jim had done. He had not been angling for a place to stay – Stephen had offered to book him into a hotel – but Toby had insisted: Jim should come out with his friends; a bunch of them were meeting in a pub, then going on to someone's thirtieth birthday party. 'It'll make a nice change,' Toby had said drily, 'from all those sheep.'

Jim had resisted the urge to correct him, to explain that there were no sheep at Trelawney House: just fields, and cliffs, and an indolent black-and-white cat named Marcel who had appeared at the kitchen door one day, skinny and threadbare, and refused to leave. But Toby was right about London being a change: just how much of a change, Jim hadn't quite imagined. The train lurched into Paddington at six a.m. Blinking sleep from his eyes, Jim opened the curtain of his compartment window to the city, its grime and bustle, its crowds already surging and parting under the high vaulted roof. Back at home, in Cornwall, everyone would still be sleeping; Dylan would be curled like a comma against the bracket of his mother's warm body.

It was years since he'd last been to London, and Jim found that he was not prepared. After stepping from the train, he stood on the platform awhile, taking it all in. Out on the Bishop's Bridge Road, he found a café, sat drinking coffee and eating a greasy bacon sandwich while the traffic ebbed and flowed, and strangers strode resolutely by in suits and high-heeled shoes. *Why*, he wondered, *are they all in such a hurry?*

Toby's friends, he discovers now, are mainly colleagues from the BBC: a TV producer, a script editor, a news presenter named Martin Saunders. They are incredulous when they hear that Jim doesn't even own a television, hasn't watched it in years, but they listen with growing interest to his description of Trelawney House: the shared studio, the vegetable garden, the strict division of duties.

'A *commune*,' one of them says; Jim can't recall his name.

Jim shifts uncomfortably on his seat. He knows what 'commune' means to most people. 'We prefer "colony". An artists' colony.'

The man is nodding at him, but Jim can see he's not really listening. 'A colony. Right. So how did you end up there?'

That Bristol warehouse: the still shadows of the boats, the black water, the wonderful freshness of Helena's lips on his. Later, she had taken him to bed – she was staying at a friend's house in Redland; a crowd of people waved at them from the living-room through a cloud of dope. Helena's skin was pale and warm to the touch; the feel of her body, moving with him, was something entirely new, something wonderful. Afterwards, they lay awake, and she said, 'Why don't you come to Cornwall with me, Jim? Today?' He'd opened his mouth to say no, of course he couldn't, and instead he'd heard himself saying, 'Yes, all right, why not? Just for the weekend.'

On Monday, he'd called Arndale & Thompson from St Ives to say that he was sick, and would return the following day. And he had; but a week later, he'd handed in his notice, and the month after that, he'd packed his things into his car and left Bristol for good. There had been none of his mother's histrionics – his aunt Patsy had made sure of it by coming to stay – and even Vivian's doctor had wished him well. 'You've done much more for her,' he'd told Jim, 'than many sons would have done.'

Now, to this man whose name has quite slipped Jim's mind, he says only, 'Oh, I met a woman, of course. Followed her there. How else?'

The man grins, raises his glass. 'Well, I'll drink to that. And you've got an exhibition opening soon, on Cork Street?'

'Yes. The private view's on Monday.'

'Great. Do you know, Jim, I'd really like to talk to my editor about you. See about getting a crew down there. Could be great for our culture slot.'

'I'm not sure . . .' Jim can just imagine Howard and Cath's reaction: Howard's fleshy face colouring, his fist slamming down on the tabletop, with its topography of ancient scars. *Absolutely not. How can you even suggest such a thing?* 'I don't think that's quite our style.'

'Well, let's see, eh? Why don't I come to the show on Monday anyway, take a look?'

Jim lifts his beer, says untruthfully, 'You'll be very welcome.'

When their pints are finished, Toby tells them it's time to go. 'Whose birthday is it again?' Martin asks.

'Anton Edelstein's,' says Toby. 'My friend from school – you remember, you met him at my Christmas party. The shipbroker.'

'Oh yes.' Martin nods vigorously. 'Eva Katz's brother. Or should that be Eva Edelstein now?'

Jim's heart seems to lodge in his mouth. Slowly, carefully, he chances saying her name aloud. 'Eva Katz?'

Martin turns to look at him. 'Yes, Eva Katz, the writer. David Katz's wife – or *ex-wife*, I should say. He watches Jim, his grey eyes shrewd. 'Why – do you know her?'

He shrugs. 'Not really. We met once, in New York. I went to see *The Bohemians* on Broadway.'

Martin gives a slow nod. 'Lovely woman. Thought I might have had a chance with her, once. But I hear she's hooked up with Ted Simpson from the *Daily Courier*. Good on him, I say. He's at least fifty if he's a day.'

On Regent Street, they hail two taxis in quick succession. As his cab ducks and noses its way across Trafalgar Square, White-hall, Millbank, Jim is quiet, thinking about Eva Katz. How long has it been since they met? Eight years – and even then it was only for, what, an hour? And yet if he reels through all the people he has met in the interim, all the fleeting conversations he has had at parties – there have been fewer of those in Corn-wall, but still, those brief, inconsequential meetings must be in the hundreds – it is *her* face, *her* conversation that has lingered in his mind with greater tenacity than any other.

Jim even painted Eva once, from memory. (Well, not entirely: he had seen a photograph of her in a newspaper, in a slip of a dress, at some film premiere, standing next to Katz.) Helena was intrigued, possibly even a little jealous. But the painting did not turn out well: he couldn't quite catch the expression – intel-ligent, a little stern – that had so intrigued him, and eventually, caught up in fatherhood, in the daily demands of his work, she slipped from his mind. But now that the taxi is drawing up outside a narrow Georgian house, its windows ablaze with light and the trailing party-sounds of music and voices, he feels a sudden excitement at the prospect of seeing her again.

Inside, the house is aggressively elegant, the sparse furniture white, sleek. Jim is introduced to Anton Edelstein – heavy-browed, friendly; Jim can see Eva in his dark brown eyes – and his wife, Thea, slender, coolly blonde. Toby and his friends con-gregate by the food, laid out on a trestle table in the walled garden. Jim stands with them, loading a plate with cheese, cold meats, Coronation chicken, but he is distracted, looking around him, searching the unfamiliar faces for hers. And then, turning, he sees her: there she is in the kitchen, talking to Anton, refill-ing her glass.

She is taller than he remembers, wearing a black jumpsuit and high wedge shoes. Her dark hair is piled up, exposing her neck; he had forgotten the even, ceramic hue of her skin. Per-haps sensing that she is being watched, she looks round; she catches his eye and stares back, but doesn't quite smile. Jim looks away, reddening. Clearly, she doesn't remember him.

'Hello.' Eva's voice, coming from somewhere near his shoul-der; he looks round, and there she is. She's smiling now, but tentatively, as if not quite sure of his reaction. 'It's Jim Taylor, isn't it? We met in New York once, at the Algonquin. You prob-ably don't remember. I'm Eva Katz.'

The pleasure of being recognised, known, floods through him. Jim opens his mouth to tell her that he does remember her, of course he does, but he is interrupted.

'Eva.' Martin is lowering his plate in order to step forward, kiss her on the cheek. 'You're looking lovely.'

'Thanks, Martin. It's good to see you.'

For a few minutes, Eva is lost to Jim: the group shifts and re-forms around her, and she swaps stories with the BBC men about people they know, names that pass over him, diffuse and meaningless. In listening, however, he learns several interesting things: that Eva has just published a novel (how could he not have noticed this? He must talk to Howard about getting the papers delivered); that before that, she was working on the *Daily Courier*'s books pages; and that she is here, at the party, with a man named Ted Simpson, who is some kind of star reporter.

'Where *is* Ted?' Martin asks, looking around. Eva smiles – Jim notices that she has done so at each mention of Ted's name – and says vaguely, 'Oh, somewhere. Inside, I think.'

After a while, she turns to Jim, noting his silence. She asks what he is doing these days: he's a solicitor, isn't he? As he begins to explain about leaving the law, about moving to Trelawney House, he senses Toby's friends' attention wandering. Gradually, they all drift away, until just he and Eva are left, and she is nodding as he tells her about the Cork Street show. 'That's wonderful,' she says. 'Living down there must be doing you a power of good.'

'Yes.' He holds her gaze. He remembers now this very direct stare of hers: level, penetrating, as if it could cut through any amount of bluster and untruth. He wonders what that idiot Katz did to lose her. *If she were mine*, he thinks, *I'd never let her go.* And then he catches himself in the thought, and his conscience wounds him. And so he says, 'My partner lives there, too. Our son, Dylan, loves it.'

She rewards him with a mother's high-watt beam. 'You have a son! How wonderful. I have a daughter, Sarah. How old is Dylan?'

He tells her, produces the photograph from his wallet. It is a Polaroid, taken by Josie, hazed by sunshine, a deep crease etched across the lower half of the frame. Dylan at nine months, fat and curly-haired, waddling across the back lawn towards Helena's outstretched arms.

'He's lovely,' Eva says. 'They both are.'

'Thanks. How old is yours?'

'Eight. Here, I'll show you.' She reaches for the small purse hanging from her wrist. As she opens it, he admires the smooth curve of her neck; the plain silver pendant – a heart – resting against the swathe of bare skin that stretches enticingly from her chin to the low neckline of her suit. The pendant is discreet, probably expensive, and yet Jim feels instinctively that it was not her choice – a gift, he supposes, from this man. Ted.

'Oh.' She looks up, and he shifts his gaze to her face. 'Of course – it's in my other bag. What a shame. I so wanted you to see Sarah.'

'I can picture her. If she's anything like you, she must be beautiful.' He has spoken without thinking. Jim has grown used, in Cornwall, to not censoring himself – it is one of the policies of the house, this candour; Howard has no time for what he terms 'petty bourgeois niceties'. Now, sensing her unease, Jim regrets the compliment. Eva is looking down at her empty glass, and he is filled with the fear that she will turn to go, and be lost to him once more.

But instead she says, in a low voice, 'You said something to me, that time we met, in New York – something that stuck with me.' She looks back at him, and a new seriousness in her expression prevents him from reaching instinctively for a joke: *Oh dear – that bad, was it?* 'I was telling you about my writing – about how badly it was going, how I couldn't finish a book – and you said, "Surely it only ever needs to be good enough for you."'

He remembers now, of course he remembers – he'd winced about it afterwards, cursed himself for sounding insufferably pompous.

'I never did finish that book,' she says. 'I just couldn't make it work, for myself or anybody else. But when I started writing this one – the last one – I wrote those words on a card, in black marker pen, and pinned it to the wall above my desk. I kept the card there the whole way through.'

'I'm sure you're giving me far too much credit. But I remembered what you said to me, too. The way you told me I should just get on with my painting, stop making excuses. I remembered it for a very long time.'

Their eyes lock for a few seconds, and then Eva looks away, at the patio, where people are gathering, dancing to the Rolling Stones. Jim has forgotten them, forgotten everyone but her; he is seized by the desire to place his hand on the soft nape of her neck, to draw her to him. But she has seen someone: a man, waving from the patio, beckoning her to join him. He is older (Martin's fifty was an exaggeration: late forties might be more accurate), and his hair is silvering, but Jim can see he's still handsome, his face animated, expressive, lit with the confidence of a man who has secured his place in the world, but is still ready to be surprised by it.

'Ted,' Eva says, though Jim already knows who he must be. 'I'd better go and . . . We'll talk later, all right? It's wonderful to meet you again, Jim.'

She presses his hand, briefly, with hers, and then is gone. He's left alone in the garden, under the flickering lights – in the time they've been talking, someone has lit candles, placed them in glass holders all around the perimeter fence, under the coloured bulbs already hanging from the trees. Jim takes his cigarette papers from his pocket, his tobacco, the tiny nugget of grass he brought with him for the weekend. He rolls himself a joint, tries not to look at her, there on the patio, now moving close to Ted, his arms around her waist, their faces inches apart.

He makes a great effort not to look, and yet Eva is there each time Jim lifts his head, as if the other guests are all in tones of sepia, bleached out. And even when he closes his eyes – which he does, taking the first sweet drag, letting it linger in his mouth – he can see her, spinning and twirling, dozens of tiny candle flames glancing off the shine of her hair.

Thirty
London, July 1971

Eva sees him before he sees her.

He has only just arrived, and is standing a little uncertainly in the hallway with a group of men, his cousin Toby among them. His hair is longer now, brushing his shoulders, and he is wearing bellbottom jeans. He removes his jacket, revealing a tight brown T-shirt with a low, scooped neck.

Jim never used to look like such a hippy, but of course he moved to Cornwall several years ago, joined some sort of commune. Eva heard the news from Harry: he had brought it up casually one evening, over dinner at the flat, before David left for Los Angeles; not calculatedly, she thought, but with his customary indifference to other people's feelings.

'Remember Jim Taylor,' he'd said, 'that guy from Clare you went out with for a while?' Eva had said nothing, just stared at him, as if it were possible for Jim to have slipped from her mind. 'He's only shacked up with some artist bird and joined a hippy commune. Free love and all that. Lucky *bugger*, if you ask me.'

Now, before Jim can look up and see her, Eva turns, runs back up the stairs. She stands at the bathroom mirror, gripping the basin; her heart is beating too fast; her mouth is dry. She meets her eyes in the glass; the colour has drained from her face, and her eyelids – she has copied a smoky effect she saw in a magazine, layered grey shadow over lashings of mascara and kohl – are smudged and stark.

It hadn't occurred to her that Jim would be at the party, and she realises now that it should have done. He has an exhibition opening soon – quite a big solo show; they ran a piece on it in the *Daily Courier* – and of course he could easily have looked up his cousin Toby while he was in London. Yet surely he should have refused an invitation to her brother's birthday party. *Unless* – Eva grips the basin harder at the thought – *he wants to see me. Unless he has come here for me.*

Immediately, she dismisses the idea as absurdly self-regarding: Jim has a girlfriend now, possibly even children. She is sure that the thought of her, Eva, never even crosses his mind. And she has her own ties: not that she will allow herself to think of Rebecca and Sam as such, even on her darkest days.

Eva splashes her face with cold water, then takes her compact from her bag, dusts her cheeks with blusher. She thinks of Sam as he was when she left: putting on his pyjamas, his hair still damp from his bath. 'Come back soon, Mummy,' he said fiercely, clinging to her as she leaned in to kiss him. She said she would, of course; told him that Emma, the babysitter, would be up in a minute to read him a story.

Rebecca was in her room, painting her toenails an arresting shade of purple. Eva thought they made her feet look gangrenous, but she said, 'That's an amazing colour, darling. I'm off now.'

Her daughter looked up, her expression softening – already, at twelve, she is concerned with her appearance (*Like father like daughter*, Eva thinks), and spends hours on the telephone with her friends after school, whispering boys' names. 'You look pretty, Mum. I love that dress.' Eva had thanked her, gone over to kiss her goodbye, to breathe in Rebecca's sweet, mingled scents of Silvikrin shampoo and Chanel No. 5. (David had bought her a bottle, duty-free, on his last trip home. It is far too mature a perfume for a twelve-year-old, but Rebecca insists on wearing it every day, even to school.)

Back out on the landing, Eva looks down at the hall: more people are arriving, laughing and talking, carrying bottles of wine, but Jim is no longer among them. She readies herself, lifts her skirt to avoid tripping as she goes downstairs. She smiles at the newcomers, though she doesn't recognise them – friends of Thea's, she supposes; they have her sister-in-law's loose, elegant air. In the kitchen, she ladles out another glass of punch.

Her brother: thirty years old. She can hardly believe it – sometimes, when she thinks of Anton, she still sees the small, determined child who wanted everything she had. But of course that boy is gone, as are the earlier versions of herself. The girl with plaits and a brief, fierce passion for horses. The teenager writing feverish screeds in her notebooks, and terrible poetry that would later make her wince. The young student falling from her bicycle, sensing the shadow of a man pass over her. Looking up, not knowing who he would be.

'Hello,' Jim says, and for a moment Eva is confused: she is still on the Backs, looking at a boy wearing a tweed jacket and a bee-striped college scarf, wondering whether to accept his offer of help. But that boy disappears, resolves himself into the man standing before her, in the open door that leads out into the garden, under the coloured lights Thea has woven through the trees.

'Hello,' she says.

A couple Eva doesn't know edge past Jim, holding hands. 'Sorry.' The girl is young, bare-footed, her hair a white-blonde sheet. 'Just after some more punch.'

Jim steps back into the garden. 'I'll get out of the way.' To Eva, he adds, 'Come outside?'

She nods wordlessly, follows him. It is not a large garden,

but most of the guests have congregated on the patio: someone has turned up the music, and people are dancing; Penelope and Gerald are whooping and twirling among them. But it isn't difficult to find a quieter, darker corner, beside a pair of bay trees in white pots. They can almost imagine they are alone here, and she remembers the last time they were, in the Algonquin, at that godforsaken party. *Nothing's quite right*, he had said, and she had known exactly what he meant, but couldn't find the words to tell him so.

'I didn't mean to come.'

Eva looks at Jim properly for the first time: at his skin, pale as always, with its scattering of freckles; at the faint laughter lines creeping across his forehead. His expression is not friendly, and she hears her own voice hardening. 'Why did you, then?'

'Toby brought me. He said we were going to a birthday party. He didn't say it was Anton's. By the time he did, we were already on our way.'

But you could have turned back, she thinks. Aloud, she says, 'You never did meet Anton, did you?'

'No. I never did.'

They are silent for what seems a long time. Eva can hear her blood pulsing in her ears. 'I'm so sorry I didn't come.'

Jim sips his red wine, his expression inscrutable. 'How do you know I went?'

She swallows. In picturing their meeting – and it is pointless to pretend she hasn't pictured it – she has never quite imagined this coldness. She had known Jim would be angry, yes – but she had, in her mind, seen his anger fade quickly to forgiveness, even joy. 'I wasn't sure.'

More gently, he says, 'Of course I went, Eva. I waited for you. I waited there outside the library for hours.'

She holds his gaze until she can't any longer. 'I was afraid, suddenly . . . I'm so sorry, Jim. It was a terrible thing to do.'

From the corner of her eye, she sees him nod. She thinks, *Perhaps it was no worse than that first terrible thing – but I did that for the right reasons, Jim. I really believed that I was setting you free.* She considers saying this aloud, but it is surely too late, too little. She blinks hard, takes a sip of punch to distract herself from the incessant thrumming of her heartbeat. She has never pictured him like this: not only his manner, but his appearance. In her mind, he is either as he was in New York – casually bohemian in his jeans and loose shirt, his hair messy, unbrushed – or in Cambridge, layered in shirts and jumpers to keep out the Fenland chill. Some mornings, when she woke before him in his narrow bed in Clare, his skin would look so pale and cold, it was almost blue; and she loved, too, the dark tracery of veins on his forearms, spanning down from his elbow to his wrist.

'I read about your exhibition,' she says now, with some effort. 'I'm so glad you found a way to set out on your own.'

'Thanks.' Jim sets down his wine glass. From his pocket, he takes a cigarette paper, a pouch of rolling tobacco, a small nugget of grass. 'It was easy, in the end. Easier than I'd thought it would be, anyway.'

Eva breathes a little more easily, noting the slight thaw. 'You met someone . . .'

He lets the ellipsis hang; she watches the deft movement of his fingers as he pats down the tobacco, breaks off a portion of the grass and worries it into crumbs, lays them at intervals along the shaft of the joint. 'I did.' Holding the open paper in one hand, while with the other he closes the tobacco pouch, returns it to his pocket. 'Her name's Helena. We have a daughter. Sophie.'

'Sophie.' She thinks for a moment. 'After your grandmother.'

He looks at her as he rolls the paper, pinching out the joint expertly between his thumbs. 'That's right. Mum was over the moon.'

Vivian. Eva had met her once, in Cambridge: she had come up from Bristol for the day, and Jim had taken them all to lunch at the University Arms. Vivian was skittish, high, dressed in clashing colours: a blue suit, a pink scarf, red artificial roses twined round the brim of her hat. After coffee, while Jim went to the bathroom, she'd turned to Eva and said, 'I *do* like you, dear: you're ever so pretty, and very clever too, I can see. But I have the most terrible feeling that you're going to break my son's heart.'

Eva had never mentioned this to Jim, fearing that it would constitute a small betrayal. But she thinks of it now, and his mother's prescience strikes her with some force. 'How is Vivian?'

'Not too bad, actually.' He has lit the joint now, taken a couple of deep drags. He hands it to her, and she takes it, though weed doesn't tend to agree with her – and what will Emma think if she rolls home stoned? Still, just a little can't do any harm. She takes a puff, and Jim says, 'They put her on a new drug – it seems to help. She's met someone, too: they got married. He's nice. A retired bank manager, of all things. Steady.'

'That's good. I'm really glad.' Beneath its vegetable tang, the grass carries a pleasant sweetness. Eva takes another drag, hands it back to Jim.

'No more?' She shakes her head, and he shrugs, continues smoking. 'What about you, anyway? I heard you had another child. A boy, is that right?'

'Yes. Sam. He'll be four next month.'

Sam: her gorgeous boy, her surprise. It had happened soon after her mother's birthday weekend in Suffolk. She had decided to speak to David when he got back from Spain – to tell him that she was leaving. But on the night of his return, he was in a grand, expansive mood: he'd taken her to dinner at the Arts Club, bought champagne, told her amusing stories about Oliver Reed. That night, Eva had seen her husband as he'd been when they first met: the shiny brilliance of him; the way the head of almost every woman in the room turned to observe his arrival. How deeply she had wounded him, all those years ago, by leaving him for Jim; and how resolute David had been later. There, under the club's great glass chandeliers, Eva could recall his eyes shining as he agreed emphatically that the only option was for them to marry. *Let me take care of you*, David had said. *Let me take care of you both.* And he had meant it, in his way; perhaps he still did. Later that night, after stumbling home from the Arts Club in the early hours, they had made love for the first time in months. Sam was the result.

Eva knew, then, that she wouldn't ask David for a divorce. She didn't want her son to grow up knowing only the idea of a father; nor did she want to have to explain the whole sordid business to Rebecca, who still idolises David. And David himself appeared to be happy enough with the arrangement: it suits him to stay married, to keep the flocks of admirers at bay (or to provide cover for one admirer in particular). But since he took the house in Los Angeles last year – he had several films lined up, and was tired of living in hotels – he has already become a husband and father more in theory than in practice. He is supposed to fly home to London whenever he can; but in the last nine months, he has spent only two weekends there.

Eva could have moved to America with him, of course, but the idea was never mooted, and she certainly applied no pressure. On her first trip there, she had disliked Los Angeles intensely: the strip malls, the featureless freeways, the exhausting sense that everyone was grafting, wheeler-dealing, out for what they could get. And David, of course, has a particular reason to keep the house in LA for himself: Juliet Franks. Eva knows they are lovers. She has known it for a long time.

'The full set,' Jim says, and Eva looks up sharply, wondering if he is mocking her. She wouldn't blame him if he were. 'And you? What are you doing these days?'

'Still reading manuscripts for publishers. The odd book review.'

He must know, better than anyone, that it is not enough.

'And your writing?'

'I'm not really . . . It's tough, you know, with the children . . .'

'No excuses. If you've got to do it, you do it. It's that simple.'

She feels her cheeks flush. 'It's always simpler for a man.'

'Oh, I see. It's like *that*, is it?'

They are glaring at each other now. Eva's blood is rising again, but with anger this time, so much hotter, so much purer, than the blend of guilt and fear and loss. 'I don't remember you being such a chauvinist.'

His joint is almost finished. Jim takes a last puff, drops the butt onto the ground, crushes it under the sole of his shoe. 'I don't remember *you* being such a wet rag.'

Eva turns then and walks away, striding back up the garden, pushing through the crowd on the patio – past Penelope, who says under her breath, 'Are you all right? What did he say?' Pen must have seen them – they were deluded to act as though they were alone in the middle of a party. But Eva doesn't care: she is running upstairs, thinking only of finding her jacket in the spare room, then walking out into the cool shadows of the square, hailing a taxi, checking on her sleeping children before crawling gratefully into bed, drawing the covers over her and leaving all this behind.

I'll apologise to Anton, she thinks as she rifles through the pile of jackets and cardigans, *though he's probably so drunk by now, he won't even notice I'm gone*. And then she feels a hand on her shoulder, pulling her round. An arm around her waist, warm lips on hers, and there is grass and tobacco and red wine, and that other familiar, indefinable taste that is his, and his alone.

Invitation
London, July 1971

'Are you sure you don't mind?'

Ted, settled on the terrace with a gin and tonic and the evening paper, looks up, smiles. 'Of course not, darling. You go. Enjoy yourself. Sarah and I will be fine.'

Eva leans forward, places a kiss on his warm cheek. It is just after six, and still hot, though the sun is dipping behind the trees, and the terrace will soon be in shadow. 'There are stuffed tomatoes in the fridge. All you need to do is put them in the oven for a few minutes, make up a salad.'

'Eva.' He cups her face with his hand. 'We'll be *fine*. Go.'

'Thank you. I'll see you later.'

Sarah is in her room, reading; she is a thoughtful, rather private child, and Eva worries for her a little, forgets that she was just the same, preferring the world of books to the tough, disordered world of other children. She wishes they had a garden for her to play in. *In Paris*, she thinks, *might we have a garden?*

'I'm off, darling. I won't be late. Ted will get dinner for you.'

'All right.' Sarah, tearing her eyes away from the page – she has almost finished *Little Women*, and is transfixed by the plight of Beth – fixes her with an expression that seems, in its quiet resignation, terribly adult. 'Have a nice time, Mum.'

In the hallway, Eva slips on her sandals, checks her bag for the invitation Jim Taylor pressed into her hand at Anton's party, just before he left. She has resolved to walk: Cork Street isn't far, and she has spent most of the day indoors, editing a tricky section of her second book. Her central character, Fiona, is an actress who finds fame, and is forced further and further away from her husband, a barrister – flatteringly devoted, but rather dull: a playful reversal of Eva's own situation with David. But Eva is, to her frustration, struggling to make the husband step out from the page. *Why*, her editor, Daphne, had written in her last sheaf of notes, *would he put up with Fiona's selfishness for so long?*

Eva is finding it difficult to answer Daphne's question, and today she has allowed herself to fall prey to distractions: a clutch of letters, delivered by the postman just after lunch; a telephone call from Daphne, asking how she is getting on. Eva has accomplished little of any substance, and the day has bequeathed a sense of unease, multiplied now by Eva's suspicion that she should not be leaving Ted to look after her daughter while she goes off alone to meet another man – however innocent their meeting might be. From the street, she looks up at the terrace, hoping to catch Ted's eye. But he is engrossed in the paper, and does not return her gaze.

It is almost a year now since Eva first agreed to have dinner with Ted. He'd been asking for weeks, scribbling little notes that she'd find in her office pigeonhole, or tucked inside a book on her desk; sending bouquets that flooded the office she shared with Bob Masters, the literary editor, and Frank Jarvis, editor of the women's pages, with their sickly perfume. They reminded her – not unpleasantly – of the roses David used to bring to her on Friday nights. Frank begged her to put the man out of his misery, if only to keep the office from becoming a florist's shop. (Lilies made him sneeze.) Bob was more circumspect, but he seemed to think well of Ted: they had been colleagues for more than twenty years. There was, he told Eva as if it were reason enough to accept Ted's advances, no better reporter on Fleet Street.

Eva, however, was unsure. The divorce had taken more than a year to come through; the whole thing had proved more difficult, more upsetting – especially for Sarah – than she'd imagined, and Eva had no intention of rushing straight into a new relationship. And besides, she wasn't at all sure she even liked Ted Simpson – he seemed humourless, even arrogant. He was a man whom even the editor stopped to listen to, whose opinions, stated with a politician's persuasive rhetoric, mattered. Also, though Eva wasn't sure of his exact age, she suspected he was at least fifteen years her senior.

Then, of course, there was Sarah. Eva still wondered whether her daughter had truly grasped the facts of the divorce, and was wary of confusing her any further. She still woke in the night, sometimes, calling for David; Eva would go to her, stroke her hair until she fell asleep – or even carry her to her own bed, read to her as she hadn't since Sarah was a small child. How might Sarah react to the presence of a new man in their home, disturbing the fragile domesticity that Eva has worked so hard to protect?

And yet, as the weeks went on, Eva found that she was beginning to revise her first opinion of Ted; even to look forward to receiving his flowers, his notes. She began to notice that he was rather handsome; to look for him in the corridors, and return his greetings, his smiles. One day, she discovered a particularly amusing card inserted into her review copy of *Lives of Girls and Women* by Alice Munro. *A most disappointing read,* Ted had written, *given that not one of these lives is Eva Edelstein's, and hers is the only woman's life this reader is interested in discovering.* She found herself laughing out loud, and then composing a short, careful note back. *I'm sorry to hear you didn't enjoy the book – but your review made me smile. I've been thinking that it might be very nice to have that dinner after all.*

For several days, she received no reply. She looked for Ted around the *Courier* building, but didn't see him, and the extent of her disappointment surprised her. And then, one morning, there he was at the door of the office. (Both Bob and Frank were out.) He'd booked a restaurant for Friday night, if that worked for her. It did, she said. When Ted had gone – stepping away as briskly as he had appeared – Eva had telephoned her mother, asked whether Sarah could spend Friday evening with them. Miriam asked no questions, though she must have suspected something – especially when Eva requested the same favour again several times over the following weeks. All she said, one day a few months into the affair, was, 'You look happy, *Schatzi.* This man is really making you happy.'

It was true, Eva realised: she was happier than she'd felt for years. Her reservations about Ted had been entirely misplaced: he took his work seriously, and was unapologetically knowledgeable about world affairs – but he was also funny, considerate and playful. The only thing she struggled to understand was why he had never married.

'I came close a few times,' he told her one night at his flat in St John's Wood – it was large, high-ceilinged, filled with souvenirs from his travels (he had lived in West Berlin, Jerusalem, Beirut), but also seemed empty, and somehow unloved. 'But travelling all over the world isn't really conducive to making a relationship work.'

She looked up at him – they were in his bed, drinking red wine – and said, 'But you're based in London now, aren't you? For good?'

Ted leaned down to kiss her. 'I am, Eva. I am.'

He spoke too soon, Eva thinks now, on her way to the gallery, as she turns onto Marylebone High Street. Last week, Ted was asked to go to Paris: the *Courier*'s incumbent correspondent, an ageing Francophile with a notorious penchant for good burgundy, is retiring to his chateau in the Dordogne.

'It's a plum job, Evie,' Ted said when he told her: his excitement was palpable, though he added quickly, 'but I'm not sure I can go if you won't come with me. Both of you.'

It took a few moments for the implication to sink in. 'You'd like us to move in together, you mean? In Paris?'

Ted grasped her hand. 'You silly thing, I don't just want to move in with you. I want to *marry* you. Be a proper stepfather to Sarah.'

Eva's first instinct was to say yes – that she was falling in love with him; that it would be a wonderful adventure – but she held back: the decision, after all, was not only hers to make. There was Sarah, of course; and her parents; her friends: all the tangled roots of their London lives. And David, though he would be unlikely to object: he could fly as infrequently to Paris as he had done to London.

And so she had kissed Ted, and said, 'Thank you – really. It's a wonderful offer. But let me think about it, darling. I need to talk to Sarah first.'

'Of course,' he said. 'I don't want you to feel rushed.'

The next night, after school, Eva had taken Sarah to the cinema – they were showing *Willy Wonka and the Chocolate Factory* at the Curzon Mayfair – and then for hamburgers at a Wimpy bar.

'How do you feel about Ted, Sarah?' Eva had asked, as casually as she could.

Sarah sucked hard on her milkshake. Then she said, 'I like him. He's funny. And I like the way he makes you happy, Mum. You smile more when he's around.'

On the other side of the Formica table, Eva found herself

struggling to hold back tears. 'How did you ever get to be so grown-up?'

'Watching you, I suppose.' Sarah picked up her burger, regarded it for a second in anticipation, and then took a bite. Still chewing, she said, 'Why are you asking, Mum?'

'Well.' Eva laid down her own burger. 'Ted and I are talking about getting married.' Across the table, Sarah looked down at her plate. 'What would you think about that, darling?'

Sarah said nothing, just kept staring down at her half-finished burger. Eva watched her daughter – the spun silk of her dark hair, the soft curve of her cheek – and reached forward, covered Sarah's small hand with her own.

'Darling,' she said again, more quietly. 'If Ted and I did get married, he would like us to move with him to Paris.'

'Paris?' Sarah looked up at her mother then. Her old au pair, Aurélie – a provincial girl herself, and rather in awe of Paris – had spoken often of the city, and Sarah had, for a period, become obsessed with the place, asking over and over again why she couldn't live in Paris like Madeline in her favourite picture book. 'Would I have to learn French?'

Eva chose her words with care. 'You wouldn't *have* to – we could try to find you a school where they speak English. But I think you'd probably want to, wouldn't you?'

Sarah seemed to consider this. 'Maybe. Then I could write to Aurélie in French.' She was silent for a while, finishing her burger, then returning her attention to her milkshake. Eva let the silence stand. *It's too much for her*, she thought. *I'll tell Ted it's too soon.* But just as she was about to speak, Sarah had looked up at Eva once more, her gaze clear and direct, and said, 'All right, Mum. I think it would be all right, as long as Dad could still come and see us.'

'Of course he could,' Eva said, and letting go of her daughter's hand, she had reached up to stroke her cheek.

And so, when Ted came to pick her up before Anton's party, Eva had greeted him with a long kiss. *Tonight*, she thought, *I will give him an answer*. But then there was the party – there was Jim Taylor – and everything was thrown into disarray. Talking to Jim – aware of him, even at a distance – Eva felt just as she had in New York: the intensity of their connection, one that seemed beyond reason, rooted in some wordless instinct. It made no sense. She barely knew Jim Taylor, and yet she was inexplicably drawn to him. When he handed her the invitation to his exhibition, she felt a flash of excitement so pure, so physical, that a blush rose to her cheeks.

Afterwards, back at the flat, Ted had asked her, casually, who she had enjoyed talking to so much at the party. 'Oh – just an old friend,' she said, matching his lightness of tone. Ted seemed to think nothing more of it, and Eva has been careful to offer him no reason to. And yet as she rounds the corner of Cork Street, where people are already gathering outside the gallery – a red-haired woman in white bellbottoms, gold jewellery glinting at her neck; the man beside her jacketless, rolling up his shirtsleeves – she is suddenly afraid. She wishes Ted hadn't insisted that she go alone, hadn't suggested, with his easy, guileless generosity, that he give her time to catch up with her 'old friend'. What on earth is she doing here? She ought to turn round, right now, and go back to her daughter, to the man she is planning to marry.

But Eva doesn't walk away; she steps inside. She sees Jim almost at once, closed tight within a knot of guests. Her fear slips into shyness; she takes the glass offered by a waiter, turns her attention to the paintings. She stands in front of a portrait of a woman with a broad, symmetrical face, standing at an open window; behind her, a swathe of cliff, a blue-green sea; beside her, a shock of yellow wildflowers in a vase. Jim's partner: Eva remembers her from the Polaroid photograph Jim produced from his wallet. She doesn't remember him telling her the woman's name.

'Eva,' he says. 'You came.'

'I did.' She leans in to kiss him on each cheek, and there it is again: that hateful blush. 'Congratulations. It's a great turnout.'

'Thanks.' He looks at her for a moment, then at the painting. '*Helena, with lady's bedstraw*. It's a wildflower that grows on the cliffs down in Cornwall: great clumps of it. Such an amazing colour.'

Eva nods, affecting interest. She is keenly aware of his physical presence, of the wide collar of his shirt, opening onto several inches of pale, freckled skin. An image flits into her mind, unbidden: her fingers tracing the diameter of his collarbone. She shivers, looks away. 'Don't let me keep you. You must have lots of people to meet.'

'Come and meet some of them with me.' Before Eva can reply, Jim takes hold of her wrist, leads her off towards unfamiliar faces: faces at whom she will smile, offer a hello, then slip into the comforting channels of polite conversation.

By nine o'clock, the gallery is almost empty; the waiters are gathering up wine glasses, stacking emptied platters of vol-au-vents, and Eva, unaccountably, is still standing next to Jim. He turns to her. They're going for a late dinner, he says, at a restaurant round the corner – he and his gallerist, Stephen Hargreaves, Stephen's wife, Prue, and a few others: won't Eva come too?

Eva hesitates, thinking of Ted, of Sarah. She didn't say what time she'd be home, but Sarah will fret if she's not there in time to say good night. And, more to the point, her daughter has taken such a leap in accepting Ted, in accepting this move to Paris: what would it mean to her to pull all that apart? And what would it mean to Ted, to the man Eva herself has so carefully, so gradually, allowed to know her, to love her?

Really, she thinks, *there is no choice to be made.*

'Thank you, but I really should get back. It was a lovely evening, Jim. Look after yourself, won't you?'

Then Eva brushes each of Jim's cheeks with her lips, and steps quickly from the gallery, looking for the cab that will take her home.

Invitation
London, July 1971

'Come to dinner,' Jim says.

They are standing in a quiet corner of the gallery; the crowds are thinning. (He can't quite believe how many people came: the evening has already acquired the surreal, underwater quality of a half-remembered dream.) Discreetly, the waiters are beginning to gather up dirty glasses, stack the empty platters.

The names of the people Jim has met are circling wildly in his mind – artists, gallerists, collectors. (Stephen has already placed red stickers next to several of the larger paintings.) Jim absorbed their praise; their interest; their memories, in some cases, of his father. One elderly gentleman – a painter, with a narrow, beakish nose and a head of thick white hair – said he had taught Lewis Taylor at the Royal College. He had grasped Jim's hand for longer than felt quite polite. 'I remember you, boy, when you were knee-high to the proverbial. Your father could be a shit – you don't need me to tell you that – but he was a real artist. Such a tragedy, what happened.'

Aunt Frances arrived as the doors opened, and stayed for an hour or so, with all three of his cousins: Toby was fresh from Television Centre, still in his suit, loosening his tie. Jim kissed his aunt, thanked his cousins for coming, agreed it was a shame that his mother and Sinclair hadn't been able to make the journey. But as he did so, he was aware only of *her*: a small figure in a blue dress, moving alone through the crowd, her arms bare but for a row of silver bracelets, her long dark hair hanging loose around her shoulders.

'I can't,' Eva says now, in a low voice. 'Won't they wonder why I'm there?'

'They know you're an old friend from university, that I invited you to see your portrait. They won't suspect anything.'

She looks over at Stephen, directing a waiter as he carries a teetering pile of platters through to the back room. 'I'm not sure.'

'Please.' Jim places a hand on her arm, lightly, but the touch is enough for her to look round.

'All right. But I can't be late. Mum's with the children.'

Stephen has booked a table in a smart French restaurant in Shepherd's Market. They are six for dinner: Stephen and his wife, Prue; Jim and Eva; Max Feinstein, an American collector, in town from San Francisco for a few days with his Japanese girlfriend, Hiroko. Despite his protestations, Jim is a little nervous as they sit. He sees Stephen's eyes travel from him to Eva and back again, and knows that he is not convinced; but he hopes he can trust him: surely it is nothing Stephen hasn't seen before. And as it turns out, Feinstein is such a dominant presence that Eva's appearance at the table is, at first, barely noted: he is an immense, looming man with a deep, monotonous voice that rattles the glassware. Beside him, Hiroko is mouse-like and silent, with an oddly mirthless smile.

'Stephen here tells me you're living in some kind of commune, Jim,' Feinstein says over the starters. His eyes shine like buttons in the fleshy cushion of his face. 'Free love, is it?'

Jim lays his fork down beside his plate. He doesn't look at Eva. 'No, not at all. It's not a commune – it's an artists' colony. A place where artists can live and work together, sharing ideas, ways of working.'

Feinstein is undeterred. 'Bet that's not all you share, eh?' He spears a garlic mushroom, lifts it to his lips. Jim watches the buttery sauce trail down the man's chin. 'I know what you hippies get up to. Seen it all back home, haven't we, Hiroko?'

Hiroko says nothing, just continues to smile. Across the table, Prue – a natural diplomat – interjects. 'You'll know of the St Ives colony, of course, Max? Hepworth et al.? Well, Trelawney House is just down the road, and it isn't at all dissimilar.'

'Hepworth,' Feinstein says, as if trying to place the face of an old fraternity buddy. 'Yes.' He begins a lengthy story about the time he spotted a Hepworth at auction, and was cruelly robbed by a telephone bidder from Panama. Jim lets the rough cadences of Feinstein's voice wash over him, barely taking in the words: every so often, he allows himself to look across the table at Eva, her head cocked politely in Feinstein's direction, her fingers gripping the stem of her glass.

He could see that the portrait had shocked her: when she saw it, she stopped still and stared. He should have warned her. He had thought about saying something at the party, when they got up from the bed (it was a miracle nobody had come in and seen them), and he pressed the invitation into her hand. But he had said nothing. Perhaps he had *wanted* to shock her: to make her see, in that enormous portrait – *Woman, Reading* was by far the largest painting in the room – what she had meant to him then, what she meant to him still. As soon as he could, he had slipped from the group, joined her in front of the painting.

'You remember I drew you like this, once?' Jim said.

Eva was silent for a moment. Then, 'I do. Of course I do.'

Now, in the restaurant, Max Feinstein is looking across the table at her, a slow smile of recognition creeping across his face. 'Hey – aren't you married to that actor guy? David Curtis? Last I heard he was shacked up in Los Angeles. What's he doing leaving a girl like you all alone over here?'

There is a silence, during which even Prue seems at a loss. But Eva replies, evenly, 'Oh, I'm not really *alone*, Mr Feinstein. Our children are here, and David comes home as often as he can. But it's very kind of you to worry for me. I do appreciate it.'

Feinstein – a stranger to irony – simpers, and Prue swiftly changes the subject; but Jim can sense Eva's unease, and begins to regret having asked her to come. There is his own conscience, too: he could feel it tugging at his sleeve last night, when he phoned Trelawney House (they have finally had a telephone installed) and listened to Helena talk about her day; about the great mess Sophie had made of her dinner, and how they had all laughed at the sight of her, food-smeared and beaming. 'Come home soon, Jim,' she said. Thinking of Sophie now – her small, lively body; her mother's clear, uncomplicated face – Jim feels a faint dread of what might ensue should Stephen mention that Eva came to the exhibition, and to the dinner. And yet it is not enough to undermine his gratitude for the fact that Eva is here, or to divert him from the course he has resolved to take.

After dessert, Stephen asks whether anyone would care for a digestif, and Eva rises from her seat, politely excuses herself. 'Thank you so much for a wonderful evening, but I really must be getting home.'

Jim sees her out. They walk silently down onto White Horse Street. There, he stops, and takes her in his arms. 'I'm sorry if that was difficult. I just couldn't let you walk away.'

She has buried her face in his chest; her voice is muffled as she says, 'I know. I didn't want to walk away either. But it's so hard, isn't it? Pretending.'

He lifts her face with his hand. He loved her as soon as he saw her with her bicycle, all those years ago in Cambridge, and he loves her still.

'Come away with me.' He leans down to kiss her. 'I'll find

a cottage somewhere. You could leave the children with your parents.'

Eva looks away, towards Piccadilly, towards the endless stream of taxis, the coughing hulks of buses and beyond them the expanse of Green Park, the trees' feathered outlines waving in the darkness. 'I don't know, Jim. I really don't.'

He says nothing, though fear courses through him: the fear of losing her for a second time. The loss would be so much worse, now, he knows, for having found her again. He can't quite think how he could bear it, but he would have to, of course. People bear loneliness every day. They think they won't be able to, that they won't survive, but somehow one second slips into another, becomes an hour, a day, a week, and they are still living. They are still alone, even in the middle of a crowd of people. Even with a partner, with a child.

But he is not alone now. Eva is looking back at him. '*Yes*, all right. I'll make it work somehow. Telephone me when you've sorted something out. Let me know where to be.'

He kisses her again. 'I will,' he says. 'As soon as I can. You know I will.'

She turns to go, and he watches her as she broaches the corner of the street, and disappears. Then he goes back into the restaurant, where Stephen has ordered a bottle of dessert wine, and Feinstein is telling everyone about his Miami beach house: 'You should *see* the women there, man – they're like nothing else on earth.' And if Stephen looks at him curiously, and Prue studiously avoids meeting his eye, Jim doesn't care: he is thinking only about when he will see Eva again. For all the years he has spent without her are dulling now, losing their shape and colour – as if he were sleepwalking through them, and has only just remembered what it is to be fully awake.

Expecting
Bristol, September 1972

Eva wakes early on Saturday morning.

She hasn't slept well, and neither, it seems, has the baby: she could feel the kicking, lay for hours with her hands splayed across her stomach as the dawn broke, and the grey light began to reach through the slats of the blind. When it is acceptably early – the alarm clock on the bedside table is ticking towards seven – she swings inelegantly out of bed. (She is too large, by now, to do anything elegantly.) Jim doesn't stir. On the back of the door, she finds the padded nylon dressing-gown thoughtfully left by Sinclair, shoulders it on over her nightdress. In the next room – Sinclair's home office: pin-neat, his folders arranged in obedient lines on the shelves he built himself – Jennifer is still asleep, sprawled on her back across the camp-bed, her face animated by unknowable dreams.

Downstairs, in the kitchen, Eva fills the kettle, finds the jar of instant coffee, spoons dark granules into a mug. Like the rest of the house, the room carries the faint, sterile whiff of bleach, and is equipped for every possible eventuality. She was surprised, the first time they came to visit Vivian and Sinclair here, to find this plain box – just built, one of seven identical properties arranged around a sweeping cul-de-sac, the continuing excavation of the fields beyond obscured only by a row of tiny, stunted saplings. It was as if Vivian had deliberately chosen the most conventional of settings, had decided to sweep away her years in that lovely old Sussex cottage, with its flagstones and rose-bushes and attic studio, and then those in the dark Clifton flat, with its mildewed, cobwebby corners and decaying Georgian grandeur. But this house had, it turned out, really been Sinclair's choice. 'We like the fact,' he told them, 'that the place is new. It feels like starting again.'

Eva saw Sinclair's point – he'd been married before, too. Like the house he had chosen, he was a man of conventional, unclut-tered outlook: a former bank manager. (Vivian had come into the bank to discuss her account, and Sinclair had suggested, with uncustomary daring, that they do so over lunch.) He wears his soft grey hair clipped short, like rabbit's fur; his pale, insipid features are the sort that, when recollected, never quite retain their shape.

After meeting Jim for the first time, Sinclair had telephoned to declare the seriousness of his intentions towards Jim's mother. He explained that he had researched her condition extensively, and was planning to press her doctor to prescribe a new drug that had just completed its first successful trials. 'I'm sure you'll agree,' Sinclair had said in the reasonable, measured tone he'd once used to discuss withdrawing overdrafts, 'that this should be a good deal better for her, in the long term, than ECT.'

Eva could see that Jim didn't quite know what to make of Sinclair – she suspected he felt a certain filial resentment at the fact that this man, this stranger, had walked into his mother's life and taken charge. But she knew that he was also relieved. Sinclair had taken early retirement, the better to look after Vivian, so she would no longer rely exclusively on Jim and his aunts. And when Vivian's doctor finally agreed to prescribe the new drug, the change in her was almost immediate, miracu-lous. Nobody, least of all Eva, could object to the ironing out of those wild highs and lows, the impossible cycle of her moods

– though Eva found that she could never quite separate her mother-in-law's new docility from the clean, beige ordinariness of this house.

The kettle boiled, Eva pours water into the mug, watches the coffee granules fizz and spin. They arrived later, last night, than they'd intended: she had wanted to finish the last batch of revisions to the draft, have it ready to send back to her editor on Monday. Vivian, opening the door, had immediately begun a fractured, gabbling monologue: as she helped Jennifer off with her coat, and Sinclair and Jim carried the bags in from the car, Eva could barely keep hold of the thread of what Vivian was saying. And Vivian had been unable to sit still for more than a moment at the dining-room table, where Sinclair had laid out a late supper. Even Jennifer had noticed; curled with difficulty on Eva's diminished lap – it was past her bedtime, really, but Eva was too tired for tantrums – she'd said in a loud whisper, when Vivian was out of the room, 'Why is Grandma being so funny?'

Eva and Jim had not had a chance to speak to Sinclair about this new change in Vivian's mood: she was still awake after they went upstairs. Even as Eva fell into an unsatisfying, depthless sleep, she was still picturing poor Sinclair, pinched and drawn from a recent episode of flu, attempting to persuade Vivian to come to bed.

'Up already?' Sinclair says now. Eva turns – she is still standing at the counter, absently stirring her coffee. He is smiling at her from the doorway, already fully dressed. 'I thought you'd be sleeping in.'

'I'm afraid I don't sleep much at the moment.'

His eyes travel to her bump. 'Ah. Silly old me. Nearly there now, aren't you?'

'Yes. A month, all being well.'

'Which of course it will be.' He comes over to her, gently prises the coffee spoon from her hand. 'Won't you sit down,

Eva love, and let me bring this over? Can I get you something to eat?'

She allows him to settle her on one of the kitchen chairs, to fuss around her, offering orange juice, eggs, toast. There is a character in her novel – set in a newspaper office that bears more than a passing resemblance to the *Daily Courier*; she has just settled on the title, *Pressed* – that she is aware of having drawn in part from Sinclair: John the letters editor, a mild man, easy to underestimate. He is one of her editor Jilly's favourite characters, though she has suggested Eva rewrite him a little, to allow him a fraction more backbone. But the book is really about women: four of them, from the clever young secretary with dreams of becoming a reporter, to the chain-smoking the-atre critic with a string of no-good lovers behind her.

'It's wonderful, Eva,' Jim told her when she showed him the first draft. 'It's all there. It's the real thing.' And she – high on her husband's praise, on this new turn in him, back towards her, closing the distance she had sensed between them – kissed him, feeling happier than she had in months. 'Thank you, darling,' Eva said. 'It means a lot to me.'

He had kissed her back, and suddenly they were back in that dingy old pub on Grantchester Road, laying their plans – every trace of David falling from her mind as Jim kissed her, and kissed her, until the landlord rang out for last orders, and then hurried them away.

'I wonder,' Sinclair says now when he has laid a plate of toast in front of her, sat down opposite with his own mug of coffee, 'which you are more excited about, Eva – the baby, or the book?'

'Oh, the book, of course.' She is spreading her toast with butter; looks up at him, smiling, to ensure he knows she is joking. Half joking, anyway. For the baby, welcome though he or she will be, is a surprise, and one drawing particular antici-pation from Jim, whose old ennui – so all-encompassing, just a year ago – seems to have evaporated. He has ploughed all his energy into turning the old box room at the top of the house into a new nursery, to allow Jennifer to stay in her own room. He is no longer making any pretence of going out to his shed (even Eva has stopped calling it the 'studio'), but he doesn't seem to mind; he says, in fact, that he is happier not forcing himself to spend all those hours out there after school. Eva, by contrast – though she has not said as much to anyone but Penelope – has struggled a little with the pregnancy; has resisted the slow cotton-wadding of her brain that has frustrated her progress with revisions to *Pressed*. But it is, she hopes, finished at last. She will send off the final version on Monday, and then turn her attention fully to the coming of this child.

For a few minutes, the kitchen is silent, Eva eating her toast, Sinclair drinking his coffee. Upstairs, Eva thinks she hears Jennifer stir. She waits for a moment, ears straining for her daughter's small cry, but no other sound comes.

Into the silence, Sinclair says, 'I'm a little worried about Vivian. You'll have seen how she is . . .' Eva nods, but says nothing; he is not given to unexpected confidences. 'It's this blasted flu, I think. Takes it out of her too, you know.'

'Yes. I can see it would.'

'I'm thinking of speaking to her doctor again. In confidence. Just to see if he can throw any light on things.'

Sinclair is looking down at the tabletop. Eva feels the sudden desire to reach out to him, and she does so, takes his hand in hers. He glances up at her, surprised. 'It must be so very hard for you, all this.'

He swallows, squeezes her hand lightly, then lets go. 'Not so hard, really. That's what marriage is, isn't it? Taking the rough with the smooth. At least, that's what it should be.'

The cry comes then: a muffled 'Mummy' drifting down through the fitted carpet. 'I'll go up to her,' Eva says.

She holds Sinclair's words in her mind as she climbs the stairs. *Taking the rough with the smooth.* They *have* been rough, these past years; there were moments when she forced herself to consider the fact that they might not make it. It wasn't that Eva doubted their love, but she began to fear that it might simply not be enough to carry them through. And yet her fears have proved unfounded: that stormy, rudderless time is behind them, and Eva can now observe it with relief, from the safe berth of calmer waters.

In Sinclair's office, she finds that Jennifer – four years old, but acting younger; disconcerted, Eva suspects, by the imminent arrival of a little brother or sister – has thrown off her bed-clothes, and is standing, red-faced and teary, behind the door.

'*Mummy,*' Jennifer cries, and her tone – wailing, disconsolate – reminds Eva, suddenly, of Vivian. 'You didn't come.'

'I'm here now, darling.' She keeps her voice low, soothing. 'I was only downstairs.'

Jennifer, uncomforted, watches her mother through narrowed eyes. 'I don't like it here. I want to go home.'

Eva goes over to her, kisses the top of her head. 'No you don't, Jennifer. What you want is some breakfast. So why don't you come downstairs and let Grandpa Sinclair make it for you?'

She helps her daughter on with her dressing-gown and slippers – these, embroidered with a picture of Minnie Mouse on each toe, are a beloved present from Penelope and Gerald, and guaranteed to resolve any tantrum.

'Does Grandpa Sinclair have Frosties?' Jennifer asks hopefully.

'I think he might,' Eva says. She leads her daughter out onto the landing, where Jim is emerging from their bedroom, mussy-haired, yawning. 'Morning,' he says, offering them both a drowsy smile. 'Where's my kiss?'

'Daddy!' Jennifer launches herself at her father, throwing her arms around his legs; and as he lifts her up, presses his nose against hers – their special, private form of greeting – Eva watches them together, father and daughter, and thanks whomever there is to thank that she and Jim have planed out those rough edges of their marriage, leaving it – she hopes; no, she *knows* – smoother, better, stronger than it was before.

VERSION TWO
||||||||

Montmartre
Paris, November 1972

Eva has taken to spending her mornings writing in a café on the Place du Tertre.

She was self-conscious about it at first: it seemed ostentatious, somehow, to sit with her notebook and pen in a café where so many great writers had almost certainly sat drinking pastis half a century before. She could almost picture Ernest Hemingway tapping her on the shoulder, shaking his head, saying, 'Think you can write one true sentence, do you, *madame*? Would you even know what one looked like if it bit you on the leg?' But when she had confessed as much to Ted, he'd laughed out loud. 'Eva, darling, why can't you get your head round the fact that you have every right to call yourself a writer, too?'

Eva had laughed with him, knowing that he was right: writing is her only work now, though the income from her first book is not quite what she would have hoped, and she has abandoned her work on the second. A few months later, she started on a third novel, about a woman in middle age who decides, quite suddenly, to abandon her safe, conventional marriage, and moves to Paris to start a new life alone.

'Too autobiographical?' she said to Ted one night over dinner, describing the plot.

He was faintly hurt. 'Surely not,' he said. 'You're not moving to Paris alone, after all – unless there's something you'd like me to know?'

She began the new book in London, writing fluidly, in a burst of enthusiasm; but her work quickly ground to a halt. Her first excuses were sound: the wedding (a small, elegant affair, just family and close friends, at Chelsea Town Hall, followed by an excellent lunch at the Reform Club); the move to Paris, with all the attendant packing and unpacking. Settling Sarah into her new school; allowing herself and Ted time to adjust to life in an unfamiliar city. But her more recent reasoning – the redecorating of the *Daily Courier* apartment; Sarah's struggle to make friends – rings hollow, even to Eva. The truth is that she is stuck, and the café, with its constant distractions – the whirr and screech of the coffee machine; the high ring of the bell above the door; the rise and fall of conversation, only half understood – is a good place to hide.

This morning – a Friday – she sits at her usual table by the window. She drinks two bowls of *café au lait* and eats a croissant slowly, tearing it into sections, layering each one with butter and jam. Out on the square, the usual painters are sitting before their easels in coats and fingerless gloves, dashing off knock-offs of Picasso and Dalí and Matisse for passing tourists. At eleven, Eva watches an elderly lady inch past the window as she does at the same time each morning, swaddled in a rabbit-fur coat. At twelve, Eva gets up, returns her notebook to her satchel, draws on her coat, leaves the coins on the metal dish beside the bill, and steps out into the fresh Paris air.

Three hours have passed since she arrived at the café, and she has written precisely two paragraphs. *I am turning doing nothing into an art form*, she thinks as she hurries towards the small supermarket on the corner of their street. And then she turns her thoughts to other, happier things – this afternoon, Penelope and Gerald are arriving at the Gare du Nord with the children.

They will all have a splendid weekend, and she will know how lucky she is to have Sarah and Ted, to have Paris, to have the company of good friends.

In the supermarket, Eva fills a basket with cheese, ham, yoghurt, a tub of olives, two bottles of red wine and those long, unwieldy baguettes that she has not yet learned to love more than a solid English loaf, or her parents' favoured Austrian rye. Beside the vegetable rack, she almost collides with Josephine St John, whose husband, Mitch, is the correspondent for the *Herald Tribune*: he and Ted share an office in the foreign press house, and Josephine – a witty, warm Bostonian, who married Mitch straight out of Harvard, and has travelled with him ever since – has become a friend. They stand together, exchanging news, until it is almost one o'clock, and Eva says she must get back: she's meeting Ted at home for lunch.

Josephine lifts an eyebrow, then leans in to kiss her on both cheeks. 'You *must* be newlyweds. I can't get Mitch to come home for lunch for love nor money.'

But as it turns out, Ted can't come home. The telephone is ringing as Eva enters the apartment: he has a story to file for tomorrow's paper – will she mind picking up Sarah alone, meeting Penelope et al., and bringing them home in a taxi? Of course she doesn't mind – but Ted is apologetic, promises to treat them all to dinner at Maxim's.

Putting down the phone, Eva is struck again by the contrast between this marriage – the ease of it; Ted's basic consideration of her needs, even when he has to put his work first – and the way things had been with David: his narcissism; the suffocating presence of his mother, always there, with her instructions about how things ought to be done. Though Judith Katz had surprised Eva completely by appearing at the door of the Regent's Park flat a few days after David left, when things were still raw and black and Sarah couldn't stop asking when Daddy was coming home. She was carrying a stack of Tupperware boxes: chicken soup, Russian salad, shepherd's pie.

'I thought you could use these,' Judith had said; and then she had pressed Eva to her, and the embrace – so utterly unexpected – had threatened the fresh onset of tears. 'I want you to know, Eva dear, that I'm thoroughly ashamed of him. As for that *woman* – well, Abraham and I won't be having anything to do with her.'

Eva had reminded Judith that if David and Juliet were to marry, as it seemed they were, then none of them would really have much choice in the matter. Judith, sweeping into the kitchen with her Tupperware, nodded. 'Yes, I suppose you're right,' she said, and her expression was so nakedly sad that Eva had understood, at once, that Judith was also in need of reassurance. 'You mustn't worry about seeing Sarah, Judith. She adores you, adores you both. You and Abraham will see her as often as you like.'

That isn't quite so easy now, of course, Eva thinks, moving around her Paris kitchen, putting away the shopping, loading a plate with bread, ham, tomatoes. But Judith and Abraham had, to her surprise, raised no objection when she told them about Ted, about the move to Paris. 'Oh, *Paris* – we'll be over so often you'll be sick of us,' Abraham had said at once, in his good-natured way; and they have, in fact, already flown out for two weekends – stayed, by mutual consent, in a good hotel on the Île de la Cité; been polite, even friendly, with Ted. It had all gone a lot better than Eva could ever have anticipated; and she has been left with a residual gratitude towards Judith, her old adversary.

The apartment is chilly, even with the gas heater on and the doors closed: she carries her lunch through to the living-room, wraps a shawl around her shoulders, and then opens the shutters, admitting the thin, wintry afternoon, the car horns and the distant cries of children out for their lunchtime break.

Ted has left today's papers in a pile on the table: he has them delivered to the apartment rather than the office. He likes to read them carefully, over breakfast: the French papers first, then the British ones, and finally the *Wall Street Journal* and the *Herald Tribune*. Eva tends to limit herself to the British papers, looking out for the bylines of the people they know – and for her own, on Saturdays: Bob Masters is still sending her two or three novels a month to review. Now, she takes the *Daily Courier* from the top of the pile, reads the main stories as she eats: the fallout of Richard Nixon's victory; the deaths of six people in an IRA bomb. And then, on the first of the culture pages, she sees his name. 'Jim Taylor: Breathing New Life Into the Art of Portraiture.'

Eva's hand stills on the page. She thinks of how Jim had looked when she refused his dinner invitation, left him on the steps of the Cork Street gallery. Younger, suddenly, and somehow lost. He'd written her a postcard, afterwards, care of the *Courier*: *Thanks so much for coming to the exhibition. I wish you every happiness, which seems to me no more than you deserve – J.*

The photograph was of a Hepworth sculpture: an egg-like oval (its title, she saw, was *Oval No. 2*) bisected by two smooth holes, as if termites had eaten through it. Eva had stared at the image for some minutes, searching for a deeper meaning – other than the St Ives connection, of course – but none came. It was as if Jim had deliberately chosen an image with the least possible significance. And perhaps that was just as well, for Eva could not deny the excitement she had felt at receiving it, though she quickly placed the postcard in the bottom drawer of her desk – where it would stay, evoking only the faintest memory of their mutual attraction. She had already given Ted her answer. And Jim – well, he had his own family to think of. His own life.

At two, Eva clears away the lunch things, then performs a quick tour of the apartment, plumping cushions, smoothing down the fresh bed linen in the guest room that will be Penelope and Gerald's; she has set up twin camp-beds in Sarah's room for Adam and Charlotte. Then she puts her coat back on, finds a scarf and gloves, and heads out onto the street.

Sarah's international school is a short walk away. Eva sees her daughter immediately, standing huddled in the playground with two other girls, their small heads bent close together, brown on blonde. She doesn't want to disturb them – Sarah has only just started to make friends – but then her daughter looks up, sees Eva, begins her lengthy, girlish goodbyes.

They take a taxi to the station: Penelope and Gerald's train is due in at half past, and Sarah's bag is heavy with the weekend's homework.

'Those girls look nice,' Eva says when they are settled on the back seat. 'Maybe you should invite them home for tea.'

'Maybe.' Sarah shrugs, and in her studied nonchalance Eva has a sudden vision of the adult Sarah will one day be, and the child she herself once was. She wraps her arm around her daughter's shoulders.

'What's that for?' Sarah says, though she is still young enough to lean in, to rest her head in the dip of her mother's collarbone.

'Just because,' Eva says, and they watch the rushing cityscape, framed by the car window: the white apartment buildings, the bright flashes of shopfronts, and the gleaming domes of Sacré-Coeur, standing sentinel on the hill.

Interview
Cornwall, February 1973

The interviewer is not quite what Jim was expecting.

She is a sensible-looking, solid woman in late middle age, dressed in navy slacks and a pale yellow twinset. Her hair is cropped short, and as she steps from her car – she has just pulled up in the drive; Jim is watching from the front-room window – she looks around with a curiosity she doesn't bother to disguise.

Jim goes out to meet her, shakes her hand. Her small blue eyes are unblinking beneath untamed, greying brows. 'Ann Hewitt. You thought I'd be younger, didn't you?'

Wrong-footed, he smiles. 'Perhaps. But I'm sure you thought I'd be better-looking.'

Ann Hewitt cocks her head and waits a few seconds, as if deciding whether to allow herself to be amused. 'Perhaps I did.'

He takes her through to the kitchen, fills the kettle for tea. Helena has left a plate of biscuits on the table, a vase of flowers on the dresser. 'She's not an estate agent, Hel,' Jim said to her before she left; she had been moving around the house since early morning, cleaning, tidying, making good. 'We don't have to impress her.'

Helena had looked up at him then, incredulous. 'Oh, we *do*, Jim,' she said. 'And you're a fool if you think otherwise.'

'Is nobody home, then?' Ann Hewitt is standing in front of the housework rota. The names are fewer now – Finn and Delia left last year, after Howard accused Delia of stealing money from the housekeeping for grass – but the duties are as neatly delineated as ever, spooling out in an unending cycle that Jim is beginning to find depressing. In fact, if he is truthful, he has found it depressing for quite a while.

'Afraid not. It's market day in St Ives. We have a stall.' He pours water into two mugs, finds the milk. 'Do you take sugar?'

'No.' From her handbag, the interviewer produces a pencil and a small black notebook. She flips to the first page, and he watches the quick march of her pencil; places a mug on the counter next to her, thinking of how the kitchen must look through her eyes. The ancient stove, so unreliable that they are often reduced to eating cold food for days, even when frost is starching the ground outside. The curtains that Josie tie-dyed and hand-stitched, now badly in need of a clean. The regiment of empty wine bottles on the dresser, hoarded by Simon, who fashions sculptures from fragments of glass (when he can be bothered to rouse himself from his bed). Jim is suddenly grateful to Helena, guilty for chiding her when she was only thinking of him, of all of them. But guilt is so often his overriding feeling towards her, these days, that he is able to suppress the impulse almost as quickly as it appears.

He sips his tea. 'Shall we go out to the studio?'

'I wonder . . .' Ann Hewitt offers him a thin-lipped smile. 'Would you give me a little tour of the house, perhaps, while the others are out?'

Jim hesitates. Stephen Hargreaves had insisted he do the interview at home – 'They're just keen to see where you work, Jim – nothing salacious.' But Howard had been furious – had forbidden Jim from doing it, until Jim had quietly reminded Howard that he was *not* his father, and couldn't forbid him from doing anything; and that Trelawney House was his home, too, and had been for the last five years. 'Bloody right I'm not your father,' Howard had thundered back. 'But if he were here, I'm sure he'd say the same bloody thing – you're an *artist*, not a celebrity. You seem to be having trouble remembering the distinction.'

They had not spoken for days – though that was not so unusual, now. It was Howard who eventually broke the silence. 'If you're set on having this woman in our home, for God's sake keep her to the kitchen and the studio. Don't let her wander round, taking it all in, judging us. And get her here on market day. I'm bloody well not going to sit here making small-talk.'

Damn Howard, Jim thinks now. *Damn his self-importance. Damn his petty bloody rules.*

'Yes, all right,' he says aloud. 'I suppose you'll get a good feel for the place.'

Later, Jim will wonder what on earth he was thinking, showing Ann Hewitt from room to room – as if *he* were a bloody estate agent – answering her questions, so politely, so innocently phrased: 'So whose bedroom is this?'; 'Your daughter, Sophie – where does she sleep?' He had even opened the door to Josie and Simon's room: they had not pinned back the gaudy, batiked sheet they hung as a curtain, and the room was in semi-darkness, the smell of weed still sweetening the air.

His only excuse, later, will be the one he can't share with any of them – that he was thinking of Eva. Jim's mind was full of her, as it is always now – and was especially that morning, when only a few hours stood between him and the moment she would step out from his mind and become real once more.

And so now, Jim barely notices as Ann Hewitt scribbles away in her notebook, is hardly aware of what he is saying as he leads her to the studio. This, at least, is tidy, everything scrubbed and put away: Howard even allowed Cath to sweep up his wood-shavings, to neatly arrange his tools.

As they talk, time seems to warp and bend: when a knock

comes at the door, he feels that hours, even days, might have passed. Jim is suddenly alert: this is his cue – pre-arranged, at Howard's insistence – to ask the interviewer to leave. And it means that Jim will be leaving shortly, too.

He accompanies Ann Hewitt back to her car, where she shakes his hand again, thanks him for his time. 'You have a very interesting place here,' she says as she climbs into the driver's seat. 'Our readers will be fascinated, I'm sure.'

He waves her off, thinking nothing of her parting words. He will think nothing more of Ann Hewitt at all until weeks later, when the article is spread across the kitchen table, sending its shockwaves out across the room.

Josie has prepared a Spanish omelette for lunch. Jim sits, eats, dismisses their curiosity about the interviewer with a vague, 'Oh, it was fine, I think.' Sophie climbs onto his knee, and he feeds her forkfuls of omelette, though he can feel Helena's irritation: she prefers Sophie to feed herself, but he loves to sit like this, carrying his daughter's small weight, pressing his nose to her head, inhaling the sweet baby-smell of her hair.

With Sophie, Jim's feelings of guilt are stronger than they are with Helena, more difficult to ignore. Guilt about raising her here, at the colony – a place that had once seemed so liberating, but is now beginning to seem like a dreadful place to raise a child. At two and a half, Sophie is becoming needy, difficult: at night, she often climbs from her cot, walks wailing from room to room until Jim – or, more usually, Helena – staggers sleepily from their bed to find her, then settles her under the covers between them. And there are so many lurking dangers: knives left out in the kitchen overnight; the terrible drop of the cliff-edge, and the sharp, unforgiving rocks below.

Until recently, Sophie was allowed to wander in and out of the studio at will; but one day in January, she dipped her hand in Jim's oil paints, and stamped multicoloured prints all over one of Howard's driftwood sculptures. Jim had found it hilarious, but Howard most definitely hadn't. 'Can't *someone*,' he thundered, his fleshy cheeks turning a dangerous shade of puce, 'keep an eye on that bloody child? She runs around here like a barefoot Indian.'

But if Sophie isn't to be admitted to the studio, then one of them – he or Helena, usually, though Cath and Josie pitch in when they can – must watch her; and that duty falls most often to Helena, who has all but stopped painting since having Sophie. All of this weighs upon Jim's conscience – not to mention the fact that, for almost two years now, he has been able, over and over again, to hold his daughter close, to love her with everything he is – and then to set her down, leave her, drive off to the woman he also loves. The woman who is not her mother.

Today, Jim leaves as soon as he can without arousing suspicion. Sophie waddles out to watch him, and Helena holds her back, away from the car wheels. 'You'll be home tomorrow, then? In time for dinner?'

'Yes, in time for dinner.' He kisses her, then leans down to kiss his daughter, whose face is already crumpling, preparing for tears. He watches their reflection in the mirror as he reverses, swings the car round, edges it out onto the drive. Sophie is crying now, beating her tiny fists against her mother's legs; for a moment, Jim considers turning back. But he does not. He drives on, watching their twin figures grow smaller and smaller, and then disappear.

In Bristol, he spends an hour or so with his mother and Sinclair. He tells them what he told Helena: that he is driving on to London, to spend the evening with Stephen and discuss next month's exhibition. He dares not think how many times he has used that excuse – Stephen, of course, knows everything – but neither Vivian nor Sinclair seems particularly interested. His mother is distracted, her eyes darting around the room as they talk; in a brief moment alone with Jim, Sinclair confides that he is worried about her, that the extremities of her moods seem to have returned.

'We must get her back to the doctor, then. Soon.' Jim speaks with concern, but he is ashamed, privately, by how unaffected he is by the news. He is thinking only of how quickly he can get away.

It is seven o'clock when he arrives at the hotel – their hotel, as he has started to call it in his mind, though they have only met here a couple of times. An entire night away together is a luxury they can rarely afford.

He finds her in the bar, looking out at the grey reaches of the sea, a gin and tonic on the table in front of her.

Eva turns, hearing him approach, and Jim feels something burst inside him: the euphoria of seeing her for the first time in too long. The narcotic rush of looking at her face and knowing that, for one night at least, and one blur of a morning, it belongs to him.

VERSION ONE

\\\\\\

Island
Greece, August 1975

On the boat from Athens, they sit on the upper deck, at the back, just as they did that first time. The bright Nikon colours are exactly as they have lived on in Jim's memory: the deep blue expanse of sea; the bleached yellows of the retreating land; the cerulean splash of sky.

He closes his eyes, feeling the sun on his face. The thrum of the engine is like the purr of some great, benign creature, blotting out the chatter of the other travellers – an American woman, close by, is reading aloud from Dr Seuss to a small child; a Greek family on his other side is sharing *spanakopita* and crumbling hunks of feta cheese. He reaches for Eva's hand, remembering how, on that first visit – their honeymoon; everything so new, everything still possible – she wore a blue and white checked dress, and her feet were bare and brown in her white sandals.

'Do you still have that dress?' he says, not opening his eyes.

'Which one?'

'The one you wore on honeymoon. Blue and white checks. I haven't seen it for years.'

'No.' She lets go of his hand. He can hear her reaching for her handbag, rummaging through its crowded depths. 'I gave it to Jennifer's school jumble sale, Jim. It must have been twenty years old.'

As the ferry approaches the island, they move with the other passengers to the prow of the boat: still that childish rush of excitement at the first sight of land. There is the crumbling watchtower at the mouth of the harbour; there are the scrubby hills rising above the town, so unexpectedly green after the parched streets of Athens. (An Athenian they met on the ferry, the last time, had made a joke in impressively scatological English: 'They say that when God made Athens, he opened his bowels, and shat out concrete.') There is the town itself – if you could call it that, this small collection of houses, rising in tiers like an amphitheatre around the harbour; the dome of the church; the bar and taverna at the dockside, where old men grumbled over backgammon in the late afternoon.

Jim remembers donkeys, too: rickety and fly-blown, left to stand in the midday sun; he had been quite upset, and Eva, surprising him, had said he mustn't judge by his own standards. But he can see no donkeys now, and the town itself appears to have doubled in size: new houses – some still unfinished, metal struts rising up from bald concrete blocks – line the upper tiers, and the bars and tavernas have proliferated. A few feet back from the quay, a couple dressed entirely in white are sipping cocktails in the shade of a striped awning, to the sound of an Elton John record spilling from the bar's open door.

He has a sudden memory, bright and clear. He and Eva sitting by the harbour at sundown with their glasses of retsina. Petros the barman pouring out measures of ouzo to fishermen, their faces thick and pocked as tooled leather. But there is no sign of Petros now: the man emerging from the bar with a tray of glasses tipped by cocktail umbrellas and glacé cherries is young, muscled, seal-sleek. Petros's grandson, perhaps. Or no relation at all.

As they wait in line at the gangplank with their suitcases, Jim turns to Eva. 'God, it's really changed, hasn't it?'

'We had to expect that, after all this time.'

A boy is waiting for them, carrying their name, misspelled, on a white card. He loads their suitcases onto a trolley, sets off without a word. They follow behind, and Jim feels his spirits dip. It was his idea, and a good one, he felt, to spend their fifteenth wedding anniversary on the island they had loved so much: a week together, just the two of them. Eva had been unsure at first; Daniel wasn't quite three – too little, she felt, to be left for a whole week. But slowly, Jim had convinced her: Daniel would be with Juliane. (The au pair, the Dührers' granddaughter, had arrived from Vienna four years ago, and by now they couldn't imagine life without her.) They would both be fine, he said. Eventually Eva had agreed, on the condition that they didn't stay in the same hotel as before. 'It would be too awful,' she said, 'if we found that it had changed beyond recognition.'

It seemed that she was prepared for the changes worked by time in a way that he was not. He is, Jim knows, far more afflicted by nostalgia than his wife: it is he who captures each new episode in the children's lives – birthdays, first steps, outings to the theatre – with his camera, who sends off each roll of film to be developed, pores endlessly over each clutch of photographs. It is, Jim supposes, the same urge that once drove him to paint – the need to capture a moment, whether real or imagined, before it disappears. And yet the attempt, it seems to him now, is always doomed to fail, whether in art (those meaningless abstract daubs on which he'd wasted so much time, and which now induce in him only a slight embarrassment, and, yes, a certain sadness) or in those family snapshots. There is always a slippage between the image in his memory – Eva brushing a lock of hair away from her face; Jennifer in her school uniform, so smart, so quietly grown-up; Daniel grinning messily from his high-chair – and the photographs he spreads out on the kitchen table.

Now, as they walk up the steep cobbled street to their apartment – he had telephoned the island's tourist office, asked for a place with a sea view, a terrace to breakfast on – a phrase slips into Jim's mind. Some fortune-cookie aphorism: *nothing is permanent except change*. It plays on repeat, a stuck record, until they reach the apartment – admire its dazzling whitewash; the blessed coolness of the shuttered rooms; the terrace, bright with red bougainvillea; the sea below mirrored and glinting. And then a weight seems to fall from Jim's shoulders, and he thinks, *But surely change needn't always be for the worse.*

When the boy has gone off with his tip, dragging the empty trolley, they fall gratefully into bed, exhausted from the long journey. Jim wakes first. It is still warm – to air the room, they opened the shutters, drew the lace curtains between the bedroom and the terrace – but the sun is lowering, a light breeze lifting the curtains. He lies for a while, halfway between sleep and dream. He had been dreaming of their garden at home: he was there with Jennifer and Daniel, playing hide and seek; his mother was there too, and Sinclair, and everyone was asking where Eva was, but he didn't know. Jim moves onto his side, gripped by irrational anxiety; but she is there, of course, soundly sleeping, her right arm crooked above her head as if frozen in the act of waving.

He would like to reach for her, draw her warm body to his. He would have done so, fifteen years ago, without thinking – or, if he thought of anything, it would only have been how lucky he was to have met her; how inconceivable it was to live his life alone. But now, he hesitates – Eva is so deeply asleep, and he knows how exhausted she is: two radio interviews this week, and all that toing and froing with the BBC about the screenplay for *Pressed*. As the date of their departure loomed, Daniel was fractious, troublesome: waking in the night, asking for Eva, consoled only by crawling into their bed, where he would shift and snuffle, robbing them both of sleep. So now, Jim does not reach for his wife. Instead, he gets up from the bed, finds his cigarettes, and goes out onto the terrace.

It is a beautiful evening; the flagstones are warm beneath his feet, the light soft and diffuse. Snatches of sound travel up from the houses below – a mother calling her child, a girl laughing, the jaunty burble of a television cartoon. Jim watches a small speedboat round the harbour wall, carve its V-shaped path through the still water. His mind is also beautifully still, and he remembers now that this was the effect the island had – the ability to pause the maelstrom of thought, to focus the mind on this moment, this place.

On their honeymoon, he had assumed that it was because he was so in love, so happy, drunk on visions of the future; and so he is surprised to find, now, that it still has a similar effect, everything falling away. All the silted build-up of the intervening decades: the years of teaching; the heavy disappointment of his failed ambitions; his infidelity, distant now (he has not taken anyone but his wife to bed since Greta); his jealousy of Eva's effortless success (not effortless, surely – he, of all people, knows how hard she works – and yet, in his darker moments, he can't help feeling how *easy* it has all been for her). All of it simply evaporates, leaving only these warm tiles, this indigo sky, this stretch of darkening sea.

He could cry with relief, but does not. He goes back into the bedroom, moulds his body to the shape of Eva's, rests his head against the dip of her collarbone until she wakes, turns to him sleepily, and he says, 'I'm glad we came.'

VERSION TWO
||||||||

Homecoming
Paris & London, April 1976

The call comes just after nine o'clock.

It is lucky that Eva is at home to answer it. She has just dropped Sarah off at school, and would have gone straight to the university had her first tutorial not been cancelled – Ida, the faculty secretary, had telephoned earlier to tell Eva that two of her students were unwell, her slow Mississippi drawl conveying her contempt for their excuses. And so Eva had found herself with several spare hours: time, she resolved on the short walk back to the apartment – stopping at their favourite *boulangerie* for croissants and fresh rolls; admiring the cotton-bursts of blossom on the trees that line their street – that she would dedicate to tackling the new biography of Simone de Beauvoir that Bob has sent from London for review.

But she has only just removed her jacket, laid her keys and shopping bag on the hall table, when the telephone rings.

'Eva?' It's Anton. She knows immediately, from his tone, that something is wrong. 'Where've you been? I've been ringing for half an hour.'

'I'm just back from taking Sarah to school, Anton.' There is a chair beside the hall table: a beautiful, rickety old thing Eva picked up at Les Puces flea-market, with the intention of reupholstering its balding seat. She sits down, aware of a cold, gaping sensation at her core. 'Didn't you try the office? What is it? Is it Mama?'

There is a pause, during which she hears her brother sigh. 'She's in hospital, Eva. The Whittington. Pneumonia. It's not good. Can you come today?'

Pneumonia: such a curious word. All through the making of arrangements – telephoning Ted, telephoning Ida, telephoning Highgate, because she wants to hear Jakob's voice, and has forgotten that he won't be at home – Eva sees the word projected in her mind, in chalk-white letters, imagines a bearded professor pointing at it with a stick. *Observe the Greek* 'pn' – *strange to our ears. From* 'pneumon', *meaning* 'lung'. Miriam's lungs: she has spent decades wheezing into bags, gasping on inhalers, shaking her head as she did so, as if it were no more than a minor inconvenience.

Ted, back early from the office, holds Eva in his arms, strokes her hair. She pictures her mother's twin lungs, disembodied, failing, like two limp, punctured balloons.

They decide, after some discussion, that Eva will go to London alone. It is a Thursday: Ted has two pieces to file for the Saturday paper, and Sarah has a French test the next morning.

'Come on Saturday,' Eva says firmly as she shuts her case. 'Just let me see how she is.'

Ted, doubtful, frowns at her across the bedroom. 'Well . . . if you're sure, darling. But I'd much rather we came with you now.'

On the train to Calais, the de Beauvoir biography lying unopened on her lap, Eva wonders why she insisted they didn't come. Ted might have held off his deadlines, or filed from London, and Sarah could surely have missed her test. But she had, for reasons she couldn't quite articulate, felt an instinctive need to go to her mother unaccompanied.

She thinks of the last time she saw Miriam. Christmas – or 'Hanumas', as Ted has affectionately dubbed it; since his arrival in the family, along with Anton's wife, Thea, the Edelsteins have incorporated into their celebrations turkey, fairy lights, even a tree. They had all crowded round the sagging dining-room table, eating by candlelight; Anton's daughter, Hanna, was button-eyed and gurgling on Thea's lap.

Afterwards, as was their custom, they had gathered in the music room. Jakob played his violin – the sad old tunes that seemed to come from some deep well of collective memory – and Sarah stepped up to the piano, performed the Satie *Gymnopédie* with which she had recently earned distinction at grade six. Miriam had sat curled in her usual chair; she looked tired – Eva and Thea had insisted she let them cook – and seemed a little short of breath, but not unusually so. She had watched her granddaughter's hands intently as they moved over the keys. Then she had closed her eyes and leaned her head back against a cushion, a small smile arching her lips.

And yet, thinking back now, Eva remembers that her mother had gone to bed very early – and on Boxing Day, she had bowed out of their usual walk in Highgate Wood. '*You* go, darlings,' she had said brightly over breakfast. 'I'll be fine right here with my new books.' Jakob, Eva sees now, had been worried. 'Your mother's doing too much,' he had said to her as they walked the short distance to the wood, arm in arm, the rest of the group striding out ahead. 'Talk to her, Eva. Make her understand that she needs to rest.' And Eva, patting Jakob's arm, had agreed that she would; but the rest of the day had been lost to eating, clearing up, watching Sarah and Hanna play together, and her promise had slipped from her mind.

The train pursues its steady, rhythmic course north, and regret – so useless, so impossible to ignore – grips Eva. Why did she not press her mother, ask her how she was really feeling; offer to stay with her, even, for a few weeks; insist that she take a break? But really, Eva knows her efforts would have been futile.

Miriam has always gone her own way, made her own choices. Eva can't begin to criticise her for it: it is one of the qualities she most admires.

At Calais, Eva joins the queue of foot-passengers waiting to embark. It is a bright, still day, as it was in Paris: the Channel is dark blue and glassy, and the crossing smooth. At Dover, it takes her a moment or two to recognise her brother: he is wearing a new, expensive-looking camel coat, and is standing beside an unfamiliar car, low-slung and sleek.

'How is she?' she asks as they embrace.

Anton swallows. Close up, he does not carry his usual gloss: he is pale, and dark thumbprints are stamped beneath his eyes. 'She seemed a little better when I left.'

In the car, they talk of other things: Hanna, who is still not sleeping through the night; Thea; Ted and Sarah; Eva's work at the university. She tells her brother about the writing course she has designed, about the joy she feels in bringing on the better students, and coaxing the weaker ones. She is surprised to note the pride in her voice: teaching was only meant to be a stopgap, a way to fill the empty hours after she and her agent, Jasper, parted ways. It was not a complete separation; he still passes on the occasional cheque, and asks, from time to time, whether she has started working on anything new; and Eva is still in touch, too, with Daphne, her old editor and friend. But in both cases, their brief, affectionate telephone calls are underpinned by the tacit acceptance that another book is now only a remote possibility, that Eva just doesn't seem to have the same urge to write. The stories in her mind that had once seemed so insistent, so impossible to ignore, have faded to faint shadows, if they are there at all. She has become self-conscious: looking over the last draft of the third book – she had limped through it, aware with each paragraph that it was becoming less and less of a pleasure – Eva felt that she could so clearly see the joins; that, in short, she was less interested in creating this fictional version of a woman's life than in living out her own.

When she had finally admitted this to herself, Eva couldn't decide whether she was disappointed or relieved. Over coffee with Josephine, she mentioned that, without her writing, time seemed to stretch before her, unmarked and limitless. A few days later, Josephine had telephoned with a plan: her old sorority sister Audrey Mills now taught English at the American University in Paris, and was looking for a literature tutor. 'She's desperate to meet you.' Josephine's brisk tone seemed to brook no argument. 'Shall I set something up?'

At Ashford, Eva drifts into sleep, lulled by the soft purr of the car. She dreams that she is back in the Paris apartment, tucking Sarah into bed (at thirteen, she will still sometimes allow such babying), turning off her bedside light, leaving the door ajar, then joining Ted in the living-room for a drink. But it is David she finds there, not Ted: dressed as he was on their wedding day, light grey suit and tea-rose buttonhole, hair slicked just so. 'Shall we play some music, Mrs Katz?' he says, and moves forward to take her in his arms. But as she steps away in the dance, to swing back to him, she sees that his face has changed: it is Jim Taylor looking back at her.

She wakes as the car pulls to a halt. Disconcerted, Eva blinks at Anton. 'We're here, sis. Time to wake up.'

It is almost evening: the streetlights are blinking on Highgate Hill, and the sky is a deep, thickening blue. Inside, the hospital is strip-lit and bustling. Eva matches her brother's quick stride towards the lifts. They pass two nurses, crisp and efficient in their uniforms, and an old man in slippers and gown, making for the exit with a packet of Woodbines.

Eva grips Anton's elbow. 'Can we wait a moment? I don't feel well.'

'I know you don't. I felt the same when they brought her in. But visiting ends at seven, and Matron's terrifying.'

They have just entered the ward, given the sister their names, when a grey-haired woman in a blue uniform approaches. The word 'matron' is stamped on a metal badge above her left breast.

'You must be Mrs Edelstein's daughter.' Matron holds out her hand. 'Thank goodness you're here. She's been asking for you ever since she came in.'

They've managed to find Miriam a corner bed, Matron explains as they walk over, with a window, a view. She says it with some pride, but Eva can see only the metal bed frame, the tangle of wires, her mother's small bulk beneath a mass of blankets – how is it that she seems no larger than a child? Jakob is next to her, sitting on a hard plastic chair. He rises as they approach, comes over to kiss her, but Eva is watching Miriam's face, white as the pillows she's resting on. Her lips are dry and parched, but she is trying to smile.

'Eva, *Schatzi*,' she says. 'I'm very sorry to be such a bother.'

There is another chair on the far side of the bed. Eva sits, takes her mother's hand. 'Don't be silly, Mama. You're no bother at all.'

Jakob kisses Miriam lightly on the forehead. 'We'll be back in a minute, *Liebling*,' he says, and then melts away, taking Anton with him.

'Don't let her talk too much,' Matron says softly before she too turns away, and Eva tries to obey, noting the shuddering rise and fall of her mother's chest. But there is so much she'd like to say, and so she says it silently. *You're the woman I most respect in all the world. I love you. Don't leave me.*

Miriam says nothing, but her eyes are half closed, and Eva knows she is listening. Then she opens her eyes fully, squeezes Eva's hand, and says in German, 'He tried to make me take you

213

away, you know. He said, "She'll be a nasty unclean little thing, just like you: best you get rid of her."'

A pain is rising in Eva's chest. She strokes her mother's hand, hoping to hush her, but Miriam continues, undeterred, the twin beams of her eyes fixed on her daughter's face. 'That is why I left. Not for any of the other reasons – and there were many, of course. I left because of you. And I'm so glad I did, *Schatzi*. You've made me proud every day of your life.'

Eva would like to say, 'You make me proud, too, Mama. How can I ever truly thank you?' But Miriam's eyes are twitching shut, and there are no other words: only the slow, rhythmic movement of Eva's hand on her mother's, the high beeping of another patient's machine, a woman moaning softly somewhere down the ward. Eva watches Miriam sleep until Matron returns, Jakob and Anton following behind, and tells her gently that it is time to go.

Geraniums
Worcestershire, May 1976

The day after Miriam's funeral, they meet in Broadway, at an inn.

It was Jim's suggestion: he had driven through the town once last year, tracing a long, dawdling route from Bristol to London, filled with the peculiar blend of despair and exhilaration that has become, in recent years, the keynote of his moods. The fatly thatched roofs; the stone walls, the colour of clotted cream; the geraniums spilling from hanging baskets outside timber-framed pubs: all this seemed to project an image of old Englishness that he found comforting.

But it must have been summer then: the geraniums are not blooming now, though the hanging baskets and the thatch are as he remembers them. He has booked them into the grandest pub, but when the landlord takes them upstairs to their room under the eaves, with its mahogany four-poster bed ('The honeymoon suite, sir'), Jim knows instantly that he has made a mistake.

Eva, at the window, doesn't acknowledge the landlord's goodbye. After the man has gone, closing the door behind him, Jim stands in silence for a few moments, watching the stiff set of her back.

'We can check out now.' He walks over, threads his arms around her waist, breathes in the scent of her. 'Go somewhere else. Anywhere you like.'

'No.' She has grown very thin: he can feel her ribs through her clothes. Shame washes through him. How he hates not being able to take care of her. 'Really, Jim. It's fine.'

She shifts in his arms, turns to face him, and he looks down at her, at her small, pinched face, her eyes carrying none of their usual light. He remembers reading somewhere that grief ages a person, but that's not how it is with Eva. In her jeans and duffel coat, she looks impossibly young – no older than a schoolgirl.

'Why don't we go to bed?' he says.

She stares at him: she has misunderstood.

'No, I mean to sleep. You look exhausted.'

'I am.' She crosses the room, unbuttoning her coat. 'Yes, perhaps I'll sleep.'

The bed is hard and ungiving, the pillows thin, but Eva falls asleep almost at once. Jim lies next to her, on his back, staring up at the canopy: the fabric carries a pattern of leaves and flowers that is vaguely familiar – William Morris, he thinks, suddenly remembering an armchair that his mother used to sit in on winter nights in Sussex, in front of the fire. He can distinctly recall sitting there with her, safe in her lap, drawing a finger across the twist and flourish of each stem. Now, he traces the pattern with his eyes while Eva's breathing slows, grows steady. He knows he will not sleep. After a few minutes, he rises gently from the bed, retrieves his shirt and trousers, his shoes, his cigarettes, and closes the door as quietly as he can, hoping she will not wake before he returns.

Outside, the High Street is busy with tourists, flocking from parked coaches, weaving in and out of giftshops and tea rooms. Jim lights a cigarette, watches the backs of two elderly ladies as they make painstaking progress along the pavement. They are like twins, with their identical crop of grey curls, fine as carded wool, their matching raincoats. As he passes, he hears one say to the other, 'What do you think, Enid? Will a scone spoil our lunch?'

Hurrying on, Jim does not catch Enid's reply. Ahead, he spots another pub; he stubs out his cigarette, goes in for a beer, carries it to an empty table outside. It is almost midday. At home – if he can call it that: when he is with Eva, Cornwall seems as remote as a foreign country – Helena will be basting the chicken, peeling potatoes, Sophie hovering next to her. Helena's parents are coming over for lunch – it had been her main source of complaint when he told her that he would be away on Sunday, that Stephen wanted to go over the hang of the next show. (Jim is careful not to reach for Stephen too often now, among his repertoire of excuses.)

'Must it be *this* Sunday?' Helena had said. They were standing in the kitchen – *their* kitchen, and only theirs; it is almost three years now since they left Trelawney House, after Ann Hewitt's awful interview was printed, making them look like 'freaks, junkies, the bloody Children of God'. Howard, spluttering across the kitchen table as he'd asked Jim and Helena – no, instructed them – to leave. Helena, red-faced and furious: 'How *could* you?' she'd hissed at him. 'I told you to be careful with that woman.' Sophie, wailing inconsolably as they packed the car and drove away from the colony, away from everything, everyone, she knew.

Jim, in the kitchen, had looked away, out at the small patio garden where Helena had planted herbs in pots, lined potato plants along a deep trough. He hated himself as he said, 'Sorry, love. Stephen's flying to New York on Monday.'

But even then, he hadn't been sure that Eva would be able to get away. It was almost two months since they'd last seen each other, just four days since Miriam had died, and Eva had withdrawn into her mourning, busying herself with death's myriad small tasks: the finding of a rabbi; the ordering of flowers;

the making of endless rounds of tea for the many friends and neighbours who came to call.

David had taken the first flight he could back from LA. Jim couldn't help feeling jealous: the man had all but left Eva alone on the other side of the world, and only now decided to step in. *But really*, he thinks bitterly, sipping his beer, *I should be grateful to David*: his presence had provided Eva with a legitimate opportunity to leave her children for the night and come away. She had told David she needed to spend some time on her own. Katz had not, apparently, seen fit to argue.

Sometimes, the absurdity of their situation threatens to overwhelm Jim: there is Eva, all but raising her children alone, in the full knowledge that her husband is in love with another; and there he is, living his own lie with Helena and Sophie. And yet, when he is not with Eva, it doesn't feel like a lie: at home, he is fully present, entirely absorbed in fatherhood. Sophie is more settled, it seems, in the cottage – less prone to waking in the night – though there have been problems at school: another girl's mother has accused Sophie of bullying, of constantly stealing her daughter's toys. The teacher called them both in for a meeting, asked if there were any problems at home. 'Oh no,' Jim had replied smoothly, grasping Helena's hand. 'None at all.'

How easily the lies slip from his lips now; and yet perhaps, he tells himself, he is actually warmer with Helena, more considerate, than he would be if he were being faithful to her, were Eva not brightening the outlook of his life. And his work certainly hasn't suffered – Jim has been careful, since *Woman, Reading*, not to allow Eva's image to creep into any more of his paintings. But she is still there, of course, in every one of them: while he works, it is her face he sees in his mind, her fathomless, intelligent eyes, with their absolute trust in his ability.

Many times, he has said to Stephen – still the only person in whom Jim has confided – that it is as if he has split himself in half, has become two people, each fully functioning in his own, separate world. The last time he said it – they were sitting over late-night whiskies at Stephen's club – his friend had sighed, leaned back against his chair. 'Like father, like son, eh?'

Stephen's words have echoed in Jim's mind ever since, bringing with them a sense that something must be done. And yet each time he thinks of raising the subject with Eva, he shrinks from it. They have so little time together – sometimes just an hour in Regent's Park between his meetings, before she collects Sam from school – and he doesn't wish to spoil it by speaking of the future. It is as if, when they are together, they exist only in the eternal present. And he knows, in the deepest part of himself, that this very fact carries its own particular allure: that it might never be matched by the humdrum rhythms of the everyday.

Draining his glass, Jim thinks of Miriam Edelstein. Earlier, in the inn – they had drunk a coffee in the saloon bar before going upstairs to their room – Eva had produced the order of service from her handbag, smoothed out its creases. There was a photograph of Miriam and Jakob on the front page: young, smiling; Miriam the mirror-image of Eva in a sleeveless summer dress. Jim had sat silently for a few moments, absorbing the photograph, his eyes lingering on the unfamiliar words printed inside: this other faith's vocabulary for death. *El maleh Rachamim. Kaddish. Hesped.* He wished he could have met Miriam. He wished it had been him standing next to Eva on the registry-office steps, smart in his suit, narrowing his eyes against the sun as his new mother-in-law, Miriam Edelstein, reached up to kiss him, to wish them the happiest of lives.

Now, his glass empty, Jim gets up from the table, makes his way back down the High Street to their inn. The landlord looks up as he walks in, but Jim doesn't meet his eye. Upstairs, he opens the door carefully, unsure whether Eva is awake – but she is still sleeping, her mouth open, her hair a dark fan against the pillow.

He undresses again, lays his clothes over the back of a chair, and climbs into bed. As he moulds his body to hers, she stirs, and he says, in a half-whisper, 'Come away with me, Eva. Let's start again.'

A few seconds of silence, during which he can feel his heart thudding in his chest. And then the silence stretches out, broken only by the soft sound of her breathing, and he realises that she hasn't heard.

Poets
Yorkshire, October 1977

'Another?' he says.

Eva looks down at her empty glass. She should say no. She should say good night, walk the two flights of stairs to the safe, carpeted silence of her room. 'Yes. Why not?'

So many reasons why not. She watches Leo's back as he walks over to the drinks cabinet, pours two generous measures of single malt. He is tall, well built, with a sportsman's loose-limbed swagger. There is a disproportionate number of middle-aged women in his group, and she has seen them watching him. On the first day, she overheard two of them in the ladies' loos, giggling like schoolgirls: 'God, that Leo Tait's even better-looking in the flesh.' The other: 'He's married, though, isn't he?' The first, disdainful: 'Since when did *that* stop any of them?'

Washing her hands in the basin – she'd waited a tactful few minutes before leaving her cubicle, to ensure the women had departed – Eva had wondered what the woman meant by *them*. Men? Husbands? Poets? She supposed the latter had a certain – well-founded – reputation for promiscuity (just think of Byron, for God's sake, or Burns) but Eva dislikes the new fashion for defining all men as a distinct, and rather disappointing, species. She had stared at her reflection for a few seconds, wondering whether the thick line of kohl she'd applied to each eye before breakfast was a little *de trop*; thinking of Jim, at home with the children and Juliane; feeling the old, mostly forgotten fury at his betrayal. And then she had collected herself, gone off to find her own group, lost herself in the intricacies of line and paragraph – she was leading a week's course on self-editing – and thought nothing more of Jim, Juliane or Leo Tait.

But that night, at dinner, she had found herself sitting next to Leo: meals were served at long benches, to encourage the mingling of the course leaders and their students, but the tutors still tended to huddle together at one end. This was where Eva was sitting – next to Joan Dawlins, a crime writer with whom she had once appeared on a television review show, and opposite the playwright David Sloane, a dark, lugubrious type who had said not a word to either of them – when Leo approached, carrying a glass of wine.

'May I?' he said, indicating the empty chair next to Eva. Joan had simpered, 'Of *course*, Leo.' Sloane still said nothing. But Leo did not sit; he hovered behind the chair, as if awaiting Eva's permission. 'Eva?'

She had looked up from her casserole, registering his presence for the first time. 'The chair's empty, isn't it?'

As soon as she had spoken, she realised she had sounded rude. Unbecoming red patches had appeared at Joan's throat. (Eva remembered them, suddenly, from the television programme: the make-up artist's frantic dabbing of pan-stick under the bright studio lights.) Sloane was actually smiling – Eva would learn, by the end of the week, that he was the sort of man who thrived on others' discomfort. And so she had turned to Leo, ready to apologise, but he didn't look in the least perturbed.

'I was *so* glad to see you were teaching this week too,' he said sunnily, sitting down. 'I really do love your books. I missed Tube stops reading *Pressed*. And the TV adaptation was great. They did a good job.'

Carefully, Eva laid her knife and fork across her empty plate.

She couldn't quite decide whether he was sincere: she has a hatred of false flattery – of which she has seen quite a lot, since her 'success'. Indeed, she doesn't really think of herself as 'successful' – she fears that if she did, she might never write another word again – but she enjoys the praise, the reviews, the interviews. Deep down, though, she is aware that none of that matters as much as the writing itself: as sitting down in the mornings at her typewriter, Jennifer and Daniel at school, Juliane moving around in the kitchen downstairs, and allowing herself the luxury of time spent entirely alone. It is more than many women are permitted, after all.

'Thank you.'

Eva must have sounded doubtful, because he turned to her – she noticed that his eyes were a shining, gunmetal grey, and that boyish dimples appeared when he smiled – and said, 'You think I'm a fake. But I'm not, you know. It's just my face. Nobody ever takes me seriously.'

'I don't believe that for a second.'

'Well.' Leo sipped his wine, still looking at her. 'Perhaps you'll be the exception, then.'

He was flirting with her, of course, quite shamelessly, and continued to do so for the rest of the week. Perhaps the women she'd overheard had judged him accurately: Leo certainly seemed to know what he was doing. He paid Eva just enough attention at mealtimes and during the evening gatherings to make her feel singled out, but not so much that anyone would notice. Eva observed his courtship – if she could give it that quaint term – with amusement. She did nothing to encourage him (he knew she was married, as was he; surely he was only playing), but neither did she tell him to stop. Later, she would see that she could easily have done so, had she really wanted to; which must have meant that what she really wanted was for the flirtation to continue.

And anyway, Eva has grown used, since her mother's death, to this odd feeling of detachment, to the sense that nothing that is happening to her is fully real. It is as if she has been split into two, even three versions of herself – living, breathing simulacra – and lost sight of the original. She tried to express this to Penelope, and it just came out sounding like science fiction. She could feel her friend watching her cautiously, as if unsure how to respond. 'Grief, darling,' Penelope said eventually. 'Grief does the strangest things. Don't fight it. You just have to let it play out.'

Was it grief, then, that encouraged Eva to play this game with Leo Tait; to nod when he offered her, and only her, a drink; to enjoy the warmth of his leg pressing against hers, safely out of sight beneath the dinner table? Perhaps at first, but on the fourth night – the Tuesday – his hand had slipped down onto her knee, and Eva had felt a lightning jolt that made her catch her breath; yet she had not brushed his hand away. After that, the game intensified: on a group outing to Haworth – Lucas, the foundation's director, was a Brontë obsessive – they had somehow found themselves alone for a moment in an upstairs passageway. Leo had caught her at the waist, said fiercely into her ear, 'I have to kiss you, Eva. I *have* to.' She had shaken her head, slipped away to rejoin the group. For the rest of the day, she had kept her distance, guilt already creeping over her, though she had done nothing, not even let him kiss her; but that night, in bed, she realised that her guilt was pre-emptive. She wanted Leo. Her decision was already made; and as she lay there sleepless in her room, she thought about Jim, and whether, with Greta, he had felt the same way.

And so, tonight: Friday. As is the foundation's custom, the end of the course has been marked by a series of readings: two students from each course – novelists, playwrights, poets, crime writers – tactfully selected by their tutors; and then the tutors themselves. Leo was the last to read. Everyone was rather the worse for wear, and the women didn't bother to hide their anticipation as he stood up, holding the latest slim volume of his poetry. 'He can read to me anytime he likes,' one woman, sitting just behind Eva, said in a stage whisper.

Eva was looking too, of course; admiring Leo's fine, tuneful baritone as it rolled out across the room. She had never read his poetry (though she had not admitted as much to him), and was unprepared for its effect: for the words' soft ebb and flow, their unexpected delicacy. She had imagined muscular rhythms, all 'sod' and 'hoe' – not this wavelike form, pushing and pulling, building to a crescendo that left the room silent for one beat, then two, before the clapping began.

Now, Leo is returning with the whiskies: their third, or their fourth? It is almost three a.m., and everyone else has gone to bed: even Lucas retired a few minutes ago, several sheets to the wind; they heard him stumble on the landing. Every moment Eva spends here, alone with Leo, is dangerous, but she makes no move to leave.

When he reaches their table, he doesn't sit down. 'Perhaps we could take these up to my room?'

They are silent on the stairs. His room is on the third floor, at the front of the house: the high bay windows, now framing the black night, overlook the car park, the road. Her own room is larger, with a view over the gardens, and the knowledge of this gives her a hot, shaming sense of pride.

Eva stands by the closed door, holding her whisky glass, as he moves around the room, closing the curtains, turning on the bedside lamp. *There is still time*, she thinks. *I could reach for the door-handle, go back out onto the landing.* But she does not: she lets Leo come over to her, take the glass from her hand, match the length of his body to her own.

'Are you sure?' he says, and she nods, draws his face to hers.

225

And then she is lost to pure sensation, to the charting of this new, undiscovered stretch of skin, and there is no room for thought at all.

She wakes in his bed. It is early – she can hardly have slept – and the room is cast in a cool, purplish light. Leo is still sleeping, breathing softly through his half-open mouth. In repose, his face seems absurdly young, though he is a good few years older than she. Eva dresses quietly, careful not to wake him; she barely makes a sound as she closes the door, walks as quickly as she can to her own room. She sees no one, but realises that she would not care if she did: the shame that she has carried through the week has, curiously, evaporated.

In the shower, soaping the body he has touched, Eva feels a sudden rush of exhilaration. She will not see Leo again, except by chance, at parties, on other such courses: they made no promises they couldn't keep. Tonight, she will be home with Jim and the children; she will step back into her other life, pick up its familiar refrain. What happened here, in Yorkshire, will be something she will keep for herself. Something to carry with her silently, like a pebble slipped into the pocket of an old coat: tucked away, and then mostly forgotten.

Gingerbread
Cornwall, December 1977

Christmas Eve: the sky is a pale, iced blue, the sea polished and still. In the harbour, a fine layer of frost is melting on the swept decks of the boats.

Holly wreaths hang in the front windows of the Old Neptune, and a sprig of mistletoe dangles from the front porch, brushing the heads of the fishermen as they duck in for a pint, leaving their wives to the plucked turkey and gift-wrap. Each time the heavy oak door is opened, a tinny blast of music rolls out across the quayside. 'When a Child Is Born'; 'Mull of Kintyre'; 'Merry Christmas, Everybody.'

In their cottage on Fish Street – how they all laughed at the name, the first time they saw it – Helena, Jim and Dylan are making gingerbread. Helena tips the sugar into the bowl, stirs the mixture with a wooden spoon. Her face is flushed with the effort, and a lock of hair, loosened from her low ponytail, is damp against her cheek. Jim would like to lean across the countertop, brush her hair back behind her ear, and feel the warmth of her skin under his hand. But he does not.

'Can I have a go, Mum?' Dylan is eight: tall for his age, with his mother's clear china skin and light brown hair. *Mousy,* Helena calls it: she has taken to dying hers with henna, leaving the bathroom smelling unpleasantly of bitter herbs. Dylan's eyes, though, are Jim's – that startling blue – and so are the freckles scattered across the bridge of his nose. Sometimes, looking at his son, Jim has the unsettling feeling that his own reflection is staring back at him. They are alike in so many other ways, too: in Dylan's talent for drawing (his set of HB pencils, bought by Jim for his last birthday, is among his most treasured possessions); in the boy's sensitivity, the way he looks to Helena and Jim as the twin weathervanes of his own moods.

'Thought you'd never ask.' Above Dylan's head, Helena catches his eye, and smiles. She seems relaxed today, playful, and he can feel the tension between them easing: it is a perceptible shift, like the sun coming out from behind a bank of cloud. There have been times, recently, after Helena has left the room, that Jim has noticed he was holding his breath.

'Here.' Helena draws her apron over Dylan's head, fastens it loosely. He isn't quite tall enough to reach the counter comfortably, so Helena sets him on a stool. 'Keep stirring.' To Jim, she adds, 'Smoke?'

They stand shivering by the back door, watching their breath writhe in the cold air. Helena's herbs are huddled inside the makeshift greenhouse she has built from pallet boxes and a couple of discarded windowpanes, only a little cracked, that she found in a skip. She is good like that – practical, much more so than he. But the smoking outdoors is a new thing: Iris's suggestion – no, *instruction*. At the thought of Iris, Jim tastes the familiar, bitter tang of dislike.

'Iris still coming round, is she?' He tries to keep his voice light.

Helena glances over. 'Yes. In a minute.' She draws deeply on her roll-up. 'Did Sinclair say what time they'd be here?'

'Teatime.'

'Fiveish, then.' He watches her profile: her full, arched eyebrows, the wide slopes and furrows of her lips. When they had met in Bristol – that warehouse exhibition; dingy rooms filled with bad art and worse wine – he had been overwhelmed by her vitality, by the way she seemed to carry the sea air in the pores of her skin. It had not been entirely fanciful: at Trelawney House, after a heavy night, Helena would still rise early for one of her walks on the beach, her face carrying no sign of the night's excesses. He remembers her as always sunny then – had painted her as such. *Helena with Lady's Bedstraw*: her beauty bare, simple, captured with a few brushstrokes. He can't quite decide when the tension between them appeared, unbidden, a hairline fracture webbing across a sheet of glass. But he has a name for it: *Iris*.

He is upstairs when Iris arrives, pulling on a jumper before heading out to the studio: it is an old whitewashed outhouse, and always draughty, though Jim goes out early each morning to switch on the electric heater. Instinctively, he stiffens, picturing that woman in his hallway, greeting Helena, leaning down to kiss his son.

Iris is short, thickset, with a large, square face and bobbed hair dyed an unflattering shade of orange. She makes fat, bulbous pottery she calls 'sculpture'; he and Helena have bits of it squatting hideously all around the cottage. She has a stall at the Saturday craft market where holidaymakers, to Jim's great surprise, sometimes part with their money for a bowl or a mug, but it is by no means a thriving concern: Iris lives, as far as he can tell, on a generous legacy provided by a great-aunt. This allows Iris to adopt the hippy's professed indifference to material things, with which Jim suspects she disguises her envy of his own modest commercial success. *Art is for the people, not for sale. Property is theft. I work on a higher spiritual plane.*

Sometimes, when Iris talks like this, Jim is gripped by the wild desire to punch her: he has never, in all his life, disliked anyone with such vehemence; and it's a feeling he can't quite explain. Helena, of course, can sense this, and her response is to dig in her heels. She certainly appears, these days, to reserve the larger part of her good humour for Iris rather than for him.

In the hallway, Jim greets Iris, one Judas kiss on each cheek. Her skin is unpleasantly clammy, and smells of patchouli. She squints at him. 'I hear you've been making gingerbread, Jim. Didn't have you down as a baker. Women's work, isn't it?' Iris half smiles at him, her head on one side. Always she goads him like this, with her gloopy, masticated feminism, as if Jim were some kind of woman-hater, when really, the only woman in the world he hates is *her*.

'Dylan's helping too,' he says, 'so does that make *him* a woman?'

Without waiting for Iris's reply, he turns to Helena. 'Heading out for a bit. Let me know when they get here, won't you?'

In the studio, the heater is breathing out its bitter smell of burning dust, and Marcel is sprawled on the old rag-rug, belly up. 'Hello, boy.' Jim leans down, tickles him under the chin, and the cat preens, shifts. 'We'll have some music, shall we?'

He slides *Blood on the Tracks* into the cassette player (his gift, last Christmas, from Sinclair and his mother), presses play. He tugs the sheet from his easel – an old habit, never broken, though Helena rarely comes in here any more – reaches into his pocket for his rolling tobacco, papers. *Early one morning, the sun was shining, I was laying in bed* . . . He sings along, pinching the tobacco, laying it along the shaft of the paper, narrowing his eyes at the canvas. *Wondering if she's changed at all, if her hair was still red* . . .

The woman's hair is not red; it's a deep, dark brown, with a conker's lustre. She is turning away, looking towards the man who sits behind her, on their living-room sofa; he is facing her, and the viewer, with an expression that Jim wishes to be un-readable. At the moment, his main fear is that the man – who is both him and not him, just as the woman is both Helena and

Eva Katz, and any of the women he has ever met – looks too miserable.

This is the third panel of the triptych. The other two, standing sheet-wrapped against the studio wall, are almost the same, but for minor variations: in the first, it is the woman seated on the sofa, and the man standing; in the second, they are both sitting. Jim has changed small details about the room, too: the position of the clock on the wall behind the sofa; the cards and photographs on the mantelpiece; the colour of the cat stretched out on the armchair. (Only one is black and white, in homage to Marcel.)

'Like a spot the difference,' Helena had said when he first outlined the idea: she was joking, but he felt the sting. His aspirations for the triptych are much grander. The painting is about the many roads not taken, the many lives not lived. He has called it *The Versions of Us*.

Jim has only just started working on the man's face – dabbing lightly at the shadows around his mouth, trying to lift its corners – when Helena puts her head round the door. She has to raise her voice to be heard over the music. 'They're here.'

He nods at her, turns reluctantly from the canvas, dips his brush in the jar of turps. He stoops for Marcel, and turns off the heater; it will be days before he can come out here again.

Jim has never liked Christmas – the endless hours of eating and drinking, the enforced good cheer. The Christmas after his father's death, Vivian was only just out of hospital, and she hadn't even bothered to get up. There was nothing in the larder to eat but a jar of Marmite and a box of stale water biscuits, which he had finished by the time Mrs Dawes next door, with her unerring ability to sense his distress, had rung the bell and insisted he come over for his dinner.

Now, Jim holds the cat's warm, writhing body, presses his

chin to the top of Marcel's head. 'Come on, boy. Let's get you inside.'

In the kitchen, there is the smell of cooling gingerbread, the low chorus of carols on the radio. (Helena is surprisingly traditional about Christmas: when Howard and Jim had tried to ban any mention of it one year at Trelawney House, she and Cath had very nearly packed their bags and left.)

Vivian is talking very loudly to Dylan. 'You mustn't peek at your presents, darling. You simply mustn't peek.' She is wearing a green jumper with a reindeer motif clumsily hand-knitted through the front, a pink woolly hat and a pair of earrings in the shape of holly leaves. She turns to kiss him, and he sees that she has scrawled two thick blue lines of kohl unevenly around her eyes, and that her pink lipstick has bled into the deep wrinkles on either side of her mouth.

'Darling,' she says.

Sinclair, coming through from the hallway with the suitcases, catches Jim's eye and mouths silently, 'Not good.'

It is Dylan who carries them through the evening: he adores his grandmother, and insists on producing his favourite toys – his Etch A Sketch; his Slinky; his Luke Skywalker action figure – for her inspection. Helena serves plates of ham, cheese, salad; they eat the cooled gingerbread with mugs of tea, and play a game of charades that disintegrates when it is Vivian's turn, and she tells them the name of the film before she has acted it out. 'Oh dear,' she says, realising her mistake. Her eyes fill with tears. 'Stupid, stupid me.'

Jim – remembering a disastrous childhood game of twenty questions that had left his mother sobbing in the front room – creates a distraction by offering everyone a drink. After her second sherry, Vivian falls asleep on the sofa, gently snoring.

Later, when Vivian has been persuaded to go to bed, Dylan

is asleep, and Helena has turned in, too, Jim and Sinclair sit in the kitchen, sharing the last of a bottle of single malt.

'How long has she been like this?'

Sinclair shrugs. Jim has seen his stepfather's expression before, on his own face, back in the years he spent with his mother in that miserable Bristol flat. 'Three weeks, maybe. Four. The medication was working wonders – you know it was – but I think she's stopped taking it. She says it makes her feel like she's inside a bubble, that she just wants to *feel* again.'

'You haven't found the tablets?'

'No. You know how clever she is. She's emptying the bottle. I think she must be flushing them away.'

The kitchen clock ticks on; in the old armchair in the corner, Marcel yawns, then settles back into sleep. 'We'll have to call Dr Harris in the new year,' Jim says. 'She'll crash soon. It's too much for you.'

'Too much for all of us.' Sinclair drains his glass. 'She keeps calling for your father at night, you know. First time she's ever done that. When I try to comfort her, she hits out.'

'I'm sorry,' Jim says, because he is, and because there is nothing else to say. Then they go upstairs to bed – Jim to climb in with Helena, seeking the warmth of her body; Sinclair to the room where Vivian is sleeping quietly, at least for now.

In the night – or perhaps it is the early morning – Jim is woken by the sound of a woman crying. He lies still for a few seconds, suddenly alert; but Helena sleeps on, and he does not hear the sound again.

VERSION THREE
//////

Afterglow
Los Angeles, December 1977

On New Year's Eve, David and Eva attend a party at the Hancock Park home of David's agent, Harvey Blumenfeld.

The house is large – of course – and half-timbered, in a turreted, faux-Florentine style that reminds Eva, incongruously, of a school trip to Stratford-upon-Avon: Anne Hathaway's cottage, thatched, fat plaster belted by dark timber beams. Enormous palm trees surround the pool, which is flanked by a low building of pretty red stone, with an open wood-fired oven on which Harvey himself – a man of immense appetite, especially for dramatic gestures – has been known, at his more intimate summer gatherings, to bake pizza for his guests.

Eva wears a long blush-pink gown with bell-sleeves and a plunging drawstring neckline. It seemed perfect in London – she had found it in a tiny boutique off Carnaby Street – but is not, she realises as soon as they arrive, at all right for Los Angeles.

The other women are in pantsuits or fifty-dollar peasant blouses. Their hair is expertly blow-dried; their bare arms and décolletages are, for the most part, the warm, even colour of milky coffee. To say they are beautiful feels inadequate, and not, in all cases, strictly accurate: theirs is something beyond beauty. They are gilded, luminous; it is as if, Eva thinks, looking round at the guests – there is Faye Dunaway, gazelle-limbed in white bellbottoms; there is Carrie Fisher by the pool, blinking at Warren Beatty – they have somehow ingested the heat of the studio lamps through their skin. David, too, has always had this quality, and both women and men are drawn by it, moth-like. There he is now, across the room, talking animatedly to a rail-thin actress in a low-cut white blouse, her eyes not wavering from David's face.

Eva stands alone, drinking champagne, looking down at her hateful pink dress. She has an uncomfortable vision, suddenly, of her entire relationship with David as an unspooling sequence of these moments: a shifting film-strip of inappropriate dresses, worn to parties at which she knows no one.

Well, not quite *no one*: there's Harvey, of course, who treats Eva with an exaggerated courtesy that she fancies he considers European. ('The beautiful *Frau* Curtis! How *are* you, loveliest of ladies?') Harry is here, though not Rose; they parted three years ago, after she caught Harry in bed with his latest young actress. And Eva has, over the years, met enough of David's people to be able to make her way around the room, drifting from group to group. She knows they do not really consider her one of them – how could she be, the little woman back home in England, bringing up two children – but they are, for the most part, gracious with her. Once, at an Oscars party, a young actress named Anna Capozzi – effortlessly elegant in a backless black gown – had come up, taken Eva by the arm, and whispered into her ear, 'It's absurd, what they're saying about David. None of us believe a word.' She must have known that it was true – that David was, *is* in love with Juliet Franks – but it was, Eva felt, kind of her to deny it.

At least Juliet isn't here: she has gone home to London for the holidays – a tactful absence for which Eva is grateful, but not fooled. She knows that Juliet is all but living with David. She has found expensive lotions and perfume in David's en suite, and Rebecca – callously frank, as if she wants to goad her mother into reacting – has told Eva that Juliet is often there in the mornings, making them breakfast. Stacks of blueberry pancakes, freshly blended juices. Once, the thought of that woman making breakfast for her daughter would have made Eva want to scream out loud. Now, she is aware only of the essential *rightness* of the scene: of Juliet as the true wife, while she is the other woman, the interloper.

It was Eva's idea to spend Christmas and New Year in Los Angeles. She would have no proofreading to do, and it would, she thought, be a chance for Sam to spend some time with his father (David has not been back to London for more than a weekend, squeezed between castings, since Miriam's funeral), and for both of them to spend time with Rebecca, who is currently living with her father. She is eighteen now, taller than Eva, with David's dark eyes and wide, insouciant lips. She has already done some modelling in London, and David has been touting her around his Hollywood friends like a ... well, 'like a pimp' was how Eva put it during their last argument, by telephone. David was righteously indignant, as only a father who has observed his children's lives from the safe distance of five thousand miles can be. 'If you try to stop her doing what she wants, Eva,' he said, 'you'll only drive her away.'

She didn't want to admit it, but Eva knew that he was right. Rebecca's teenage years have been punctuated by tears, door-slamming, threats of running away to Los Angeles. Their worst argument came when Rebecca was just fourteen: David had not flown home as promised for her birthday. The usual apologetic phone call had followed – 'So sorry, darling, but Harvey has set up a meeting with George Lucas'; then an oversized bottle of Chanel No. 5, his usual peace offering, had arrived in the mail. Eva, by way of recompense, had organised an elaborate dinner party for Rebecca and four of her friends:

prawn cocktail, chicken chasseur, baked Alaska. But, on the night, Rebecca and her friends had not materialised; and only one of the friends – a sweet, nervous girl named Abigail – had had the decency to telephone. 'I'm so sorry, Mrs Katz,' Abigail had said. 'Rebecca's gone out to a club with the others. She'll be so angry that I told you, but I felt bad.'

Slowly, carefully, Eva had wrapped the uneaten food in cling film, returned it to the fridge; disassembled the place settings; removed *Aladdin Sane* (her birthday present to Rebecca) from the record player. Sam had helped – he was five at the time; still in awe of his beloved elder sister, but precociously sensitive to his mother's moods – and then Eva had put him to bed, and sat up smoking, waiting. It was almost two a.m. when Rebecca arrived home; when she saw her mother, she had pursed her lips – painted a lurid, glittering pink – and said, 'I wish I lived with Dad instead of you.' And Eva – with a candour she would later regret – had replied, 'Well, if that's how you feel, why don't you just bloody well fly over there?'

Rebecca's eyes had turned to slits. 'Maybe I will. And then you'll be sorry, won't you?'

But Eva had never thought that Rebecca would make good on the threat – until four years later, her A levels dutifully completed, Rebecca did. She had packed all her things – her jean-shorts and fringed suede waistcoats; her Bowie cassettes; Gunther, her ancient, fraying teddy bear – and set off for Heathrow one Saturday morning with the plane tickets David had, apparently, airmailed to her.

It was lucky Eva had caught her: she'd been out taking Sam to football practice. Opening the door, she saw her daughter heaving a backpack down the stairs, and caught her by the arm. 'Where on earth do you think you're going?'

'Los Angeles.' Rebecca had stared at her mother – challenging her – and Eva had seen David's resolve, David's confidence, in those black-brown eyes, in the firm set of her daughter's chin. She was so like her father; she was eighteen; perhaps she *should* go and spend some time with him. And so Eva decided not to fight. Loosening her grip on Rebecca's arm, she said, 'What on earth possessed you to leave without saying anything?'

Rebecca had softened a little, then. 'Sorry. I thought you'd try to stop me.'

Eva, sighing, had reached forward, tucked a loose strand of hair behind her daughter's ear. 'Come on, I'll drive you to Heathrow. Not that you deserve it. And as for your bloody father . . .'

At the car, Eva had stowed the backpack in the boot. Rebecca had climbed into the passenger seat, her bare legs brown, un-blemished, and said, quite matter-of-factly, 'You do understand that I need to get away, don't you, Mum? You smother me, you see. You smother me with your love.'

Eva had turned away, pretended to check her wing mirror as she blinked away her tears. They were silent as Bowie accom-panied them up the M4. (How romantic that unlovely stretch of road still seemed, for the fact that it led to Cornwall, to Jim.) At the terminal, Rebecca was contrite – 'I really am sorry, Mum' – and Eva, not wanting anger to sour their parting, had bought her a few gifts for the trip: a Christian Dior compact; a pair of Ray-Bans. Rebecca had even cried a little as they said goodbye. And then she was gone: a tiny figure in shorts and boots, stoop-ing under the weight of her enormous rucksack.

All the way home, to Sam and an empty flat, her daughter's words had played over and over in Eva's mind. *You smother me.* It struck Eva then that she had made her choice, not once, but twice: invested not in Jim, in the chance of their finding hap-piness together, but in her children, in her certainty that their happiness must lie with a mother whose primary loyalty – at least on paper – was to their father. Oh, she had considered divorcing David, and bringing her love for Jim into the bright, clean light of day; but each time she did so, she saw her children – the way Rebecca glowed each time she saw her father; the way Sam treasured each of David's film posters and theatre programmes, his autographed ten-by-eights. She had thought about bringing Jim into their lives – about building a home; threading together the disparate wefts of their broken families – and felt a rush of pure fear.

She was putting her children first – they both were: Jim his daughter, Sophie, too – and that fact, Eva thought now, had made her over-protective. She remembered the time, just back from one of her rare nights away with Jim, that she'd insisted Rebecca stay at home for the whole weekend rather than go out with her friends; she'd wanted her daughter's presence, in some way, to make up for how deeply, how painfully, she was missing Jim. She also remembered the afternoons when, returning from a snatched hour or two in Regent's Park, she had forbidden Sam from going to a friend's house after school. Guilt had made her draw the children too closely to her. As she drove back down the M4, it had occurred to Eva that she need do so no longer. That perhaps the best mother was not one who tried, against all odds, to protect her children; but one who was honest, happy, true to herself and to her own desires.

In Los Angeles, the party rolls on with champagne, and a band, and fireworks at midnight. At one o'clock, the spent Catherine wheels are still smouldering, and the guests are beginning to disperse: those who wish to continue the party will do so at the Chateau Marmont, or in motel rooms scattered along the freeway. Eva and David will not be among them: Sam and Rebecca are at home (if Rebecca *stayed* home – Eva suspects she will have slipped away in the too-fast car David bought her for her eighteenth birthday). And so they make their way to David's red Aston Martin, the Californian night cool and damp, and smelling of oleander and gasoline and the fireworks' bitter afterglow.

David has left the top down; Eva draws her wrap closer around her shoulders as he eases the car out onto the drive, the gravel loud beneath the tyres.

'Cold?' he says, glancing over.

'No. I'm fine. It's refreshing.'

From the road, they can see the lights of downtown LA, blinking like the tail-spots of distant planes. Eva thinks of Jim, of course, as she always does: of the solid, safe shape of him; the way that every time she sees him, it's as if the rest of the world has faded to a blur.

She thinks of that day and night in the hotel in Broadway, the day after her mother's funeral: how Jim had come back in after his walk, stretched out next to her, and asked her to come away with him, and she'd pretended she hadn't heard. She'd loved him for asking – of course she had – but she had just lost her Mama, the children their beloved Oma, and the idea of forcing upon them another loss, another sudden shift in circumstance, had simply been too awful to contemplate.

She thinks of what Jim might be doing right now; of whether he is lying next to Helena, thinking of the last time they – he and Eva – made love.

She thinks of how it felt to write him that letter, all those years ago, to bicycle with it down King's Parade as the street-lights blinked on, and to feel that her heart was breaking – not in some metaphorical sense, but with a pain that was physical: a tearing in two.

She thinks of Jim standing outside the New York Public Library, his cold hands sheathed in his pockets, waiting for her, scanning the crowds for a face that would not appear.

She thinks, *It has been too long*.

She thinks, *Now*.

'It's time to stop this, David.' Eva's voice seems unnaturally loud, floating out to him across the silent road. 'I can't do this any more. I'm not even sure what it is we're doing.'

David watches the road unspool. His profile is almost as familiar to her as her own – she will be forty this year; she has known him for more than half her life – and yet she is struck, now, by how little she really knows the man he has become. His is the face on the movie poster, his eyes expressionless, unfathomable.

'You're right,' he says. He speaks carefully, as if choosing words in a language he doesn't fully command. 'We've let things lie for too long.'

'I love someone.' She wasn't expecting to say this now.

'I know. And Jim deserves you, Eva. I mean it. He's loved you all this time.'

Eva runs a hand over the smooth pink fabric of her dress. A scrap of poetry – T.S. Eliot; how devoted she had been to him at Cambridge – drifts into her mind: *Footfalls echo in the memory / Down the passage which we did not take.* All the efforts they have made, all the secrecy, those tissue-thin layers of lies and half-truths. All of it gone – just swept away.

'When did you find out?'

'I think I always knew.'

She swallows. They pass a motel missing half its sign, the neon letters *TEL* floating ghostlike in the darkness. 'Does Rebecca know?'

'I'm not sure. She hasn't said anything.' Eva breathes a little easier – she will tell her daughter, and Sam too, but in her own time. 'We haven't been honest with them, have we?'

'We haven't been honest with each other.'

'Oh, I don't know about that.' David reaches into the dashboard for his cigarettes. He lights one, passes it to her. 'We both did what we thought was right, Eva. And it wasn't just out of some dusty old idea of duty – I did love you, you know. I probably still do. We just don't fit, do we?'

They are silent as they smoke. *He is a decent man, underneath it all*, Eva thinks. *He really did the best he could.* Another open-top car passes, blaring its horn: four teenagers are hanging out, Deep Purple thrumming from the stereo. Eva scans their faces for Rebecca's, but her daughter isn't among them. She leans back against the headrest, smoking the cigarette down to its last sour gasp, thinking of how suddenly everything can change; thinking of what Jim will say when she tells him what she has done.

Outside David's house – that modernist box of steel and concrete and glass; it has always been David's place, not hers – the car purrs gently to a halt. They sit for a moment, neither of them quite ready to go inside.

'Be happy with him, Eva,' David says. 'I really want you to be happy.'

She reaches out, touches his face with her hand. It is the first time she has touched him in months – years, even – and the feel of David's cool skin beneath her palm sends a shiver through her: fear, regret and the sweet remembered pleasure of loving him, or believing she did. Believing she had to.

'I think we will be, David. I really think we will.'

Ground
Bristol, February 1979

They bury Vivian on a Friday morning: the coldest of February days, the sky grey and the air damp, moistening the skin, though no rain has fallen.

The grass of the churchyard is frozen hard; it snaps beneath their feet as they walk from the church. All through that slow procession – Jim is at the front left-hand corner of the coffin, bearing his portion of its weight, allowing its sharp edges to press uncomfortably against his shoulder – he can think only of the diggers; of how long it must have taken them to break the ground, to cleave through the iced topsoil to the warm, crumbling earth below.

He has never been to a burial before. Funerals, yes – Miriam's was almost three years ago – but all of them cremations: brief services building to a theatrical denouement, the coffin disappearing behind a pair of curtains as if in a conjuror's trick. Of his father's funeral, Jim remembers only that slow dance of red velvet, the mechanical whirr as the casket moved off to places unknown. His mother still and silent on the pew beside him (the doctor had come to the house that morning, given her something 'to keep her calm'); the dark-grey worsted of his shorts rough against his thighs.

When the police telephoned with their news, Jim had assumed – when he was able to think anything at all – that his mother's funeral would follow the same pattern. But it turned out that plans had been made, promises given. Vivian had been attending church for more than a year. Jim had not been surprised when she told him: his mother had often, in her high periods, developed sudden, unpredictable fanaticisms. There had been a particularly uncomfortable phase in his early teens when she'd flirted with Wicca, and he'd found strange little offerings around the house – plaited twigs, a nest of quail's eggs, a heap of dried daisy-heads.

And so Vivian had wanted, Sinclair said, to be buried at her new church: she had a horror of cremation, of being wheeled off to meet the flames while still alive, her cries going unheeded.

Jim did not say, *Well, if my mother wanted a Christian burial, perhaps she should have thought twice about throwing herself off a bridge.*

He is at pains to be solicitous of Sinclair, who feels responsible – though Jim does not hold him so, any more than he does himself; perhaps rather less. It was Vivian who had refused to take her tablets: they had found her stash hidden in a plastic bag inside the cistern of the downstairs toilet. It was Vivian who had wanted to be able to *feel* again. It was Vivian who had ground a sleeping tablet into powder, slipped it into Sinclair's bedtime single malt, and then crept from the house at three a.m. to walk barefoot across cold black tarmac to the bridge.

It was a plain footbridge, spanning an unremarkable stretch of A-road: goodness knows why she had chosen such a place. A driver, naturally, found her. He told the police he'd seen her fall – watched a woman drop, her nightdress luminous in the streetlight. 'She was smiling,' he said. 'I'm sure she was. I'll never forget it.'

Jim knew this because he'd asked to see the driver's statement. Reading it, he'd been reminded, suddenly, of a story he'd once heard in a Bristol pub: he was back from Cambridge for the holidays, had gone out alone one night to the White Lion for a beer. The man was tall, good-looking, about his age; sitting among a group of pasty-faced office boys in cheap suits. He was telling these boys, in his soft Bristol burr, about a factory girl, jilted by her lover, who had thrown herself from Clifton suspension bridge and floated gently down, her wide Victorian skirts forming a kind of parachute. She had, incredibly, survived. 'Lived to eighty-five,' the man had said. It was curious how vividly Jim could see the man's face in his mind. 'A legend in her own lifetime.'

At the graveside, the undertaker's boys step forward to lower the coffin into the ground. Someone – one of the diggers, Jim supposes – has lined the bare hole with baize: against the black earth, the green fabric seems cheap, artificial. Jim releases his share of his mother's weight to the boys' care – they are men really, muscles straining under their black suit jackets – and feels a hand slip into his. Eva. Sinclair is on his other side – a husk of a man, hollowed out, as if air is whistling through him. Jennifer and Daniel are behind them, each holding one of Jakob's hands.

'What is that man doing, Opa?' Daniel whispers loudly to Jakob as the priest – a large, ungainly man with a soft, kind face; of course he must be kind, to have permitted Vivian a proper funeral – steps to the side of the grave.

'Saying goodbye, Daniel,' Jakob whispers back. 'We're all saying goodbye to your grandma.'

Afterwards, the black cars take them back to Sinclair's house – Jim has never quite grown used to thinking of it as his mother's – where Eva and his aunts have prepared the buffet, set out wine, sherry, beer. He pours himself a whisky – the last of a bottle he gave Sinclair for Christmas, but has almost polished off himself over the last few wakeful nights – and watches Eva as she moves among the guests. She is still slender, compact; her dark hair – gathered now into a low bun – throws up the odd streak of grey, but really, she could still be taken for a girl.

His girl. His wife. The woman he knows better than any other – better, certainly, than he ever knew his mother, with her fathomless reserves of sadness. She has come so far from the girl she once was, out there with her bicycle on the Cambridge Backs. Eva is now, in some way, public: a person known, recognised. A few weeks ago, a man of about Jim's age had come up to them while they were out to dinner, and told Eva how much he admired her without so much as glancing in Jim's direction. And he hadn't minded – not as he might have, once. He'd put paid, on that wonderful holiday in Greece, to his unsightly bitterness. And he had come home feeling better, truly, than he had in years – closer to his beautiful, brilliant wife; filled with love for his children; finding satisfaction in his teaching, in the possibility of inspiring in others his own love for art, and all that it means to him.

And yet still it has crept back, gradually: that old sense of failure, of ambition unfulfilled. *A husband, a father, an art teacher*: dull, plodding, reliable. Not a *real* artist; not like his old friend Ewan, with his exhibition at the Tate. Recently, at a party, Jim had overheard some new acquaintance of Eva's – a TV producer, blue-suited, shiny – ask why her husband had never considered becoming a 'proper painter, like his father'.

'Oh, but Jim *is* a painter,' Eva had replied. 'And a very good one too.'

Jim had been proud of his wife's loyalty, of her deliberate, tender blindness. (He hasn't painted anything in years.) And yet her words had also stung. For days he had wondered whether Eva truly believed what she had said – whether this was, in short, her version of the truth, and what that meant about the person she must still believe he was. For what claim, now, could Jim truly lay to being any kind of artist?

The wake passes in a blur of faces. 'At least she is at rest,' someone says – a woman about his mother's age, grey-haired, her small blue eyes pink-rimmed. Jim nods, unable to think of a response. Only his aunt Patsy seems to have anything meaningful to offer. 'You did all you could for her, Jim. You were her darling boy – her everything – but in the end, even that wasn't enough, was it? Nothing was ever enough.'

She frowns as Jim pours another whisky: he brought a second bottle with him from London. 'You'd better watch that. Drinking yourself into a stupor won't make it hurt any less.'

He knows his aunt is right: he is drinking too much. He can't blame his mother for that, either – convenient as that would be. For months now, Jim has been uncomfortably aware of the relief that comes with the first drink – the sense that he is re-configuring the world, making it comprehensible.

After dinner is the best time (earlier, sometimes, at weekends). The day's stresses passed, Daniel in bed, Jennifer sitting dutifully with her schoolbooks, Eva out somewhere – usually, Jim can't remember where; maybe she asked him to come, maybe she didn't – and the kitchen quiet, calmly lit. The second drink is good, too, and the third: then, the room's colours grow warmer, and the evening is filled with possibilities. It is only with the fourth drink, the fifth, that those possibilities seem to recede, and the room's shadows lengthen. It is then that he wonders where Eva is, where everyone is, why the house is so silent. It is then that Jim feels the great, deep loneliness creep over him, and with it the unnerving sense that it is not his father he takes after, but his mother. For surely this is how Vivian must have felt in those darkest times, on that moonless night when she closed the front door behind her and walked out in her bare feet. Jim thinks then that he really is his mother's son, and the thought fills him with fear; and so he pours himself another drink.

Sometime later – it is dark outside, and the kitchen windows are throwing pools of light out over the neat front lawn – Eva makes coffee. She places a mug in front of Jim – he is sitting at the kitchen table, as he has been for a long time. The other mourners must have left: he is aware only of his wife, and of Sinclair, and of the low chatter of the television from the living-room.

'I failed her,' Sinclair says. 'I'm so sorry, Jim.'

Jim looks at his stepfather, at his gentle, unremarkable, un-memorable face. 'You don't have to be sorry, Sinclair. There was nothing you could have done. Nothing anybody could have done.'

He has said the same thing, or variations of it, over and over again, for weeks. He will keep saying it, but it will never be enough. He will never be able to make Sinclair understand, really understand, that the darkness lived inside Vivian, and that although she feared it, hated it, there were moments, too, when she wanted nothing more than to dive down into it, allow its waters to close up over her head. Jim understands, and that is why he reaches for the whisky bottle, pours a generous dose into his coffee mug.

'Jim . . .' Eva's voice is soft, concerned, but he shakes his head. He gets up, takes the mug, goes out to the hallway, opens the back door.

The cold is the slow, seeping kind: he doesn't notice it at first, but his fingers shake as he takes out his rolling tobacco, his papers and filter tips. He is clumsy, fumbling; curses his hands, the cold, everything, until Eva comes, takes the tobacco from him, and rolls them both a cigarette. Silently, they smoke, look-ing out at the dark, frosted outlines of wintering shrubs. They smoke because there is nothing left to say. They smoke until their faces are aching with cold, and it is time to go back inside.

VERSION TWO

||||||||

Breakfast
Paris, February 1979

It is Ted who finds the notice in the newspaper.

They are having breakfast: coffee and brioche, the World Service turned down low, the papers spread across the dining-room table. Ted still prefers to read the papers at home, but Eva can join him only on Fridays, now – on other days, she is due at the university by nine o'clock. Often, she gets there earlier, for an hour of reading, preparation: the quiet gathering of her thoughts.

Eva's office is on the third floor of the English faculty: small but well lit, its windows framing the splayed upper branches of a plane tree, its walls lined with framed film posters and book-cover reproductions. The pleasure Eva takes in this little room, furnished exactly as she likes it, surprises her. She loves their apartment, with its miscellany of family life (Sarah's guitar, propped against the sofa; Ted's papers; the washing strung from the kitchen ceiling on the old-fashioned laundry rack), but none of it feels as fully hers, and hers alone, as this shabby faculty cubbyhole.

Even now, as she scans an article about striking lorry drivers, Eva's mind is already in that room: considering the pile of first-year short stories she has left on her desk, the reference she has agreed to write for a Harvard master's application. And so she isn't fully listening when Ted says, 'Jim Taylor. Don't you know him from Cambridge?'

'Jim Taylor?' Eva looks up, notes that her husband's expression is serious. 'What about him?'

'His mother's died. Killed herself, apparently. What an awful thing.' He folds his copy of the *Guardian* neatly in half, passes it to her. *Vivian Taylor, artist's widow, dies at 65.* It is not the lead obituary, but a down-page article, accompanied by a small black-and-white photograph of a slender woman in a patterned dress, the man beside her shorter, stockier. *The coroner has ruled the cause of death to be suicide. She is survived by her son, Jim, a prominent painter in his own right, and by her sisters, Frances and Patricia.*

Eva looks again at the photograph. Vivian is not quite smiling, but the man with his arm around her – her husband, Lewis Taylor – is beaming. He isn't handsome – he is short, blunt-featured: nothing like Jim – but he has a certain ragged, leonine power, tangible even in three inches of grainy newsprint. But Vivian: *artist's widow, artist's mother. How dreadful*, Eva thinks, *that her life should be defined only in relation to the men she loved.*

Across the table, Ted is watching her face. 'Did you know her at all?'

'No.' Eva lays the paper down. 'I barely know Jim, really. We didn't even meet in Cambridge – it was later, in New York.'

'Oh. Sorry.' He is moving on, already, to the French papers, taking up the morning's edition of *Libération*. 'My mistake.'

Later, in her office – it is lunchtime: traffic lining the street below as the weekend exodus begins, students whooping and laughing in the corridors – Eva takes out the obituary, places it on top of the unfinished Harvard reference. There is Jim, surely, in Vivian's expression, in the cast of her slender body. She is surprised they didn't use a photograph of Jim, too – his is the more familiar face; Eva recently read an article stating that a painting of his had sold at auction for a staggering sum. Perhaps the editor thought it would be too painful for him, for his family. *Strange, too*, she thinks, *that there should be no mention of Helena, or their son. What was his name? Dylan. A beautiful boy: dark hair and bright, curious eyes, dazzled by sunlight, reaching out for something beyond the frame.*

From her desk drawer, Eva takes a postcard printed with the address of the university. *Too plain*, she thinks. *Too businesslike*. Instead, she finds a card she picked up at the Rodin Museum: *The Wave*. Three women crouched beneath a frozen surge of greenish onyx. Not by Rodin, but Camille Claudel. *Artist's widow, artist's mother*: will Jim find the resonance significant? She decides to take the chance that he will not.

Dear Jim, Eva writes. *I was so sorry to read of your mother's passing*. She crosses out 'passing', stares for a moment at the spoiled card. She has no other card to send him; he will have to forgive the mistake. She writes 'death' instead: surely anything else is euphemism. *I have no other words to offer: it's at times like these, I think, that we see how inadequate language really is. Art says it all much better, doesn't it? I hope you are still able to work. I think of you . . .*

Eva pauses here, taps her chin with the blunt end of her pen. 'Often' would be an exaggeration: she thinks of Jim Taylor only rarely, and fleetingly – while washing up, or closing her eyes for sleep; in those unguarded moments when she allows her mind to wander to what might have been. She will leave the statement as it is: truthful, but ambivalent. Then she adds, *With all my sympathy and best wishes, Eva Simpson*. The address of Jim's Cork Street gallery on the right-hand side of the card, and it is done.

She turns the card over, stares at it for a few seconds – she can't quite read the expressions of the three bronze figures caught beneath that solid overhang of water – and then places it in her coat pocket to post later.

The next few hours pass quietly. She is interrupted only by a student – Mary, a nervous freshman from Milwaukee, anxious to know what Eva thinks of her story ahead of Monday's class; and by Audrey Mills, bearing coffee and pastries from the local *patisserie*. Audrey is a large, good-natured woman whose thick grey hair always hangs in a plait drawn across one shoulder. They talk of the usual things: students, midterms, the repairs Audrey's husband is making to their country house south of Versailles; Ted's book (he is halfway through a tongue-in-cheek Englishman's guide to the French character); Sarah. 'It's the half-term concert tonight, isn't it?' Audrey is finishing a mouthful of millefeuille.

Eva nods. 'Starts at five. I'd better get this reference done and head off. My life won't be worth living if I'm late.'

At four o'clock, Eva unspools the finished Harvard reference from her typewriter, folds it neatly, and places it inside a good cream envelope. Then she shrugs on her coat, checks her handbag for car keys, purse, compact. Outside, the corridor is empty, echoing; her heels click efficiently on the parquet as she makes her way downstairs, wishes the lone security guard, Alphonse, *un bon weekend*.

The Friday afternoon traffic is still heavy: it takes her an age to manoeuvre her little Renault out onto the Avenue Bosquet, and the queue of cars slows to a halt on the Pont de l'Alma. It's already half past four. Eva taps out an anxious rhythm on the steering-wheel, tries to remind herself that there are worse places to be stuck in traffic: it is a dull, colourless day, but the tall grey buildings along the Rive Droite are austerely beautiful, a study in monochrome.

She watches a small boat plough the grimy waters of the Seine, and finds herself thinking about her mother – about a visit Miriam and Jakob made to Paris one summer, soon after she and Ted were married. They had taken a bateau-mouche from Notre-Dame to the Eiffel Tower. The heat on the unshaded boat was intense, and Sarah was being difficult, whimpering endlessly about ice cream. To mollify her, Miriam had produced a carton of orange juice from her handbag, which Sarah then – deliberately, Eva suspected – managed to spill across the front of her new white dress. Eva had snapped at her daughter, and then at Miriam; at the Tower, they had aborted their plans to take the lift to the top, and sought instead the cool interior of a nearby café.

Eva can see her mother now: reaching into her bag for a handkerchief; looking pointedly at the tabletop while Ted and Jakob made tactful conversation, and Sarah busied herself with the ice-cream sundae Eva hadn't had the heart to refuse her. She had suddenly felt thoroughly ashamed of herself; she'd reached across the table, taken Miriam's hand, said in German, 'I'm sorry, Mama. Forgive me.' And Miriam had replied, 'Don't be so silly, *Schatzi*. What is there to forgive?'

She is still thinking of Miriam at five fifteen, when she arrives at the school. Ted is standing by the main doors, his shoulders hunched against the cold.

'Don't worry,' he says when she reaches him, exhausted. 'They haven't started yet. Thank God for French timing, eh?'

Eva kisses him, loving him for always remaining calm. Ted is impossible to argue with: he listens, considers, never raises his voice. She has seen him really angry only a handful of times, and even then it was perceptible only in the deepening colour of his cheeks, the emphatic slowing of his speech. *He is such an easy man to love*, she thinks, and she takes his arm, walks with him down the corridor to the main hall. And he is easy for Sarah to love too, reserving for her a relaxed, unstudied affection. Seeing them together makes Eva fleetingly regret, sometimes, that he was unable to have children of his own. Ted told her this on one of the very first nights they had spent together at his flat in St John's Wood, in a dull, broken tone that seemed to speak of a fear of losing her, losing what they were, so carefully, tentatively, embarking upon. But Eva had drawn him to her, said with a certainty that she would only later truly come to feel, 'I have a daughter, Ted. Be a father to her. Let's just be grateful for what we have.'

Sarah is one of the last students to perform. Eva can hardly breathe as she watches her emerge from the wings and sit down on the stool in the centre of the stage, settling her guitar on her knee. She is so like David – his height, his loose elegance and sculpted features – and yet she has so little of her father's unshakeable confidence. *Why would she*, Eva thinks, *when she has barely seen him more than twice a year since she was five?*

Eva wonders, sometimes, whether her daughter's shyness – it took her music teacher weeks to persuade Sarah to take part in the concert – has developed as some kind of reaction to David's fame. Here at the international school, among the children of writers and diplomats and businessmen, Sarah's parentage is barely noted. But it had not been so in London: there was bullying, nudges and whispers, name-calling. Eva had drawn information from Sarah slowly, stealthily. *Think you're it, don't you, just because your dad's on the telly?* Eva had wanted nothing more than to run straight to the school – to take the headmistress by the scruff of the neck, and make her end her daughter's suffering at once. But she'd resisted, for Sarah's sake. They'd waited it out. Not long afterwards, Ted had asked her to marry him, raised the possibility of their moving to Paris; and here they are.

Now, Sarah sits motionless on stage, staring down at the floor. For ten seconds, maybe twenty, silence rolls out across the room. Eva is gripped by the fear that her daughter will simply get up and leave; she grasps Ted's hand so tightly that later he will show her the red welts she raised on his palm. But then, after a few long moments, Sarah begins to play. And she is good, as

Eva knew she would be, with a certainty that was surely beyond a mother's natural pride. Sarah has her Oma's natural aptitude for music; as she plays, there is a perceptible shift among the other parents: a collective drawing-in of breath. And later, there is applause, for which Sarah stands red-faced, blinking, as if she had quite forgotten that she was being watched.

As promised, they take Sarah out to dinner, with her best friend Hayley, and Hayley's parents, Kevin and Diane. Kevin and Ted discuss real estate – Kevin is a broker from Chicago, specialising in acquiring 'high-spec' apartments for fellow expats. Hayley and Sarah share secrets at their end of the table, their faces half hidden by curtains of hair. Diane – a tiny, skeletal woman with the precise manners of a Southern belle – leans in to Eva, her Hermès scarf trailing her Chanel scent. 'Can you *believe* how grown-up they are?'

'I can't.' In Eva's mind, her daughter is still the plump-cheeked toddler crawling across the living-room carpet, or the five-year-old thrusting out her fat little legs on the Regent's Park swings. Sometimes, when Sarah walks into the room, Eva has to blink a few times to erase the memory of the girl she once was.

She has forgotten, now, about the postcard she wrote to Jim Taylor a few hours earlier, still lying unposted in the pocket of her coat: a coat that, when they get back to the apartment, Eva will hang on the hall stand, and not wear again for almost a week. She will not reach her gloved hand into her pocket until the very end of that day. Then, taking out the card, she will read it over, and wonder what on earth possessed her to write such a thing. *What use could Jim Taylor possibly have*, she will think, *for empty platitudes from a woman he barely knows?* And so she will place the postcard in the wastepaper basket beneath her desk, and not think of it again for many years.

//////

Ground
Bristol, February 1979

'What can I do?' Eva says.

It is the first time either of them has spoken in some time. He heard her approach – her shoes crunched crisply on the gravel – but she did not come to him at once. She stood behind him, at a slight distance, but he could feel her there as surely as if she had spoken: there was that same narcotic rush of joy, potent as always. At once, he was ashamed: to stand alone at his mother's graveside, while the other mourners were filing slowly away, and to feel *joy*?

'Just be here.'

Eva's gloved fingers curl around his, black suede against thick grey wool. She bought him both the gloves and a new coat, handed them to him in a smart striped bag. Jim had tried to say it was too much, but she shook her head. 'Just take them, darling. Please just let me do this for you.'

He is glad of the coat now: the air is icy, snatching at his face, his neck. He hardly knows how long he has been standing here, how much time has passed since the last scattering of earth, the vicar's sober summing-up. *Through our Lord Jesus Christ, who will transform our frail bodies that they may be conformed to his glorious body*. Ten minutes? Half an hour? The vicar – a gentle, soft-faced man – had closed his book and moved away. The undertaker's boys had stepped back in smart unison. There was a low murmuring among the guests: Sinclair, beside him, had turned to Jim expectantly, as if awaiting his cue. Sophie began to tug at his hand. 'Dad, I'm *cold*.'

Jim didn't move. He had stood silently until everyone was gone: even Eva, who hadn't been standing next to him, where he'd have liked her, but towards the back, holding Jakob's arm. (He'd had a fall a few weeks before, and was still walking with a cane.) On her other side was Sam, quiet and grey-faced in his undersized black suit. Rebecca stood behind, her dark hair dramatically coiled and pinned, her fingernails painted an ugly brownish red. She hadn't wanted to come – her RADA year group was deep into rehearsals for *The Winter's Tale* – but Eva had insisted. Jim heard their whispered discussion in the dark: the Regent's Park flat isn't really large enough for four people – certainly not five, now that Sophie has come to live with them. Resentments simmer in the small rooms: sometimes, on opening the front door, Jim can feel it thickening the air like trapped smoke.

Arguments erupt with exhausting frequency, but only between certain adversaries: Rebecca and Eva; Sophie and Jim. Between the rest of them, the dynamic is too fragile, too uncertain, to permit the open airing of grievances. With Eva, Sophie is shy, monosyllabic, unresponsive to her stepmother's gentle overtures (a day out shopping for school shoes, endured in stony silence; a cinema trip; a concert by Jakob's orchestra). He and Eva are both patient with her, suspecting that Sophie's decision to move to London – to give up her school, her friends, her whole life in Cornwall – was prompted less by her forgiveness of Jim than by the fraying of her relationship with her mother. Helena is now immersed, Jim knows from Sophie and from the vitriolic letters Helena still writes to him, in a series of affairs with younger men. The latest is Rebecca's age – an electrician named Danny, whom she met, Sophie says, when he repaired some faulty wiring in the cottage. 'It's *disgusting*,' Sophie told Jim, with a bruised dignity that touched his heart. 'I don't want to see her ever *again*.'

Meanwhile, Rebecca – furious that Eva has insisted she live at home through her RADA course, rather than throw money away on an expensive flat – appears to have decided, for the most part, to act as if Jim simply isn't there. And Sophie seems rather afraid of Rebecca, with her glamour and her insouciance and her habit of declaiming her audition speeches, loudly, in front of the bathroom mirror. Sam is the only one who seems relatively unperturbed by the changes in the household – he is sweet-natured, studious, preoccupied with football, space travel, engineering: enthusiasms that Jim doesn't share, but in which he does his best to show an interest. So no, the flat will not do: Jim and Eva have agreed that they will have to find their own place – somewhere fresh and light. Somewhere to start again.

Standing alone at the graveside – all these thoughts, and others (Vivian, mixing paints in the pantry of the Sussex cottage; Vivian, thin and glassy-eyed, unseeing, in the hospital), shifting through his mind – Jim was dimly aware that he was making a spectacle of himself. He could almost see his own image, caught in long shot: the grief-stricken son standing sentry by his mother's grave. But as he stood there beside the freshly dug hole, with its lining of bright green baize, he was aware not so much of grief as of a curious emptiness. Exhaustion. Relief. The stillness that falls when a long-expected event finally comes to pass.

'The car is waiting,' Eva says softly now.

Jim nods: he has forgotten all about the black car, about the driver in his peaked cap. Eva squeezes his hand, and they turn to go. The church car park is almost empty now: just Eva's little Citroën (there wasn't space for all of them in the family car), and that black saloon, where dimly, through the rear passenger window, he can see a woman's face pressed against the glass. Pale skin, wide-set blue eyes. There is a quickening in his gut: Helena. He blinks a few times, looks again. The woman's features rearrange themselves into those of a girl. Sophie.

When Jim told Helena he was leaving her, her face had crumpled and twisted as if he had landed her a physical blow. He had wanted to feel pity, and yet Helena had seemed so ugly, her grief so vengeful and uncontrolled – *a woman scorned* – that it was all he could do not to simply walk out the door and close it behind him. And in the end, that was more or less what he had done: closed the kitchen door on her tears, on the shattered crockery littering the flagstones. (Helena had thrown plates at him; later, in his studio, she would take a knife to several of his canvases.)

Jim had looked up the stairs, to the open door of Sophie's room – she was at school – then picked up his suitcase and left. Earlier, he had placed a letter on her pillow, setting out, as best he could, his reasons for leaving; telling her that she would always be welcome to stay with him and Eva. Much later, he would realise what an error he had made in not talking to his daughter face to face. He hadn't known then that it would be three months before he saw Sophie again, or that six months after that, Helena would call to tell him, her voice low and venomous, that Sophie wanted to leave Cornwall, and come to him. 'She's chosen *you*,' she said. 'So that's it, Jim. You've taken everything I have. I hope you're happy now.'

The awful truth was that Jim *was* happy: not in some bland, superficial way – fixed Kodak smiles under the bluest of skies – but in his deepest self. This kind of happiness was less a state, he realised, than a form of honesty: a sense of essential rightness. He had known it when he was with Eva in Cambridge, and had looked for it again with Helena: he had found something real with her, something true, but not that. And then, all those years later, Jim had found that happiness again with Eva – or at least a version of it, however muddied, complicated.

All that complexity had fallen away, though, on 8th January, 1978. The precise date was etched on his mind. Eva was just back from Los Angeles, and they had reserved a whole night for each other at their Dorset hotel. He knew at once that something had changed – feared that she had finally resolved to leave him. But the opposite was true: she was leaving *Katz*.

'It's you, Jim,' she had said. 'It's always been you.' And there it had been: that honesty, that slippage of two discrete objects into congruence. Jim had driven back to Cornwall the next day, and packed his bags.

Now, he walks Eva to her Citroën, where Jakob, Sam and Rebecca – her family, now his – are waiting. 'See you there,' he says, and kisses her. Then he slides onto the back seat of the family car.

'Home, sir?'

Jim wants to tell the driver, 'That house was never my home.' But instead he says, 'Yes, please. Sorry to keep you waiting.'

Vivian and Sinclair's house isn't far from the church; they might have walked, in fact, but the undertakers were quite insistent on the cars. This is the farthest edge of Bristol, where ring roads and new-builds bleed into overgrown culverts and scrubby fields. Through the car window, a short parade of shops – a Chinese restaurant, a launderette – gives way to a school's sprawling estate, disembodied shouts coming from an unseen playground. It is half past twelve: lunchtime.

'Hungry, darling?' Sophie is sitting very straight and still beside him, her cheeks still mottled from crying. She shakes her head, and Jim wants to reach for her, as he would have done, unthinkingly, just a few years ago.

It was only when Jim drove to Cornwall to collect her that he'd begun to understand the full extent of Sophie's anger. He'd loaded the boot and back seat with her cases, her schoolbooks, her collection of hideous troll dolls, with their wizened plastic faces and fluorescent shocks of hair. In the hallway of the cottage – Helena, to Jim's relief, was out – he'd held his daughter to him, felt her rigid and unresponsive in his arms. 'I'm so glad you're coming,' he had whispered into Sophie's hair. 'We both are. Eva and I.'

'I'm only coming,' Sophie had replied stonily, 'because Mum makes me *sick*.'

Vivian, too, had been angry, to an extent that took Jim by surprise. She and Helena had never, he thought, been particularly close; but when she learned of what she called Jim's 'desertion', Vivian had made an ugly telephone call to Eva's flat. ('You *beast*,' she'd hissed at him; he could hear Sinclair in the background, his voice calmly soothing. 'Now, Vivian, come along, there's no need for this.') She had also written letters – sheet after sheet lined with her oversized, looped handwriting. *You are no better than your father. Selfish, both of you. Heads full of nothing but yourselves and your bloody paintings.* Finally, she had come to see them in person. Eva had opened the door; Vivian had pushed past, imperious, her mouth an uneven pink line beneath a wide-brimmed hat.

'What,' she'd said, 'have you done with my son?'

Had Vivian been a different kind of woman – her illness a different kind of illness – the scene might almost have been comical: a skit from the pen of Oscar Wilde. *A handbag?* But nobody was laughing.

'You have *ruined* your daughter's life,' Vivian said to Jim, while Eva made tea, watching her with cautious concern. Then, drinking the tea, Vivian added, 'You have ruined my life. Both of you.'

Jim had known then, as he'd suspected all along, that it was really his father Vivian was angry with: his father and herself.

He'd driven his mother back to Bristol that evening – she'd left the house while Sinclair was taking a bath, without telling him where she was going. Vivian had fallen asleep in the car almost at once, the lights of the motorway flashing orange on her face as the miles passed. Jim had spent the night in the spare room, woken to find his mother's equanimity restored – for the moment, at least. Before he left, Sinclair had taken Jim aside. 'I don't think she's taking her medication,' he'd said, 'but the doctors won't do anything unless she tries to harm herself. I'm at my wits' end.'

All Jim had been able to do was tell Sinclair not to worry: that she would surely even out, over time, with or without her medication, as she had always done before. But almost a year later, Vivian had slipped a sleeping tablet into Sinclair's night-time drink, and stolen from the house in the small hours. A driver had found her the next morning at the base of a nearby road bridge. She had not left a note.

At the house, Jim's aunts are handing round plates of sandwiches and sausage rolls. Eva, having arrived a few minutes before, is slicing a Victoria sponge. The house is not full: there are perhaps twenty people, standing in small, hushed groups. Stephen and Prue are here, and Josie and Simon from Cornwall. Even Howard and Cath have sent their condolences, in the form of one of Cath's intricate pencil drawings – a milk bottle, a clutch of tulips, *We're sorry* sketched underneath with a fine-nibbed pen.

Jim stands with Stephen in a corner of the living-room, smoking a cigarette.

'It was a good service, Jim.' Stephen's voice is low, serious; he is wearing a sober charcoal-grey suit. Jim thinks of all the many nights he has sat with Stephen – too many to count – speaking of his love for Eva; his indecision; his feelings about his mother, his father. Stephen, it occurs to Jim now, is the only person who really knows every part of him – even with Eva, he must edit himself, expunge those facts that might cause her pain (the erotic content of Helena's angry letters; the fact that Jakob had taken Jim aside, the first time they met, and warned him – politely, discreetly, but a warning all the same – never to do to Eva and her children what Jim had done to his other partner and child). Stephen knows all of this – knows everything – and he is still here. Still standing next to him. Jim feels a rush of affection for his friend. Touching his arm, he says, 'Thanks for coming. I mean it.'

Stephen clears his throat. 'You don't need to thank me. Least I could do.'

Across the room, Jim's aunt Patsy is asking the vicar if he would like tea; Jim, watching, catches her eye, nods. 'Excuse me a minute, Stephen, won't you?'

In the kitchen, Jim finds Sinclair filling the kettle.

'Let me do that,' he says, but his stepfather places a firm hand on his arm. 'For God's sake, Jim, I'm capable of making a bloody pot of tea.'

'Of course you are. Sorry.'

Jim busies himself with the cups and saucers; someone – Patsy, Jim assumes – has laid them out on the counter in neat rows, beside a milk jug and sugar bowl. The bowl is part of a larger set, hand-painted with a pattern of small yellow flowers. Jim remembers this china from the Sussex house: Vivian would take down the cups from the dresser for guests. She smashed one of them, once; sent it flying across the kitchen towards his father's head. She missed, of course, and the broken pieces had lain on the floor for days.

He'd thought of this as he drove away from Helena, that day a year ago – away from the plates she'd sent flying across the flagstones, from the scorched earth of their relationship, their love – and felt, then, the full weight of his decision settle over him. And yet, as London approached – London; Eva; their chance, at last, of a life together – Jim had felt his sorrow gradually fade. *Was that how my father felt when he left us, when he drove away with Sonia?* he thinks now. *And yet he returned, and I did not. Does that make him the better man?*

'I'm sorry, Jim. That was unfair of me.'

Jim has, for a moment, forgotten that Sinclair is in the room: he looks up, sees his stepfather watching him, contrite. Sinclair's hands are shaking as he places the kettle on its stand. Jim has never heard him swear.

'It doesn't matter. What can I do?'

He has, unconsciously, echoed the words Eva spoke to him at the graveside. Jim looks back to the living-room, through the open serving-hatch, seeking out her face. She is always present in his mind, but this is a sharpening of focus, a small tug on the invisible thread that connects them – that has always connected them, from the very first moment he saw her in Cambridge. How lovely she was that day, with her watchful eyes and neat, ballerina's poise.

He sees her now, handing a slice of cake to an elderly woman he doesn't recognise. She has her back to him, but, sensing she is being watched – or perhaps feeling that same tug – she turns.

With you, I can face anything, he tells her silently. *Stay with me.*

Eva gives him a small smile – barely a twitch of the lips – as if to say, simply, *Yes.*

PART THREE

VERSION ONE
\\\\\\

Bella
London, September 1985

Bella Hurst enters Jim's life on a fresh September day, the sky high and cloud-swept, the playing fields still damp from last night's rain.

It is the first day of term: the smell of paint lingers in the classrooms, and the parquet in the great hall is newly lacquered, shining. The corridors are almost silent – the boys won't arrive until the following day – and Jim is in the art-room store cupboard, lining the shelves with pots of poster paint, tubes of oils. He is taking his time, enjoying the quiet, the sense of order; tomorrow, all will be noise and bustle once again.

'Mr Taylor?'

The girl – later, he will know her as a woman, but it is as a girl that he first sees her – is standing just beyond the open door, as if unsure whether to come in. The light – the high windows have just been cleaned, and the easels and workbenches and screen-print tables are doused in sunshine – is behind her, so he can see only her outline. A shadowed cloud of curly hair, a loose white shirt. Leggings, ankle boots. A leather satchel dangling from her left shoulder.

He lays down the box of paints. 'Yes?'

'Bella Hurst.' She extends her hand, and he offers his own. Her grip is firm.

'Ah,' he says.

'Weren't you expecting me?'

'I was. Well, I knew you were coming. But I didn't . . .'

He wants to say, *I didn't have any idea you'd be so absurdly young.* Alan's secretary, Deirdre, had telephoned back in August to say that Gerry, Jim's deputy head of department, had broken his leg on a cycling holiday in France, and that a supply teacher would have to be found. It hadn't taken long: a few days later, she had phoned again to say that a new teacher had already been secured. Jim, Eva and the children were just about to leave for Cornwall – a fortnight at Penelope and Gerald's beach house near St Ives. And so, with Eva standing beside him in the hallway, staring pointedly at her watch, Jim had nodded at the name – *Bella Hurst* – thanked Deirdre, and not thought of it again.

'Do call me Jim,' he says now, to fill the silence. 'Only the boys call me Mr Taylor.'

'All right. Jim.' Bella steps back, shrugs off the satchel. 'Do you want to give me the grand tour?'

He shows her round, opening drawers and cupboards, switching on the projector, indicating the stacks of coarse paper for the lower years, and the good drawing sheets for the sixth form. She is not quite as young as he imagined (in silhouette, she seemed barely older than Jennifer): mid-twenties, perhaps. Her hair is a dark, unruly mass, and when he meets her gaze, he notes that one of her eyes is blue, and the other almost black.

'Like Bowie,' she says. He has just switched on the projector, throwing a lopsided image of Van Gogh's *Sunflowers* onto the far wall.

'What?'

'My freaky eyes. David Bowie has one blue and one dark eye, too.'

'Oh.' Jim flicks the switch, and the flowers disappear. 'I really wasn't . . .'

'Staring? No, I know you weren't. I just like telling people that Bowie and I have something in common.'

Back in the store cupboard, he sets the ancient, paint-spattered kettle to boil, makes two mugs of tea. They sit on tall stools before the pupils' workbenches, arranged in a C-shape, with Jim's desk completing the square. Bella tells him she did her foundation course at Camberwell, her degree at St Martin's and her master's at the Royal College. She rents a studio space in Peckham and lives in a squat in New Cross. (Jim shudders instinctively at this, picturing loose floorboards, mice, a leaking roof, and will later chide himself for his small-mindedness. *Since when*, he'll think, *did you become so bleeding bourgeois?*) She rides a bicycle; has never taught before (it was her tutor at the Royal, an old schoolfriend of Alan's, who suggested her for the job); and disapproves wholeheartedly of private education.

This she says with a smile, lifting her mug to her lips. 'I suppose that makes me an awful hypocrite.'

'It does, rather.' Jim has finished his tea: drunk it in awed silence, mute before this whirlwind of a girl – woman – with her mobcap of curls, her loose, artless clothes, her scattergun speech, veering wildly from one subject to the next. 'I'd maybe keep that to yourself.'

Bella lays down her mug. 'Yes. Maybe I will.' From her satchel, she takes a packet of tobacco. 'Roll-up?'

Jim smiles. 'Don't mind if I do.'

They smoke on the fire escape, where Jim and Gerry usually take a breather during morning break, steeling themselves before confronting the next batch of bored adolescent boys. They are, Jim has decided, simply unaware of how lucky they are; of how rare a privilege it is to attend a school such as this, with its red-brick turrets, ancient oak trees and wide swathes of lawn. These boys are the sons of bankers and barristers: sleek, entitled men, men with money, men whom Thatcher is making richer by the month.

Art, for most of Jim's pupils, is a subject devoid of meaning: an easy ride, a chance to muck around with paints and scissors before getting back to the serious business of maths tests, debating societies, rugby practice. But there is always the odd boy – perhaps one or two a year – who stands out, who bends his head low over his life-drawing (an ageing actress, fully clothed), as his pencil brings her form to life. It is for these boys that Jim is able to keep getting up in the morning, looping his tie, smoothing down his hair. It is for these boys – as much as for Eva, Jennifer and Daniel – that he is able, most evenings, to stop at the fifth drink, before the sixth and seventh deliver him to sweet, obliterating sleep.

'You were at the Slade, weren't you?' Bella is standing in a strip of sunshine, lifting her face to its warmth. Always, afterwards, Jim will think of her as a pattern of light and shade. A Man Ray photograph, caught in grainy monochrome.

'I was. How did you know that?'

She opens her eyes. The contrasting colours of her irises lend her face a disquieting, lopsided look. 'Victor said. My old tutor. He knows your work. And we all know your father's, of course. The great Lewis Taylor.'

He wonders whether she is teasing him. 'It's years since I did any real work.'

'Well.' Bella has finished her cigarette, stubs it out in the sand-filled plant pot he and Gerry keep out here for that purpose. 'I'm sure you have your reasons.'

Jim nods, unsure whether to say more; but she is turning to go. 'Got a one-to-one with the colonel.' Noting his confusion, she laughs. 'Alan Dunn, of course. Victor says he still runs the place like a regiment.'

And then she is gone, and the art room feels suddenly empty.

Jim returns to his work in the store cupboard. Soon it will be lunchtime, and the rest of the day will be lost to meetings, time-tabling, preparation. It will only be when he climbs into his car and waves to Bella Hurst, pedalling off on her bicycle, that he will think again of what she said.

He must have his reasons. And yet, as he draws the car out onto the steep road home to Gipsy Hill, Jim will find himself struggling to remember what they are.

Pronto soccorso
Rome, May 1986

'Darling?'

Eva lays her shopping bags down on the tiled floor of the hallway. She stands for a moment at the foot of the stairs, listening to the silence.

'Ted, I'm making lunch – are you coming down?'

Still no answer. He must have gone out: Ted's schedule is unpredictable, dictated by the morning headlines, or by urgent phone calls from London. His latest editor, Chris Powers – an impossibly youthful, smooth-featured type just in from the *Mail* – manages to make Eva feel she is wasting vital time even in the seconds it takes her to climb the stairs with the telephone.

She gathers up the shopping, carries it through to the kitchen. Umberto, lying prone on the worktop, lifts his head and mewls out a greeting. She ought to tell him off; they have been unsuccessfully trying to teach him some manners since taking him in shortly after their arrival in Rome. He was a pathetic, stringy little thing then, riddled with fleas and mange. But Eva rarely has the heart to chide him: instead, she tickles the cat under his chin, finds the velvet-soft place behind his ears. Umberto purrs and preens, rolls over onto his back. It is then, while running her hand over the cat's belly, that her gaze rests on the kitchen table. Ted's wallet, keys and driving licence. The three things her husband never leaves the house without.

Eva's hand lies still on the cat's fur. She strains to catch a sound from upstairs: the low murmur of Ted's voice on the telephone; the typewriter's artillery patter. (He is wary of the word processor she bought him for his sixtieth, says he mistrusts the speed with which the blurred green letters imprint themselves on the screen.) But there is nothing – only the purring of the cat, the shudder and hum of the ancient fridge, a muffled bellow from Signora Finelli next door, calling her half-deaf husband to *pranzo*. And then she hears it – the most peculiar sound: a deep, inarticulate keening, like the whimper of an injured animal.

In seconds, Eva has crossed the hallway, climbed the stairs. Outside the closed door to Ted's study, she hesitates, catching her breath. The keening has acquired greater urgency: it is as if he is trying desperately to reach for words, and finding only senseless, elongated vowels. She opens the door, rushes over to his desk, where Ted is sitting perfectly still, his back to her. Her first thought is, *There's no blood.* Her second, as she reaches him, takes his face in her hands, is, *My God.*

Ted's face is rigid, expressionless: only his eyes seem alive. He stares at her, bewildered as a child (she thinks fleetingly of Sarah at two, with chickenpox, wrapped in sweat-soaked sheets), as she strokes his cheek.

'Darling, what on earth's happened? Are you in pain?' Eva does not expect an answer: at least none other than the sound still coming from his mouth, which is half open, as if he were midway through framing a word when his body froze. 'I'm calling an ambulance. Please try to be quiet, darling. I'm here now. We'll get you to hospital, all right? As soon as we can.'

Ted watches as she reaches across his desk for the phone. Next to it is his spiral-bound notebook; as she dials the emergency number, she sees that the uppermost page is covered in a tiny, crablike scrawl. Not a single word is legible.

She takes Ted's left hand in hers. '*Ambulanza*,' she says into the telephone.

Hours later, Eva is sitting on a hard metal chair in the waiting area of the *pronto soccorso* hospital. It is a low, modern building, not five minutes' walk from the house – she has passed it countless times on her usual, ambling route to Trastevere. Their house clings to the steep hill of Monteverde Vecchio; it is tucked away behind iron gates, and accessed by a vertiginous series of steps. Here, their neighbours have planted fragrant herbs, tufted grasses and a purple bougainvillea that, in the last days of summer, strews the cobbled path with discarded blooms.

Eva traces that same route most mornings – her descent leisurely, pausing to offer Signora Finelli, out sweeping her front step, *buongiorno*; and to admire the Roman light, soft and yellowish, glancing off loose roof-slates and crumbling *palazzi*. She orders a cappuccino and a *cornetto* at the bar in the piazza, sometimes with a friend, but most often alone. She tours the market with her shopping bags, lines them with peppers, tomatoes, courgettes and seeping balls of mozzarella suspended inside polythene bags like prize fish. Then she walks slowly back, passing the hospital where the words *pronto soccorso* glow red and urgent from the perimeter wall.

She has taken note of those words – filed them away in her mind, with the many other Italian words she's encountered every day for the past four years. (Her Italian is not quite as fluent as her French, but it is good enough to plane away the rougher angles of life abroad.) Not once had Eva considered what might be concealed behind that wall, or thought that she might find herself, one day, sitting here in the waiting-room, observing the steady rhythm of the second hand on the wall clock.

The wait for the ambulance had seemed interminable. *How*, Eva had thought, sitting with Ted, uselessly stroking his face, *can they take so long to get here, when the hospital is so close?* When the paramedics had finally arrived, they'd complained at length about the impossibility of finding a place to park. They were armed with a stretcher, first-aid kit and breathing apparatus – but by then, Ted's condition seemed to be improving. He had regained feeling in his limbs, could move and speak, and attempted to persuade both Eva and the paramedics that he didn't require hospital attention.

'*Non è niente*,' Ted had assured them, in his clumsy, school-boyish Italian.

But the lead paramedic shook his head. '*Signore*, we must take you in now, even if we have to strap you to this stretcher.'

In the ambulance, and since – waiting here on this hard chair, while the doctors run their endless tests – Eva has tried not to allow the fears circling in her mind to gain purchase. As soon as he could move again, Ted was dismissive, even angry: she shouldn't have called an ambulance; he had a piece to file by two o'clock. But Eva, in her turn, was firm. She had telephoned Chris Powers herself; insisted that, at the very least, Ted must allow the doctors to establish what had happened.

No one said the word 'stroke' aloud, but she could hear its echo in the air. It was there, too, in the paramedics' exchange of glances as Ted described the sensations that had overcome him; and in the face of the kindly, handsome doctor who had ushered Ted through those implacable double doors – '*Prego, signore*' – and urged Eva to wait outside. She had wanted to go in with him, of course, but apparently that was not how things worked. 'Better the family waits here,' the doctor had said, letting the doors swing shut behind him.

Now, in the waiting-room, the matronly *signora* sitting opposite Eva leans forward, offers her a foil-wrapped parcel. '*Mangia*,' she commands, as if Eva were another of her children. There are two here with her: a girl, about six years old, her hair tugged into tight plaits; the boy a little older, fidgeting on his chair. A third, Eva assumes, must be beyond the closed doors to the ward.

Eva opens her mouth to refuse, but she doesn't wish to offend; and besides, it's hours since breakfast, and she has had no lunch. '*Grazie mille*,' she says.

The *panino* is delicious: salami and mortadella. The *signora* watches her as she eats. '*Grazie*,' Eva says again. '*È molto buono.*' The *signora*, taking this as an invitation, issues a detailed set of instructions as to where to acquire the best produce: the Trastevere Market, apparently, does not pass muster. Eva is considering how to politely disagree when she sees Ted emerging from the double doors.

'Darling.' He looks tired but calm: if there had been bad news, surely the doctor would have called her through? 'What did they say? Aren't they keeping you in?'

He shakes his head. 'They don't know much yet. They want me to see a neurologist.' Noting her expression, he adds, 'They don't think it was a stroke, Eva. So that's something.'

'Yes. That's something.' She takes his hand. 'How are you feeling now?'

'Shattered.' He offers a thin smile. 'Home, please.'

They take a taxi, unable to face the long flight of steps. At home, Ted settles heavily on the living-room sofa, Umberto curling into a tight circle on his lap. Eva puts on a cassette – Mozart, to lighten the mood – and sets a saucepan to boil for pasta. She thinks about calling Sarah in Paris, and decides against it – it is almost nine o'clock; she'll be busy getting ready for the gig, and Eva doesn't want to worry her. And she *would* worry. Even now, she turns to Ted with her problems as often as she does to Eva, and there are many: Sarah's life in Paris is chaotic, her band's career as fraught and stuttering as her relationship with its guitarist, Julien.

Ted has been there for Sarah, solid and reassuring, all these years – and for Eva, too, of course. *I can't believe it took me so long to find you*, he had said to her one night years ago, when it was all just beginning. *I'm afraid that if I make one false move, you'll disappear.*

Now, taking the packet of fettuccine down from the cupboard, Eva tries again to dispel the image that has been spooling through her mind since she called Ted's name, and heard only silence in response. An open road ribboning endlessly across flat desert lands: the blank, featureless landscape of life without him.

Landing
Sussex, July 1988

'Well? How was it?'

Sophie, settling on the back seat, waits a few seconds before replying. 'Fine.'

Jim catches Eva's eye. 'And your mother?'

Another brief silence. Then, 'Yeah. She's fine.'

He sets the car into reverse, edges it out. It's Saturday, and the airport is busy. Jim and Eva arrived early to meet Sophie; they sat in the arrivals hall, drinking bad coffee, watching a family – two parents and three children, each scalded a raw, uncomfortable shade of pink – navigate the concourse with a trolley piled high with luggage, duty-free bags and a stuffed donkey wearing a sombrero. Behind them came three men in vests and shorts, sipping on cans of Stella.

'Christ,' Jim said to Eva, his voice low. 'I hope they weren't on Sophie's plane.'

'Don't worry. The Alicante flight hasn't landed yet.'

Alicante: a city of dust and heat and unfinished skyscrapers. This, at least, is how Jim imagines it: he has received only one postcard from Helena, sent soon after she moved to Spain. A tall, mud-coloured hotel of brutal ugliness; on the back, she had written, *For Jim – because even the most hideous building here is lovelier than the home I shared with you. H.*

Jim had been furious – not so much with the sentiment (that

he could understand), but with the fact that Helena had put it on a postcard, where their daughter could see her mother's hatred plainly inscribed. He'd composed an angry letter back, but Eva, reading it over at his request, had suggested he wait before posting it. 'Helena has every right to be angry,' she said. 'There's no point in alienating her even further, is there?'

And so he had waited, and after a few days, had consigned the letter to the bin. But Helena must have felt she had made her point. Since then, she has written only to Sophie – enclosed photographs of her small whitewashed house in a village in the mountains; of old women dressed in black, their faces a contour map of wrinkles; of skinny goats framed against rocky, grassless land. And then, two years ago, of a dark, narrow-faced man, his skin a deep brown, his eyes narrowed against the light. 'Juan,' Sophie said when she showed him the photograph, her expression giving nothing away. 'Mum's new boyfriend.'

Helena, of course, is free to do as she likes; Jim's only real concern, then, was for Sophie – for this new shift in the unstable ground of her young life. He tried to ask her how she felt about Juan – this was two years ago; she had just turned sixteen – but she would not be drawn. Sophie turned her slow, heavy-lidded eyes on him and said, with an indifference that seemed absolute, 'Why should I care what she does?'

'Indifferent' is the word Jim reaches for most often, now, to describe his daughter. She is morose and apathetic, barely speaking other than when spoken to, and even then in the curtest of monosyllables. She has put on weight: her face – that simulacrum of her mother's – has filled out, and she hides her broadening hips under loose T-shirts. But what alarms Jim most is her lack of passion for anything, for anyone: she is average at school, and has few friends; she's at home most weekends, watching television in her bedroom on the small portable set. Had Sophie even set herself squarely against Eva – made her stepmother the object of vivid teenage tantrums – Jim might have had a clearer idea of what they were dealing with; but she addresses Eva with the same robotic brevity that she accords the rest of the family. Only Sam, now studying geology in London, seems able to reach her; on the weekends when he comes home to Sussex with his textbooks and dirty washing, Sophie is transformed: smiling, almost animated, trotting puppy-like after her adored stepbrother, who responds in kind with a genial, amused affection.

At first, he and Eva were careful not to press Sophie too hard: to consider the impact that their move to Sussex must have had on her. (They had finally sold the Regent's Park flat in 1984, bought a dilapidated farmhouse not far from the village in which Jim grew up.) 'Don't you remember how hard it was, starting a new school?' Eva had said. 'And she's had to move around so many times. I think we should give her a little time.'

And they had given her time – let her settle into the new house; waited out the first term at the new school. But that's exactly what Sophie seemed to be doing: waiting; marking time. She brought no friends home, nor was invited out. (Years later, Jim would think of this with an uncomfortable stab of irony.) Eva and Jim began to worry. 'What's it like at school, Sophie?' they would ask, at regular intervals; or, 'If you really hate it here in Sussex, you know we don't have to stay. We can talk about going back to London.' But Sophie gave only bland non-answers – 'It's fine'; 'I'm fine' – until Sam – still living at home then, finishing his A levels – warned them to stop asking. 'She thinks you're always getting at her,' he told Jim. 'She feels like nothing she can do is good enough for you and Mum.'

And so they had tried hard to take a step back; to give her the space to work through whatever it was she was working through. 'She's a teenager,' Eva said, remembering her own tricky phases with Rebecca. 'It will pass.' But it didn't; the years rolled on, and Sophie became more and more remote. Through her final months of A levels she displayed no interest in applying to university, or taking alternative steps to find a job. Jim and Eva abandoned their tactic of cautious distance, and tried, again, to take her in hand. 'You can't just bury your head in the sand about this, darling,' Jim said. They were sitting at the dining-room table one Sunday afternoon, the roast lunch cleared away, their pudding bowls empty in front of them. 'You really need to have some kind of plan.'

Eva, at his side, nodded. 'Can we help you, Sophie? Can we try to work out together what you'd like to do next?'

That had reached her: Sophie had turned to her stepmother, and said, her voice clear and calm, 'Is that what you did? Did you sit down with my dad and *work out* how he was going to leave my mum?'

It hurt, of course – later, in bed, Jim had held Eva as she cried – but they continued, undeterred. Did Sophie want to go to university? Would she rather get a job? But her exams came and went, and still Sophie had made no decisions. Even this trip to Spain came about only because Helena and Juan sent the plane tickets as an eighteenth birthday present. Jim could not imagine his daughter taking the initiative herself, even if he and Eva had offered her the money. (They had done so more than once, and she had flatly refused to take it.)

Now, joining the queue of cars waiting nose to tail at the exit, Jim can't stop himself from saying, his grip closing on the steering-wheel, 'Well, Sophie. Is that really all you've got to say about two weeks in Spain? That it was "fine"?'

In the rear-view mirror, he sees his daughter roll her eyes. 'What else do you want to know?'

Eva places a hand on his knee: a warning. 'I'm sure you're tired, aren't you, love? Why don't you close your eyes for a bit? Maybe you can tell us more about your trip over dinner.'

They are quiet then. On the motorway, Jim concentrates on the shifting brake-lights of the cars in front. It is a warm day, softened by a stiff breeze from the sea: as they turn off, following the road home, he opens the window, breathes in deeply. The road narrows, hunkering down further into the countryside; the tall trees on either side, heavy with sap, bow to meet in the middle in places, forming a tunnel through which the greenish light dimly filters.

Jim loves this place, loves it with a deep, unquestioning certainty that he has never felt for London, or even Cornwall. His being here feels in some way the natural extension of his love for Eva, but also – and this he had not expected, when Eva first mooted the idea of moving to Sussex – for his mother. The initial, shaming relief he had felt after Vivian's death – the sudden lightness in his shoulders, as if a heavy burden had been removed – had given way, very quickly, to guilt. For months, he was unable to paint, had spent his days moving listlessly about the Regent's Park flat, until Eva – working on a manuscript in Rebecca's old bedroom – could stand it no longer. She had asked Penelope for the number of a therapist, a distant mutual acquaintance from Cambridge. He had gone to see the woman in her flat in Muswell Hill – shadowy, book-lined, calm – and found, after some initial resistance, that there he was able not to dispel the guilt, exactly (guilt not just for what he had done, or not done, for his mother, but to Helena and Sophie, too), but to turn down its volume so that on good days it was barely audible. And, more importantly, after six months of therapy, he had begun to paint again.

Years later, as the situation with Sophie worsened, Jim had suggested to Eva that Sophie might also like to talk to someone; even asked whether, God forbid, they should confront the fact that she might be developing the early signs of his mother's illness. 'Yes,' Eva said. 'It has to be worth a try.' But when he raised the possibility with Sophie – this was just before Christmas last year – she had eyed him with withering disdain. 'So what you're saying, Dad,' she said, 'is that you think I'm some kind of nutter, like Grandma Vivian?'

Jim couldn't contain his anger then. 'Don't you *ever* use that word about your grandmother. You don't know what you're talking about.'

Sophie, fleeing through the kitchen door, paused then, looked back at him. 'Well, neither do you, Dad. So why don't you just leave me alone?'

Now, home from the airport, Jim carries Sophie's suitcase upstairs to her room, then asks if there's anything he can do to help with dinner. Eva shakes her head. 'I'm just heating up a lasagne.'

'I'll pop outside for a bit, then.'

Eva nods. 'I'll knock when it's ready.'

His studio occupies the old barn that came with the house; it was this, together with the rambling grounds – an overgrown orchard, a meadow waist-high with grass – that had made them fall in love with it. The barn was in a terrible state – roof-tiles missing, timbers rotting, the carcass of an ancient John Deere quietly rusting under cobwebs. But they had set to work – he, Eva, Anton, Sam and a team of builders from the village. Slowly, painstakingly, they had turned the barn into a functional studio: punctuated the sloping roof with enormous sheets of glass; plumbed in a toilet; and even – such luxury – installed central heating. For the first few weeks after they had finished, Jim could hear Howard's voice in his head, as it had once sounded on winter mornings, when they had moved about the freezing communal studio at Trelawney House. *Bit of cold never did anyone any harm. Don't go round grumbling, for God's sake – put on another jumper . . .*

Almost as soon as he began working in the new studio, Jim

found himself moving away from painting, and into sculpture: working with great hunks of limestone, then granite; turning them into tall, smooth-sided monoliths that carry, in his mind, the quiet power of ancient monuments. The critics have not been so kind: 'A tedious exercise in priapic pointlessness' was how one of them had described his last exhibition. Jim had laughed on reading the review; he remembered his father telling him, on one of those afternoons when Jim had sat silently watching him paint, that 'The opinions of critics are fit only for lining a hamster's cage.' Stephen's first reaction, however, had surprised him. 'The sculptures are interesting,' his old friend and gallerist had said, and Jim knew faint praise when he heard it. 'But you're a painter, really, Jim, at your core. Better, perhaps, to return to what you know?'

Now, Jim stands before the piece he has been working on for three weeks: a narrow shard of black granite, planed and smoothed, its blank surface littered with tiny splinters of colour: grey, white, charcoal. He thinks about something else that Howard used to say at Trelawney House, over and over again, to whomever would listen. *With sculpture, you're not creating something out of nothing. You're just chipping away at what's already there.*

The words struck Jim, and stayed with him: he felt, when his hands first itched to move over solid stone, that they also expressed something about the way he feels for Eva. Jim wouldn't allow himself to regret the years he'd had without her – his years with Helena; his daughter, Sophie – but in his mind, his new sculptures are monuments to the essential simplicity, the rightness, he feels in being with Eva; to the overwhelming gratitude he feels for this, their second chance. He only wishes there were some way he could have struck out for that chance – for his own happiness – without causing his daughter so much pain. That he could find some way, in short, to make it up to

Sophie, other than by trying his best to show her, each day, each week, how much she means to him. But she does not seem to want to listen. *Or*, he thinks darkly, *perhaps I'm just not trying hard enough*.

At half past seven, they gather in the kitchen to eat; Eva serves the lasagne, salad, pours white wine. Eva asks again about the holiday, and Sophie tells them a little more – about the black chickens Helena is keeping in the back garden; about Juan, whom she describes as 'All right – a bit weird, but all right.'

Jim watches his daughter, pale and awkward in her black T-shirt and leggings. He feels a rush of affection for her; reaches over to take her hand, tells her he is glad to have her home.

Sophie regards him coolly, and then removes her hand.

VERSION ONE

\\\\\\

Man Ray
London, March 1989

A few days before her fiftieth birthday, Eva invites Penelope over for lunch.

'Don't bring Gerald,' she says. 'Jim's in Rome. School trip.'

The next day – a Saturday – she bakes a quiche, prepares a salad, and sets a bottle of Chablis to cool. They eat. They drink. They discuss Gerald's bad back; Jennifer's wedding plans: she is engaged to Henry, a fellow trainee solicitor – polite, steady, his hair already thinning a little at the crown – but devoted to Jennifer, and she to him. Last month, while they were out shopping for bridal gowns, she had turned to Eva and said, 'I love Henry so much, Mum, I'm almost afraid to marry him; afraid that marriage won't match up to the idea I have in my head. Is that how it was with you and Dad?'

Eva had looked at her daughter, standing there before the rack of dresses – so young, so lovely, so dear to her – and experienced a rush of feelings she couldn't quite define: love, sadness, happiness and something else, a kind of nostalgia, the sense that she was winding back to the moment in her own past when she had stood beside Jim, and vowed to make their love last for a lifetime, and beyond. No, she had never been afraid. 'Don't worry so much, darling,' she told Jennifer. 'Marriage isn't a thing to match up to some perfect image in your mind. It will be what you make it. And you and Henry will make it *wonderful*.'

Too painful to think about that moment now. Eva pours herself and Penelope a fresh glass of wine, and then produces the postcard that she has tucked into the back pages of a proof copy of her latest book. (Non-fiction, this time: a survey of the ten best women writers of the twentieth century.) She lays it down on the table between them.

It is a reproduction of a black-and-white photograph. A woman, shown in profile, her lips and eyebrows dark and full, her hair fashionably shingled. The whole image is a little blurred, unfocused, as if shaded with the softest pencil point.

'Lee Miller, no?' Penelope says. 'Man Ray?'

Eva nods, impressed. 'Turn it over.'

On the back of the card is written, in a sloping, familiar hand, *For B – because I will always think of you in beautiful monochrome. Thank you for bringing me back to life. All my love, always, J.*

They are silent for a moment. Then Penelope says, 'Where did you find it?'

'In the car. Yesterday. I was cleaning out the boot.' Eva drains her glass, watches her friend across the table. She feels oddly calm, as she had been the previous afternoon, when the disparate cogs of her mind had finally seemed to slip into oiled synchronicity, and she'd climbed into the car, knowing at once where she had to go.

'I won't insult you by asking whether it's definitely Jim's writing.'

'No.'

Penelope sits back in her chair, runs a finger up the stem of her glass. 'And do we know who this "B" could be?'

'Bella Hurst.'

'The girl with the studio?'

'The very one.'

She should have known, of course: any wife would say the same. And yet Eva is uncomfortably aware that she really *should* have known, that when she had begun to sense a change in Jim, through that autumn term – he seemed lighter; he drank less; he even cleared the shed, dug out his easel, and began, tentatively, to paint – there would be something, or someone, more behind it than the gradual fading of his grief for Vivian. She had known of the supply teacher, of course – he had mentioned her a few times at first; nonchalantly, she'd thought ('Oh, she's quite sweet – very young – lives in a ghastly squat in New Cross'), and then more regularly, with greater enthusiasm. Jim had begun, occasionally, to go to the pub with Bella Hurst; had visited her shared studio in Peckham; had met up with her, once or twice, after Gerry returned to work, and she was no longer at the school. Eva must, she supposes, now presume that there were also other meetings of which she was not informed.

It was, Eva had believed, a friendship – perhaps this Bella Hurst (she thought of the girl always, for some reason, with her surname attached) was looking for a mentor. And Jim: well, she'd had no reason to doubt him since that long-ago dalliance, or whatever it had been, with Greta. And Jim had been quite open with her about Bella – had told her how much he enjoyed talking to her about art, that she had ideas he'd never really debated before – ideas about practice, deconstruction, about the dissolution of the old boundaries between high and low art. Privately, Eva had thought these ideas rather pretentious, but she had stopped short of saying so aloud.

Jim had even invited the girl to dinner: Bella Hurst had sat there, drinking their wine, eating the food Eva had prepared. She was impossibly young and tiny in her workman's vest and loose dungarees; her eyes, beneath that unruly thatch of hair, were entrancingly mismatched, one blue, one black. Eva had felt a twinge of something then – even if it was only shameful envy of her youth, her freshness, something that she and Penelope might try to emulate with lotions and night-creams, but could never retrieve – but she had filed it neatly away at the back of her mind. She was just too *busy* to be bothered with suspicion: busy with research for the book, with newspaper articles, with radio series and discussion shows and the Booker. (She was a judge for the 1987 prize, and spent much of 1986 working through a teetering stack of novels.) Even when Jim had come to Eva last year, told her that a space had come up in Bella Hurst's studio – that he wanted to rent it, go there on weekends, during holidays – even then, her reaction had only been one of delight that he was working again. 'That's a fantastic idea, Jim,' she'd said. 'Of course you must take it. Perhaps a fresh start, in a new space, will be just what you need.'

Eva can only think, now, that it had been a case of deliberate blindness on her part, and their hiding in plain sight. How stupid they must have thought her – if they had thought of her at all. Or perhaps Bella Hurst had considered their marriage a permissive one; perhaps Jim had even told her it was such. Could he have found out about Leo Tait, about their brief liaison in Yorkshire? Eva doesn't think it likely – she has never mentioned that night to anyone, and can't imagine that Leo would have done so. But now, anything seems possible. And had it been, with Bella, just a one-night thing – a physical urge that Jim couldn't resist, as she herself had been unable to with Leo – then she might feel differently; but there is no way that Jim's note can be attached to a casual affair. *Thank you for bringing me back to life.* Each word a bullet to Eva's heart.

Yesterday, in Peckham, she had found Bella Hurst unruffled, implacable. Eva had rung the bell to the studio, told a bored-looking man in paint-spattered overalls whom she was there to see. He had left her standing at the open door – she had read the name on each pigeonhole in the hallway with its peeling paint, its greenish sproutings of mould, over and over again; watched the letters of her husband's name rearrange themselves into an incomprehensible jumble.

She had felt light-headed; had put a hand to the wall to steady herself, wondering what she would do when she was face to face with Bella Hurst; wondering what she could possibly say that might lessen the weight of her pain. There was nothing, surely – this was the end of everything, the ripping apart of the life Eva and Jim had worked so hard, for so long, to build, and to maintain. The giddy joy of falling in love, of finding each other; their honeymoon; their months in New York; their beloved house in Gipsy Hill. Jennifer. Daniel. The loss of Vivian, of Miriam. Those terrible years in which Eva had feared they were drawing apart, and yet they'd found a way back to each other, hadn't they? They'd pulled through. What could she possibly say that would make this girl – this *child* – understand what it meant to be shown a picture of your life as you know it – a picture of substance and beauty; the hours and weeks and years that make a shared life, a family – and then see it ripped unceremoniously from its frame?

When Bella had eventually appeared, she had done so smiling, her naked face serene above a loose white shirt, black leggings, a man's tweed waistcoat (not Jim's). Eva had showed her the postcard – told her, in a voice she couldn't keep from trembling, that she had found something that she presumed belonged to her.

'Well,' Bella said, those blue-black eyes hard as marbles. 'It's useless to say I'm sorry, I'm afraid, because I'm not. But I hope it won't be too hard on you.'

Telling all this to Penelope, Eva can feel herself wincing at the crass banality of it all: the middle-aged man, just shy of his fiftieth birthday, falling for a girl just a few years older than his daughter; the wife finding the lovers' note, rushing to confront her rival. She pictures herself, standing there in that foul hallway in her oldest, least flattering jeans, her hair unbrushed – emptying the car boot had been the last stage of a spring clean, and she hadn't thought to change. Jim has turned her into the oldest cliché there is – the wronged wife – and she hates him for it; hates herself for playing the role. But that doesn't make it hurt any less.

She is crying now. 'Oh, Pen. I must have looked such a state.'

Penelope covers Eva's hand with her own; with the other, she reaches into her handbag for a tissue. 'I'm sure you didn't. But that's hardly the point, is it?'

'No.' Penelope hands her the tissue, and Eva wipes her eyes. From the hall comes the squeal of the telephone.

'Shall I get it? Tell whoever it is that you'll call them back?'

'It's all right.' Eva scrunches the tissue into a ball. 'It's probably Jennifer. I don't want her to know anything's wrong. Not yet.'

It is Jennifer, calling about the arrangements for Tuesday night: they are to celebrate Eva's birthday in the upstairs room at the Gay Hussar. At the sound of her daughter's voice, Eva's fragile composure falters; she smothers a rising sob, but not before Jennifer catches the sound. 'Are you all right, Mum? You sound upset.'

Breathing deeply, looking at the framed photograph on the wall above the hall table – the four of them a few years ago, on the beach at St Ives – Eva draws on her last reserves of strength in order to say, her voice strong, unwavering, 'I'm fine, darling. Thank you for asking. Penelope's here for lunch. I'll call you later on.'

In the kitchen, Eva slumps into her chair, places her head in her hands. 'God, Pen. The children. I can't bear it. What am I going to do?'

From her handbag, Penelope produces a packet of cigarettes. She lights one, hands it to Eva, then lights another for herself.

'We've given up,' Eva says, but Penelope bats her objection away. 'For God's sake, Eva – if we ever needed a smoke, it's now.'

After a moment or two, she adds, 'What do you want to do?'

'Apart from punch him in the guts?' Eva looks up, meets Penelope's eye, and even now, even here, they can exchange a thin smile. 'I don't know. I really don't. I mean, I'll have to speak to him, of course – see if he really means to leave. Bella certainly seems to think he does. But I'll have to hear it from him.'

'Of course.' From her red-painted mouth, Penelope emits a small cloud of smoke. Eva can sense that she'd like to say more, that Penelope is holding herself back from revealing the depth of her own sense of betrayal – her anger on Eva's behalf, of course, but her own anger too. Penelope has always adored Jim; has always strived to see things from his point of view. They have all been such good friends, and for such a long time, but now, a line must be drawn in the sand. 'And if he says it's over with Bella? That he'll end it?'

'Well.' Eva draws deeply on her cigarette. 'Then I'll have to see what's left between us. I simply don't know whether we could carry on.'

Eva's words hang in the air unanswered; unanswerable. Out in the garden, beyond the French windows, the weak spring sun is lowering over Jim's shed, over the steeply inclined sweep of lawn. The tree where Daniel's old rope-swing still hangs is just coming into blossom; the borders are lush with the shrubs Eva and Jim planted together years ago. The terrible realisation strikes Eva that she may not be able to keep this house if they divorce; not for financial reasons – she is the greater bread-winner, has been for years – but because it will be too full of all the things that had, until yesterday, defined the contours of her life. The furniture, the photographs, the children's younger selves practising scales at the piano, filling each room with their shouts, their smiles, their heartfelt babyish demands: all this, now, she will have to reassign to memory.

A key turns in the front door. Eva looks back at Penelope, quickly stubs out her cigarette. 'Daniel. Don't say anything, Pen.'

'As if I would.' Penelope takes a last drag, then extinguishes her own cigarette.

Here is Daniel, sloping into the room – all sixteen-year-old, five foot eleven of him, his bare knees black with mud beneath his rugby shorts. He loves the sport, and Jim, though indifferent to it, takes him to matches at Twickenham; stands for hours on the side of the pitch at Daniel's school games, cheering him on, clapping his hands inside thick wool gloves. *Will Jim still do that if he leaves us?* Eva thinks. *How can anything ever feel normal again?*

'All right, Aunty Pen?' he says. 'Mum?'

'We're all right, darling.' Eva reaches for a smile. She keeps her voice light, steady, as she turns and says, 'How was the match?'

VERSION TWO
||||||||

Father
Cornwall, November 1990

Jim wakes at six a.m., just as the train is leaving Liskeard.

He lies still in his bunk, enjoying the warmth of the covers. He has slept well: lulled, no doubt, by the whisky he and Stephen consumed over an evening at the Arts Club, not to mention the champagne and wine they'd had with dinner. He had taken a taxi to Paddington at eleven o'clock, found his way, a little unsteadily, to his first-class, single-occupancy cabin; noting, dimly, that he was growing used to such luxuries. There had barely been time to change into his pyjamas, accept the hot chocolate offered by a uniformed guard, before sleep claimed him.

A knock comes at the door: muted, polite. 'Breakfast, sir?'

'Yes. Thank you.' He swings his legs down from the bed. 'Just a moment.'

It is a sorry meal – dry, coagulated scrambled egg, cold toast, bacon doused in fat – but Jim clears his plate, drinks the watery coffee. His head is pounding; as he dresses, he finds the packet of aspirin in his wash bag, takes three tablets with the mug's last dregs. Then he slips on his coat, packs his few belongings into his overnight case, and steps out into the morning.

It is a clear, still winter's day, of the kind that he has always loved: the sky hazed and distant, the low sun dazzling, the last red and yellow leaves still clinging to the trees. And the ice-fresh air of Cornwall: in the car, Jim lowers the window despite the cold, takes in great gulps of it. This is what he can't explain to Stephen, whenever his friend asks him, for the fiftieth time and counting, why Jim insists on continuing to live out here, hundreds of miles away from London. (Stephen seems to have conveniently emptied his memory of his own years at the Bristol gallery.) The air, the light, the striated seascape of water, rock, grass. The sense of standing right at the furthest limit of the land.

The house is cool and quiet, the kitchen spotless – yesterday was one of Sandra's cleaning days. Caitlin has filled the fridge; a note lies on the counter, in her neat, sloping hand. *Congratulations again! I'll be up around 10. C x.*

Jim makes a pot of coffee, carries it through to the living-room, where the light is so bright it hurts his eyes. The huge plate-glass windows frame a painter's view: a rocky outcrop of garden, stretching down to the cliff edge; a solitary gull, caught on a thermal; the sea inky, borderless. He sits, sips his coffee. His headache is receding to a faint memory of pain, and he is home, with good news, and all is gloriously silent.

He had been surprised, in the months after Helena left, by how quickly he grew used to living alone. He'd moved out as soon as he could – couldn't stand another night in the cottage on Fish Street, where the silence was not the warm, expectant kind he has come to prize, but one born of painful absence: of half-empty wardrobes, of stripped cupboards and, worst of all, of his son's vacated bedroom, cleared of all but one dog-eared drawing, left sellotaped to the wall above Dylan's bed. On the worst days – there were several in those weeks, after the terrible afternoon when he'd come in from the studio to find Helena packing, Dylan crying, Iris standing tight-lipped and resolute in the hallway, telling him that he mustn't 'stand in the way of love' – he had carried his duvet through into Dylan's room, slept fitfully on his sheetless bed. Waking in the night to that same freighted silence, Jim had taken Dylan's drawing down from the wall. It was an early scrawl – he, Dylan and Helena on the beach at St Ives, the sun round and weightless. Jim knew it was absurd to believe that this crumpled sheet of paper could somehow stand in for the presence of his son, and yet he found he slept better with the drawing beside him.

From Fish Street, then, Jim had moved to a house on the outskirts of town – newly built, nondescript; a stopgap, where he turned the living-room into a makeshift studio. He was keeping the spare bedroom free for Dylan: Helena had promised to send him down from Edinburgh to visit, as often as Dylan wished. (Iris, it turned out, owned a house in the New Town; Jim had, at the height of his anger, observed to Helena that she *could* have moved further away – 'to bloody Timbuktu'.) And Dylan wanted to come; he told Jim so on the telephone, their brief, truncated conversations pointing so clearly to his son's confusion and homesickness that they were almost more than Jim could bear. But Jim forced himself to put his son's needs before his own: it would, he agreed with Helena, be too disruptive for Dylan to come back down to Cornwall until they'd all found their feet, and settled him into his new school.

Jim wondered, at times, whether he could have fought harder for his son; whether he should have contested Helena's assumption, as Dylan's mother, that she had the right to take him with her, even though she was the one leaving Jim. But he was determined not to make Dylan a witness to some awful custodial tug-of-war; and Helena, to her credit, felt just the same. She'd written him a letter, after she left. It was measured, controlled; she asked Jim to forgive her, to understand that she had fallen for Iris quite suddenly, with her whole heart, and felt that she had no choice but to leave, to strike out for happiness. She asked him not to forget that they'd had so many good years together, and produced their wonderful boy. Jim, once the flame of his anger had burned down, would eventually find some comfort in that letter.

But for the time being, Jim had only the unlovely house, with its empty, magnolia rooms. Working there was difficult, but was also the only thing he had. He had channelled his fury (it was still burning brightly then) into a series of portraits: dark, full of shadows. Iris, fat-cheeked and orange-haired. Helena, shown from behind, her hair tugged into an unflattering ponytail. Dylan at her elbow, his nine-year-old face turned towards his father (unseen, beyond the frame). And Vivian, stealing from her bed in the blackest moment of the night, Sinclair sleeping on beneath a mound of blankets.

He had called the series *Leaving, in Three Parts*. When it was done, Jim found that he began to sleep better, even to appreciate the order and peace of living alone. At his next exhibition, in September 1980, Stephen had sold the series, intact, to an undisclosed collector, for £150,000. This, together with the proceeds from the sale of *The Versions of Us* – that figure had made the papers, and Jim's reputation; he had wanted to change their lives with it, buy them a house – had made him rich. And when Sinclair died a few months later – neatly, with minimal fuss, just as he had always lived – Lewis Taylor's small legacy passed to Jim, together with Sinclair's portfolio of investments, carefully managed, and left to Jim in lieu of any children of his own.

It all amounted to a sum Jim had never imagined might be his. And with it came the uncomfortable sense – inherited, like so many other things, from his father – that art was not, in its essence, something that ought to bear any connection with money. Jim put the larger part of it away in a trust, for Dylan; with the rest, he bought this house. The House (the literal name amused him): low-slung, boxy, built in 1961 of wood and concrete and glass by a local architect obsessed with Frank Lloyd Wright; perched incongruously on a clifftop like a beached boat. The nearest village was eight miles away, and Jim, nursing his solitude, was glad it was no closer.

Now, the coffee finished, he carries the pot and mug back through to the kitchen, takes his overnight case upstairs. In his bedroom, he undresses, steps through into the shower. What was it the man from the Tate – David Jenson; unctuous, smooth-mannered – said last night? *A landmark show, bringing father and son together for the first time. Great British portraiture spanning two generations.*

Jim had not seen it coming – like Stephen, he had thought the gallery's board was simply considering adding a new painting to their collection. His shock had been so great that he had, for several seconds, been unable to speak; and so Stephen had stepped in. 'What a wonderful idea, David. We'll find a date for you to come down to Cornwall, see the work. Set the wheels in motion.' That was when Jenson had ordered the champagne.

In the shower, Jim thinks about his father. There is so little about him that he remembers clearly: his lopsided, goblin face; his smell of turpentine and pipe tobacco. The way he stiffened when Vivian shouted; Lewis rarely shouted back, but when he did, his voice was deafening, sent Jim scuttling to his room. The day Mrs Dawes had collected Jim from school – Vivian was away, visiting her parents – and he'd found a strange woman in the kitchen, naked under his mother's blue silk robe, layering a slice of bread with butter and jam. Lewis had made them all tea. Jim remembers the woman's black hair and slender neck, the creamy expanse of her skin. He doesn't remember her name, but he remembers Sonia's: recalls watching his father pack a case while she waited outside in the car, and Vivian screamed, and the good china shattered on the flagstones.

His father's paintings formed the landscape of Jim's child-hood: their muted blues and greys, their warm-eyed women, their soft washes of English sky. But since his father's death, he has seen them only in books and postcard reproductions: Vivian had sold them all, every single one. Now this David Jenson is going to find them and bring them together, like estranged relations to a family reunion. To place them alongside Jim's own paintings. To ask people to stand and stare, to assess how much of the father has remained in the son.

Dressing, Jim thinks, *I am older now than my father was when he died*. Fifty-two years old: he celebrated his fiftieth in this house, with champagne and margaritas and a band strumming out Rolling Stones covers until four a.m. Single (more or less) for a decade. A lesbian ex-partner living in connubial pottery-making bliss on the isle of Skye. A twenty-one-year-old son studying printmaking in Edinburgh, and already a great deal more mature than either of his parents were at his age, or – Jim laughs to think of it – any time since.

Dylan had come down for Jim's party; they'd stood together in the garden, drinking beer, and his son had said, 'You know, Dad, I've been thinking about how you were after Mum and I left – how you never tried to poison me against her. You could have made things really difficult, and you didn't. I think that's kind of amazing. And I've had fun, coming down to see you in the holidays. I still do. Watching you in the studio, and stuff. It's been great.'

Jim, looking back at his lovely, handsome son – he has Helena's clear skin, and Jim's blue eyes, and the combination, to Jim's mind, makes Dylan much better-looking than his father has ever been – had felt so full of pride and love that for a moment he'd been unable to speak. And so he'd simply slung his arm around Dylan's shoulders, thinking that he'd never expected things to turn out like this; but then he'd lived long enough to understand the futility of expecting anything at all.

Anything, or anyone. In the years since Helena left, Jim has found his imagination straying to one particular face. His cousin

Toby had also come down for Jim's birthday party; he'd stayed on at the House for a few days afterwards, with his elegant French wife, Marie. It had occurred to Jim, late one evening, to ask after Eva. He'd watched Marie and Toby exchange looks. 'She's having a hard time,' Toby said. 'Ted Simpson's not well at all – Parkinson's, I think. They're back from Rome. He can't work. She's looking after him more or less full-time.'

Jim had found it difficult to articulate his feelings: sorrow for Eva, he supposed, overridden by a sense that it was not his sorrow to feel. What claim could he really make to knowing her? He sees her often in his mind, with her large, calm eyes, her intelligent smile; but he hasn't painted her likeness for years – not since his triptych. Recently, he has wondered whether that painting was an exorcism of sorts: a conclusion put to the possibility of a relationship between them; one he had intuited, in meeting her, but that had withered before it had even had the slightest chance to take root. Eva Katz – Simpson – was the partner that might have been, against whom, existing as she did only in Jim's imagination, no other woman could ever quite measure up. Helena had sensed it, he was sure. But Caitlin – well, Caitlin is different.

His studio assistant, his secretary, sometimes his model, and then quietly, unobtrusively, a little more. Thirty-eight years old; a more than decent painter in her own right; her body slim and supple. (She begins each morning with a run along Carbis Bay.) A brief early marriage behind her. No children, no demands.

Jim can hear Caitlin now, moving around downstairs: making more coffee, no doubt. She has her own key, but keeps office hours – unless they should, by mutual consent, wish her to stay a little longer. She has never spent the night. It is a delicate, tender arrangement, carefully calibrated to their respective needs.

'Coffee?' she calls redundantly up the stairs: she will already have made a pot.

'Yes, please,' he calls back. And then he follows his voice downstairs, to where Caitlin is waiting, and outside, in the studio, is an easel, a fresh canvas, a new working day.

Hamlet
London, September 1995

David is standing at the bar, talking to Harry, wearing a checked cotton scarf knotted over a smart black coat.

For a moment, Eva has the odd sensation of watching the years roll backwards – almost four full decades – until she can see them quite clearly as they were in the ADC bar: young, puffed-up, full of grand plans. Then, just as quickly, those boys are gone, and here before her are two men in late middle-age: grey-haired, confident, satisfied. It strikes Eva now that neither man had ever shown the slightest doubt that his plans would come to pass exactly as he willed them.

'Eva.' David's charm is undimmed by age: he leans forward to kiss her as if she were the one woman responsible for his happiness. Eva supposes, at one time, that she was, but she knows this ability of his now for what it really is: a reflex action, the product of his indefatigable urge to be adored. Many women have fallen for it – and she was among them. One Cambridge play; one summer; those dizzying after-noons in twisted sheets that would force them to become so much more to each other than they ought to have been. They had been happy then; and they had tried, for too long, to re-capture that happiness. What was it he'd said in the car in Los Angeles, that night when they both gave up trying? *We just don't quite fit, do we?* It is because of Jim, of course –

her second chance – that Eva knows how true this is.

'David.' She offers her cheeks to be kissed. To Harry, she says, 'Excited?'

He nods. 'Nervous. Press night and all that. But Rebecca's been a *darling*, of course, from start to finish.'

'Of course.' Eva throws him an assessing glance. Harry has put on weight, and his thin hair is standing up behind his ears, like an owl's tufts. Rebecca said he had married again: a much younger woman, barely out of her teens. An actress, naturally. His last Ophelia. 'Until he gets bored, of course,' Eva had said, and Rebecca frowned. 'Harry's all right, Mum. I don't know why you've always had it in for him.'

Now, Harry is shifting uncomfortably under Eva's gaze. 'Well. I'd better get back, rally the troops. See you at the party – and *enjoy*.'

David slaps his old friend firmly on the shoulder. 'Go to it. Mind they all break a leg. And give my daughter a big hug from me.' When Harry has gone, he says to Eva, 'It's only the half. I bought you a gin and tonic. Shall we sit?'

They find a table by the window. It is just beginning to grow dark: the sweep of concrete stretching down to the Thames is webbed with shadow, and the river path is busy with couples, their twin silhouettes shifting in the fading light. Inside, the foyer is filling up; Eva is aware of the looks, the conspicuous nudges. They have only just sat down when a woman in a scarlet jacket – about Eva's age; smiling, red-lipsticked – approaches their table, brandishing a programme.

'So sorry to bother you both.' The woman blushes to match the jacket. 'Would you mind awfully . . . ?'

From her pocket she produces a pen. David beams at her – his professional smile. 'Not at all. To whom should I make this out?'

Eva looks away. It is a long time since she was last out with

David alone; she has forgotten the minor disturbances his presence so often causes. Once – this was in the mid-sixties, at the very height of David's fame: Rebecca could only have been six or seven, and Eva wasn't yet pregnant with Sam – a woman had followed the three of them home from Regent's Park. She had planted herself on their doorstep and rung the doorbell over and over again, until they'd had no option but to call the police. David had laughed it off – 'Just part of the job, Eva, stop fussing' – but she could still remember the fear and confusion on her daughter's face. Still, it doesn't seem to have done Rebecca any harm: she's gone on to choose the same kind of life for herself, after all. What was it Garth – Rebecca's husband, a playwright, and the perfect, deadpan foil to his wife's natural exuberance – said last year, when Rebecca's agent telephoned to tell her that she now had her own official fan club? 'Finally – a load more people to love her almost as much as she loves herself.' Garth was laughing as he said it, of course. Rebecca had scowled at him, but then she had softened and smiled.

'It's good to see you,' David says when the red-jacketed woman has turned reluctantly away. 'You look well.'

'Do I?' Eva is in the last throes of a summer cold: pink-nosed, her eyes watering, no doubt loosening her make-up; she'll have to reapply it before the party. But, wary of sounding ungracious, she adds, 'Thank you. Nice coat.'

'It is, isn't it?' He runs a hand over one of the crisp lapels. 'Burberry. Jacquetta chose it.'

'How is Jacquetta?'

'Good.' He sips his gin and tonic. 'Really good.'

'And the girls?'

He smiles; a real smile, this time. 'Perfect.'

It was Rebecca, again, who informed Eva that David and Juliet were to divorce. The wedding had been a very public affair

– a poolside ceremony at the Chateau Marmont; an exclusive cover story in *People* magazine – and the divorce was to be no less so. Each painful thrust and parry was played out across the newspapers; David had slunk back from America, gone to ground at his parents' house in Hampstead. Eva had felt so sorry for him, despite herself, that she had found herself inviting him to spend a weekend with them in Sussex.

It was not a success. David had drunk all their good wine; told Jim repeatedly that he should never have let Eva go (she found this part of the performance particularly unconvincing); and then spilled a mug of coffee across the new living-room carpet. Since then, Eva has restricted their meetings to family gatherings: the children's weddings; the grandchildren's blessings; the odd press night and film screening. To the last blessing – of Miriam, Sam's youngest daughter; named after her own mother, in a gesture that had moved Eva deeply – David had brought a woman none of them had seen before. She was six foot tall, with a blonde lion's mane of hair, and an incipient baby bump leavening the austere lines of her frame.

'This is Jacquetta,' David told the family, with some pride. 'She's having twins.'

Now, he says, 'And Jim? All well back at the ranch?'

Eva nods. 'All well.'

This isn't strictly true, but she has no wish to discuss with David how disappointed Jim had been with his last sculpture exhibition. (No sales, and not a single national review.) Or their continued anxiety over Sophie, now twenty-five and scratching out a chaotic life in Brighton, changing jobs and partners with the same irredeemable lassitude they have for so long struggled to address. Or Eva's own quietly prolonged grief for Jakob, whose death came two years ago, and whom she still misses, every hour of every day.

And anyway, how could Eva convey to David the fact that,

difficult as they are, such problems do not seep beneath the foundations of what they have built together, she and Jim? The breakfasts shared in silent companionship, voices speaking softly on the radio. The mornings spent separately – he in his studio, she in her study, but each still acutely attuned to the other's presence. The evenings of cooking, eating, watching television, seeing friends: all the minute permutations of their life together.

'Rebecca tells me you're working on something,' David says. 'A book?'

She nods. 'Perhaps. They're short stories, but I think they'll hang together.' She is unable to keep the excitement from her voice: to find her way back to writing after so long, and to enjoy her writing, to hope that it might even be good; it is almost more than she could have hoped for. And it was Jim, of course, who made it happen; Jim and his absolute intolerance for any of her weary excuses. *You're a writer, Eva. You've always been a writer. So go upstairs and write.*

David places a hand on her arm. 'Eva, that's wonderful. I always said you shouldn't have given up your writing.' She smiles – how like David that is. 'Anything about me in there?'

She laughs. 'Oh yes. I'd get your lawyer on the case as soon as possible.'

'All right.' He sits back, eyes shining with amusement. 'I deserved that. But seriously – what are the stories about?'

'Oh . . .' How to answer that; how to reduce months of work, of thinking and worrying and refining, to one polished sentence? 'Love, I suppose. One woman, and the men she has loved. Each story is about a particular moment, experienced with a particular man.' Seeing his eyebrows lift, she adds, 'Don't look at me like that. There haven't been a *lot* of men. Most of the stories are about the one man she loves most deeply.'

'Her Jim, then.' She holds David's gaze, and then the

three-minute bell rings out across the foyer. Around them begins the general bustling of the crowd. The atmosphere between them breaks, loses its charge.

'We should go in,' Eva says.

'Yes, let's.'

They are in the usual house seats: row F of the stalls. At row H, David stops to greet a man Eva doesn't know. She smiles faintly in his direction, and then settles herself, removing her jacket, placing her bag under the seat. The set is brightly illuminated: high faux-brick walls, violent splashes of dreadful conceptual art, a battered metal kitchenette. New York, circa 1974: Hamlet as a chain-smoking queen, lazy artist and sometime protégé of Andy Warhol. Gertrude – Rebecca; a little young for the role, really, at thirty-six, but the loyal Harry had overruled his casting director's qualms – as a drunken soak.

Rebecca has described Harry's concept for the production to her mother at length, and Eva isn't at all sure what she will make of it. But she knows, however bizarre the production might prove, that Rebecca will be good: her daughter has three Olivier awards lined up on her mantelpiece at home. And yet the old, familiar anxiety for Rebecca – costumed, nervous, waiting in the wings – is still there, just as it always was for David. How clearly Eva can see herself and Penelope, sitting in the stalls at the ADC, silently running through the lines as David and Gerald spoke them aloud; their eyes roaming around the stalls, seeking out anyone who might dare to criticise.

David comes to sit beside her, and she says, 'Remember that production of *Oedipus Rex* you were in at Cambridge?'

'Yes. What about it?'

'You did all look a fright, didn't you?'

He looks pointedly at her, and Eva worries for a moment that he won't take the joke: he has never been good at laughing at himself. But he does laugh. 'Bloody hell, you're right, we did. Callow youth, eh? We didn't have a clue.'

Then Eva finds herself laughing too. They are both still spluttering as the house-lights dim, and Francisco and Bernardo stride out in biker boots, their hair tugged into high, punkish crests. Then David leans in to whisper, 'Not as much of a fright as this lot, though, eh?'

She has to smother her laughter with her sleeve. The elderly woman in the next seat turns to glare at them, and Eva falls silent, watching, wondering how it is that their own grand drama – a marriage for convention as much as desire; a divorce too long in coming – has faded to nothing but laughter, and the faint residue of shared memory.

Snowball
London, January 1997

'You're not looking, Daddy.'

A Tuesday afternoon, a quarter to four; Jim is walking his daughter home from school. It hasn't snowed for days, but the last covering is still banked up against the edges of the pavement in sooted drifts; where the kerb meets the road, it has turned to ugly yellow slush. Robyn has caught a handful of fresher, paler snow from a garden wall. He looks down at her small, mittened hand, at the misshapen ball slowly melting into pink and purple wool.

'I am, darling. That's very good. But put it down now, all right?'

Robyn shakes her head, and the bobble on her pink hat shifts violently from side to side. 'No, Daddy. You don't put a snowball down. You *throw* it.'

She lets go of his hand, takes aim; he reaches out to stop her, but is too late. The snowball traces a low arc through the air, threatening to collide with a passing dog.

'Robyn,' Jim says sharply. 'Don't do that.'

Luckily, she's not much of a shot: the ball lands fatly on the kerb, several inches wide of the dog. Still, Jim meets the owner's eye as he passes. 'Sorry about that.'

The man smiles from beneath his pork-pie hat, showing three gold teeth. 'Don't worry, mate. Kids, eh?'

'Kids,' Jim agrees.

Robyn stops still, sucking on the damp wool of her mitten, watching the dog owner's retreating back. 'Daddy,' she says loudly, while the stranger is still within earshot, 'did you see that man's teeth? They were made of *gold*.'

'Come on, missy.' He tugs on her other hand. 'Let's get you home.'

Home, for seven years, has been an early Victorian house in Hackney: two-storeyed, with a snubbed, flat facade, white-painted trim and a high wrought-iron side gate dividing it from its twin next door. The house had been empty for some years when he and Bella moved in – not as squatters: Jim had drawn the line at that; had bought the place with a portion of the inheritance that came to him after Sinclair's death. The wallpaper in the back bedroom was a world map of mould, bare wires were hanging perilously from ceilings, and the floorboards were rotting away to nothing. But Bella had fallen in love with it, and as it was Jim who had insisted they move out of the New Cross house – at weekends, the crumbling walls shook to deep bass while he hid upstairs with earplugs, trying to read – he felt he should not stand in her way.

Bella had at once set about restoring the house: chipping off the wet plaster, stripping back the wallpaper, painting the living-room ceiling from the top rung of a ladder even when she was eight months pregnant, and stubbornly ignoring Jim's pleas to take care. He'd been reminded, inevitably, of the summer of 1962 (his mind struggled to compute how distant that was now), when he and Eva had moved into the house on Gipsy Hill, with its salmon-pink stucco, and the old artist's shed in which Jim had expected to achieve great things. He had lived in that house for almost thirty years; he couldn't just banish all memory of the place. He and Eva had worked so hard, together, to make it their home: she'd come back from the *Courier* in the evenings, change into one of his old shirts, tie a scarf over her hair, and set to painting.

He'd made the unsettling mistake, one day, of coming downstairs, seeing Bella up on the ladder – her back was to him, her dark curls wrapped in a scarf – and calling out Eva's name. Bella hadn't spoken to him for four days. Sending him to Coventry – he believes the modern term is 'stonewalling' – is something she does with unnerving frequency. He didn't know it when he fell in love with her, but he certainly knows it now.

In the hallway, Jim strips his daughter of her rucksack, her hat and mittens, her plump padded coat. She stamps her feet in her tiny striped wellingtons, sending nuggets of stale snow spinning across the floorboards. So much about Robyn – her clear blue eyes (she has not inherited her mother's mismatched irises), the pink-lined seashells of her ears, her comically intense expression of deep thought – reminds him of Jennifer, even of Daniel. And yet he is wary of making too many comparisons: Bella had snapped at him the first time he saw Robyn smile and said – giddy with paternal joy – that it might have been Jennifer looking back at him. 'Don't make me feel,' she'd replied, 'that everything we do together must be measured against the life you had with her.'

Later, Bella had apologised, put her overreaction down to postnatal exhaustion. But he'd remained unsettled; for this was not at all the woman – the girl – who'd walked into the school art room that day in September, who'd talked to him for hours in the pub, the studio, even over that ill-advised dinner with Eva, about art, freedom, a life uncircumscribed by convention. The time Jim spent with Bella had been as refreshing as a cool glass of water to a dreadful thirst: her youth, her beauty, the sheer *ease* of being with her, with none of the responsibilities, the expectations, of a long marriage.

He was, for many months, unable to believe that his

fascination might be reciprocated: and yet it seemed, joy of joys, that it was. One Saturday afternoon, while they were working in the studio – it was early spring; they'd thrown open the windows for the first time in months, put on a CD (something loud, jarring: Bella's choice) – she had come through to his room from hers and stood silently for a while at his elbow, watching him paint. He'd said nothing, instinctively aware that something was about to change. She'd moved closer until he could feel her breath on his neck. Then, into his right ear, she'd whispered, 'I think I love you, Jim Taylor. Do you think you could love me?' Turning, drawing her into the circle of his arms, he'd given her his answer.

Then, Jim would not have thought Bella capable of petty jealousy, nor through the delirious early months of their affair. And when he went to Bella – when he arrived at the New Cross house with his suitcase, his marriage over, his choice made – she had welcomed him: folded him into her arms, and told him the next morning – over a fried breakfast in a nearby greasy spoon – that she had never been happier than in that moment.

He can't quite work out when things changed. Perhaps, he thinks now, he's never really known Bella, seen her clearly for who she is, rather than who he wishes her to be: his saviour; the woman who restored his faith in art, and in his own ability to create; who's cured him of his need to drink – he stopped drinking to excess as soon as they met, as if afraid of losing even a second in her company. Or perhaps there has simply been a shift in her, brought on by motherhood, or by the pressure of Jim's ending his marriage. Whatever its source, the result is much the same.

The night he returned from Rome to discover Eva sitting in the kitchen, her eyes fierce, a Man Ray postcard lying on the table in front of her, had taken Jim entirely by surprise.

He hadn't recognised the card at first: it was only when Eva turned it over that he'd felt his stomach fold in on itself. He had simply not, during his snatched evenings with Bella (he had usually gone to the New Cross house after school, told Eva he'd been caught in a staff meeting) allowed his fantasy vision of the future to collide with the present as it actually was. He had pictured himself making great work, with Bella at his side; had imagined telling Alan Dunn where he could stick his job. But he had not prepared for this moment – and so he had stared at his wife, the sound of his heartbeat loud as the roar of the sea.

Eva hadn't wanted an explanation – she had driven straight off, apparently, to confront Bella herself. At this, Jim had felt a nausea so profound he'd been convinced that he was about to be sick. Eva hadn't even, in that moment, seemed angry; she just wanted to know what he was going to do.

'Do?' he'd said dumbly.

Eva had fixed him with those eyes, the eyes that had looked up at him that first time, on the path, as she crouched beside her stricken bicycle. The eyes that had watched him for thirty-one years – wise, quizzical, almost as familiar to him as his own.

'Surely the one thing you owe me now, Jim,' she said crisply, her tone carefully measured, as if her composure depended on choosing the correct words, and then placing them in the correct order, 'is to tell me whether you are planning to leave.'

He'd left at once – it had seemed the kindest thing. He'd simply turned round, told Eva that he was sorry and that he loved her – had always loved her. She was crying, and he'd wanted so much to go to her, to comfort her – but he could not, of course, and he'd had the awful realisation that he would probably never hold her in his arms again. And so he'd made himself turn and leave; had picked up his weekend case from the hallway. Only after he'd closed the door had it occurred to him that he hadn't taken the car keys – and then that the car was probably no longer his to take. Eva had bought it. Eva had bought so much of what was theirs.

He'd wheeled his case out onto the pavement, looking for the amber light of a taxi, feeling utterly empty, exhausted, and yet aware – he couldn't deny it – of a creeping sense of elation. Bella was his: there could be no going back. He was turning the page, opening a new chapter in his life. At the New Cross house, one of Bella's flatmates had opened the door; told him, with dull-eyed disinterest, that she was asleep upstairs. He'd carried his case up, quietly pushed open her door, sought the warmth of her small, slender body.

Now, in the Hackney kitchen, Jim makes Robyn a sandwich: brown bread and strawberry jam, without crusts. He sits with her at the table as she eats and twists around on her chair, pausing to offer him cryptic snapshots of her day at school: 'We drew Australia, Daddy'; 'Harry did throw up at break time'; 'Miss Smith has a hole in her jumper. Under the arm.'

Jim doesn't remember many of these moments – the ebb and flow of everyday life with a small child – from Jennifer and Daniel's childhood. He has come to realise that he was rarely alone with them in their early years: Eva, and then the au pair, Juliane, had done so much of the day-to-day parenting. He wonders now how Eva managed it – she was as busy as he was, with her work at the *Courier*, and her writing. And yet she did, and he can't remember her ever chiding him for his lack of involvement. No, the resentment had been all on *his* side, and the knowledge of it shames him now, adds to his mounting debt, one that his older children won't easily let him forget. Jennifer, appraised of his betrayal, had withdrawn his invitation to her wedding; on the telephone, her voice icy, remote, she had told him she never wanted to see him again. (This hadn't lasted – they now see each other every few months – but she'd held firm for a good year.) Daniel had been less emphatic, but

314

no less upset. 'Mum's in pieces, Dad,' he'd told Jim over a rather desolate lunch at a carvery near Gipsy Hill. 'Why can't you just come home?'

Impossible to explain to his sixteen-year-old son why Jim couldn't come home; why – despite his regret at hurting Eva, at hurting his children – he was happier with Bella than he'd been in years. He had already left the school by then – he'd handed in his notice before the end of the spring term, and hadn't been asked to return for the summer. Alan's disapproval had been etched on his face as he accepted his resignation, and Jim had not found the courage to say any of the things he'd imagined. But then they had discovered that Bella was pregnant, and, all at once, their future had come into sharp focus. At the hospital for their first scan, Bella had held his hand tightly, watching the tiny image of their child appear on the screen. 'I knew it, Jim,' she'd said later. 'From the first moment I saw you, I knew I wanted to have your baby. She – or he – is going to be so beautiful. Our very own work of art.'

After tea, playtime: Jim settles Robyn in her bedroom, surrounded by her dolls. On the landing, he pauses before the door to the spare room. It is here, among boxes and broken umbrellas and Robyn's discarded playthings, that he has set up his easel, laid out his paints, his brushes, his turps-soaked rags.

It was a temporary arrangement at first: the new studio space they'd rented in Dalston was smaller than the one in Peckham, and Bella had started working on a larger scale – her last piece, a minute reconstruction of her childhood bedroom, had occupied the entire space. There wasn't room for them to work side by side, and his working from home would leave Bella free to spend longer hours at the studio.

Jim felt dwarfed by her work: its scale, its swagger, threatened to overwhelm his quieter, more tentative efforts. The sculptures he had attempted in the Peckham studio, in the first flush of energy brought by falling in love with Bella, with all that he felt she represented, had not come to life, and he had, with an unspoken feeling of failure, returned to painting. But even here, at home, that sense of diminution has remained – his work just seems too small, somehow; an inaudible whisper next to Bella's full-voiced shout. He is still painting, dutifully, on the days he is not supply teaching, or looking after Robyn, but he is aware of it as exactly that: a duty. To his long-held ambitions; to Bella; to the version of himself he has offered her: the artist thwarted by fatherhood, by marriage, by responsibility, looking for a chance to start again.

On the landing, he turns from the spare room, goes back downstairs. It is half past four: still hours until dinner, which he has promised to prepare (if Bella comes home at all: she has begun to spend several nights a week sleeping at the studio). In the kitchen, Jim makes himself a cup of tea, carries it through to the living-room, sits down. A great feeling of tiredness washes over him, and he suddenly feels that he couldn't possibly get up. His eyes twitch shut, and he is aware of nothing, until a small hand is tugging at his sleeve, a small, shrill voice shouting, 'Daddy, wake up! Why are you sleeping?'

Rising slowly from a dream, he says, 'I'm coming, Jennifer. Daddy's coming.'

When he opens his eyes, he is surprised not to see Jennifer there. He blinks at this tiny girl, her eyes a pure, clear blue beneath her mass of dark curls, and for a few seconds, he has no idea at all who she is.

VERSION TWO
|||||||||

Advice
London, July 1998

She carries Ted's lunch through on a tray: leek and potato soup, blended to a fine purée; a slice of buttered bread that she will break into small pieces and moisten with the soup.

'Ready for lunch, darling?' Eva places the tray down on the meal trolley beside Ted's bed – wheeled, hospital-issue; ugly but functional. She does not expect a reply, but when she turns, she sees that he has fallen asleep.

She stands for a moment, watching the shuddering rise and fall of her husband's chest. He has pressed the right side of his face against the pillow, so that only the left side – the good side – is visible. With his eyes closed, his mouth half open, he looks exactly as he always did: she is reminded of the first morning she woke beside him in his unfamiliar bed, traced the planes and contours of his face as he slept. When he woke, he had said, 'Please tell me that you're really here, Eva. That I'm not dreaming.' She had smiled, drawn a finger lightly across the curve of his cheek. 'I'm here, Ted. I'm not going anywhere.'

In the kitchen, she lays his tray back on the countertop: she'll check on him again in half an hour, heat up the soup; or perhaps he'll prefer it cold. It is a beautiful day, warm but not oppressively so: she has opened the kitchen windows, hung the washing – Ted's sheets, laundered on endless rotation; his striped pyjamas; his support stockings – out to dry. Now, she

317

takes her own bowl of soup out to the garden, lays the patio table with placemat, spoon, neatly folded napkin.

Eva made a point of mentioning this routine in the book. *You will mostly be eating alone, but don't neglect those small rituals that make a meal feel special. You'd have done it when your husband, wife or parent was well, so why not do it for yourself now?* Daphne had worried that it sounded too prescriptive. 'Will most carers really be fretting about folding napkins, Eva?' she'd said on the telephone: they were working on edits to the second draft. 'Aren't you just putting them under even more pressure?'

But Eva had held firm. 'It's the small things like that, Daphne, that keep you from going mad. At least, that's been my experience. And that's what I'm writing about, isn't it?'

Eva had sounded more certain than she truly felt: her deeper worry was about the fact that she was writing the book – working title, *Handle With Care* – at all. She had been caught completely off guard when Emma Harrison – a young woman who had taken over clients from Jasper, Eva's former agent and friend – approached her with the idea. It had only been six months since Sarah had bought Eva the laptop computer and set her up with something called Outlook Express. (The name had made Eva laugh. 'Sounds like a film by Sergio Leone,' she had said.) Only a handful of people had Eva's email address, but the enterprising Emma Harrison had managed to track it down. She had, she explained tactfully, joined the agency soon after Jasper's death. *I do hope you don't mind my contacting you out of the blue*, she wrote. *But I wondered whether you might like to have lunch one day soon? I have an idea that I'd like to put to you.*

They met at Vasco & Piero's in Soho, Jasper's favourite haunt. (Eva had to hand it to the girl: she had done her research.) Emma had ordered an expensive Sancerre, and said that her idea was simple. 'A book about caring. Part memoir, part practical guide. It must be *so* difficult, doing what you're doing, Eva – and there are thousands of wives and husbands and children up and down the country doing the exact same thing. Quietly, nobly – for no money, mostly. This would be a chance to speak to them. To offer them support.'

Eva had drawn the line at 'nobly' – she was, she said rather primly, 'no Florence Nightingale' – but she had promised to think about it. That night, after Ted's bath – Carole, the evening nurse, had come to help lift him in and out, and now Eva was rubbing E45 cream into his legs – she had said to him, 'Darling, they're asking me to write a book about you. About what looking after you is really like. I'm not sure it's a good idea. What do you think?'

Ted had become quite agitated then: the voiceless sounds that had become his only mode of expression increased in volume. (She would start the book with this: the terrible fact that a man who had built his career on the ability to communicate had been left unable to speak.) His eyes had moved rapidly from side to side, in the blinking action she had come to associate with assent.

'You think I should?' she said. The blinking continued. 'Well.' She moved her hand up his body, began massaging the cream into his right arm. 'We'll see, then.'

Now, in the garden, she eats her soup. She has left the radio on, and the news travels softly through the kitchen window: three children killed in a petrol bomb attack in Northern Ireland; famine in Sudan; Brazil to meet France in the World Cup final. (*Stay interested in the world*, she had written in chapter three. *Listen to the radio, watch television, subscribe to a newspaper. The important thing is to remember that you and the person you care for aren't the only people left in the world – and certainly not the only people in pain.*)

She thinks about those poor children in Ireland and Sudan;

about Sarah's Pierre, now a bright, bilingual seven-year-old; about the frightened woman who wrote to her a month ago, saying that her husband had returned to Pakistan with their two children, and she believed she might never see them again. Eva did not choose the letter for her column. Instead, in accordance with the policy she has developed with the *Daily Courier*'s lawyers, she wrote back to the mother, urging her to go to the police. The woman's reply came yesterday. *Thank you for your advice, Mrs Simpson. I can't tell you what it means to me. But it's no good. He says he'll kill them if I come after him. And I really think he could.*

Advice. This is what Eva deals in now, though she feels, deep down, that she knows no more than anyone about anything; less, even, than she did when she was twenty, and everything seemed so plain and clear and simple. It was *Handle With Care* that did it, of course: the book's success had exceeded even Emma Harrison's expectations. The critics loved it (most of them, anyway); the readers adored it. Eva was invited to appear on television, and to join the boards of three charities. The 'care issue' was debated in Parliament. Even Judith Katz – now ninety years old, and measuring out her days in a rather chic sheltered housing development in Hampstead Garden Suburb – telephoned to offer her congratulations. And then the *Daily Courier* got in touch, in the shape of Jessamy Cooper, the thirty-four-year-old editor of the new Saturday magazine. (*When*, Eva couldn't help wondering, *had the whole world grown so absurdly* young?)

Over another expensive lunch, Jessamy had said, 'How would you feel about being our new advice columnist?'

Eva thought for a moment. 'Agony aunt, you mean?'

'If you like.' Jessamy had smiled. 'But "agony" sounds a bit gruesome, doesn't it?'

The irony, Eva thinks, finishing her soup, is that the more

time she spends issuing advice and talking about care, the less time she spends actually *caring*. They now employ Carole for three full days a week, and to help Eva give Ted his bath. When he is in a particularly bad phase – there was a bout of pneumonia just after Christmas – they book her for nights, too, and she stays in the spare room.

The book has made this possible – that, and Ted's payout from the *Daily Courier*, which proved more than generous. Eva had been invited in to see the new editor, a recent import from the *Telegraph* whom Eva had never met; she had sat at a cautious distance from his desk, watching his small, rheumy eyes shifting uncomfortably around the room. 'Great man, Ted Simpson. Much missed.' *But you never knew him*, Eva had resisted the temptation to say. *What do you know of how much he is missed?*

It would seem, however, that even Ted prefers Eva to keep busy with her writing. He had told her, back when he was still able to speak, that his greatest fear was not for himself, but for the fact that she might be forced to devote herself to his care. There had been a terrible incident – Eva had related it in the book – a few weeks after they'd returned from Rome: they had taken a train to King's Cross one morning, and he had lost control of his movements as they crossed the platform. She had known exactly what to do – grip his arm tightly as she helped him inch backwards across the concourse, find a place for him to sit; above all, try to keep him calm. But a businesswoman – Eva can still picture her now in her trim black suit, her sharp spiked heels – had tutted as she passed; said loudly, 'Fancy being drunk at this time of day. It's a disgrace.'

Ted had shrunk from the woman's voice, as if from a physical blow. When they finally found somewhere to sit, he had placed his head in his hands, and said, 'You should leave me, Eva. I'm no use to you. I'm ruining your life.'

Eva had taken his hands from his face; they were cold, blood-less, so she had warmed them with her own. 'Ted. I told you I wasn't going anywhere. And I'm not. You're stuck with me, all right?'

And yet Eva could not pretend, in the deepest part of herself, that the thought of leaving him had not occurred to her. One afternoon a few weeks later, she had snatched a few hours for herself, made the slow climb uphill to Alexandra Palace. She had sat on a bench under a wide plane tree that made her think of Paris, looking down over the city. *I am too young for this*, she told herself. *I never asked for it. It isn't fair.* And it wasn't, of course – but then she made herself think of how much more unfair it was for Ted. She pictured herself leaving, handing his care over to a nurse of whom they could expect no more than a distant, anonymous kindness; leaving him in a hospital some-where, reassuring herself with that terrible euphemism 'home'. Ted was an only child – his parents dead, no children of his own – and she and Sarah were all he had; they would not desert him. And Eva loved him. That fact was beyond question.

From the radio, now, comes the theme music to *The Archers*. Eva listens, closes her eyes, enjoying the warmth of the sun on her face, the soft farmyard sounds of summer in Ambridge. Opening them, she sees Umberto – a venerable old man now, scrawny and placid as an Italian *nonno* – stretch and turn in his favourite shady spot under the clematis. She goes over to him, tickles the cat under his chin. 'What do you say, *caro mio*? Shall I go and see if your *papà*'s woken up?'

He is awake. She replaces his lunch tray on the trolley, puts a hand to Ted's face. 'Gosh, darling, you're burning up. Shall I open the window?'

He blinks rapidly at her. She goes over to the window, lets in the street sounds, the faint promise of cooler air. She looks back at him, at his bad side, where, since the last stroke, his features seem to have slipped, resettled. His eyes watch her with an inexpressible sadness. She says, 'My darling. Please don't look at me like that. I can't bear it.' He blinks again, and then closes his eyes.

Missing
Sussex, April 2000

They have heard nothing from Sophie for six weeks when Jim comes in from his studio and says, 'I think we should go and look for her.'

It is a Tuesday, just gone eleven. Eva is standing by the kitchen window, holding a mug of coffee: her mid-morning break from writing. She is almost at the end of what, after all these years, she hopes will be the final draft of her collection of short stories. 'Are you sure that's a good idea, darling?'

'No.' He places a hand on the door frame, steadying himself. 'I'm not sure it's a good idea at all. But it's the only idea I've got.'

Eva drives. The morning is bright, windswept; the trees that line the narrow lanes bend and sway as they pass, and blossom is falling from the hedgerows. Jim thinks about the last time he saw Sophie, just before Christmas. She had resisted all their attempts to invite her over for Christmas Day – her mobile never seemed to be switched on – and he had decided to take matters into his own hands. He'd driven to Brighton alone – Eva was in London for the weekend with Sam and the grandchildren, and Jim had stayed to finish a commission that he was meant to have ready for shipping the following week. He'd followed these same roads, slippery then with a fine layer of frost.

The address he had for his daughter was on a road called Quebec Street: a tiny terraced house, its blue-painted facade cracked and peeling. For a long time, there had been no answer. He had begun to wonder if she had moved without telling them: it would not have been the first time. But then, there she was – or a shadow of her, bone-thin and shivering in a long-sleeved T-shirt.

'Dad,' the shadow said. 'Didn't you get the message? I don't want to see you.' And then she had closed the door in his face.

Now, as they turn onto London Road, Eva says, 'Quebec Street, then?'

'Only place to look, isn't it?'

She reaches across for his hand. 'Darling. Please don't expect too much.'

He grips her hand tightly. 'I know.'

They park at the far end of the street, in front of a neat, whitewashed house, a pair of wooden model boats beached on the living-room windowsill. On the short walk along the pavement, Jim feels his legs grow heavy; two doors down, he stops, suddenly afraid that they might give way. Eva takes his arm. 'Do you want to sit down? Come back later?'

Jim shakes his head. He will not be afraid of his own daughter. 'No. Come on. I have to try.'

For the second time, then, he rings the doorbell. They stand on the pavement in anxious silence. A girl passing on the other side of the street – leather-jacketed, her hair a luminous shade of green – watches them without smiling.

He presses the doorbell again, waits. Then, finally, there is the sound of footfall on the stairs, a shape looming in the hallway through the frosted glass. Jim holds his breath. The door swings open. Here is a man he doesn't know – a man wearing a black T-shirt, grubby jeans; his skin unnaturally white.

'What?' the man says.

Jim regards this stranger; tries, and fails, to get the measure of him. 'I'm Sophie's father. Is she in?'

'Got the wrong house, mate.' The man has a strong London accent and a faint smirk. 'No one called Sophie here.'

'I don't believe you.' Jim takes a step forward, but the man bars his way.

'Mate. Don't try it. I'm telling you – you've got the wrong house.'

Eva places a hand on Jim's arm, urges him back. 'If that's the case,' she says, 'we're very sorry to have disturbed you. But we're confused, you see. My stepdaughter used to live here. My husband saw her just a few months ago.'

The man looks at her, openly smiling now. Jim would like to reach out and punch him, feel the crack and splinter of bone and tooth beneath his fist. But Eva's restraining hand remains on his arm.

'Well. I can see why that would be confusing. But she doesn't live here now.'

'Do you think,' Eva says in that same reasonable tone, 'we could come inside and see for ourselves?'

'No. I don't think so. Now why don't you both run along back to your nice comfy middle-class lives?' And the door clicks shut.

Jim barely hears the man. He is looking at Eva, so brave, so dear to him. Suddenly it all seems dreadfully clear: he has chosen Eva – the certainty of happiness with her – over his daughter. He has brought this terrible moment on himself, on all of them; it is the logical conclusion. He should not have left Helena. He should never have tried to go back in time, to the moment when he and Eva had their entire lives before them. He has gone against the natural law of things: the law that says you get one chance at happiness, with one person, and if it falls apart, you do not get that chance again.

In his mind, he spools back through the years, to Anton's birthday party, to the moment he saw Eva standing in the kitchen in her long dress, her shoulders bare, her hair gathered at the nape of her neck. He should have turned away from her then, gone back home to Helena, to their baby daughter, to the life he had made his. But he knows he could never have done it. He could never have turned from Eva as he had that time in Cambridge, outside Heffers bookshop: she was pregnant with Rebecca, staring after him, watching the back of his departing head. It had taken all his strength then not to look back. He could never have been that strong again.

'Jim? Darling. Are you all right?'

He says nothing. He stumbles, and Eva catches him. 'Come on. Let's get back to the car.'

She drives down to the promenade, parks on Brunswick Square; takes him by the elbow, like an invalid, and leads him to the seafront. Down a set of steps to a café: a hard metal chair, fish and chips in a yellow polystyrene box. The beach is bare but for a dog walker, throwing a stick; the agile arc of the dog; the sea wide and grey and angry.

'Where is she?' he says.

'Somewhere we can't get to.'

'Drugs.' It is the first time Jim has said the word aloud, but it has been there between them for months – years, even. Sophie's erratic behaviour. Her weight loss. The sallow hue of her skin.

Eva nods. 'I think so.'

'It's my fault,' he says.

'No.'

'It is. Everything. Sophie. Mum . . . I let them all down, Eva. I wasn't there for them. I've never cared about anyone but myself.'

'And me.'

He looks at her. The wind is whipping at her hair. She is everything to him: his whole world, or the best version of it. Surely he never really had a choice. 'And you.'

They are silent for a moment. Eva gathers up the empty boxes, carries them over to a bin at the path's edge. He watches her small, deft movements. With her back turned, she could be twenty still; even when she turns, she does not really betray her sixty-one years.

Sitting down again, she says, 'Jim, you can't blame yourself for everything. You just can't.'

'I should have put Sophie first,' he says quietly. 'I should have been a better father.'

'Darling.' Eva turns to him, cups his chin with her palm. 'I don't think there's a father, or a mother, alive who doesn't feel that way. You did the best you could.'

'I wish I'd done better.' He stands, and she does the same. Her hand drops from his face, and he reaches for it. 'I'm sorry. I'm just so worried about her.'

'Of course you are. And we'll do everything we can to find her. When we get home, we'll call everyone we can think of. Helena. The Ship: that's where she was working, wasn't it? Sam might have some ideas. It'll be all hands on deck, Jim, all right? We'll find Sophie, and we'll bring her home.'

Relief floods through him: the relief of having Eva, loving her, sharing a life. He takes in a great lungful of air.

'Let's go down to the sea,' he says. And he leads her onto the pebbles of the beach, where they stumble as they tread, clumsy as infants taking their first steps.

VERSION ONE
\\\\\\\\

Sixty
London, July 2001

'Ready for the big speech?'

'As I'll ever be.' Eva takes a sip of champagne. 'I've got cue cards in my bag.'

'Clever girl.' Penelope lifts her glass, chimes it against Eva's. 'You've had tougher audiences, anyway.'

They are standing on the top deck of the ship, at the prow. Around them move men in dinner suits – men of their own age, mostly, with slicked grey hair (if there is any left to slick) and comfortable, reddish faces – and women in evening dresses, their décolletages gamely exposed. Watching a woman across the deck – her white hair piled into an elaborate chignon, the neckline of her red gown plunging deeply over the fine crêpe-paper skin of her breasts – Eva feels an odd blend of pity and admiration. She and Penelope have exercised careful restraint: Pen, now resignedly stout, is neatly encased in black spun through with fine gold thread. Eva is in dark green silk. Expensive: a treat to herself, bought on impulse.

'Lovely dress. You look so tiny. Damn you.'

'Hardly. But thanks, Pen.'

Penelope smiles. She watches Eva for a moment, her head fractionally tilted, considering. More seriously, she adds, 'You're beautiful, darling. Age shall not wither you. It might have got to the rest of us, but it's leaving you alone. Remember that.'

'All right, Pen. I'll try.' Eva places a grateful hand on her friend's arm. She has always been there when Eva needed her; and how many times, in recent years, has Eva had reason to be thankful for that? 'I'd better nip to the loo before dinner. See you down there, OK?'

'OK. Good luck with the speech. Picture them all naked.' They stare at each other; Penelope is the first to laugh. 'Actually, on second thoughts, don't.'

The toilets are on the lower deck, beside the ballroom, where waiters in white jackets are flitting between round tables heavy with glassware; in the centre of each table rises a single calla lily in a tall white vase. Through the wide glass windows, the chimney of the new Tate Modern thrusts up against the darkening sky; across the river, the answering dome of St Paul's is stately, palely glowing. Eva stands for a moment in the doorway, watching her city; taking it in.

'Eva. There you are. Thank goodness.' Thea: greying hair discreetly highlighted, the fine straps of her slip dress exposing the taut contours of her upper arms. Fifty-eight years old, and she still works out every morning in the basement gym of the house in Pimlico. In the weeks after Jim left – those first terrible days, when time had seemed to collapse in on itself, and Eva couldn't even bring herself to change her clothes – Thea had tried to instil a similar discipline in her sister-in-law. Three mornings a week, she had come to collect Eva, bundled her into the MG, and set her going on the rowing machine. 'Exercise cures *everything*,' she'd assured Eva, in her brisk, Norwegian way. But it wasn't true: Eva had not been cured. She had simply redistributed the pain around her body.

'It all looks wonderful,' Eva says now.

'Do you think so? I'm so glad.' Thea comes over, lays her head on Eva's shoulder. She is given to such sudden gestures of affection; at first, Eva found them a little disconcerting – not very

British, and certainly not very Austrian – but she has grown to like them very much. 'There's someone on our table we'd like you to meet.'

Eva steps away, stung. 'Oh, Thea, you haven't . . .'

'Don't look at me like that. Just keep an open mind.' Thea lifts the neat arc of an eyebrow. 'Now it's almost time for dinner. Will you come and help me round up the troops?'

The family is seated together at the top table, as at a wedding: Anton and Thea; Jennifer and Henry; Daniel and his new girl-friend, Hattie, a fashion student with a small lace hat of her own design balanced elegantly on her cornrowed hair. Thea's mother, Bente – a retired neurosurgeon in her eighties, with her daughter's excellent bone structure and formidable intelligence – has managed to make the journey from Oslo. She sits beside Eva's niece, Hanna, now twenty-six and in the final year of medical training. On Bente's other side are Anton's old schoolfriend Ian Liebnitz and his wife, Angela, who have grown, like many long-married couples, faintly to resemble each other. Between Angela and Eva, an empty seat, and a name Eva recognises, etched in careful longhand. *Carl Friedlander.* Anton's new partner in the firm, the man who, if Eva remembers correctly, lost his wife to cancer, not more than a year ago.

Across the table, she catches Anton looking meaningfully at Carl's vacant chair. 'Just you wait,' she mouths at him, 'until I do my speech.' Eva is angrier than she's letting on: angry that, rather than simply enjoying her own brother's sixtieth birthday party, she'll be forced to endure the agony of a set-up in plain view of her son and daughter, and just about every friend she and her brother have ever had (excepting Jim, of course. Jim has not been invited). But Anton smiles at her, shrugs. He is suddenly so like the little boy he used to be – chubby, red-cheeked, forever seeking out some new source of mischief – that Eva is unable to resist the urge to smile back.

Carl Friedlander arrives just as the starter is being served. He is extremely tall – more than six foot, Eva surmises, as he offers breathless apologies to the table: he was coming in from his daughter's place in Guildford, and the train had simply sat outside Waterloo. A spare, fleshless face, almost gaunt; a crop of thick white hair. Shaking his hand, Eva is reminded of a photograph of Samuel Beckett that used to stare out across the *Daily Courier* office from above Bob Masters's desk: a Cubist composition of monochrome planes, cross-hatched with blocks of shadow. But Carl Friedlander's expression is not, she notes with relief, quite so severe.

Sitting down, he says, 'Lovely to meet you.' He settles himself on his chair, smoothes out a crease in his jacket. 'I know of you, of course. I mean, I did before I met Anton. My wife read every single one of your books.'

He flinches, a little, at 'wife', and so, to spare his embarrassment, Eva says quickly, 'How kind of you to say so. And did you read any of them yourself? Men are allowed to, you know.'

Carl looks at her, judging her tone. He gives a short, dry laugh. 'Is that so? I wish I'd known. I hid *Pressed* under a copy of *Playboy* while I was reading it. In case anybody saw.'

It is Eva's turn to laugh now. She can feel Jennifer, always finely attuned to the nuances of her mother's moods, watching them from the other side of the table. 'Well, now you know, you can reread it in public as often as you like.'

Between the starter and the main dish, Eva learns that Carl Friedlander was born and raised in Whitechapel, to German (he doesn't need to say Jewish) parents. That he joined the merchant navy in 1956, and remained there for thirty years, until he left to run his own shipbroking firm. That when Anton's company took over that firm two years ago, he'd thought he would retire, but Anton had twisted his arm to stay on. That he adores Wagner, despite knowing that he probably shouldn't. That his granddaughter's name is Holly, and she is the brightest, most precious thing in his life. And that he is profoundly, inexpressibly lonely.

This last, of course, is perceptible only to someone who can read the signs, who knows what it is to reach the latter portion of one's life (morbid to think that way, but there it is) and find oneself suddenly, unexpectedly alone. Eva knows it is absurd, really, that this should come as such a shock: we are alone when we enter the world, and alone when we leave it. But marriage – a good marriage, at any rate – obscures that basic truth. And Eva's marriage to Jim *had* been good: she can see that now, at a distance of more than ten years from its unceremonious finale.

In the months after Jim left, Eva had experienced what she might now grudgingly call a breakdown, though the term feels imprecise. It was less a breaking down than a cleaving in two: she'd had the surreal sense that the route of her life had bifurcated, and she had found herself stuck on the wrong path, with no means of tracing her way back. Easy to think of Dante – and she had, of the *via smarrita*, the right road lost. She had been unable to work (her publisher had been forced to put out her survey of women writers without a single interview); quite unable to function at all. It had taken the combined efforts of Penelope, Anton, Thea and an expensive psychotherapist to shake Eva out of it: to remind her that there were things to be done, decisions to be made. That, and her overriding need to be present for her children; not to mention her determination not to allow Jim to see that she was failing without him.

Eva would, she had decided, spare herself that last indignity. So she had roused herself, put the pink house they had loved so much on the market; bought a smaller place in Wimbledon, near the common, with a spare bedroom for Daniel, who was just off to university in York. She had even sent a card, when required, to Jim and Bella, to mark the birth of their baby daughter, Robyn.

For a year or so, Jim had kept his distance. Jennifer had even withdrawn his invitation to her wedding. But then, gradually, he had reappeared in their lives: at Daniel's graduation (Bella was at home with Robyn), Jim had taken Eva's hand during the ceremony, leaned over and whispered in her ear, 'Thank you, Eva. Thank you for not making it any harder than it had to be.'

She had felt a rush of anger then, so powerful she'd wanted to shout out loud. *You walked into my life when I was nineteen years old. You were the only man I ever loved – the only man I ever hope to love. You took everything we did together, everything we were to each other, and scorched it to nothing: left it a cloud of ash.* But she had said none of this. She had simply squeezed Jim's hand, and then let it go.

When the main course has been cleared, Thea gets to her feet, and silence falls across the room. She proposes a toast to Anton, and there is the high glockenspiel ring of glasses, a ragged chorus of cheers. Then Thea looks over at Eva. She stands in her turn, and all thoughts of Jim, of loneliness, of this stranger seated next to her – a fellow traveller on the wrong road – fall from her mind as she speaks of her brother: the boy, the man, the father, the son. And of their parents, much missed.

'Great job,' Carl says when Eva sits back down; as she spoke, his eyes never left her face.

Later, when the meal is over, the round tables have been cleared from the ballroom, and everyone is a little drunk, Carl will ask Eva to dance. He will hold her a little self-consciously at first, and then closer, moving fluidly, elegantly, in a way that Eva will find entirely unexpected.

Afterwards, she will break away, aware of the curious eyes of her son and daughter, her niece; and Carl will nod, disappear back into the crowd. She will feel his absence then, will scan the upper deck for a glimpse of him, even as she pretends she isn't looking. As the party draws to a close – the guests spilling unsteadily back onto the embankment; the boat's lights spreading washes of colour across the night-black surface of the water – Carl will come to say goodbye, will tell her that he would very much like to see her again.

Then, Eva will find herself saying, *Yes. Please. I'd like that too.*

VERSION TWO

||||||||

Detour
Cornwall, July 2001

Early on the morning of Anton's sixtieth birthday, as Jim is packing his overnight case for his trip to London, he receives a phone call from his son.

For a few moments after hanging up, Jim sits in silence, a slow smile creeping across his face. Then he dials his cousin Toby's number.

'So sorry,' he says. 'The baby's come. Yes, a fortnight early. You'll send my apologies to Anton and Thea, won't you? Have a good time.'

At the station, he attempts to exchange his train ticket to London for one to Edinburgh, but the clerk purses her lips. 'That's an advance return, sir. Non-refundable, non-exchangeable. You'll need to buy a new ticket. And there's only the sleeper from Penzance now.'

'Fine.' In his excitement, Jim forgets to be irritated. 'Just book me a return from London to Edinburgh, then, please. First class. I need to get there today. My son and daughter-in-law have just had a baby. Their first.'

The clerk's expression softens a little. 'Your first grandchild?'

Jim nods.

'Well.' She jabs at her keyboard, waits as the ticket printer whirrs and sputters. 'You've got it all to come, then, sir, haven't you?'

The next London train leaves in half an hour. Jim buys a newspaper at the kiosk, orders a large cappuccino with an extra shot. The morning is fine, bright, the promise of warmth leavened by the brisk Cornish breeze; standing on the platform with his overnight case, the coffee in his hand, Jim feels a tide of pure happiness rise up in him. His granddaughter, Jessica. (Dylan and Maya chose the name in the sixth month of pregnancy, after seeing a production of *The Merchant of Venice*.) He closes his eyes, feeling the wind on his face, breathing in the station smells of engine-grease, bacon and disinfectant. He thinks, *I will hold on to this moment and remember it. I will catch it before it disappears.*

He has a table seat on the train: spacious, comfortable. He accepts fresh coffee from the waiter, though his cappuccino isn't yet finished, and orders the full English. It is only then, as Jim sits back, unfolds his newspaper, watches the gorse and the slate cottages and the distant glittering sea, that he realises he hasn't told Vanessa he'll be away for longer than one night. He takes his new mobile phone (it was Vanessa who persuaded him to buy it; he is still rather wary of the thing, with its tiny keys and sudden inexplicable noises) from his overnight case. Slowly, painstakingly, he taps out a text message. *Jessica's come two weeks early. I'm on my way to Edinburgh. Not sure when I'll be back. You'll hold the fort, won't you? J.*

Of course she will. Vanessa is bewilderingly efficient: she has quit her job, as PA to the head of a London investment bank, for Cornwall and 'a more creative life'. Jim isn't entirely sure how managing his studio – ordering materials, archiving paintings and correspondence, preventing the relentless surge of email and paperwork from engulfing him completely – constitutes a 'creative life', but Vanessa seems happy enough. She's no Caitlin, who left abruptly two years ago, after announcing that she'd met someone who would be 'hers, and hers alone'. Vanessa is married, for one thing – not that Jim would have chanced his luck even if she weren't. But he enjoys her company, and is grateful for the uncanny way she manages to anticipate his needs.

Here she is now, popping up on the phone's screen, asking whether he'd like her to send flowers to Anton Edelstein. *Great idea*, Jim types back. *Thanks, V. Speak soon.*

Anton Edelstein: sixty years old today. Odd that Jim should find this so difficult to take in, when he passed the sixty-year mark two years ago. (Caitlin had only just left him; he was still licking his wounds, and had a doleful celebration in an Indian restaurant with Stephen Hargreaves.) In Jim's mind, Anton is still a thirty-year-old in flared trousers and paisley shirt, doling out rum punch in his Kennington kitchen.

Jim has seen little of Anton in the intervening years – at a party or two at Toby's; at the private view of Jim's first solo show at the Tate. There, in the dim shadows of the gallery's basement foyer, Jim had found himself asking after Eva.

The question had taken Anton by surprise. 'I didn't realise you knew my sister.'

'Not very well,' Jim said quickly. 'We've met a few times over the years.'

'Yes. I suppose you would have.' Anton's gaze had shifted uncomfortably to the ground. 'Well, in that case, you'll know that it's all been very hard for her. Very hard indeed.'

Jim had nodded, though really he could hardly imagine how hard it was. He had first heard Eva on the radio two years before – he usually listened to Radio 4 while he was painting, and had switched on his set one morning to hear her voice, clear and eloquent and utterly unexpected. She was talking about a book she'd written: a book about caring for her husband, Ted Simpson, the former foreign correspondent, now severely disabled by the combined effects of Parkinson's disease and several strokes.

Jim had stood quite still, forgetting to breathe, thinking of what Toby had said at his own fiftieth birthday party – *Ted Simpson's not well at all.* Thinking of the man he'd seen take Eva in his arms at Anton's thirtieth, all those years ago: grey-haired, stockily handsome, with a firmness about him, a solidity, that even Jim could see was attractive. The heart-shaped pendant he was sure Ted must have given her, lying coolly against Eva's warm skin.

Now, on the train, eating his breakfast, Jim thinks again of Eva, allows himself to acknowledge the fact that he had been looking forward to seeing her at the party. His invitation hadn't come from Anton directly – Jim doesn't really know him well enough – but from Toby: Marie was taking their daughter, Delphine, to France for a fortnight, leaving Toby behind to finish the edits to his latest documentary. 'Come with me, old man,' Toby had commanded over the telephone. 'We can be two old crocs together. Show those young things what we're made of.'

As he agreed to go, Jim had thought of Eva, whose voice he heard often on the radio, whose *Daily Courier* advice column he had taken to reading carefully each week. He liked the woman he had come to know through her writing: wise, self-deprecating, empathetic. He'd imagined seeing her again at this boat party of Anton's, carrying this deeper knowledge of her. Ted had died just over a year ago: Jim had seen his obituary. He wanted to tell Eva how sorry he was. He pictured her eyes on him – dark brown, insightful – speaking (and here, perhaps, his imagination had departed entirely from reality, and yet he'd allowed himself that indulgence) of a possible future.

But now he is travelling north, to his son, his granddaughter. Dylan insisted that Jim didn't have to come right away – 'We're all over the place. You could wait a few days if you want' – but his need to go to them was immediate, instinctive. He adores his clever, sensitive son, already making a name for himself as a printmaker; is fiercely proud of his talent, his vision; of the precocious maturity with which Dylan had, so quickly, adapted to his parents' parting and his mother's relationship with Iris, and found a way to keep them all close. Jim loves his daughter-in-law, too: loves Maya's warmth, her intelligence, the many small ways – a glance; an encouraging word; the light touch of her hand on Dylan's back – in which she shows Jim how deeply she loves his son. Jim wants to see his granddaughter *now*: that tiny girl, Dylan's girl, looking out at this strange new world for the first time.

And so it is of Jessica – with Dylan's blue eyes and Maya's dark skin and her own messy crop of black hair (Dylan has emailed a photograph of her, propped in the crook of Maya's arm) – that Jim thinks now, as the train carries him north, past fields, over bridges, skirting the fleeting sprawls of towns; carving its silvery path through the life he is already living, not the one that might have been.

VERSION THREE

//////

Sixty
London, July 2001

She finds Jim standing alone on the top deck, at the prow.

'Darling, are you coming? Thea's calling everyone in for dinner.'

He turns, and she is shocked for a moment by how tired he looks, how defeated. The situation with Sophie has aged him. In the weeks after her disappearance, it was as if Eva suddenly saw the decades written on Jim's face, where before she had seen him only as he always was: angular, tousle-haired, fired by his own particular form of inner energy. Pulling her through that gap in the hedge outside Clare; squinting at her in the half-light of his attic room, as his pencil moved fluently over his sketchpad. Slowly tracing the line of her collarbone with his hand.

'Just taking a breather,' he says. 'I'm coming.'

They go down to the ballroom together. The family is seated at the top table, as at a wedding: Anton and Thea; Rebecca and Garth; Sam and his wife, Kate, their two daughters, Alona and Miriam, arranged between them, fidgety in their smart summer dresses. Thea's mother, Bente, over from Oslo, sits beside Eva's niece, Hanna. On Bente's other side are Ian and Angela Liebnitz; and on Eva's right, a man named Carl Friedlander, Anton's new partner in the firm. (Eva is surprised, at first, to see him seated with them – later, she remembers Anton saying that Carl

341

had lost his wife to cancer, and admires the gesture.)

'You have a lovely family,' Carl says to her, as the wine is poured, and Eva, thanking him, looks around the table, and thinks, *Yes, I do.* Rebecca is glamorous in a red sheath dress, her dark hair swept up into a chignon; Garth is leaning in close, sharing a private joke. Sam is quieter, more reserved, as he has always been. (How keenly Eva remembers him as a small boy: compact, chubby-kneed, patient; never grasping for things or issuing imperious demands, as his sister had done.) But Sam's reserve, Eva knows, is the product of a certain innate shyness – he certainly didn't inherit that from David – that he wears only in public: with Kate and his girls, and with Sophie, too, he is easy, open, affectionate. There he is now, reaching across to Alona, placing a firm hand on her shoulder: 'Sit quietly, darling.' And she, rather than scowling or complaining, inclines her head to meet her father's hand, brushes her cheek against it, in a small gesture of love that touches Eva deeply.

Their family: the family she shares with Jim, who now slips his hand into hers. All of them here but one: Sophie. She could not be persuaded, though Sam went to visit her in Hastings, told her how much it would mean to him – to all of them – if she would come; and bring Alice with her too.

It was Sam who had found Sophie. She had phoned him, about six weeks after Eva and Jim's fruitless trip to Brighton, and had given him an address, but told him not to pass it on. He'd kept his promise. 'What choice do I have?' he'd said to Jim, who had been cold with impotent fury. 'If I tell you, she may not speak to any of us again, and where would that leave us?'

Painful as it was, Jim had been forced to concede that Sam was right. So Sam had gone to her – taken Kate, Alona and Miriam to Hastings, as if for an ordinary family day out. From the seafront, he had driven on alone to the address Sophie had given him. It was a small flat on the third floor of a rather daunting block: 'Clean, though,' Sam had reported later. 'Very clean.' Sophie, too, was clean, in every sense. She was also six months pregnant. 'Tell them I'm not using,' she'd urged Sam, and he had; but she hadn't wanted them to know anything more.

When the baby was born, Sophie had named her Alice, and emailed Sam a photograph. That is all Jim has of his grand-daughter: a small, grainy image of a two-day-old girl, wrinkled, faintly cross-eyed. Sophie will not allow Helena to see her either – she has cut herself off from both of them, like a branch sliced cleanly from a tree. Eva had thought at first that the fact Sophie would see neither of her parents – that her hatred wasn't reserved for Jim alone – might offer him some meagre comfort, but Jim takes none from it at all.

It is an excellent dinner: lobster cocktail, rump steak, key lime pie. 'Anton's death-row meal,' Thea explains, placing an affectionate hand on the back of his neck. She is still slender, unfussily elegant in a slip-dress of fine grey silk. 'My husband should really have been born an American.'

Anton smiles, strokes his wife's arm. He is the image of a successful businessman in late middle age: sleek, signet-ringed, running comfortably to fat. Eva has to strain a little to re-member the boy he once was, standing in the hallway of the Highgate house in his cricket whites; tunelessly intoning the Torah at his bar mitzvah. But then sometimes her brother will look at her, and she will see that the boy is still there: restless, mischievous, ready for anything.

'She's a feeder,' Anton says now. 'There's no way I can call this puppy fat any more.'

Jim spends much of the meal talking to Angela about his last exhibition: a small, strictly commercial assembly of paintings at Stephen's gallery, at which it had been impossible to pretend that Jim's work still inspired the interest it once had. 'How *do* you decide what to paint?' Eva hears Angela asking as she turns back to Carl: a tall, rather austere-looking man, with a perceptible air of sadness. He asks if he is right in thinking that she recently published a novel (a small nod from Eva at this: she can still hardly believe it is true); wonders shyly whether she was once married to the actor David Curtis. Accustomed to the question, Eva says yes, indeed she was; selects a few of the usual stories about Oliver Reed ('charming'), Los Angeles ('desolate somehow'), David Lean ('quite brilliant').

Eva asks Carl how he is finding the business, and he tells her about his time in the merchant navy; his German background (they exchange a couple of jokes dredged up from their respective childhoods: his German is not as fluent as hers, but she laughs all the same); his wife, Frances, with whom he shared twenty-seven years of marriage.

'You must miss her very much,' Eva says as the pudding plates are cleared away.

'I do.' Carl turns to thank the waiter hovering at his right elbow. 'But life is for the living, isn't it? We all have to find some way to carry on.'

After the coffee, the speeches. Thea stands first, proposing a toast. Then it is Eva's turn. She rises to her feet, suddenly nervous. Across the room, she catches Penelope's eye; her friend smiles her encouragement, and Jim, next to her, reaches up to squeeze her hand. It is enough: the words return to her. Afterwards, Eva raises her glass to her brother, and the whole room does the same.

Back up on deck, Eva and Jim share a cigarette. It's getting late: the band is playing slow tunes, and the embankment is deserted, strobe-lit by the headlamps of passing cars. Behind them, on the boat's starboard side, is the looming tower of the old Bankside power station, now the new gallery, Tate Modern. Eva would have liked to stand and look at it, this grand symbol of a London transformed, but Jim is resolutely facing the other way.

'Great speech,' he says.

'Thanks.'

She hands him the cigarette. 'Can't believe Anton's sixty. Can't believe *we're* sixty.'

'I know.'

She watches Jim's profile: the fine lashes framing his blue eyes, the softening contours of his chin and neck. 'Doesn't seem real, does it?'

They are silent for a moment. From the ballroom, a Paul Weller song – *You Do Something To Me* – floats out over the upper deck.

'I miss her, Eva,' Jim says. 'I miss her so much.'

She thinks of Carl Friedlander, alone for the first time in almost thirty years. Of Jakob and Miriam. Of Vivian and Sinclair. Of Jim's father. Of the absences torn from the weft of all their lives. 'I know you do.'

He passes her the dwindling stub. 'Do you think Sophie will ever come round?'

Eva drags in the last puff of smoke. She is reluctant to be the carrier of false hope. 'I think so. Eventually.'

'She's just so *angry* with me.' Jim turns to look at her, and his face, eerily struck by the flicker of the car lights, seems deflated, structureless. 'And with Helena. We did everything wrong, didn't we, Helena and me? We lived in that absurd hippy set-up, with people coming and going, and all of Howard's petty rules, and me out in the studio all day, never spending any time with her.'

Eva crushes the cigarette into an ashtray mounted on the handrail. On the riverbank, a young couple is walking slowly past: the man in low-slung jeans and baseball cap; the woman tottering in high heels. The woman looks round at the boat

– takes them in, standing there on the top deck, with a bold, appraising stare – and Eva is reminded of the time Sophie had stood in the doorway to their bedroom in the Sussex house, watching Eva carefully apply her make-up before a party. Eva had turned, beckoned her in, thinking she might like to try on some lipstick. But Sophie had shaken her head. 'Mum says wearing make-up is slutty,' she'd said, her voice monotonous, matter-of-fact. 'I suppose that means you're a slut.'

And then she had turned on her heel and disappeared back into her room, before Eva could work out how to respond; in fact, Eva had not responded, and had never told Jim about the incident, either. It was one of the few times Sophie had shown Eva, overtly, how much she disliked her – and though Eva hopes she has done everything she could, over time, to make an ally of her stepdaughter (and still believes that she may yet), the memory of it has never quite deserted her.

'Jim, she was a baby then,' Eva says. 'She'll hardly remember any of that. And anyway, you were working hard at something you believed in. She should be proud of you. Her father, the artist.'

This, too, is a misstep: Eva sees him wince. 'Well.' His voice is tight with contained emotion. 'We both know how well that's turned out.'

She reaches for his hand. He takes it in a firm grip, says with greater intensity, 'Sometimes I wish so much, Eva, that we were back in Ely, on that day we took the bus from Cambridge: do you remember?'

She nods: of course she remembers. 'I have this terrible feeling that everything from then on has just been wrong, somehow. That none of it was meant to happen.'

'You don't really believe that anything is meant to happen, do you?' Eva speaks quietly, so that only he can hear.

'No. Maybe not. Who knows?'

Eva folds her arms around him. He smells of shaving foam and toothpaste and, faintly, of the generous measure of whisky he drank after dinner. 'No regrets, Jim, all right?'

Into her hair, he says, 'No regrets, Eva. Not now. Not ever.'

Rescue
London, November 2005

A gunshot wakes him.

Jim lies still, listening to the loud thrumming of his heart. He'd been standing in an underground car park, thick with shadow; someone was chasing him – a faceless figure in a black hooded top, the twin barrels of a shotgun glinting in the gloom . . .

More shots: two of them, in quick succession. A voice. 'Dad. *Dad*. It's Daniel. Open up.'

He opens his mouth to speak, but no sound comes out. Jim stays where he is, breathing, letting his pulse slow. The drawn blind is casting wide slats of light and shade across the living-room floor. He wonders why he isn't in his bedroom. He wonders why his son is banging on the door. If he has lost his key, why doesn't Eva let him in?

'*Dad*.' The voice is louder now: Daniel must have come round to the living-room window. 'Are you there? Let me in, please.'

Consciousness is returning slowly to Jim, in patches, like a child's drawing sloppily coloured in. He is aware of the rough fabric of the sofa, then of a small patch of drool that appears to have gathered stickily on the arm, beside his open mouth. Then of the regiment of bottles assembled around the sofa, shaded prettily in the half-light like a still-life, pencil-sketched. Then of the fact that this is not his house.

'Dad. Come on. I'm worried about you.'

But this must be his house: why else would he be here? So where, in that case, is Eva?

'Dad. This is serious. Open up.'

This *is* his house, but not Eva's. It is the house he shares with Bella and Robyn. So where are they?

'*Dad.*' A dull thud: someone is banging on the window. 'Please. You've got to let me in.'

Bella isn't here. Neither is Robyn. Jim is quite alone.

'I'm serious, Dad. If you don't let me in, I'm going to come back with the police, and make them break down the door.'

'*All right.*' Jim's voice emerges in a low croak. The voice of an old man. The voice of a man he doesn't know. 'I'm *coming.*'

From beyond the window, he hears Daniel sigh. 'Dad, you're there. For God's sake.'

Getting up from the sofa, Jim becomes aware of the pain: the deafening clash of it. He sits for a moment, concentrating on remaining upright. His breathing is shallow, ragged, and he seems to be naked except for a pair of underpants and his dressing-gown, on whose right sleeve a large, brownish stain appears to have bloomed. When he gets to his feet, his head spins woozily, and his pain redoubles its infernal rhythm.

He staggers across the living-room to the hall, opens the door. There, on the front step, is his son: jeans, brown leather jacket, his dark hair artfully styled. Beyond him, a bright wintry Hackney morning. Sun thinly glancing off flaking stucco. The front path inches deep with mulching leaves.

'Jesus Christ, Dad.'

Jim squints at his son, but the light hurts his eyes, and he finds he can't quite look at him.

'Come on. Let me make you a coffee, or something.'

He can feel the effort Daniel is making to say only this. He moves aside to let him in, follows him back down the hallway.

The kitchen is not as bad as Jim had feared. Unwashed plates stacked beside the sink, the remains of the Indian he ordered last night – or was it the night before? – congealing in plastic containers. Bottles lined up along the windowsill. This confuses Jim: he quite clearly remembers throwing bottle after bottle into the recycling bin, wincing as they crashed and splintered. Odd how the bottles always seem to reappear.

Daniel hands Jim a mug of black coffee – of course there's no milk – and a packet of Nurofen, then sits down opposite him at the table. Jim takes two tablets with the coffee. The crashing inside his skull is quieting a little, and the colours are slowly bleeding back into the day. With them come snatches of memory. The blank look on Bella's face the morning she left, as if she were looking at a man she barely knew. Robyn fiddling with her hair (Jim took her out for pizza some days ago) while he asked about school, her friends, her dance classes, struggling to find the right words with which to reach his own daughter. He'd been reminded, painfully, of that awful pub lunch he'd shared with Daniel all those years before, after leaving Eva, leaving Gipsy Hill: dry roast chicken, rugby on the television, and his teenage son quietly uncomprehending. *Mum's in pieces, Dad.* But Bella wasn't, was she? She was A-OK; he was the one falling to pieces. He'd driven Robyn home – 'home': the glossy Islington mews house she and Bella were sharing with that man – and then gone back to Hackney. There, Jim had heard the siren call of the bottles neatly shelved in the newsagent's on the corner. The sweet righting of the world, its shifting back into balance, that had come with the first sip.

'Dad, you look awful.'

'Do I?' It is a while since Jim last looked in a mirror. He has been having trouble, lately, with his own reflection: an unnerving sense that he doesn't recognise himself. 'I suppose I must.'

'When did you last have a wash?'

What a thing for a son to ask his father. A lump forms in Jim's throat. 'Come on, Daniel. It's not as bad as all that.'

He can feel his son watching him. Daniel has Eva's eyes, her direct, uncompromising gaze. What does he have of Jim's? Nothing, Jim hopes, for the boy's sake.

'Hattie and I would like you to come and stay with us for a bit. We don't think it's good for you to be on your own.'

Hattie: that lovely, sweet-faced girl with the wide smile, the easy laugh. How can Jim take this ugly face of his into her home, let the blackness that surrounds him flow out over that light, beautiful flat, with its white walls and sanded floors and dried flowers in jars?

He shakes his head. 'No. I don't think that's a good idea. I'm fine where I am.'

'You're not, though, Dad, are you? You're not fine at all.'

Jim says nothing. Through the back window, he watches a sparrow settle on a branch.

Bella and Robyn had left after breakfast one day, while he was out buying a newspaper. She must have had their bags ready in the spare room; how, Jim wondered for weeks afterwards, could he not have noticed? Her note was on the kitchen table, scrawled hurriedly – her writing was almost illegible – on the back of a used envelope; later, it occurred to him to wonder whether she had been planning to leave a note at all. *We both know it's over. I suspect we should really never have started it. But we did, and it was good while it lasted. We're moving in with Andrew. You can see Robyn whenever you like.*

'Andrew' meant Andrew Sullivan, of course. Jim knew about him: he'd been collecting Bella's work for years, and she'd been perfectly open with Jim about the fact that she was sleeping with him. When she'd told him, she was stretched out, cat-like, on their bed; Jim was standing up, folding clean washing, feeling somehow at a disadvantage. She'd been sleeping with Andrew for months, she said. But he knew that, didn't he?

He didn't.

'Oh.' Bella had seemed genuinely perplexed. 'I'm sure I never made you any false promises, Jim. We promised to make each other happy, didn't we? Well, this makes me happy.'

'Come on, Dad,' Daniel says now. 'It's no good, you being stuck in the house on your own.' He doesn't need to add, *surrounded by memories of that woman*. He and Jennifer made their feelings about Bella perfectly clear: Jennifer overtly (she and Henry had planned their infrequent visits carefully, choosing times when Bella was unlikely to be at home), Daniel with a little more tact. They had even had a good dinner together – he, Bella, Robyn; Daniel, Hattie – for Jim's last birthday. But that had been in an Italian restaurant in Soho; thinking about it now, Jim can't remember the last time his son was in this house.

'Have a shower. Let me put a few things in a bag for you.'

'Daniel.' Jim looks directly at his son for the first time. Daniel's open, unlined face – his compassion, his youthfulness, his sheer bloody *optimism* – makes Jim want to weep. 'I know what you're doing, and I am grateful. But honestly, I don't think I should come. Look at me. I'm a mess. I can't bring this crap into your house. It's not fair on Hattie.'

'Actually, it was Hattie's idea. Hers, and Mum's.'

Perhaps it is the mention of Eva that changes Jim's mind: that, or simple exhaustion. A letting go. Either way, he allows Daniel to take him up to the bathroom, to leave him showering while his son sorts a few of his things into a bag. And then they are in Daniel's old Fiat, the heaters giving out their stale, biscuity warmth while the dark-windowed boozers and fried-chicken shops of east London give way to the looming glass and concrete of the City; the wide silver river to south London's twisting roundabouts and high, blank-faced estates.

Hattie and Daniel live on the ground floor of a neat terraced Edwardian house in Southfields. The plasterwork is recently painted, the garden hedge trimmed. Hattie, waiting in the hallway, smells of face cream and fabric conditioner, so clean and fresh that Jim feels he oughtn't to touch her. But she draws him to her. 'Glad you're here. We've been so worried.'

It is then that Jim starts to cry, while Daniel carries Jim's bag in from the car, and his son's girlfriend holds him in her arms.

'I've made such a mess, Hattie,' Jim says quietly. 'Such a mess of everything. I miss her so much.'

'Of course you do,' she says. 'Of course you miss Bella.'

No, he would like to say, crediting the truth that he is only just beginning to acknowledge to himself. *Not Bella. Eva.*

But he does not say these words aloud. Instead he thanks Hattie, and he steps away, dries his eyes with the sleeve of his jumper. 'Sorry, Hattie. I'm not sure what came over me.'

Daniel, coming back through from the kitchen, places a hand on his father's arm. 'Come on, Dad. Let's get the kettle on.'

Pines
Rome & Lazio, July 2007

'Are you hungry?' Eva says after she has embraced Sarah, then held her at arm's length for a moment, noted the shape and colour of her. Her daughter has a new haircut – short, rather elegant; in the sixties, the term would have been 'gamine'. She has lost weight, too: in Eva's arms, she felt less substantial than usual, and Eva found herself remembering, with some pain, her daughter's precarious years in Paris, when she'd had to watch Sarah grow skeletal, living on coffee and cigarettes and who knew what. She and Ted had telephoned from Rome as often as they'd permit themselves, asking if they could send money; whether Sarah – and, later, Pierre – were eating enough. It is this old habit that has prompted her to ask this question now.

Sarah, knowing this, offers her mother a wry smile. 'I'm fine, Mum. We ate on the plane. I could murder a coffee, though. Pierre?'

Eva's grandson is standing a little apart: he is fifteen, all skinny legs and sharp angles, two white wires dangling from his ears. He removes one of the wires to answer his mother's moving mouth. 'What?'

'Take the headphones out, please, and say hello to Oma properly.'

Pierre rolls his eyes, makes a pantomime of stuffing the wires into his pocket. But when Eva holds him close, he is a boy again, wide-eyed and grinning, chasing the ginger cat around the tiny fifth-floor apartment in Belleville where he was born.

'Hello, Oma,' he says into her ear.

'Hello, darling. Welcome to Rome.'

They stop for coffee at the airport bar: three espressos in heavy white china cups, the barman eyeing Sarah with lazy interest. Sarah admires the fluency with which Eva places their order, asks after the man's day.

'Not too rusty, then?'

'It seems to have come back. Like your French, no? When you've lived somewhere, I don't think the language ever really goes away.'

Eva had been afraid, at first, that it would have: that not only her Italian, which she had not had cause to use for many years, might have deserted her, but also her love of Italy, the ease with which she and Ted had navigated the complex paths and channels of Roman life. And, more than that, she'd feared that she would simply not be able to face navigating them without Ted.

For all these reasons, Eva had told herself to turn away from the window of the *agenzia immobiliare* – she and Penelope were on a week's holiday in Rome, 'exorcising demons', as Penelope put it. They'd hired a car, taken a day trip out to Bracciano. But she had not turned away: she had gone in, asked to view the house in the hills south of the town, with the small swimming pool, and the lemon trees standing sentry in pots on the sun terrace. Later that day, they had stood beside those lemon trees, smelling the resiny sweetness of the pines that screened the house from its neighbour.

'You've got to do it,' Penelope said. A few days later, Eva had.

Now, she drives north, through the scrubby outskirts of Rome: past billboards from which slender women in bikinis pout and pose; past run-down *casali*, old farm machinery rusting in front yards; past walls daubed with obscure political graffiti: *Berlusconi boia!, Onore al Duce*. It is Eva's favourite time of day: the threshold of evening, when the sun is dissolving into shadow, and the light is soft, the sky streaked with pink and orange. They have wound down all the windows, and the breeze is warm on their faces, the air carrying heat and diesel fumes and the honking of horns.

Sarah is stretching out in the passenger seat, arching her back like a cat. 'God, it's good to be here.'

'Busy week?'

She closes her eyes. 'Busy *year*, Mum.'

'Still tough at the council?'

'You have no idea.' After a moment, she reaches across, touches Eva lightly on the arm: an apology. 'Didn't mean to sound snappy. I'll tell you all about it later. Just let me close my eyes for a minute.'

'Of course. We have all week, don't we?'

They are silent for the rest of the journey: Sarah dozing lightly in the front, Pierre plugged back into his music, the minutes elapsing to his own private soundtrack. When they reach the house, it is almost dark. Eva goes in ahead, switching on lights, while Sarah and Pierre stand out on the terrace, yawning, taking it in.

'Wow, Oma.' Pierre has removed the headphones; he is staring at the swimming pool, open-mouthed. 'You didn't tell me you had a pool.'

'Didn't I? I hope you packed your trunks.'

'Don't worry.' Sarah taps her son playfully on the shoulder. 'Clever old Mum packed them for you.'

For supper, Eva fills plates with cheese, bread, tomatoes, thin slices of prosciutto. She shopped carefully at the market in Bracciano that morning, enjoying her good-natured discussions with the stall-holders about quality and price; thinking about the market in Trastevere, and about the kindly *signora* she had encountered in the waiting-room at the *pronto soccorso* hospital, bossily informing her that she ought to do her shopping elsewhere.

There is sadness everywhere, of course – sadness and memory, the echo of Ted's voice in her head, the remembered pressure of his hand in hers. But there is also joy: the sense – though really Eva suspects such a feeling to be overly sentimental – that she is closer to Ted here in Italy, somehow, than in the London house where he had faltered, grown ill; where she had watched him slowly fade away. He would have loved it here. Sometimes – though she has told no one this – she even thinks she sees him, caught fleetingly out of the corner of her eye: the quick dark blur of him, walking across the terrace; the bright flash of his white shirt. Eva will stop what she is doing then, and stay quite still, as if the slightest movement might frighten him away. But she can never quite resist the temptation to turn and look; and of course, when she does, there is never anybody there.

They drink wine as they eat – rough local stuff, watered down for Pierre – and talk of Sarah's latest case. (She is a social worker in Tower Hamlets; moved to London to train after everything went to pot in Paris with the band, and Julien.) The wine loosens Pierre's tongue: he describes his plans for the summer – a drum course, a weekend at a music festival with friends. Sarah asks how the new book is going, and Eva tells her, 'Slowly.'

Later, when it is fully dark, Pierre slinks off to bed, and Eva lights the candles she has placed all round the terrace in terracotta pots.

'It's beautiful here, Mum. I can see why you fell in love with it.'

'Yes. I did, rather. I know you thought I was barmy.'

Sarah regards her mother over the rim of her wine glass. 'No. Not barmy. I was worried you'd be lonely. Are you?'

Eva takes a moment to answer. 'Sometimes. But no more than I'd be anywhere. It's difficult, of course. Without him.'

'Of course. I miss him too.' Another short silence. Then, 'Dad called the other day.'

'Did he?' Thinking of David, Eva finds herself smiling. After all these years, her feelings towards him have grown kindly; she can see David, now, for what he always was – selfish, impossibly vain, but talented, too, and driven by his need to be true to that talent. There had been good times; the fact that their marriage had not stuck had surely, Eva will now admit, been as much her fault as his. They had each simply met, and then married, the wrong person. If the years have taught Eva anything, it is that this is hardly an unfamiliar tale.

'He's bored,' Sarah says. 'Nobody's sending him scripts any more, he says. He's feeling sorry for himself. "I'm a lonely old man, Sarah." I told him to try living alone on ten quid a week, not seeing a soul from morning till night, and then tell me he was lonely. That shut him up.'

'I bet it did.' Eva sips her wine. She is familiar with the gentle battles that persist between Sarah and her father: much gentler now than during Sarah's tricky Paris years, when she had refused to see David, had insisted that her only true father was Ted. 'He mentioned Lear, the last time we spoke. Said Harry was trying to persuade the National.'

'Yes. He's hoping they might give it the go-ahead for next year.'

'Well, that'll keep him busy for a bit, then, won't it? He won't be calling for Meals on Wheels quite yet.'

Sarah gives a dry laugh. 'I suppose not.'

A few minutes of quiet: the play and flicker of candlelight, the whirr and plash of the pool's filters. From somewhere beyond the pines comes the cry of a child, and its mother's answering call. 'Anything else you want to tell me about, darling?'

Sarah glances at her mother: sharply at first, then softening. 'Mum, you're completely transparent.'

'Am I?' Eva opens her eyes wide. 'And I thought I was discretion itself.'

'All right. There is someone.'

'I knew it.'

'How?'

'The haircut.'

Sarah smiles. 'That has nothing to do with him. But he does like it.'

'Has Pierre met him?'

'Not yet. It's still pretty new. But it's good. His name's Stuart. He's from Edinburgh, originally. Lives in Stoke Newington. Works for Age Concern.'

Eva spears a sliver of prosciutto with her fork, buying time. Her mouthful finished, she says, 'Married?'

'Divorced. Two kids, younger than Pierre. So we need to move slowly.'

'Very sensible.'

Sarah nods. 'I promise you'll meet him when we're ready. Though that would mean coming back to London.'

'I'll be back. October, probably. Winters out here can be fairly grim.'

'Not as grim as London, surely?' Sarah lifts the wine bottle, refills both their glasses. Then, sitting back in her chair, she says, 'What about you?'

'What about me?'

'No flickers of romance? Long lingering glances across the piazza?'

Eva laughs. 'Romance? You make me sound like some awful hormonal divorcee.'

Sarah doesn't laugh. She is straight-faced, serious: looking at her, Eva remembers the nights she and Ted had spent on the telephone – Rome to Paris; their bill, of course – while Sarah cried and cried at the other end of the line. The worst night of all, when Sarah had told them she was leaving Julien, taking Pierre, and they had both got straight into the car and driven north through the night. The *autostrade* empty, endless. The Alps glowing white in the pale dawn.

'Come on, Mum. You did everything for Ted. You don't have to be alone for ever.'

'I know.' Eva picks up her napkin, dabs at a faint spatter of wine that has settled on the collar of her shirt. 'But I'm not looking for anyone, Sarah. I think that part of my life is over.'

Eva is aware of her daughter's eyes resting on her for a moment longer, but Sarah says no more. They are quiet again, feeling the thickening of the Italian night, drinking their wine until the bottle is finished, and it is time to go to bed.

Later, unable to sleep, Eva lies watching the shadows on the ceiling, wondering whether what she said to her daughter was true; wondering why it is that here, in Italy, she has found a particular face returning so often to her thoughts. A narrow, pale face, scattered with freckles. Eyes a vivid, violet blue.

In the last few months, she has been having a recurring dream: a high-ceilinged room, light flooding through dusty windows. A man before an easel, painting. He has his back to her; he doesn't turn when she calls out, or even as she approaches him, drawn by the desire to see what he is working on. Each time, she has the strongest feeling that he is painting her own image. But when she is standing behind him – so close that she might reach out and touch him, though she does not – she sees that there is nothing on the canvas but white space.

In the dream, the artist never turns, never shows his face. But each morning, when Eva wakes, she knows exactly who he is, and the knowledge of it leaves her with a faint, peculiar sense of longing: peculiar because it is for a man, a life, that she has never known, and surely never will.

VERSION THREE

//////

Beach
Cornwall, October 2008

For Jim's seventieth birthday, Penelope and Gerald host a picnic on the beach beside their house.

It is more than a picnic: a feast, ordered from the deli in St Ives. Four wicker baskets filled with potted crab, pork pies, pasties; fat Greek olives and crumbling hunks of feta; a great whorl of festering cheese Gerald names as 'Stinking Bishop', and which makes the younger children screw up their faces in disgust. White wine in ice buckets. Cushions and blankets layered over pebbles; a table and chairs carried down from the house. Gerald's iPod playing softly from a small battery-operated speaker: Muddy Waters, Bob Dylan, the Rolling Stones. It is unseasonably warm – an Indian summer; the sky is bright and unclouded, a thin, diluted blue.

Three o'clock, and Jim is sitting on a folding chair, talking to Howard. He is approaching a delicious state of drunkenness: had been quite unable to believe, when Howard appeared, ghostlike, at his shoulder, that here before him was his old friend and nemesis. He was much thinner now, and walking with the aid of a cane; but there were the same large, loose-knit features, the same black eyes beneath thick white brows.

Jim had, at first, found himself unable to speak. After a few seconds, he'd managed only, 'How?'

'Eva,' Howard had said. Across his shoulder, Jim had seen Eva watching them. He had smiled at her, to show that she had done the right thing – a beautiful, unexpected thing. Then he had clasped Howard to him, felt the bulk of the man, still strong, sinewy; breathed in his smell of rolling tobacco and old wool. With that came a hundred other smells: the cloying sweetness of marijuana, the sharp tang of cold sea air, the deep woody scent of the shared studio, laid with stacks of freshly sawn timber.

Holding his old friend at a distance, Jim said, 'Cath?'

Howard shook his head. 'Lost her five years ago. Cancer.'

Now, they are sketching out the contours of the last three decades. The gradual failure of Trelawney House (Jim and Helena had heard something of this from Josie), the scattering of its residents. Howard and Cath's removal to a terraced cottage in St Agnes. Jim's leaving Helena for Eva: for the great sense of freedom he has found with her. His vigorous, productive years – the exhibitions, the newspaper articles, the money – petering out, a fire dwindling to embers.

'I was working with sculpture, for a while,' Jim says. 'Found myself thinking of you, Howard. What was it you used to say? That you weren't creating something new, you were just chipping away at what was already there.'

Howard laughs. 'Did I really say that? Bet I didn't admit that Michelangelo said it first.'

'No.' Jim smiles. Over Howard's shoulder, he can see his granddaughter, Alice, splashing in the water. She is approaching the waves cautiously, with a crab's sidelong gait; her older cousins, Alona and Miriam, are taking her hand, guiding her, playing at adulthood. 'You had to rule the place, didn't you, Howard? Always had to show us you knew best.'

The old man's thick eyebrows twitch. 'Never saw it like that. I just wanted us to make good work. Something we could all believe in.' After a moment, he adds, 'That interview. Making out that we were wastrels and derelicts. Showing her the bedrooms, for goodness' sake. What were you thinking?'

'I'm not sure what I was thinking.' Howard's face the morning the interview was published. The paper spread out across the kitchen table; Cath crying softly in a corner of the kitchen. Sophie wailing, inconsolable. Helena grim-faced and silent in the car. 'She twisted everything I said. You know how these things go. You must know that by now.'

Howard, watching the horizon, slowly nods. 'Yes, I know. It was all a very long time ago.'

Jim would like to tell him how much he had always admired him; how he had always felt, deep down, that Howard was the better artist. But he can't quite seem to shape the words. 'Are you still working?'

'Oh no. Not for years.' A smile creases Howard's lips. 'Burned the lot, didn't I? Got mad at Cath one night, drank a bottle of whisky, and set light to it all. Cath called the fire brigade. Very nearly torched the whole street.'

'God, Howard.' Jim is laughing, though the image in his mind – drawn from the newspaper story he read about it, and no doubt sensationalised by memory – is a terrible one. Smoke rising above a row of cottages. Howard standing barefoot on the patio, watching his life's work go up in flames. 'I saw the story. I should have written. I should have asked how you were.'

'Oh, it was small fry, really. Nothing to bother a proper art-world type like you.'

'Howard—' Jim begins, but he is prevented from saying more by Alice, now turning from the water's edge, calling for him, the breakers nipping at her toes.

'Go,' Howard says. 'I'll find Eva. Thank her again for dragging me out of my cave.'

Jim gets to his feet, grasps the other man's hand. 'I'm glad you came. It's good to see you. And I'm sorry. About Cath. I loved her, you know. We all did.'

'I know.' Howard nods. 'Happy birthday, Jim. You've a lovely family. Never mind the bumps along the way.'

In the shallows, Jim sets a steadying hand on each of Alice's shoulders. She is a small, quivering thing, crying out again at the sudden shock of cool water on her skin. Alice is more precious to him – though he would never admit it to anyone – than Alona and Miriam, not only for the blood that connects them (odd that this should make any difference, when of course the woman he loves most in all the world is not of his blood), but for the fact that she was lost to him for so long.

Alice was two years old when Jim finally met her: Sophie had simply appeared on their doorstep one afternoon, grey-faced and shivering. A man they didn't know was waiting in a car on the drive; later, they'd remember that he hadn't even extinguished the engine. 'Take her for a bit, will you?' Sophie had said. And then she was gone, running, slamming the passenger door shut before they could reply.

The small child hadn't cried as her mother left. She had watched the car turn, spit gravel, and then disappear. Then Alice had reached for Jim's hand, and said, quite calmly, 'Hungry.'

Over the next few years, they had Alice to stay many times, their despair for Sophie still colouring each day. And then, just before Alice was due to start school – they had found a place for her in the village primary, assuming that Sophie would not have made the necessary arrangements in Hastings – she had reappeared just as suddenly to take her daughter home. 'It's over, Dad,' Sophie had said. 'Really over this time. I promise you.'

And Sophie has, as far as Jim and Eva know, remained true to her word: she has found work as a teaching assistant at Alice's school, is attending Narcotics Anonymous meetings four times a week. It was there that she met Pete. He is here now: a mild, unremarkable-looking man, not one you would ever pinpoint as an addict, but if there is anything Jim has learned, it is never to put too much trust in appearances. He has always felt the potential for addiction in himself: an inchoate longing to loosen his grip. Had things turned out differently, Jim thinks, he might easily have allowed that longing to overwhelm him.

He is grateful to Pete, too, for the calming influence he appears to exert over Sophie's life. And Alice adores him: she is struggling free from Jim's grasp now, scrambling back up the beach, calling out his name. 'Pete! Me and Grandpa went in the sea! It *bit* us . . .'

Jim follows Alice at a more sedate pace, the pebbles hard and smooth under his deck shoes. He rejoins the group around the table – Penelope and Gerald, Anton and Thea, Toby; Eva, topping up everyone's wine. Seeing him approach, Eva smiles, hands him a fresh glass. 'Having a good time?'

'The best.'

He sits in an empty chair, next to Penelope. 'Thanks so much for this, Pen. I couldn't have asked for a better celebration.'

Penelope – draped in a blue kaftan, a white silk scarf knotted at her throat – shakes her head. 'It's all Eva's doing, I promise. All we did was sit back and let things happen.'

'Since when, my darling Pen,' Gerald says mildly, 'have you *ever* just let things happen?'

Eva comes up behind Jim, places a hand on the back of his neck. 'How was it with Howard?'

'Good. Great.' He twists round to look at her. 'How on earth did you find him?'

She smiles. 'Helena, would you believe? I emailed her. She said he and Cath had moved to St Agnes – then it was a simple Google search. Howard's the president of the St Agnes Residents' Association.'

'Is he really? Well, he *has* gone straight in his old age . . .'

'Hey,' says Toby. 'Less of the old. Not *all* of us are seventy yet.'

'All right. Less of the old.'

Seventy: an age that once seemed inconceivable to Jim, that of a stooped, shuffling ancient, waiting for his moment to step quietly from the room. But Jim is neither stooped nor shuffling: a little soft around the middle, perhaps, his face pouched and lined – but still alert and vigorous, alive to the inconceivable preciousness of each moment as it passes.

He reaches back, over his shoulder, for Eva's hand; grasps it tightly, as if the pressure of his hand on hers can convey his gratitude. And perhaps it can: Eva squeezes back, holding on; both of them looking to the horizon, to where the great waves are breaking, drawing with them the deep, unanswered loneliness of the open sea.

Kaddish
London, January 2012

A colourless London winter's day: damp, windblown, the pavements slick with intermittent rain. At the entrance to the crematorium, the mourners huddle, the older women clutching at their billowing skirts. A gaggle of smokers stands a little apart, cupping their lighters with their hands.

Eva watches from the passenger window of the family car. She is holding Thea's hand tightly, and thinking of other funerals – Vivian's, in Bristol, frost clinging to the grass beside the grave; Miriam's, on a fresh Thursday in spring, daffodils in glass bowls around the synagogue; Jakob's, spare and simple, as he had wanted it. Anything not to think of the hearse, now slowing to a halt in front of them; of the flowers – calla lilies and irises, Anton's favourite, Thea had said, with a certainty Eva hadn't dared to question – arranged around the coffin. Plain oak with brass handles. They'd agreed that Anton would not have wanted anything fancier than that.

Her brother had made no arrangements for a funeral. A will, yes – they'd drawn those up shortly after they married, Thea said, during one of the blurred, wakeful nights the sisters-in-law spent at the kitchen table in the days after his death, waiting for the dawn to bleed into the next interminable day. But he'd been superstitious about funerals: hadn't wanted to think about his own, for fear of tempting fate. Eva – raw, exhausted, finishing her sixth mug of coffee – had found it difficult to reconcile this information with the man Anton had become: a grandfather, a shipbroker, a man of substance. It was, she decided, in some way comforting to think that the boy he once was – chaotic, full of mischief – had lived on in this childish reluctance to acknowledge the administrative processes of death.

Without instructions, then, Thea and Eva had put their plans into place. A cremation: non-denominational, Thea insisted, and Eva – though thinking privately of the soothing ritual motions of their parents' Jewish ceremonies – did not disagree. Thea, alert to Eva's feelings, suggested that somebody (Ian Liebnitz, perhaps?) could say Kaddish. In the first hours after Anton's heart attack – he and Thea had been at a New Year's Eve party; in A&E, the family had been surrounded by bedraggled revellers in party clothes – the sisters-in-law had found their long-established affection deepening to something wordless, the terrible intimacy of grief. They would, they had decided, write the eulogy together, to be delivered by the celebrant: neither woman felt she would be strong enough to stand up and speak herself. Hanna would read some Dylan Thomas. Jakob's recording of the Kreutzer Sonata would be played as the velvet curtains slid shut.

There was a certain satisfaction in the making of these arrangements: a tick-list efficiently completed. But none of it quite prepared Eva for how it would feel to sit in the car following her brother's body, or to step out under the crematorium's covered entrance, feeling Thea shrink and buckle beside her.

Hanna, emerging from the back seat with her husband, Jeremy, comes forward to take Thea's arm. Eva presses her niece's shoulder gratefully, and then moves among the gathered mourners, thanking them; accepting embraces, condolences, tears. Jennifer falls into step beside her; Susannah (a late baby, conceived after many fruitless rounds of IVF, and now a quiet, watchful four-year-old) is standing with her father, Henry. Beside them are Daniel and Hattie, the latter wearing a vintage fur muffler, a dark blue dress cradling the swell of her pregnancy. Next to Hattie, Jim: a slight, white-haired figure in a black coat. He has lost weight since giving up drinking; seems somehow diminished, though nobody considers this a change for the worse.

'Eva.' Jim steps forward, places a gloved hand on each of her arms. 'I'm so sorry.'

She nods. 'I know. Thank you for coming.'

The celebrant is politely ushering them inside; at the door, Eva feels a hand slip into hers. Carl. He has driven himself to the crematorium; hung back as Eva made her greetings, allowed her the air she needed, as is his way. But she is grateful for him now, for the reassuring pressure of his hand, for the tall form of him, slim and solid as a sail-ship.

'Glad you're here,' she whispers.

'Me too.'

It is, everyone will agree later, a particularly beautiful service. The florist has placed three large displays of lilies and irises around the central plinth. Ian Liebnitz says Kaddish in a fine, strong baritone. The eulogy is both informal and dignified, with a respectful smattering of jokes, and the celebrant makes no mistakes. Hanna chokes a little over the poem, but manages, after a few seconds, to gather herself, and carry on. The sound of Jakob's violin – swooping, plangent, as if mining a deep, atavistic seam of sadness – fills the room as the curtains slowly close.

The wake is held at the house in Pimlico, where the caterers have laid out roast chicken and potato salad, Norwegian meatballs, a baked salmon. Waiters move soundlessly from room to room, offering drinks. Eva, accepting a glass of white wine, thinks of the countless times she has raised such a glass to toast her brother's health; of his sixtieth birthday party, more than a decade ago, when he and Thea had so astutely seated her next to Carl Friedlander.

Carl had – quietly, unobtrusively – slipped into Eva's life with a speed and ease that had taken both of them by surprise. They had started with coffee, then a concert, then a Saturday-afternoon visit to Tate Modern that had turned into drinks and dinner; a few days later, a supper at Eva's house in Wimbledon had become an invitation to stay the night. He had taken her sailing for the weekend, out of Cowes. She had asked him to come for Christmas; he'd invited her to spend his birthday in Guildford with his daughter, Diana – a friendly, plain-speaking woman, to whom Eva had immediately warmed – and granddaughter, Holly. The following year, Carl had presented her, early in December, with an unexpected gift: flights to Vienna, three nights in a good hotel. They hid from the cold inside wood-panelled cafés, eating Sachertorte (delicious, but not a patch on Miriam's) and drinking milky coffee. They saw *Die Fledermaus*. They found the apartment where Miriam was born – a tall, unremarkable building, its ground floor now occupied by a shoe shop – and stood on the station concourse where she had said goodbye to her mother and brother, not knowing that she would never see them again. Eva had cried, then, and Carl had held her, without self-consciousness, until she had no tears left.

He is a deeply intelligent, considerate man, and essentially light of heart: the grief Eva sensed at their first meeting has eased with time, and with this new possibility of love. Eva can't help contrasting Carl with Jim: with the restlessness that always resided at Jim's core. She had loved it, once, as she had loved every part of him; had seen it as the natural undertow of his need to draw, to paint, to shape the world into a form he could understand. And perhaps it was: perhaps, had life not carried them down the path it did, that unease would simply have led

371

him towards becoming a better artist, as it had his father.

She had taken no satisfaction in the fact that Jim's leaving her for Bella had rebounded on him, that it had not afforded him the new burst of energy (for art, for love, for life) he must have believed it would. Eva's anger had long since faded. Jim was a part of her: he always would be. She had remembered, in considering this, a Paul Simon song that she had played over and over for months in the early eighties, as if it might contain the answer to a question she hadn't yet formed. *You take two bodies and you twirl them into one. Their hearts and their bones. And they won't come undone.*

Eva had felt the truth of the lyric then, and she still does, though she and Jim are now nothing more to each other than former lovers, parents, grandparents; survivors berthed in the calmer waters of old age. Though the boy he was all those years ago in Cambridge, stopping to help her on the path, has become a pale, thinning man, almost elderly. And though the girl Eva once was is now hidden deep inside herself, under loosening skin, greying hair; beneath all the accumulated detritus of time.

Sometime in the afternoon, Eva steps out into the back garden for a cigarette. (Her inability to quit is the one subject on which she and Carl disagree.) It is there that Jim finds her.

'Not given up yet, then?'

She shakes her head, offers him the packet. 'I know *you* haven't.'

'Got to be allowed some vices.' Jim takes a cigarette, accepts her proffered lighter. 'Cut down, though. Five a day.'

'I thought that was meant for vegetables.'

He smiles. It is the same smile as always, though the skin around his mouth has pouched and puckered, as has her own. How many times have they stood together, smoking, talking, making plans? Too many to remember. Too many to count. 'Yes, well. Doing what I can on that front, too.'

They are silent for a while, contemplating the cool, damp grass, the naked trees. Above them, the clouds are massing, darkening; the day has barely bothered to bring light, and the evening will be falling again soon.

'It doesn't seem right, a world without Anton,' Jim says. 'He was always so vivid, somehow. Larger than life. Remember his thirtieth? That disgusting punch he made, and everyone passing out from too much grass.'

She closes her eyes. She can see the old Kennington house: the white furniture, the walled garden, the lights strung from the trees. With the clarity afforded by time, Eva can see that things were starting to founder even then; can remember Jim holding her in his arms as they danced; can remember willing things to take a turn for the better. And they had, for a while. They really had.

'Of course I remember. God, thirty seemed so old then, didn't it? We just had no idea.'

'Eva . . .' She opens her eyes, sees Jim regarding her with a new intensity. She swallows. 'No, Jim, please don't. Not now.'

He blinks. 'No. I'm not . . . I don't want to ask for forgiveness. Not today. Not again. I know you're happy with Carl. He's a good man.'

'He is.' She takes a deep drag on her cigarette. Next to her, Jim is shifting his weight uncomfortably from foot to foot. A knot of fear forms in the deepest part of her. 'Jim? What is it?'

He takes a moment, sends a small cloud of smoke billowing from his mouth. Then he says, 'I can't tell you today. Not on Anton's day. Come and see me, will you? Next week, maybe? We'll talk.'

Eva has finished her cigarette. She drops the stub, crushes it with her foot. 'This sounds serious.'

He looks at her again, holds her gaze this time. 'It is, Eva. But not today. Come and see me. Please.'

The knot of fear has risen up in her body; loosened itself, snaked up into her chest, her throat. Jim does not need to say more. She will go to him: she will hear what the doctors have said, how much time he has. She will help him to make his plans; soothe him, if she can. *Hearts and bones*. A young woman with a broken bicycle. The man she might, so easily, have missed: cycling past, not stopping, carrying with him a whole life, a life that might never have been hers to share.

'Of course I'll come,' she says.

VERSION TWO

||||||||

Kaddish
London, January 2012

'Smoke?' Toby says. 'I reckon there's time.'

Jim shakes his head. 'Given up.'

'You never have.' Toby stares at him, impressed. 'Well, old man, I'll be damned.'

He stands with Toby while his cousin lights his cigarette, draws in his first grateful puff. There are a few other smokers, standing a little apart, acknowledging each other with an expression that is not quite a smile. It is not a day for smiling, though that is how Jim remembers Anton Edelstein, will always remember him: vigorous, expansive, grinning.

It is many years since Jim last saw Anton, but he has, in recent months, come across photographs of him on Facebook: Toby, Anton and their friend Ian Liebnitz on a whisky tour of Speyside; Anton on holiday in Greece with his wife, Thea. Dylan had set Jim up with a Facebook account on his last visit to Edinburgh. 'Good for keeping in touch with the old crowd, no?' he had said, and Jim had nodded at his son, not wanting to betray his reluctance: the fact that the larger part of him can't understand how and when the world decided to knock down the walls that had once discreetly shielded private lives from view.

Jim's only online 'friends' remain Dylan, Maya, Toby and Helena. (She is given to posting phoney motivational messages on his wall, knowing that they irritate him beyond reason. *Every time you find some humour in a difficult situation, you win. Don't let yesterday's disappointments overshadow tomorrow's dreams.*) He had demurred from requesting Anton Edelstein as a friend, still ruled by the no doubt anachronistic sense that a virtual friendship ought to spring from more than a distant, if cordial, acquaintance. He had, however, found himself lingering over Anton's photographs, looking for a particular face.

It had not taken him long to find Eva. She was sitting at a table on some sunny terrace; behind her rose the distant plumes of pine trees, and a swathe of glistening water – a swimming pool – was visible just beyond her left arm. The changes time had brought in her had, for a moment, shocked him. (He had the same feeling, often, on seeing his own reflection in the mirror.) But fundamentally, she was unchanged: still slim, narrow-featured; still fully, wholeheartedly, alive. Her grief had not, he saw, destroyed her, and for that Jim had felt a kind of gratitude.

The funeral cortège is approaching; the black hearse edging respectfully to a halt. The smokers stir, shuffle, as if caught in an illicit act. Jim, turning, sees the doors of the family car open, Eva stepping out, holding tightly to her sister-in-law's hand. She seems smaller than in the photograph, than in the many images of her he has retained in his mind. Her feet, in their smart black shoes, seem tiny; her body, neatly belted inside a coat of dark-grey wool, is trim as a bird's. She doesn't notice him: her attention is focused on the covered entranceway, where the other mourners are gathering. Beside her, Thea Edelstein is a pale ghost of a woman, her eyes red-rimmed; it feels intrusive even to look at her. The daughter, Hanna, is emerging from the back seat, with a handsome, blond-haired man Jim presumes to be her husband.

He is suddenly certain that he shouldn't have come. He is

finding it difficult to breathe: to Toby he says, through short gasps, that he will wait behind for a few minutes, follow him inside. Toby stares at him. 'You all right?'

'Yes. Just need some air.'

Jim stands alone until all the other mourners have gone in, the red-brick wall rough beneath his hand. It is the worst of London winter days – monochrome, cheerless, spurts of rain carried on an icy wind – but he doesn't feel the cold. He is thinking of the doctor's office in the hospital. Not even an office, really, just a windowless room. A desk, a computer, a bed covered with a thin paper sheet. As the doctor spoke, Jim was reading a notice on the wall. *Have you washed your hands? Everyone can do their bit to halt the spread of MRSA.*

For days afterwards, it was that notice Jim held in his mind, not what the doctor had said, though the words were there too, of course. Biding their time. Waiting, like mines, to explode the casual certainty that his life would simply roll on as it always had.

'You going in, sir?' The undertaker, extravagantly sombre in his hat and three-piece suit. 'I'm about to gather the pall-bearers.'

Jim nods. 'I'm going in.'

Inside, three large displays of blue and white flowers are arranged around the central plinth. Ian Liebnitz recites the Kaddish, which Jim knows only at second hand, through Allen Ginsberg's poem: he is not prepared for its bare, unvarnished sorrow. The celebrant gives the eulogy – written, she says, by Anton's widow and sister. (In the front row, Jim sees Eva bow her head.) Hanna Edelstein reads the Dylan Thomas poem, familiar from many funerals, made unique by her strong, determined voice, which wavers only in the final lines. The curtains close slowly to the sound of a solo violin. Later, Jim will place the music as the first movement of Beethoven's Kreutzer Sonata.

He thinks, of course, of his mother's funeral: of the iced

Bristol ground, the high wooden rafters of the church; of his anger, still jagged then. He was angry for such a long time: angry with Vivian, for making him carry the burden of her illness, and then for allowing it to overwhelm her. Angry with his father, for not showing him how to love one woman, and her alone – and for being, Jim knows, the better artist. Angry with himself for not allowing anyone – not Helena, certainly not Caitlin – to truly know him. He was able, for many years, to channel this anger into his work – but anger, Jim knows now, is a young man's game. He is no longer angry; could find no anger, even, with his doctor, or with the stark facts he'd laid out for Jim's inspection. Facts with which it was impossible to argue.

After the service, the mourners linger in the courtyard, walk slowly among the floral tributes. Jim reads the card attached to a bouquet of white roses. *To a dear colleague and friend. You are much missed. Carl Friedlander.*

'Jim Taylor.'

He looks up. She is damp-eyed, trying to smile.

'Eva. I'm so sorry.'

'Thank you.' She moves closer, places a hand on his arm. She smells of face-powder and some sweet perfume. Why has he so often dreamed of her, this woman he barely knows, sketched out her image with his pencil, mixed in oil paint the precise colour of her skin, her hair, her eyes? He has never quite been able to answer this. Now he sees that the fact of her presence is the only answer.

'It was good of you to come.' He is intensely aware of the light pressure of her hand on his sleeve. 'I've followed your career over the years. You've achieved so much.'

'Have I?' Jim can't help himself – defensiveness is the weapon he reaches for most often these days. But she looks wrong-footed, and so he pedals back. 'Thank you. It's kind of you to say. And you . . . Well. I've read all your books.'

'Really?' That half-smile plays again on her lips. 'You must be something of a glutton for punishment.'

He would like to reply, but Eva is looking over his shoulder. 'David,' she says to the man behind him: David Katz, Jim sees as he turns. An old man now, with a head of white hair, an expensive-looking black coat.

Eva is moving away from Jim. 'You'll come back to the house, won't you? Twenty-five Lupus Street. Do come.'

He was not planning to attend the wake, but he does, standing a little self-consciously with Toby, collecting a glass of red wine from a waiter's tray. It is a handsome house: Georgian, pillared, its interiors a muted seascape of white, grey and blue. Jim thinks, with a sudden deep yearning that surprises him, of the House: his beloved Cornish home of concrete and glass, with the wide picture window framing rock, sea, sky.

The house, of course, will go to Dylan, along with everything else: Jim has already informed his solicitor, asked him to check over his will. He is having dinner with Stephen tonight. He will tell his old friend then, begin to make the arrangements for his legacy (a word that lends his life's work more import than Jim suspects it truly deserves). Then, tomorrow, he will make the journey north, to Dylan, Maya and Jessica. The thought of Dylan's face as he tells him the news tugs a blankness across Jim's vision, like falling snow.

An hour or so later – it is mid-afternoon, and night is already drawing in – Eva makes her way over to him. She has removed her coat: her black wool dress is neat, well cut. Jim has been watching her as she moved among the guests, thanking them for coming, her tone light, solicitous; were it not for the tightness around her eyes, she might have been any hostess running an ordinary party. He feels a rush of admiration for her – for the sacrifices she has made, for the years she must have lost in looking after Ted. But perhaps Eva didn't see it that way;

perhaps she is one of those to whom selflessness comes easily. He knows himself well enough to admit that it has never come easily to him.

'Sorry I've not had more time to talk,' she says. They are alone, by the garden window: beyond the darkening patio are the dimming outlines of trees. 'Odd how funerals require you to be sociable, when of course it's the last thing you want to be.'

He looks down at his feet, thinking perhaps that she means him: that the presence of someone like him – a mere acquaintance – is exactly the burden he had feared it would be.

'Oh, I didn't mean you,' she adds quickly, as if he had spoken aloud. 'I'm delighted you're here. I've always . . .' Eva hesitates, and he watches the set of her chin. Below, in the soft dip of her collarbone, is a silver heart. 'Felt I knew you better than I really did, I suppose. It's a funny thing. I did get your postcard, you know. I kept it for years. The Hepworth.'

'*Oval No. 2*.' How Jim had cursed himself after writing it: waited weeks for a reply, though he knew perfectly well that he had composed it precisely so as not to invite a response.

'That was it. *Oval No. 2*. I kept looking at it, trying to work out if it contained some kind of coded message.'

It had. *Leave him. Come back to England. Love me.* He had hidden it too well.

'None other than to wish you well.' He meets her gaze, hoping she will understand his true meaning.

'Yes. That's what I decided, in the end.' A short, charged silence. Then, 'I actually wrote you a card too.'

'Did you?'

'Yes, when I heard about your mother's death. But I didn't post it. I decided there was nothing I could say that someone else wouldn't already have said.'

He can't help smiling a little. 'Do you know – I did exactly the same thing.'

Looking at him. Her eyes night-dark, inquisitive. 'Really?'

'Yes. I wrote to you again, after your husband died. Ted. I'd read your book, and I'd heard you on the radio. I felt like I knew a great deal about you both – but after I wrote the letter, I realised I didn't, really. So I tore it up.'

'Gosh.' A woman Jim doesn't recognise is at Eva's elbow: tall, with a kindly, large-boned face. Eva turns to her. 'Daphne. Thank you so much for coming.' The woman embraces her, then moves away. Eva's attention is his once more, and Jim is struck, with a violence he had not expected, by how profoundly he desires that attention.

'Opportunities lost, I suppose,' she says.

'Yes. Opportunities lost.'

Eva looks away, towards the garden. He senses the slow calibration of a decision.

'This isn't the time or the place to talk,' she says. 'Talk properly, I mean. But could we do that, perhaps? Meet another time?' Then, a little anxiously, 'Only if you'd like to, of course. I know you still live in Cornwall. And I'm in Italy a great deal. But I'll be in London for the next few months. Perhaps, if you're ever in town . . .'

It is Jim's turn to look away. He has an odd vision of the passage of both their lives as two separate tracks, now suddenly, unexpectedly, veering closer. He ought to say no. It is only coffee she is proposing – or tea, somewhere safe, unthreatening: the Wallace Collection, perhaps, or the Royal Academy café. And yet surely it is also more than that. He knows it. He knew it when they met at the Algonquin; he knew it at Anton's party, and when she stood beside him on the steps of Stephen's gallery. Then, like now, she had lingered on the brink of a decision, and had not found in his favour. Now, perhaps, she has.

He should not say yes. Eva has lost Ted: she should not have to face losing anyone again. And yet he cannot refuse her. He is simply not strong enough. Or perhaps he is simply too selfish: later, he will be unable to decide which it is. But then there will be excitement, too – the prospect of their next meeting planing the edges from his fear as he travels north to Dylan, to the conversation he has rehearsed so many times, but for whose impact he cannot truly prepare.

'I'd like that very much,' he says.

Kaddish
London, January 2012

'All right?' she says.

He turns to look at her. She senses a stiffening in him, a drawing-in of breath. 'Yes. All right.'

She moves closer, takes his hand. Before them, the flowers: white chrysanthemums, bright orange marigolds, a cascade of lilies and irises. 'Beautiful, aren't they?'

Jim says nothing. Across the courtyard, the other mourners are beginning to disperse, making their way towards their parked cars.

'We can go home now,' Eva says. 'We don't have to go on to the house.'

'No.' His grip on her hand tightens. 'No, we must go. Today is about Anton. And Thea and Hanna. We mustn't make it about me.'

In the family car, Eva sits on the back seat, beside Hanna, as she had on the journey to the crematorium. Jim is in front, beside the driver, the rigid set of his back admitting nothing. He has been this way for a week – silent, remote; since the day they sat in the doctor's office in the hospital.

Eva had known from the moment the doctor requested – no, demanded – a biopsy that the results would not be good. But she had still found it difficult to absorb her words; had found herself imagining that she was listening not from a hard plastic chair, placed at right angles to the doctor's desk, but from a great distance. *Please*, she had said silently, without knowing to whom she was speaking. Her mother, perhaps, or Jakob, with his kind, wise face. *I have just lost my brother. Don't let me lose my husband, too.*

The doctor's voice had receded to a faint echo. But Jim had been listening attentively, leaning forward, making careful notes on the pad Eva had suggested he bring with him. Afterwards, she went over those notes, filling in the gaps in her own understanding. *With chemotherapy*, he had written, *12–18 months. Without, 6–8 months.* He had underlined *6–8* three times.

They have decided not to tell the family until after Anton's funeral. 'We can't possibly put anything more on them all now,' Jim had said. 'And I need some time to take it in.' Eva agreed: she couldn't, in any case, imagine the words with which to frame such information. And so, for now, it is between the two of them, and the kindly Macmillan nurse who drove out to the house from Brighton two days ago, who sat on their sofa, drank their tea, showed them a leaflet printed in cheerful primary colours. 'The chemo,' the nurse said, 'will give you some time, Mr Taylor. It's worth having, isn't it?'

Eva had waited for Jim to agree that it was, but he did not reply.

He has not cried yet; has remained dry-eyed, even, through Anton's service, which went exactly as she and Thea had planned it. Ian Liebnitz said Kaddish. The celebrant spoke the eulogy Eva had helped Thea to write. Hanna – brave Hanna – read the Dylan Thomas poem. Jakob's recording of the Kreutzer Sonata filled the room as the velvet curtains glided shut. Eva did cry then; her shoulders shook, her breath came in short gasps. Thea placed an arm around Eva's back, and she felt ashamed: she should, she thought, have been comforting her sister-in-law, for already she was understanding what it must be like to lose a husband. With great effort, Eva forced herself to think of Anton as he would no doubt prefer her to remember him – happy, comfortable, smiling – and of Jim as he is now, sitting beside her, rather than as he might soon be.

Thea has employed caterers for the wake. They have laid out platters of food in the dining-room – roast chicken and potato salad, Norwegian meatballs, a baked salmon. Waiters are moving soundlessly from room to room, offering glasses of wine on silver trays.

Returning from the downstairs bathroom, Eva stands alone for a moment in the living-room doorway, taking stock. In one corner, Penelope and Gerald are talking to David and Jacquetta, tall and striking in a long black velvet coat. Rebecca and Garth are standing with Ian and Angela Liebnitz, Jim's cousin Toby, and Anton's business partner, Carl Friedlander. Sophie and Pete are by the French windows. Beyond, in the failing light of the afternoon – the day has been cold, damp, unremittingly grey – Alice is playing in the garden with Alona and Miriam; Hanna is upstairs with Thea, taking a moment's rest. Behind her, Sam and Kate are coming through from the kitchen. She doesn't know where Jim has gone.

'Mum.' Sam places a hand on her arm. 'You OK?'

She turns, offers him a small smile. 'Yes, darling. As OK as I can be. How about you?'

'Holding up. Come and have something to eat.'

Eva fills a plate she knows she will not be able to finish. She has eaten little since New Year's Eve, when the call came from Thea. They'd been at a party when Anton had the heart attack; Eva, Jim, Hanna and Jeremy had spent the rest of the night in A&E. Eva has eaten even less in the four days since Jim's own appointment at the hospital.

'Granny Eva.' This is Alice, her face serious, as if she has news to deliver of some import. 'Grandpa wants you to come and talk to him outside.'

Eva looks up: there, on the patio, is Jim, his back turned, a faint smoke-trail rising above his head.

'Thank you, Alice darling. Here, will you take this plate through to the kitchen for me?'

The cold is a shock after the clotted warmth of indoors. She should have put on her coat; she draws her cardigan tighter as she approaches. 'There you are.'

He nods. His cigarette is almost finished. (He had given up; started again during their long, wakeful night in the hospital.) He stubs it out with his toe. 'I'm going to have the chemo,' he says.

'Yes.' Her voice steady, not betraying her relief.

He turns his blue eyes to her. 'It seemed pointless. Eighteen months rather than eight: what's the difference?'

She moves over to him, stands close, their arms not quite touching. There is a stirring in the bushes at the far end of the garden: Anton and Thea's ancient cat, Mephistopheles, out on the chase. 'A big difference,' she says.

'Yes. I know that now.' Jim places an arm around her, draws her in. 'We'll tell them together, shall we? Not this week. Next Sunday, perhaps. We could make a sort of party of it. Well, not a party, exactly. But you know what I mean.'

'Yes, darling, I do.'

In the silence, they hear the kitchen door opening: a young man and woman Eva doesn't know – Hanna's colleagues from the hospital, she supposes – are coming out, clutching cigarette packets, their voices loud, bright, confident.

Seeing the elderly couple standing together on the patio, their arms around each other, the young woman hesitates. 'Oh. Sorry to disturb you.'

Eva shakes her head. 'You're not disturbing us.'

The young couple moves off deeper into the garden, where Mephistopheles is now sniffing the air, his tail curled neatly round his front paws.

'You,' Jim says in a low whisper, his breath warm on Eva's ear, 'have made me happier than I ever thought was possible.'

'You incorrigible old romantic,' she says lightly, because the alternative is to break down, lose herself. Then, quietly, after a moment, 'What would my life have been without you?'

He does not answer, because there is no answer to give: none but to stand together, each feeling the other's warmth; looking out to where the shadows are gathering, and the night is coming on.

2014

This is how it ends.

A woman stands in the upstairs bedroom of a house in Hackney, sorting clothes into black plastic sacks. She can hear her daughter moving around downstairs; every so often, Jennifer's voice floats up through the empty rooms. 'Mum, I'm not sure what to do with this. Come and tell me what you think.' Or, 'Shall we break for a cup of tea?'

This is not Eva's house, and yet she moves around it with easy familiarity; knows where to find the teaspoons, the mugs. She and Jennifer bought the milk that morning, together with a small packet of digestive biscuits. Clearing the house might, perhaps, have fallen to Bella, or to Robyn, but they live far away now, in New York. And anyway, Eva would not have allowed anyone else to do the job.

Shirts, suits, jeans: all go into the plastic sacks. Lone socks, a moth-eaten brown jumper, a pair of paint-spattered overalls. Holding these, Eva pauses. Here is the house on Gipsy Hill: pink stucco, bare floorboards, the filthy glass roof of the dilapidated artist's studio. Here is Jim, brush in hand, turning as Eva, home from the office, steps into a freshly painted living-room. 'What do you think, Eva? Do you like it?' Here are his arms around her, flecks of white paint in his hair. Here is her answer, as she leans in to offer him a kiss. 'I like it, Jim. I like it *a lot*.'

Eva folds the overalls slowly, carefully, running her hand over the deep creases in the navy twill, and then sets them aside. She has so few objects with which to remember Jim: a few pieces of furniture (the antique armchair he bought for her fortieth birthday, reupholstered in dove-grey velvet; the scrubbed pine kitchen table they found in Greenwich market). A box of family photographs. His ancient copy of *Brave New World*, the pages yellowing, some of them splitting from the spine.

Jim had given her the book the last time Eva was here with him, in his house. It was July, and warm: they sat outside in the garden – blowsy now with weeds; later, Eva would call Daniel, ask him to spend an afternoon tackling the mess – eating the lunch Eva had prepared. Cold chicken, tomatoes, a pasta salad. Jim ate little that day: he was already weak, his clothes hung loosely, and as she helped him outside, settled him gently in a garden chair, he kept his eyes tightly closed, as if afraid to look at her, and see her pity.

They ate; they talked. She made coffee, and then Jim asked her to go back inside, bring out the book she'd find on the table beside his armchair. 'You might recognise it,' he had called through the French windows, and she did: a Penguin paperback, bordered by two thick red stripes. *Brave New World: A Novel*.

She had carried it out to the garden.

'I found it when I was clearing out some things,' he said. 'You know, preparing.'

He didn't need to say what for. She had watched his dear, familiar face, and felt so filled with love for him that it was, for a moment, impossible for her to speak. Then, gathering herself, she said, 'I was so impressed that you were reading Huxley.'

'Were you?' He had smiled, and Eva shifted her gaze to the book in her lap; smiling, Jim was so much his younger self – the boy she fell in love with; the husband with whom she had built a life. Not a perfect life, but a life that was theirs, and theirs alone, for as long as it could last. 'I must have thought that carrying it around with me made me look deep. A way to show the world there was more to me than a degree in law.'

'Oh, any fool could see there was more to you than that.' Eva spoke lightly, but he reached across the table for her hand.

'No, not any fool, Eva. Just you. Only you.'

Jim's hand in hers was light, cool; the skin thin and papery, almost translucent in places. In that hand was everything she had once loved, everything she had believed in. Eva held it, and there was no anger, no pain, no forgiveness: just a woman holding a man's hand, offering him whatever comfort it was hers to give.

'I'm afraid, Eva.' His tone was matter-of-fact; he was looking down at his coffee mug. 'I'm so afraid.'

'I know you are.' Her grip on his hand tightened. 'We'll all be there with you, Jim. All of us.'

He met her gaze. 'There are no words to thank you, really.'

'We don't need words,' she said. And she had sat quietly, holding his hand, until he grew sleepy, his eyes twitching shut; and then carefully, tenderly, she had helped him back upstairs to bed.

Three days later, Jim was admitted to hospital. Strip-lighting, linoleum; Jim sleeping mostly, his closed face grey against the pillow. His oncologist gathered them in the family room – Eva, Carl, Jennifer, Daniel; Robyn and Bella were standing by to fly back from America – to deliver his news with a compassion, even a tenderness, for which they were all, in some small way, grateful.

The hospice. Red brick, fountains; an enormous horse chestnut tree shedding conkers onto the lawn outside Jim's room. His body seeming to grow lighter by the day, until, at the end, it was almost weightless, barely denting the mattress on which he lay.

The crematorium. A beautiful October day – pale sunshine, leaves lying in drifts beside the gravel path, stained glass throwing panes of coloured light across the polished floor. Bella, her dark curls glossy, tamed; her coat dark purple, expensive. Robyn, tall, blue-eyed: the image of her father. In the chapel, Bella had paused at the front pew. Eva turned, gave her a small nod, and Bella returned it, slid down onto the bench. And there they had sat – Robyn between them; Daniel, Hattie and Carl to Eva's left; Jennifer, Henry and Susannah in the row behind. As the celebrant took her place at the lectern, Eva felt a sense of peace draw over her: one born of sadness, yes, but also of gratitude, joy, memory. *I loved you*, she told Jim silently. *And look how much we made of that love.*

Now this: Jim's bedroom. Jim's house. The clearing-away of his belongings, of all the ephemera with which he had, for a time, secured his place in this life.

Eva has left the top drawer of the chest until last. Here, beneath piles of underwear and vests, she finds a scroll of good, thick drawing paper, tightly furled. On top of it, a note, secured with an elastic band. *For Eva. With love, always. Jim x.*

She spreads the paper out on the chest of drawers, and sees herself. Soft pencil lines. A book in her lap. Her hair half covering her face; behind her, the mullion panes of the college window. It is her, and it is not her. A version of her. His version, or the version she once offered him.

Eva stands quietly, looking at the drawing, until she hears Jennifer's voice call out again, and then she goes downstairs to find her.

✳

It also ends here.

A woman stands before the wide picture window of a house in Cornwall, looking out. Wide swathe of roiling sea. The sky huge, limitless, hung with pale grey cloud.

'So you first met in New York in 1963,' the reporter says. Her name is Amy Stanhope (she handed Eva a card when she arrived) and she is young – no more than thirty; sitting on the sofa, cradling the cup of tea Eva has just made. 'You were –' she consults her notebook '– twenty-four then, but you didn't get together until you were in your seventies?'

Eva turns her attention, reluctantly, back to the room. 'Please don't put "get together". You make us sound like teenagers.'

'Sorry.' Amy is a little cowed before this thin, rather formal woman, her white hair drawn severely back from her head, her brown eyes sharp, searching. She has read only one of Eva Edelstein's books – *Handle With Care*, her memoir about caring for her second husband, Ted Simpson. From this – and the fact that Eva Edelstein chose to become a carer for a second time, to a man with whom she fell in love so late in life – Amy has pictured someone softer. A kindly old lady, self-effacing, possibly something of a martyr. 'But that was when you ... became close, wasn't it? Eighteen months ago, just after his diagnosis?'

Eva nods. She had known, somehow, from the moment she saw Jim again at Anton's funeral. She'd seen him wrestle with himself; she'd wanted to say, *Don't do the right thing. Surely you see this means we must act quickly, before this last opportunity is lost?* Instead, she'd simply asked if he would like to meet. And they had, just a few days later: Jim was stopping off in London on his way home from Edinburgh. He'd suggested tea at the Wallace Collection café. Eva was nervous – had spent a good deal of time deciding what to wear; settled on a dark green dress she'd bought in Rome the previous winter. But when she saw Jim Taylor, sitting there in the gallery's courtyard in his long black coat, those nerves had evaporated. He looked up as she approached, and she felt her heart leap to her throat.

They had stayed together for the rest of the afternoon; met again the following day for lunch, before Jim caught his train back to St Ives. Eva went with Jim to Paddington; there, on the concourse, he had told her what he'd told his son. He'd understand if she didn't want to see him again, he said – if it was simply too much to take on. Amid the clamour and din, the commuter bustle, the high-pitched shrieks of a small child, Eva had reached out and touched his face. 'It's not too much, Jim. It's not too much.'

Back in the living-room of the Cornwall house, Amy is speaking. 'And you moved in here just a few months after that?'

'Yes. Six weeks after we met again.'

Amy smiles. 'So romantic.'

'Some would call it foolhardy. But it didn't seem so to us.' Her first visit to St Ives. On seeing him again, waiting for her at the platform's end, Eva's excitement was so pure, so revitalising, that she felt she might be twenty again. The drive had taken them past shingled cottages, past snowdrops bowing their heads beside the road; it was February, and the landscape was an Impressionist painting of shimmering whites and blues. Jim rolled down the windows at Eva's request, and the cool breeze on her face tasted of the sea. Approaching the house, he said, 'I can't tell you how happy I am that you're here. You'll stay awhile, won't you? You'll stay as long as you like?'

She had stayed; insisted Sarah and Stuart take the London house, rented out the villa in Italy. (She'd wanted to take Jim there, to rest for a time under the sun, but he was weakening, wanted nothing more than to stay at home in his beloved Cornwall.) Eva had spent hours writing, or in the garden; on good days, Jim would take himself out to the studio to paint. 'If Matisse could lie in bed cutting masterpieces out of paper,' he said, 'then I can at least try to pick up a paintbrush.'

On bad days, she had sat with him on the living-room sofa, listening to the radio, watching old films. Often, sleep would overcome him – Jim was tired so often – and he'd slump against her shoulder. Once, he woke midway through one of David's films – it was years since Eva had seen it, and she was watching her ex-husband with fascination, as if examining footage of her own past – and said, 'Isn't that David Katz?' Eva said it was, and Jim had made a sound that was somewhere between a cough and a sigh. 'I hated him, you know, when we met. I hated that he'd found you first. But this is our time, now, isn't it? I just wish we had more of it.'

The journalist, Amy Stanhope, is sitting on that same sofa now. *We had so little time*, Eva thinks, and a lump forms in her throat. By way of distraction, she offers Amy another cup of tea, and Amy says she would love one, though the mug she is holding is still half full.

In the kitchen, Eva can see Jim everywhere: stirring bolognese sauce on the stove; pouring coffee; encircling her with his arms as she stood at the counter, chopping vegetables for soup. *Ours was a good love*, Eva tells him in her mind. Not the giddy love of teenagers, or that of a married couple in middle age, frayed by work, home, children, by the hue and cry of the everyday; but its own, pure thing, true to itself, answerable to no one, to nothing. If the children had wondered at it (and they had), well, they'd simply had to accept it for what it was. Jim and Eva had agreed that this new love would not erase those that had come before; nor would they fall prey to imagining what might have been.

Last Easter, Sarah had come to stay, with Stuart and Pierre, and they had all sat out on the terrace beyond the kitchen, sharing a meal, watching the sun lowering over St Ives Bay. Jim had just finished his latest course of chemotherapy; he was gaunt and sick, but seemed happy, at ease, asking Stuart and Sarah about their work in London, Pierre about his music. Washing up at the sink where Eva is standing now, filling the kettle for tea, Sarah had slipped her arm around her mother, drawn her close, and said in a low voice, 'I can see it, Mum. I can see why you love him. I'm so sorry I made a fuss.' And Eva, leaning gratefully into her daughter's embrace, had replied, 'Darling, you've nothing to be sorry for.'

A few months later – it was July, and warm, the sea a deep turquoise, the cliffs splashed yellow with lady's bedstraw – Jim was admitted to hospital in Truro, and Eva had telephoned Dylan in Edinburgh, advising him to come as soon as he could. By September, Jim was slipping away to a place Eva couldn't reach. The hospice was so much like the place in which she'd lived out her last few weeks with Ted that Eva, standing in the doorway on the day he was admitted, felt her legs give way; a nurse had had to help her to her feet. *I'm afraid it will be too much for you*, Jim had said that day at Paddington. And it was true: it was too much. She'd known it would be, and yet she had made her choice; and as she stood, weeks later, at the crematorium, remembering his life, remembering all that he was to his family, and to her, Eva knew that if she had the chance, she would make that choice again.

And I still would, Jim, she thinks now, pouring milk into Amy's tea.

Eva carries the mug through to the living-room. 'Shall we finish our talk in the studio?'

'That would be wonderful,' Amy replies, and they walk out into the garden – the air icy, the border plants squat and shrunken, waiting for spring. At the studio door, Eva pauses. 'How well do you know Jim's work?'

'Well, I think. Like most people, *The Versions of Us* is probably the work I know best. It's so powerful, so resonant. And I read about his show at the Tate, the one that brought Lewis Taylor and Jim together. It was amazing to see the continuity between them – and the differences, of course.'

Eva smiles: perhaps she has underestimated Amy. 'Then you

396

may know that we have *The Versions of Us* here now. It was in a private collection, but Jim bought it back last year.'

The paintings are hanging on the back wall of the studio: three hinged panels, turned slightly in on themselves. Eva opens the two outer leaves, and Amy stands before them, her eyes travelling across each board. A woman with dark brown hair, looking away from the viewer, towards the man who sits behind her, his expression blank, inscrutable. This is the third panel of the triptych. The other two are almost the same, but for minor variations: in the first, the woman is seated, and the man standing; in the second, they are both sitting. Minute details about the room vary, too: the position of the wall-clock; the cards and photographs on the mantelpiece; the colour of the cat stretched out on the armchair.

'It's beautiful,' Amy says. 'Those colours . . . He painted it in the mid-seventies, didn't he?'

Eva nods. 'Yes, in 1977, while he was living in St Ives with Helena Robins. His then partner.'

'It's strange looking at it here, now, with you. The woman in the paintings – she looks just like you.'

The triptych was a present: a surprise. Jim had arranged it all with Stephen Hargreaves; he took Eva out to the studio on the morning of her birthday – he was still walking then, without his stick, and had insisted she keep her eyes closed until they were inside. Opening them, she had looked, and seen herself. Seen them both. 'Now do you understand,' he said, 'you were there with me all along?' And then he had kissed her, and she thought of all the years that had led up to this – all those seconds and minutes and hours, spent elsewhere, with others, doing other things; none of them wasted, or regretted, but none more precious to her than this moment now.

'Yes, she does, doesn't she?' Eva speaks so softly that the journalist has to strain to hear.

397

They are silent, then. In front of them, the triptych. Slicks of oil paint on canvas. Three couples. Three lives. Three possible versions.

*

It ends here, too.

A woman stands on the Cambridge Backs. A wide strip of earth and tufted grass, rutted by the heavy passage of bicycles. Behind her, the steady crescendo of passing traffic. In front, a row of trees, through which she can just make out the spire of King's College Chapel.

'It was here, I think,' Eva says. 'Hard to remember exactly where, but this seems about right.'

Penelope, beside her, links her arm through Eva's. 'It hasn't changed at all, has it? I mean, looking across at King's, we could be right back there, in the thick of it. Everything ahead of us.'

Eva nods. A girl approaching on a bicycle – dark hair flying out behind her, black satchel slung across her shoulder – rings her bell, and they step aside to let her pass. Eva hears the girl tut loudly as she cycles on, and wonders for a moment what they must look like to her: two elderly women, dawdling on the footpath. Spectators to the flow, the urgency, of younger lives.

'It's not our place any more, though, is it?'

Penelope squeezes Eva's arm. 'It'll always be your place, Eva. Yours and Jim's.'

They had planned to come here together. She'd organised a weekend – reserved a room in a good hotel, a table at a restaurant. But on the morning they were to leave, Jim had woken pale and exhausted. He'd slept poorly, as he often did: Eva had heard him in the night, turning in their bed, stumbling against the door-jamb on his way to the bathroom. She had looked at him and said, 'We'll leave Cambridge for now, shall we, darling? Rest up at home. The city's not going anywhere, is it?'

They had swallowed their disappointment; they both knew it was unlikely they'd make it back. The chemotherapy was working – Jim was still here, after all; still with her – but at a cost: aside from the exhaustion and the sleeplessness, there was the nausea, the loss of interest in food, in wine, in all the things in which he'd once taken such great pleasure. His hair had thinned, and he was losing weight: it seemed to Eva that he was shrinking before her eyes. 'Heroin chic,' Jim had said: he would retain his sense of humour to the last.

At home in Sussex. Days spent reading, and listening to the radio, and on good days, taking the car down to Brighton. The sea steely, implacable; the beach impassable now, the stones too precarious for Jim's unsteady gait, and so they had walked slowly along the pier, sat in a café and drunk tea, watched passers-by flirt and kiss and argue. They spoke less and less: not because they had nothing to say, but because they enjoyed the companionability of silence; and because so much of what lay between them was unspoken, unspeakable. There was pain, and fear, and sadness; and yet on those afternoons, in Brighton, they were not unhappy. They had each other. They had their respective children, and their grandchildren, and the endlessly shifting patterns of their lives. They had their joy that Sophie had come back to them. They had their relief that they had found a way back to each other.

At the end, the hospice. There was a huge horse chestnut tree in the garden, framed by Jim's bedroom window; he liked to lie in bed, watching the way the sun caught the conkers as they fell. He used to gather them on his way to school, he said; leave them in his pocket and retrieve them months later, their shine dulled. Alice – she was sitting by his bed, staring at her grandfather, at the wires, the machines, the metal bed frame – had grown excited then, and said, 'I do that *too*, Grandpa. I do that too.'

Eva was there every day, and most nights; she knew each of the nurses by name. They were kind, most of them, in a way that far exceeded the merely professional: one nurse, a cheerful Nigerian woman named Adeola, took a particular shine to Jim, and he began, jokingly, to call her his 'wife number two'.

'Mr Taylor,' Adeola would say with a wink when Eva appeared at the door, 'your wife number one is here. Shall I ask her to come back later?' And Jim, when he was able, would smile (how the sight clawed at Eva's heart) and tell her that perhaps Adeola should let Eva in, or she might become suspicious.

Those four walls. The chair on which Eva sat for hours; the bed on which she spent her nights, under a hospital blanket, her sleep punctuated by the low beeps and murmurs of Jim's machines. When the moment finally came, it was the middle of the night, but she was already awake: she had woken a few minutes before, knowing that this was his time. His eyes were closed, his mouth open; she placed a hand before his lips, felt the minute pressure of his breath. It was coming in gasps now, the sound strange, frightening; but she would not allow herself to be afraid. She took his hand. It wasn't long before he was gone; and then she sat there with him, stroking his hand, until Adeola came.

Now, on the Backs, Penelope says, 'Let's look at the drawing again.'

Eva reaches into her handbag; here, tucked beneath the fly-leaf of her hardback diary, is a sheet of paper. She found it just a week ago, while going through the mass of correspondence in Jim's studio. It was torn from an A5 pad: a pencil sketch, the bare outline of a woman, sleeping on her side, her hands pressed together, as if in prayer. A note on the back, in Jim's scribbled hand, read, *E, sleeping – Broadway, Cotswolds, 1976*. He had never shown it to her, had tucked it away in a folder filled with bills. She wondered whether he had even remembered it was there.

Eva stares at the drawing, then hands it to Penelope. After a few moments of silence, Penelope hands it back. 'Are you done, darling?'

'Yes, Pen,' Eva says. 'I think I am.'

ACKNOWLEDGEMENTS

So many people have helped bring this book to life, or kept me sane while I was trying to do so.

Huge thanks to my eagle-eyed team of early readers, for their encouragement and advice: Jonathan Barnes; Fiona Mountford; Doreen Green; Simon Armson; Matthew Ross (I am still impressed by his familiarity with Ely Cathedral); and Sofia Buttarazzi (apologies for the late nights!). Thanks also to David Race, Ellie and Irene Bard, and Conrad Feather.

The research and archive team at the *Guardian* and the *Observer*, and Anne Thomson, archivist at Newnham College, Cambridge, both offered fascinating insights into the history of their respective institutions. Katharine Whitehorn kindly offered me some reflections on her time at Cambridge and on Fleet Street. Many thanks to all.

I am so grateful to Judith Murray for her invaluable wisdom, support and general fabulousness; and to Kate Rizzo, Eleanor Teasdale, Jamie Coleman and all at Greene & Heaton. Thanks also to Sally Wofford-Girand and everyone at Union Literary, and to the lovely Toby Moorcroft.

I am indebted to Kirsty Dunseath and Andrea Schulz for their belief, their consideration, and their astute, careful and sensitive editing. Thanks also to Rebecca Gray, Jessica Htay and the whole team at Weidenfeld & Nicolson and Orion; and to Lauren Wein and everyone at Houghton Mifflin Harcourt.

Thanks to Jan Bild, Peter Bild and Ian Barnett for their

incalculable support and faith over the years. And thanks, above all, to my husband, Andrew Glen, for putting up with me – and, as he pointed out, tolerating the fact that a fair few of his *bon mots* have unwittingly made their way into these pages ...

Finally, this novel is infused with the memory of Peter's mother, my late step-grandmother, Anita Bild. Miriam Edelstein's story is in large part inspired by Anita's own: like Miriam, she made the journey to London from Vienna in the thirties; and the Edelsteins' house in Highgate is modelled on Anita's, where we often sat talking about music and literature. I wish I had been able to show Anita this book; I like to imagine that she'd have turned to me afterwards, told me (I hope!) that she'd enjoyed it, and then, kindly but firmly, corrected my use of German.

LB

Exclusive
Bonus Content

Read on for author interview,
book club questions and much more...

RICHARD AND JUDY
ASK LAURA BARNETT

How long have you been intrigued by the 'what if?' questions of existence?

For as long as I can remember, really. My mum and I have often talked about the 'road not taken', to paraphrase Robert Frost. When she was twenty-one, my mum's then boyfriend asked her to marry him, and move from London to New Mexico. She said no, but it's so strange to think that, if she'd accepted, I might never have been born …

I can also remember being very aware, aged eighteen, of going off to university, and seeing my future branch away from that of my friends. It was another key moment in which I became intrigued by the question of 'what if', and by how easily, even unconsciously, we find ourselves stepping off down one path rather than another.

Was the movie *Sliding Doors* an influence in the writing of this book?

I wouldn't say it was an influence, but it was certainly a useful reference point. The initial idea for *The Versions of Us* – the story of one couple's relationship, told from beginning to end, in three different ways – came to me one morning in spring 2013, more or less fully formed.

As I began to research the other books, films and TV shows that had played with the parallel lives theme, I thought, naturally, of *Sliding Doors*. I'd watched it when it first came out in 1998, and enjoyed it – as a teenager, I used to hang out with my friends by the river Thames at Hammersmith, so it was fun seeing those locations on screen – and I suspect it did help lodge that fascination with the 'what if' question in my mind. But in *Sliding Doors*, there are only two iterations of the story, rather than three; and addressing this kind of what-if scenario is a very different undertaking in a novel. In the film, just changing the colour of Gwyneth Paltrow's hair helps keep the stories distinct. I had to find much more subtle ways to distinguish each version from the others.

Do you believe our lives are ordered by purely random chance, or a deeper, pre-planned destiny?

Ah, I wish I had an authoritative answer to this (but if I did, I would probably be founding a religion, rather than writing novels!). I definitely don't believe in absolute predestination. The idea of some divine, unseen hand moving us around the globe like pawns on a chessboard has always depressed me: what point is there to living, it seems to me, if every move we make has already been decided for us? But neither do I believe in purely random chance; I see too much beauty and symmetry in life for that.

When I began writing *The Versions of Us*, I knew that I didn't want the novel to stand as an argument for fate – for the idea, suggested by a lot of love stories, that there is one perfect person in this world for each of us, and that if we don't meet him or her, we are doomed to live in misery. Our lives, surely, are far more complicated than that. In each version of my story, there is a profound connection between Eva and Jim, but it is tested by the pressures exerted by real life: by work, by family, by the passage of time. We see the characters having relationships with other people, as well as with each other. I am most interested, I suppose, in the unexpected journey life takes us on, and the different ways we all find to be happy.

Will your next novel have such a profound, philosophical theme?

Well, I am already a good way into writing my next novel, and its themes are less obviously philosophical – but still, I hope, profound. The novel is called *Greatest Hits*, and it's about a British female singer-songwriter, now in her sixties, looking back on her life and career. I'm interested in the challenges posed by living a creative life, particularly for women; and in the ways artists make sense of their experiences through their work. And I'm having great fun inventing a character who, of course, never actually existed – but is as real in my mind as Joni Mitchell, Sandy Denny or Kate Bush. That, I suppose, is the joy and the madness of writing fiction!

Download our podcast at http://lstn.at/rjversionsofus

Do you have any questions that you would like to ask Laura Barnett? Visit our website – whsmith.co.uk/richardandjudy – to post your questions.

RICHARD AND JUDY BOOK CLUB
QUESTIONS FOR DISCUSSION

The Richard and Judy Book Club, exclusively with WHSmith, is all about you getting involved and sharing our passion for reading. Here are some questions to help you or your book group get started. Go to our website to discuss these questions, post your own and share your views with the rest of the Book Club.

• The story is told from the point of view of Eva and Jim and tells of the ups and downs of their relationship. Do you find you have more sympathy with one or the other of the characters?

• Which version of the story do you like best and what do you think is the most likely outcome of their relationship?

• Has the novel made you consider the 'what if' question in your own life?

• Discuss the ending of the novel.

For information about setting up, registering or joining a local book club, go to www.richardandjudy.co.uk

MY SPOTIFY PLAYLISTS
by Laura Barnett

My second greatest love, after literature, is music, and music – from the Rolling Stones and Talking Heads to Schubert and Mozart – also punctuates the lives of Eva and Jim in *The Versions of Us*.

Here, I offer a little explanation and context for the songs that underpin particular scenes in each version – moving, with the novel, from the 1950s right up to 2014.

You can listen to a full Spotify playlist for each version at www. versionsofus.com.

VERSION ONE

Take Five by the Dave Brubeck Quartet

This smooth, slinky number, with its tricksy beat and infectious saxophone melody, is the record chosen by Eva's editor, Frank, for a spot of after-dinner dancing at Eva and Jim's Gipsy Hill house in 1962.

This Land Is Your Land by Woody Guthrie

What else might Jim expect to hear in a basement dive bar in Greenwich Village in 1963 than Woody Guthrie? With its plain, unvarnished message about nationhood and freedom, this song has proved an audible influence on just about every American folk musician since the 1940s.

Wild Horses by the Rolling Stones

This gorgeous, yearning song has – as I see it, anyway – so much to say about love enduring through the years, despite all life's difficulties and disappointments. Released in 1971, it's on the turntable at Anton's thirtieth birthday party when Eva and Jim dance together in the garden.

Don't Let The Sun Go Down On Me by Elton John

Eva and Jim have just returned to the Greek island where they spent their honeymoon when they hear this track wafting out from a harbourside bar. It was a huge hit in the mid-seventies, and perhaps a subtle indicator, here, of Jim's state of mind.

Burning Down the House by Talking Heads

Recalling his first kiss with Bella, Jim remembers that she'd put on a CD – 'something loud, jarring'. This is the track Bella played: suggestive both of the age gap between them – Bella a twenty-something conceptual artist with a love of new-wave; Jim a married man in middle age, the best of his own work behind him – and of the explosive effect she will have on Jim's life.

Harvest Moon by Neil Young

This song is playing at Anton's sixtieth birthday party in 2001, as Eva and Carl Friedlander dance together for the first time 'in a way she will find entirely unexpected'. Written when Young was in his forties, it evokes (for me, anyway) a romance that may no longer be in the first flush of youth, but is still achingly true.

Kreutzer Sonata by Beethoven

Beethoven's sonata – the inspiration for a novella by Tolstoy, about an unfaithful musician and her jealous husband – begins with a plangent refrain for solo violin. Jakob's recording of this piece is played in all three versions of Anton's funeral. Here, unlike in the Tolstoy, it stands as a hymn to love and loss.

Hearts and Bones by Paul Simon

I've long been captivated by the exquisite lyrics to this song, about a couple – possibly Simon and his former partner, Carrie Fisher – on a road trip to New Mexico, gradually coming to terms with the fact that the reality of love can't live up to their high ideals. It seems fitting that Eva should think of this song in considering her marriage to Jim, and all it has meant to her.

This Is Us by Mark Knopfler and Emmylou Harris

This song doesn't actually appear in *The Versions of Us*, but I have used an extract from it as an epigraph, as I feel it fits really well with my intentions for the novel. From *All the Roadrunning*, Knopfler and Harris's gorgeous 2006 album of duets, it's a novel-in-miniature about a couple looking back over their marriage, and all the moments, both ordinary and extraordinary – falling in love; having children; watching them grow up – that have defined their shared lives.

VERSION TWO

An Die Musik by Schubert, sung by Felicity Lott

'After the speeches, Miriam Edelstein sings a Schubert lied, accompanied by Jakob on piano. Privately, Judith Katz considers this a little *de trop*...' This is the song Miriam sings at Eva and David's wedding in 1960: a paean to music, so central to Miriam and Jakob's lives – and, naturally, something they wish to pass on to Eva.

So Sad (To Watch Good Love Go Bad) by the Everly Brothers

In their hotel room on their wedding night, David Katz puts on an Everly Brothers record. This is the song they dance to: a lovely, slow track, shot through with the Everly Brothers' characteristic close harmonies – but one that hints at the fact that Eva and David's marriage may not be entirely easy.

Jingle Bells by Ella Fitzgerald

I defy anyone to hear the reindeer-swift rhythms of Ella's brilliant version of *Jingle Bells* and not want to dance. So it proves at Eva and David's Christmas / Hanukah party in December 1962: even the heavily pregnant Eva is persuaded to get to her feet, while a young actress named Juliet Franks watches her intently from across the room.

Summer in the City by the Lovin' Spoonful

It's not summer when Jim first meets Helena in Version Two, but it is in a city: Bristol, at an art exhibition in a disused warehouse. They go upstairs for food, where the record player – with this track on it – is turned up so loud that they can't hear each other speak; Jim can only watch Helena's face as she eats.

Sympathy for the Devil by the Rolling Stones

Anton's thirtieth birthday party in 1971 appears in all three versions of Eva and Jim's story, and we hear a different Rolling Stones song each time. In this version, Jim stands alone, smoking, watching Eva and Ted dance together to *Sympathy for the Devil*.

Première Gymnopédie by Erik Satie, performed by Alexandre Tharaud

I used to play this haunting, deceptively simple piece on the piano as a child. Eva's daughter Sarah plays it – much better than I ever did, I'm sure – at the Edelsteins' house in Highgate on Christmas Day 1975. A few months later, called home from Paris by her mother's illness, Eva realises how tired and withdrawn Miriam had seemed that day.

Mull of Kintyre by Wings

Not, strictly speaking, a Christmas song, this was, nonetheless, a Christmas number one in 1977, when we hear it playing in the Old Neptune pub, close to Helena and Jim's cottage in Cornwall. Helena and Jim, however, are at home with Dylan, making gingerbread.

Tangled Up in Blue by Bob Dylan

Probably my favourite Dylan song, this traces the story of a couple drawn together and apart by circumstance: even when she is far away, the woman's red hair still lingers in the man's mind. Eva's hair may not be red, but the resonances are there, I hope, when Jim slides *Blood on the Tracks* – the superb 1975 album that this song kicks off – into his cassette player while working on his triptych, *The Versions of Us*.

Catch the Wind by Donovan

I performed this hippie anthem in a school talent contest, in my one and only live appearance on acoustic guitar (I soon switched to bass, which had fewer strings to worry about). My rendition didn't go down as well as Sarah Katz's does at her school concert in Paris; but neither, as I recall, was I quite as nervous as she is.

Adagio in E for Violin and Orchestra by Mozart, performed by Anne-Sofie Mutter

Ted Simpson loves Mozart, so on their return from hospital in Rome following his first stroke, Eva reaches for a Mozart cassette to 'lighten the mood'. But even Mozart can't undercut Eva's anxiety for Ted, and for Sarah, now living an unhappy, chaotic life as a rock musician in Paris.

Gimme Shelter by the Rolling Stones

Anton Edelstein isn't the only Stones fan in *The Versions of Us:* for his fiftieth birthday party, held – in this version – at his recently-acquired modernist house on a Cornish cliff top, Jim has a band 'strumming out Rolling Stones covers until four a.m.'

Ruby by Kaiser Chiefs

On a trip to Italy to visit his grandmother, Eva, Sarah's son Pierre is – like most teenagers in the noughties – more interested in his iPod earbuds than in his surroundings. This song is playing on Pierre's iPod as Eva drives them from Ciampino airport to her house in Bracciano, north of Rome.

Kreutzer Sonata by Beethoven

See above.

This Is Us by Mark Knopfler and Emmylou Harris

See above.

VERSION THREE

Come Fly With Me by Frank Sinatra

Who doesn't love Sinatra's exuberant 1958 classic, about slipping away in search of freedom and fun? Well, anyone, perhaps, who is woken by it playing at full volume at three in the morning – as happens to Jim when he is back living with his mother, Vivian, in her Bristol flat.

You Go To My Head by Stan Getz

I don't name the Stan Getz number performed by the jazz band as Jim arrives at the Algonquin party in 1963, but this – understated, romantic, insistent – is the track I could hear playing in my head as I wrote the scene.

Whole Lotta Love by Led Zeppelin

At a party at Richard Salles's house, Jim notices a woman 'standing by the fireplace in a green dress, her flame-red hair loose across her shoulders'. He goes over to talk to her, but they have to shout to be heard over a Led Zeppelin record – this one. Her name, of course, is Helena.

Let's Spend the Night Together by the Rolling Stones

In the third version of Anton's birthday party, it's this Stones track that's playing as Eva and Jim spar – each unsure of the other's feelings, though perhaps this song offers an indication – in the garden.

Aladdin Sane by David Bowie

On his daughter Rebecca's fourteenth birthday, David Katz breaks his promise to fly home from Los Angeles to see her. To make up for it, Eva prepares a dinner party for Rebecca and her friends, and buys her this record by her idol, David Bowie, as a gift.

Smoke on the Water by Deep Purple

After Harvey Blumenfeld's New Year's party in Los Angeles in 1977, David drives Eva home in his red Aston Martin. As they drive, they finally have the conversation they probably should have had many years before. An open-top car passes them on the freeway, with this bombastic seventies classic blaring from the stereo.

You Do Something to Me by Paul Weller

This gorgeous, unashamedly romantic song has been a slow-dance staple at weddings and parties since the mid-nineties, when Weller included it on his album *Stanley Road*. And, sure enough, the band at Anton's sixtieth birthday party in 2001 have it on their set-list: Eva and Jim can hear the song drifting up from the boat's ballroom as they talk on the upper deck.

Got My Mojo Working by Muddy Waters

To celebrate Jim's seventieth birthday, Penelope and Gerald host a picnic on the beach beside their house in Cornwall. This foot-stomping slice of Delta blues – with an encouraging sentiment, perhaps, for a man no longer in his prime – is one of the tracks playing on Gerald's iPod.

Like a Rolling Stone by Bob Dylan

Jim is, as we know by now, a big Dylan fan, and this song – one of Jim's favourites, I suspect – is also on Gerald's iPod playlist for the picnic.

Kreutzer Sonata by Beethoven

See above.

This Is Us by Mark Knopfler and Emmylou Harris

See above.

TEN NOVELS THAT MADE ME
by Laura Barnett

1. *Where the Wild Things Are* by Maurice Sendak

As a child, I found Maurice Sendak's sumptuously illustrated tale about a little boy, Max, whose bedroom magically transforms into a jungle thronged with fang-toothed monsters, terrifying and exciting in equal measure. The book fired my imagination, sending all sorts of strange creatures wandering through my dreams – and introducing me to the many weird and wonderful worlds contained within the pages of books, just waiting to be explored.

2. *Cat's Eye* by Margaret Atwood

I studied Atwood's 1988 novel for GCSE English, and her writing was a revelation to me. The novel is about a painter, Elaine, looking back on her life, and particularly on her dysfunctional childhood friendships. It's beautifully written, packed with poetic imagery, and so cleverly structured, with a non-linear narrative reflecting the chaotic processes of memory. This was the first novel to really show me that a writer needn't simply plod through a story from beginning to end, but is free to find his or her own original way to tell it.

3. *Tess of the d'Urbervilles* by Thomas Hardy

Hardy was my favourite writer through much of my teens, and I still adore his descriptive lyricism, and the fact that his female characters feel, for the most part, properly three-dimensional. I have this novel to thank, too, for a good early dose of feminist outrage. When, at fourteen or so, I first read the scene in which Tess tells Angel Clare about her treatment at the hands of Alec d'Urberville and Clare – despite having already made his own confession – rejects Tess, I was so furious at his double-standards, I threw the book across the room. Angel Clare remains my least favourite character in literature.

4. *The Millstone* by Margaret Drabble

I discovered this 1965 novel in my late teens. It's about a highly educated young woman who falls pregnant after a one-night stand, and decides to keep her baby. On the one hand, her decision – to me, at seventeen, anyway – felt like an important indictment of the social disapproval such an event still brought in the 1960s. But on the other, I couldn't quite understand why the character had, as I saw it, opted to throw her life away. This is a novel that offers no easy answers; as a young writer, it showed me how powerful – and true – such ambiguity can be in fiction.

5. *Breathing Lessons* by Anne Tyler

This isn't the first Anne Tyler novel I ever read – that was *A Slipping-Down Life* – but it's the one that has probably had the greatest influence on me as a writer. Its action takes place over a single day, as Maggie and Ira, a middle-aged couple from Baltimore, where all Tyler's novels are set, are driving to a funeral. Tyler excavates the layers of memory and shared experience that underpin any long marriage, and shows that there is beauty, pain and grandeur to be found in even the most ordinary of lives.

6. *The Time Traveler's Wife* by Audrey Niffenegger

I was twenty-one when this debut novel came out, and it had a huge impact on me. Here, like *Cat's Eye*, was a book that took the conventional precepts about narrative structure, and turned them on their head – and did so not to play the sorts of clever-clever postmodern games I'd grown tired of reading at university, but to examine the ties that bind a couple together, even when one of them keeps, well, slipping in and out of time . . . I kept my copy close by while writing *The Versions of Us*, as an inspiring example of how playing around with structure needn't mean sacrificing emotional impact.

7. *Moon Tiger* by Penelope Lively

I came to this Booker-winning novel quite late, having already read – and loved – many of Lively's other books. But this quickly took its rightful place as my favourite. At its heart is another strong, independent woman – Claudia Hampton, an elderly historian lying alone in hospital and piecing together her own history: memories of her career, her family, and the love she lost. Claudia's voice is so vivid and real, and I was – and still am – in awe of the way Lively manages to capture a whole life, in all its glorious glamour and banality, and pin it to the page.

8. *We Were the Mulvaneys* by Joyce Carol Oates

Again, I'd read several of Joyce Carol Oates's other novels before coming across this one – considered by many to be her greatest – in a charity shop. I'm so glad I picked it up: this ambitious, sprawling saga about a family in upstate New York who seem to have it all, until a tragic incident shatters their illusions, is a masterclass in pace and pathos. Oates is so brilliant at tracking the passage of time without ever making it weigh or drag, and she has a magpie's eye for detail.

9. *Olive Kitteridge* by Elizabeth Strout

I'm a sucker for novels set in New England – there's something majestic about the region, with its flame-red autumns and lighthouses and Atlantic spray. This is set in Maine; it's not a conventional novel, but a series of short stories centring around the testy, cantankerous Olive Kitteridge, her long-suffering husband Henry, and various inhabitants of their small town. My mum – a former librarian and voracious reader – loved this book and passed it on to me, and I was captivated from the first paragraph. Strout writes with such delicacy and insight about everyday life – a place that, far from being banal or uninteresting, can actually be a source of the most compelling drama and tension.

10. *The Cazalet Chronicles* by Elizabeth Jane Howard

All right, so this isn't one novel, but five – starting with *The Light Years*, written in 1990, and ending with *All Change*, published in 2013, not long before Elizabeth Jane Howard's death. I discovered them after reading a fascinating newspaper interview with Howard, and then hearing one of the early novels in the series – tracing the lives of the Cazalet family and their various friends and relatives, before, during and after the Second World War – on the radio.

I was immediately hooked: Howard's writing style is dense and detailed, and has an almost hypnotic quality, drawing us into her characters' lives until they seem almost more real than our own. I read all five books in quick succession, coming to the end of each one with a profound sense of loss – but also reminded of how the very best fiction draws us into the heads of other people, and makes us see the world through their eyes. And what greater adventure can there really be than that?

READERS SHARE THEIR #WHATIF MOMENTS...

I always think #Whatif I'd stayed at college and hadn't dropped out... Would I still have started blogging? Met my partner? Moved out? @BookLoverx

#Whatif the kitchen on my friend's floor in the New Zealand Auckland YWCA had been cleaned properly? She wouldn't have gone to the kitchen on my girlfriend's floor, they wouldn't have met, and my friend wouldn't have introduced us. @weiminga

#Whatif Rachel and I had got together after our fling at university instead of meeting again seven years later? I wonder if we would be married today with two beautiful children. @pcmurph

A six-hour coach journey from London to Manchester. One unexpected text from my university love and the words 'give us a go'. #Whatif I'd said yes? I'd still be loving you Andy, just not from afar. @charityshopgold

#Whatif I'd walked right past that Pret? I'd never have met my husband or moved to London. I'd be a Long Island housewife. Or a Brooklyn hipster... @GennMcMenemy

#WHATIF

The two of us are absolutely passionate about reading and there's something immensely satisfying about discussing books amongst friends and family.

We'd love you to be part of these conversations so do please visit our website to discuss this book, and any of our other Book Club choices. There is so much to discover and so many ways to get involved – here are just some of them:

- Subscribe to our author podcast series
- Read extracts of all the Book Club books
- Read our personal reviews and post your own on our website
- Share your thoughts and discuss the books with us, the authors and other readers using #WHSRJ
- Set up, register or join a local book club

For more information go to our website now and be a part of Britain's biggest and best book club – whsmith.co.uk/richardandjudy. See you there!

Richard & Judy xxx

WHSmithuk

@WHSmith

ⓇΩ kobo

**Read anytime, anywhere
on just about any PC,
tablet or smartphone
with FREE Kobo apps.**

**Browse and shop
over 4 million eBooks.**

**Choose from new releases
and bestsellers, including
Richard and Judy's
recommended reads.**

**Visit www.whsmith.co.uk/koboapps
or scan the QR code to download
the app and to see the latest
Kobo offers or competition.**

W&N

THE BOOKSELLER
INDUSTRY AWARDS
IMPRINT OF THE YEAR 2015

For literary discussion, author insight,
book news, exclusive content,
recipes and giveaways, visit the
Weidenfeld & Nicolson blog and
sign up for the newsletter at:

www.wnblog.co.uk

For breaking news, reviews and exclusive competitions
Follow us 🐦 @wnbooks